The Broken Land

BY KATHLEEN O'NEAL GEAR AND W. MICHAEL GEAR FROM TOM DOHERTY ASSOCIATES

NORTH AMERICA'S FORGOTTEN PAST SERIES

People of the Wolf	*People of the Mist*
People of the Fire	*People of the Masks*
People of the Earth	*People of the Owl*
People of the River	*People of the Raven*
People of the Sea	*People of the Moon*
People of the Lakes	*People of the Nightland*
People of the Lightning	*People of the Weeping Eye*
People of the Silence	*People of the Thunder*

People of the Longhouse
The Dawn Country: A People of the Longhouse Novel
The Broken Land: A People of the Longhouse Novel
*The Black Sun: A People of the Longhouse Novel

THE ANASAZI MYSTERY SERIES

The Visitant
The Summoning God
Bone Walker

BY KATHLEEN O'NEAL GEAR

Thin Moon and Cold Mist	*It Sleeps in Me*
Sand in the Wind	*It Wakes in Me*
This Widowed Land	*It Dreams in Me*

BY W. MICHAEL GEAR

Long Ride Home	*Coyote Summer*
Big Horn Legacy	*Athena Factor*
	The Morning River

OTHER TITLES BY KATHLEEN O'NEAL GEAR AND W. MICHAEL GEAR

The Betrayal
Dark Inheritance
Raising Abel
Children of the Dawnland

www.Gear-Gear.com
*Forthcoming

The Broken Land

A PEOPLE OF
THE LONGHOUSE NOVEL

Kathleen O'Neal Gear and
W. Michael Gear

TOR®

A TOM DOHERTY ASSOCIATES BOOK · NEW YORK

THE BROKEN LAND

Maps and illustrations by Ellisa Mitchell

A Tor Book
Published by Tom Doherty Associates, LLC
175 Fifth Avenue
New York, NY 10010

www.tor-forge.com

Tor® is a registered trademark of Tom Doherty Associates, LLC.

Library of Congress Cataloging-in-Publication Data

Gear, Kathleen O'Neal.
 The broken land : a people of the longhouse novel / Kathleen O'Neal Gear and W. Michael Gear.—1st ed.
     p. cm.—(North America's forgotten past ; no. 19)
  "A Tom Doherty Associates book."
  ISBN 978-0-7653-2694-2
 1. Iroquoian Indians—Fiction.   I. Gear, W. Michael.   II. Title.
  PS3557.E18B76 2012
  813'.54—dc22

                                                          2011025170

First Edition: January 2012

Printed in the United States of America

0 9 8 7 6 5 4 3 2 1

To Linda Walters
English teacher at Tulare Union High School,
California, 1969–1972

She taught an amazing course called "Supernatural Literature," where her students studied the works of writers like H. P. Lovecraft and Edgar Allan Poe. I well remember the outcry it caused in our small community, especially the charges that she was teaching Satanism. Despite pressure to stop, Mrs. Walters had the courage to stand up and continue teaching her students that classic body of literature. I know it wasn't easy.

Thank you, Mrs. Walters. You will never know how much that class meant to me.

Your student,
Kathleen O'Neal Gear

B.C.

13,000	10,000	6,000	3,000	1,500

PEOPLE *of the* WOLF
Alaska & Canadian
Northwest

PEOPLE *of the* EARTH
Northern Plains & Basins

PEOPLE *of the* NIGHTLAND
Ontario & New York &
Pennsylvania

PEOPLE *of*
the OWL

Lower
Mississippi
Valley

PEOPLE *of the* SEA
Pacific Coast & Arizona

PEOPLE *of the* RAVEN
Pacific Northwest &
British Columbia

PEOPLE *of the* LIGHTNING
Florida

PEOPLE *of the* FIRE
Central Rockies &
Great Plains

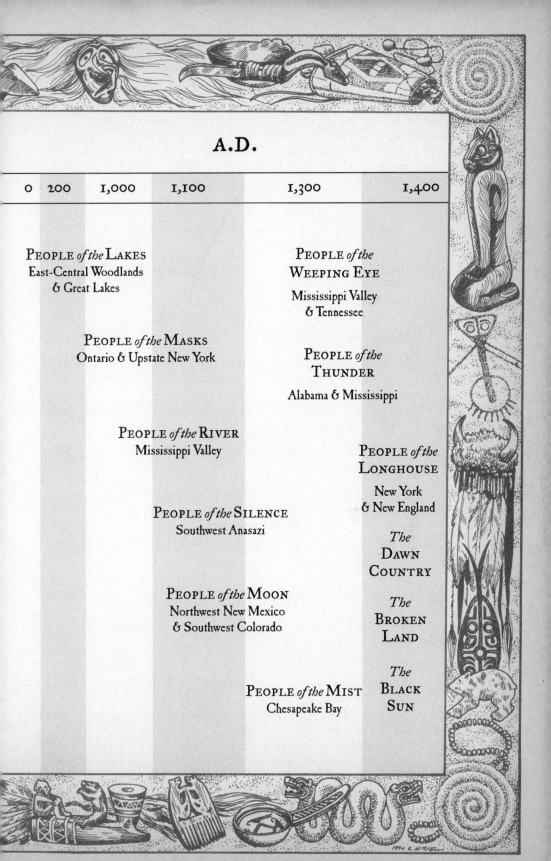

A.D.

0	200	1,000	1,100	1,300	1,400

PEOPLE *of the* LAKES
East-Central Woodlands
& Great Lakes

PEOPLE *of the*
WEEPING EYE

Mississippi Valley
& Tennessee

PEOPLE *of the* MASKS
Ontario & Upstate New York

PEOPLE *of the*
THUNDER

Alabama & Mississippi

PEOPLE *of the* RIVER
Mississippi Valley

PEOPLE *of the*
LONGHOUSE

New York
& New England

PEOPLE *of the* SILENCE
Southwest Anasazi

The
DAWN
COUNTRY

PEOPLE *of the* MOON
Northwest New Mexico
& Southwest Colorado

The
BROKEN
LAND

The
PEOPLE *of the* MIST   BLACK
Chesapeake Bay   SUN

Skanodario Lake

Coldspring
Village

Hilltop Village

Wyango Village Canassatego Village

Hansera Village Riverbank Village

Tyor Village Agweron Village Sedge Mars
Village

Wenisa Village

Shookas Village Tehana Village

Decanasora Village

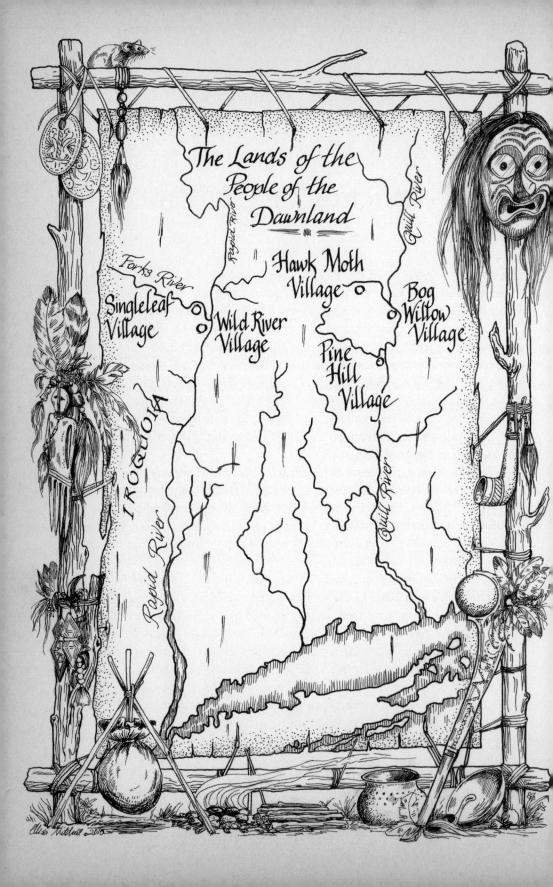

The Lands of the
People of the
Dawnland

Hawk Moth
Village

Singleleaf
Village

Wild River
Village

Bog
Willow
Village

Pine
Hill
Village

Forks River

Rapid River

Quill River

Quill River

IROQUOIA

Nonfiction Introduction

The Iroquoian story of the Peacemaker is one of North America's most beautiful epics. There are literally hundreds of recorded versions, often contradictory, and many more versions that are kept alive only by Haudenosaunee *hegeota*, storytellers. These oral historians are the Keepers of the sacred stories. Despite sometimes profound differences, most of the Keepings share two elements: the story opens in a ferocious landscape of war, and three people are struggling to end it: Jigonsaseh, Dekanawida, and Hiyawento. For more information on the grisly nature of the warfare, please see the introduction to *People of the Longhouse*.

Let's talk about "Keepings." What is a Keeping? Keeping takes many forms and is a sacred obligation.

Women were the Keepers of the Three Sisters: corn, beans, and squash. They were responsible for the agricultural fields, planting, tending, harvesting, and preserving the crops. As part of their Keeping obligations, women controlled food and its distribution. They also decided when to make war and when to make peace. Often this duty included fighting and leading warriors into battle.

As a fascinating example, in 1687 the French monarchy decided it would steal Seneca lands. King Louis XIV assigned one of his most decorated war heroes, the Marquis de Denonville, to lead the offensive. The marquis believed the best way to accomplish the task was to destroy Seneca government at the roots. He used a standard European military strategy that had proven very effective in dealing with the wild tribes of Ireland and Scotland; he invited the Haudenosaunee leaders—the Grand Council and several clan mothers—to a peace conference, then took them prisoner and shipped them to France as slaves. Fortunately, he was so ignorant of the role of women in Iroquoian society that he unwittingly left the most powerful woman in the nation, the Jigonsaseh, untouched. She made him regret it, for she called up an army of men and women warriors so powerful they virtually destroyed the marquis's forces, and chased the terrified survivors all the way back to Montreal, handing him the most ignominious rout of his life. In 1688, the marquis pleaded for peace and agreed to all of the Jigonsaseh's demands, including dismantling the French fort at Niagara and returning the captives who had survived their brutal slavery (O'Callaghan, 1: 68–69. See also, Mann, *Iroquoian Women*, chapter 3).

Men were the Keepers of the forest. They were generally responsible for the hunt and the execution of warfare. They cleared the fields for the crops, built the longhouses, constructed palisades and canoes. They hunted, fished, fought, and brought home captives to restore the spiritual strength of the clans. Men were appointed as village chiefs by clan mothers, after which they organized and planned attacks, and served on the national Grand Council, relaying the wishes of their Peoples. They were also responsible for negotiating agreements related to trade, territory, and war.

Men and women also Kept their own histories. There were "men's stories," and "women's stories," and they were generally told around separate council fires. This cultural tradition, virtually unknown to the early ethnographers, dictated which versions of the Peacemaker story survived to be passed down through the centuries. Why? Because the first recorders of the Peacemaker epic were almost exclusively European men who'd been born and bred in the Victorian era. Not only were they oblivious to the fact that women Kept their own stories, but as outsiders they may not have been allowed to sit at the women's council fires to hear their sacred stories. As a result, nearly every version of the Peacemaker epic that was recorded was a men's story. Most of Jigonsaseh's story has been lost.

There are a few fragments, however. One of our goals in this quartet of books has been to pull the fragments together and restore Jigonsaseh to her proper place in the epic. From what we can tell, she was the pivotal clan matron responsible for the success of the League. She approved the Peacemaker's mission, and he consulted her on every important decision. One fragment says he refused to begin any meeting until she arrived. Without her support and leadership, it's doubtful that Dekanawida and Hiyawento would have been able to establish a lasting peace. We owe special thanks to Haudenosaunee scholars Pete Jemison and Barbara Mann for their meticulous research on Jigonsaseh.

We know from the oral history that Jigonsaseh used food to create alliances. One story fragment says she fed every passing war party, no matter their nation. She did this to buy goodwill and keep her People safe. It is also probable that she used food to create other types of alliances. The oral history says that Jigonsaseh—at the request of Dekanawida—went to the People of the Flint, the Mohawk, to convince them to join an alliance to overthrow the evil cannibal sorcerer Atotarho. She also rallied the female leaders of the nations and convinced them of the truth of Dekanawida's vision. She was apparently a formidable politician. She used the clan system as the glue to hold the fragile alliance together long enough for the idea of the League to gain a foothold. As such, she cofounded the League with Dekanawida and Hiyawento.

The few hints we have about her personal history are intriguing. In one version of the epic (Hewitt, 1932), she is Dekanawida's mother. In another, she's his grandmother. In yet another, she doesn't know Dekanawida at all. Rather, she is from a different nation, the People of the Mountain—the Seneca. Dekanawida seeks her counsel early in his life, just as he's beginning his peace initiative. Some stories say she was born among the Wyandot Attiwandaronk, also known as the Neutral Nation. A few versions say she was the direct descendant of Sky Woman, through her daughter, the Lynx. Others say Jigonsaseh was the Lynx.

Regardless of the diversity of elements, one thing is almost certain: She was the head clan matron of the League of the Iroquois. In Chief David Cusick's Keeping ("Sketches of Ancient History of the Six Nations," 1825), the Jigonsaseh in the Peacemaker story was the ninth woman to carry that name.

The other two heroes, Dekanawida and Hiyawento, have been extensively chronicled. An excellent discussion of both characters can be found under "The Second Epoch of Time," in the *Encyclopedia of the Haudenosaunee,* edited by Bruce Johansen and Barbara Mann.

Hiyawento (Ayonwantha) became, by virtually all accounts, Dekanawida's closest friend and advisor. However, story variants picture him as either the right-hand man of the evil genius Atotarho, or Atotarho's greatest political opponent and the victim of the chief's treachery. Sometimes, as in the Johnson's 1881 version, Hiyawento is the Peacemaker. Dekanawida doesn't exist, and Jigonsaseh and Atotarho appear only at the end, and play bit parts.

Nearly every nation claims he was either born among their people, or they adopted him. The tragedy that befell his family, as you will see in *The Broken Land,* is the central feature of Hiyawento's story. Though sometimes his daughters are involved, other times it's his brothers or his wife. His grief drives him to create the "Truth belts," known in modern society as wampum belts. This term, however, is incorrect. *Wampum* is an Algonkian term. The correct Iroquoian term is *otekoa*. Hiyawento's grief was also the source for the creation of the Condolence Ceremony, which is the sacred heart of the League.

The great villain, Atotarho (Tadadaho), in most versions, is depicted as the mad tyrant of the Onondaga, whom many believed to be a cannibal sorcerer. However, in Chief David Cusick's Keeping, Atotarho is the hero of the story. None of the other characters exist.

The Peacemaker's personal history is perhaps the most interesting. His stories are certainly the most divergent. As with Hiyawento, nearly every nation claims he was born among their people, or adopted by them. The earliest versions of Dekanawida's life bear striking resemblances to the life of the Creation Hero, Tarachiawagon. He is shown as a spiritual emissary, a visionary man, who came to the aid of the Iroquois when they were on the verge of destroying themselves. Other versions say he was born of a virgin among the Wyandots north of Lake Ontario. These versions show him being abused by his people, who did not believe in him. When he left them, he paddled across Lake Ontario in a white stone canoe and made peace among the Iroquois. Afterward, he traveled across the ocean and became the person known to Christians as Jesus.

While every major plot element you encounter in these books can be found in written sources, the oral history, or the archaeological record, the profoundly different versions of the story pose unique problems for anyone trying to decipher what actually might have happened. As you read this novel, you will see how we sifted through the different versions, pieced them together, and made sense of them.

No matter which variant you believe, the Peacemaker story is astonishing. In a time of extreme climatic and cultural stress, Dekanawida managed to pull together five warring nations. We think his message of compassion and spiritual unity is as powerful today as it was six hundred years ago. Given current events, perhaps more so.

The Broken Land

Twelve summers after *The Dawn Country*...

I don't feel my body, just the air cooling as color leaches from the forest, leaving the land strangely gray and shimmering. When the blue sky goes leaden, and the rounded patches of light falling through the trees curve into bladelike crescents, I faintly begin to sense my skin. I have the overwhelming urge to run, but I can't. My legs do not exist. Instead, my fingers work, clenching into hard fists, unclenching. A great cloud-sea swims beneath me, a restless dark ocean punctured by a great tree with flowers of pure light; its roots sink through Great Grandmother Earth and plant themselves upon the back of the Great Tortoise floating in the primeval ocean below.

As though the birds know the unthinkable is about to happen, they tuck their beaks beneath their wings and close their eyes, roosting in the middle of the day. Noisy clouds of insects that only moments ago twisted through the forest like tiny tornadoes vanish. Butterflies settle to the ground at my feet and secret themselves amid the clouds. An eerie silence descends.

I lift my eyes just as Morning Star flares in the darkening sky. As though she's caused it, fantastic shadow-bands, rapidly moving strips of light and dark, flicker across the meadow.

Dimly, I become aware that I am not alone. Gray shades drift through the air around me, their hushed voices like the distant cries of lost souls. We are the last congregation. The dead who still walk and breathe.

"Odion?"

It is my friend's voice. Wrass, who is now called Hiyawento. He uses my boyhood name. I turn to see him standing beside me. He points.

Beyond the cloud-sea at the western edge of the world, an amorphous darkness rises from the watery depths and slithers along the horizon like the legendary Horned Serpent who almost destroyed the world at the dawn of creation. Strange black curls, like gigantic antlers, spin from the darkness and rake through the cloud-sea.

Elder Brother Sun trembles in the sky. A black hole opens in the universe, and he slowly turns his back to flee. There is a final brilliant flash, and blindingly white feathers sprout from his edges. Blessed gods, he's flying. Flying away. If he leaves us, the world will die . . . unless I do something.

I know this. I don't know how, but it is up to me to stop the death of the world.

A crack—like the sky splitting—blasts me. I look down and see a great pine tree pushing up through a hole in the earth, its four white roots slashing like lightning to the four directions. A snowy blanket of thistledown blows toward it like a great wave, spreading out all over the world.

I stagger as my body comes alive in a raging flood. Just as I turn to speak to the Shades . . . a child cries out. The sound is muffled and wavering, seeping through the ocean of other voices. It sounds like the little boy is suffocating, his mouth covered with a hand or hide.

Fear freezes the air in my lungs.

As though he has his lips pressed to my ear, a man orders, "Lie down, boy. Stop crying or I'll cut your heart out."

The Dream bursts. For a time, there is only brilliance. Then I see the flowers of the World Tree, made of pure light, fluttering down, down, disappearing into utter darkness . . . and I'm falling, tumbling through nothingness with tufts of cloud trailing behind me. . . .

One

Sky Messenger

Darkness is coming.

I halt at the edge of the birches and steady myself by placing a hand against a massive granite boulder, concentrating on the bright yellow leaves that whirl through the cold air. The scent of snow suffuses Wind Mother's breath. While my fingers gouge the rock, I gaze up at the deep blue thunderheads standing like fortresses above the chestnuts and sycamores that ring the meadow. Dusk's purple halo has faded to nothingness, leaving the white tree trunks steel gray, the dry grasses silver.

The old wolf who always strides at my side lifts his gray muzzle and scents the air, returning me to the acrid odor of burning longhouses. The scent is strong, mixing eerily with the cries of the wounded who scatter the battlefield. I sink against the boulder, hoping that, for the moment, shadows hide me from my warriors.

The other members of the war party have retreated to the nearby meadow to cook supper and tell stories, each trying—as I am—to forget the horror that surrounds him. My thoughts drift and, as always, return to her.

. . . long naked legs whispering through the spring grass . . . pearl-colored Cloud People scudding overhead. Struggling for air, for more of her. Floating weightlessly through the deep wildflower-scented afternoons, her lips upon my body like fire.

I'm shaking. I cast a glance over my shoulder to make certain no one is watching me. I am a deputy war chief. I cannot afford weakness. Dozens of campfires glitter. Here and there, men laugh, and their breath condenses in the cold air and glides across the fire-dyed meadow.

Beyond the warriors, near the river, the captives sit roped together, shivering, gazing around with wide, stunned eyes. Four women and eleven children. I have counted the children over and over. In the morning they will be marched off to alien villages, adopted into strange new clans, or killed, as suits the whims of the matrons. The sight always sickens me. As a boy, my village was attacked and I was captured. I know from the inside what it feels like . . . and the utter despair still haunts me. To this day, I refuse to take captives, which does not endear me to the clan matrons of the Standing Stone People. Many times my warriors have voted me war chief, but the matrons refuse to allow it. They say I am not ready.

They are right.

I clench my fists and turn my gaze to the burning village, where flames still leap through the charred husks of twelve longhouses. We arrived this afternoon. Well thought out, every possible permutation calculated and planned for by War Chief Deru, our victory required only three hands of time. Most of the villagers were still in their bedding hides, sick with the unknown fever that ravages the land. They barely put up a fight.

On the canvas of my souls I see it all again: the assault, pouring the pine pitch at the base of the palisade, setting the fires, people fleeing in all directions, arrows cutting them down like blades of grass beneath finely flaked chert scythes.

This is a Flint People village. Blessed gods, if they ever find out I was among the war party—if *she* ever finds out—my life will not be worth the price of a wooden bead. Even if the Flint matrons do not believe hunting me down is worth the lives it would cost—for I am a formidable warrior— she will be coming. She can't let me live, not after his. Not after the promises I made.

. . . *I requicken in you the great soul of Dekanawida.* . . .

The dread emptiness that often assaults warriors when the battle is done filters through me. I lean more heavily against the boulder and concentrate on breathing, just breathing. Empty cadences of the river babbling over rocks penetrate the night.

Only three moons ago, the Flint People were our allies. We fought together, lived together, protected each other's villages from the marauding Mountain People who sought to kill us all and take our lands. When the matrons ordered this attack, I was stunned, as were many, including War Chief Deru. Our people have suffered many losses in the ongoing war, and each has to be replaced. Every warrior understands that this is accomplished through adoption. Captives are taken and marched home, the best selected, and put in line for the Requickening Ceremony. During the ritual, the souls of lost loved ones are raised up and transferred to the living body of the captive, along with the name of the deceased. When relatives have their families back, it eases their grief, and restores the spiritual strength of the clan.

I wipe my mouth with the back of my hand. When I lower it, I stop to stare at the blood that cakes my fingers. Some of the people who lived in this village were her relatives. Her clan.

. . . Sunlight filtered through the scent of her hair. Flesh coming alive, the open lips that touch mine like an unslaked summer, the heart-wrenching safety of her arms enough to convince me to forsake my own people.

"Blessed gods, stop it," I murmur with hushed violence.

When the war ends, perhaps . . . But, no, that will never happen. Not after tonight. And the war isn't going to end. Great Grandmother Earth has been growing progressively colder and drier for longer than I have been alive, at least twenty-three summers, which means our corn, beans, and squash crops rarely mature. As a result we are forced to hunt and fish harder. After many summers of desperation, most of the deer are gone, the lakes fished out. The only solution is to take what we need from our enemies.

Or so the matrons tell us.

When I refused to obey the order to accompany this war party, High Matron Kittle called a special council meeting of the allied villages. What the council decided was law. "Alliances are quicksand, always shifting. You know that, Sky Messenger. We must all do our duties, including you. Don't you care about your people?"

". . . You're the only man I've ever trusted. From this time forward, you are one of my people. Her sudden embrace like wind ransacking the forest . . . ears roar. Later, pawpaws baked in hot ashes . . . happier than at any other time in my life . . ."

Two men rise from their cook fire and stretch their tired muscles. Deerbone stilettos, war axes, and clubs bristle on their belts. Every man carries in his bosom the idea of the knife and axe. How can he even think of peace when the thrill of victory beckons?

Someone makes a joke. Laughter erupts, but it is uneasy, filled with nerves and exhaustion.

When a low growl rumbles in Gitchi's throat, I reach down and pat the old wolf's grey head. He is staring out at the battlefield, his yellow eyes bright, fixed on something I do not see. "It's all right, Gitchi. Everything is—"

The words die in my throat. There, at the edge of the burning village, wreathed in blowing smoke, stands a dark wraith, his black buckskin cape flapping around his tall body. The ancient, tarnished copper beads that ring his collar flash blue in the firelight. He turns to gaze directly at me, and the hair at the nape of my neck prickles. His hood is pulled up. Inside, where his face should be, it is blacker than black, like a bottomless chasm.

Gitchi whimpers.

The figure looks one last time at the destroyed village, then turns away so gracefully I swear it is not tethered to the ground. It glides northward, toward the worst part of the battlefield.

My gaze tracks it.

The figure stops at the edge of the clearing where the cries of the wounded are unbearable. Soon, after my warriors have had suppers and drunk their fill of water, they will return here to dispatch those still alive and strip their corpses of valuables. For now, the field appears to be alive with gigantic beetles. Humped shapes crawl, topple, struggle up again. Probably trying to reach injured loved ones.

The figure turns to stare at me expectantly. *What is it he wants me to . . . ?*

Flashes catch my eye. Curious, I walk away from the fires to see better.

When I stand alone in the blackness, the blood seems to drain out of my body, leaving me ice cold and staring fixedly at the battlefield littered with dead. Lights rise from the corpses, hundreds of them. Some shoot away into the heavens and blend with the Path of Souls, the star road that the Flint People call the Road of Light. That shining path leads to the Land of the Dead. Others bounce around as though not sure where they are or what has happened.

For a timeless moment, I cannot move.

Exhausted men who've been living horror for moons often see things that are not there. I back away and shake myself. *It's the exhaustion, war fatigue.*

Four bucks appear at the far edge of the clearing. As though they've absorbed the firelight, their thick coats flicker and their antler tips shine like points of flame.

When the bucks trot out onto the battlefield and begin tossing their heads as they chase the lights, everything in me longs to cry out.

The People of the Standing Stone believe that the souls of the dead must travel the sky road to reach the afterlife, but sometimes, especially after a long illness, souls become lost. The Spirit lights roam about in confusion, weeping. When the deer hear them, they run at them, catch them in their antlers, and throw them up into the heavens where the Spirits can see the Path of Souls and begin their journey to the Land of the Dead.

A child sobs, jerking my attention back to the captives. I glance from them to the wandering souls of the dead and back. My veins are on fire.

My Spirit Helper once told me that before a man crosses the bridge to the afterlife, he must discover what he's running from and why. My gaze rivets on a boy of perhaps eleven summers. His face is terror. It might as well be my own face—twelve summers ago. I know that's what I'm running from, and have been for more than half my life. I've never truly been able to come to terms with what happened to me. The only one who ever understood was Baji. She stood guard over my pain like Hadui, Wind Woman's angry son who controls the violent winds. Any man who dared to criticize me had to face her wrath, and few were brave enough.

My feet begin to walk of their own accord. Without realizing it, I find myself loping through the trees with Spirit lights bobbing around me. *Are they following me?* When the two guards in front of the captives see me coming, they tip their heads.

I lift a hand and casually kneel by the oldest woman to test her ropes. A moan escapes her lips. She has a wrinkled oval face with graying black hair and the hateful eyes of a caged she-wolf.

Barely audible, I say, "Every man here is dead tired."

This is a dream. I'm not really betraying my people.

She stares at me with her jaw clenched.

I pull a hafted chert knife from my belt and slip it into her fingers. "Wait for the right moment."

My clan will hunt me down and kill me for this.

A soft gleam swells in the darkness around me, and I realize the Spirit lights have gathered like fireflies to watch me. They blink and twinkle.

Am I dead? Was I killed in the battle, and I am actually one of them, but do not yet realize it?

The elder's expression slackens as her hand goes tight around the knife. "Is this some trick?"

I do not answer, but rise and walk over to the two guards. "Utz, Hannock, you must both be starving. Why don't you go eat? I'll take this watch."

A grin crosses Utz's face. His two front teeth rotted out long ago, leaving ugly gaps. As he ties his war club to his belt, his blue knee-length cape sways around his stumpy legs. "It's about time. I was thinking about fainting to get someone's attention."

Hannock chuckles. "One of these days, your stomach is going to be your doom."

Utz replies, "Only if it's empty, and I strive never to allow that to happen." He slaps me on the shoulder. "Thank you, Deputy. We'll return as soon as we can."

I wave an unconcerned hand. "Take your time. After you eat, you might want to scavenge the battlefield before anyone else has a chance to make off with the best items."

Hannock, a youth of seventeen summers with long black hair, gives me a conspiratorial smile. "We appreciate that. Shall we bring you something?"

"Only if you happen upon a nice pair of seashell earrings for my little sister."

Hannock laughs. "We'll see what we can find."

They head straight for the closest cook pot. As they kneel in the circle of warriors and begin filling wooden bowls, the rich scent of cornmeal mush flavored with dried plums and hickory nuts wafts on the breeze. Utz must have said something amusing; the men throw back their heads and laugh.

I turn to the woman. She is staring fixedly at me, as though she suddenly thinks she knows me. In a whisper, she asks, "Aren't you Dekanawida? The man who was to marry Chief Cord's adopted daughter, Baji?" Perhaps forty summers old, she must be a clan leader. Of course she knows me. All gazes are focused on her, as though awaiting instructions. My Flint name moves through the women.

"Dekanawida . . . It's Dekanawida . . ."

I say only, "Be patient."

The boy glances between us. The soot that coats his oval face is tear-streaked. All of the children looked starved, their faces gaunt. Several are sick. Coughs puncture the night. The boy leans toward the woman and whispers, "Mother? What's happening? Who is he?"

She swiftly saws through her ropes and shifts to work on the boy's. When he's free, she gives him the knife and says, "Cut the ropes of the person next to you, then keep passing the knife down the line. No one is to make a sound or move until I say so." She glares sternly. "Do you understand, my son?"

The boy swallows hard. "Mother, we can't run! There are too many of them. They'll slaughter us!"

She lifts her eyes to me, and for a long time our gazes hold. Of course she doesn't trust me. How can she? But I am her only hope, and she knows it. I can see that truth clearly on her face. Perhaps, she is also praying that I still have a sense of loyalty to her people.

"What will you give to save these children?" I ask.

"Whatever I have to. Just tell me what to do, *Cousin.*"

She has just called in family obligations. As I rise to my feet, the world takes on a gauzy dreamlike appearance. The firelight blurs. Whatever I do in the next few moments will determine my fate forever. I can no longer see her clearly. Her wrinkled face is nothing more than an indistinct splotch in the night. I have experienced this strange blindness and disorientation before, after being struck in the head by a war club. *Is that what happened? At this very instant I'm lying on the ground, struggling to wake?* "Someone must be sacrificed. Probably two of you. Decide now which of you is willing to die."

The elder turns to the woman next to her. She does not have to ask. The woman swallows hard and whispers, "Of course."

The elder turns back and gives me a barely discernible nod.

Two

War Chief Deru stalked through the firelit camp like a confident bear. A big, muscular man with massive shoulders, he had a square jaw and a squashed nose, crushed by the same enemy war club that had caved in his left cheek. Across the meadow, most of the men ate with their heads down, their gazes focused on what lurked inside them. Deru was a master at assessing the mood of his war parties, and he knew many of these men were angry and disheartened. They had just slaughtered relatives of men and women who only a short time ago had saved their lives, and the lives of their loved ones. Later, he expected fights to break out. They had to relieve their frustration some way.

He halted by the fire of five warriors. Each had his cape pulled tight against the cold. Their dirt-streaked faces wore hollow expressions.

He lightly slapped a man on the back. "Jonsoc, how is your arm?" Though they'd bandaged the arrow wound, it continued to seep blood through the thick leather binding.

Jonsoc, a stoutly built youth of sixteen summers, flexed his muscles and winced. He always kept his black hair cut very short, in mourning for friends lost in battle. "I can still fight, War Chief. Don't worry." His dark deeply set eyes appeared haunted.

Deru propped his hands on his hips, and it made his red-painted leather cape flare outward. "There will be no more fighting for a few days, at least

I hope not. We'll be headed straight back to Bur Oak and Yellowtail villages tomorrow."

For defensive purposes, villages had been moving closer together, combining warriors to mount larger war parties. It seemed to be working. They'd had many successes of late. Though tonight's triumph was a hollow mimicry of true victory. It had not been a battle of skilled, passionate warriors fighting for the honor of their clans, but a slaughter of sick people who could barely lift their heads from their bedding hides. An unknown fever stalked the land, making enemy villages easy targets. That's what was eating at his men. They felt like murderers, instead of warriors.

Both Deru and Sky Messenger had spoken out against the orders, arguing that it was more honorable to wait until the Flint People were well, then attack. High Matron Kittle had barely listened. In a bored voice, she'd informed them, "The council wishes to keep our losses low. Which should be obvious to you two, since you claim to be warriors. Surely you know it's easier to kill people when they are sick and can't fight. We are also, all of us, obligated to gather enough captives to restore the numbers of clan members lost in the last battle with the Mountain People. How do you propose we do that if we do not attack someone? Get out of my sight. Both of you make me ill."

A stinking wave of smoke gusted out of the burning village, scattering the embers in the fire and flinging them about. Warriors cursed and lunged to get out of the way. Deru pulled up his cape and covered his nose until it passed. Ashes spun across the meadow like tiny tornadoes, then thrashed through a copse of leafless plum trees before vanishing into the forest.

"I wish Wind Mother would calm herself," Jonsoc said. "Her constant whining has a sickly quality that shreds my nerves."

"You're such a girl." Hannock chuckled.

Wampa's brow lifted. She shoved shoulder-length black hair away from her irritated face. She had seen twenty-four summers and distinguished herself in battle many times. Her twin sister, Yaweth, sat beside her, smiling as Wampa's hand dropped suggestively to her belted war club. "Perhaps you would like to rephrase that before I crush your skull."

Hannock grinned sheepishly. "What I meant to say is, Jonsoc, you are such an *infant*."

Jonsoc sighed. "Oh, yes, I like that much better than being called a girl. Thank you, Wampa."

Smiles replaced the hollow expressions. Warriors shoveled more cornmeal mush into their jaws and laughed as they chewed.

Deru glanced around the camp, searching for his deputy. "Has anyone seen Sky Messenger? I've been looking for him for over one hand of time."

Between bites, Hannock said, "He relieved us so we could eat. He's guarding the captives."

"Ah, good for him, always thinking of his warriors before himself."

Deru turned and saw Sky Messenger standing before the captives with his war club propped on his shoulder. Strangely, the children had stopped crying. He studied their firelit faces. They sat like small statues, still and quiet. Some must by lying down in the grass. He saw only a handful of children and two women.

Deru gave Sky Messenger a nod, and his deputy lifted a hand in return. He was a tall man, almost as tall as his legendary mother, former War Chief Koracoo. She towered over almost everyone in the village. Tonight her son had tied his shoulder-length hair back with a cord that made his round face appear moonish in the firelight. Sky Messenger's brown eyes had a tight look. Deru squinted, wondering what was wrong—other than the fact that they had just killed the families of friends.

Deru looked again at the warriors around the fire, but Sky Messenger's expression nagged at him. He rubbed his jaw. The way the children had been roped together, it would have been very difficult for any of them to lie down.

Just as he started walking toward Sky Messenger, his deputy let out a shout and pointed. *"Warriors!"*

Shrill war cries erupted on the opposite side of the camp. Wampa leapt to her feet and shouted, "We are attacked! Grab your weapons!"

Deru jerked his club from his belt and led the charge through the deep leaves toward the birches. Men ran to follow him, their own distinctive clan war yells tearing from their throats as they barreled forward, preparing to do battle with Flint warriors. . . .

Stay close to me," I hiss, and trot down the muddy bank with the women and children slipping and sliding behind me. I have my bow and quiver over my left shoulder. A war club, stilettos, and a small pouch are tied to my weapons belt. But if we are discovered, my weapons will be useless. Despite the fact that they will soon consider me to be a traitor to the Standing Stone nation . . . I will not kill my friends. These are men and women I grew up with. Warriors who have saved my life many times over.

Which means I must free these slaves quickly.

The scents of wet earth and water fill the night. The rushing river covers most of the sounds we make, and every time a child cries, one of the women runs back to shush it.

I head straight toward two dead trees that lay canted at an angle near the water. They must have blown over recently. Ax marks cover the trunks where the branches have been chopped off and used to warm longhouses, fire pottery, and cook food, but most of the trunks are intact. I stop at the thickest trunk. Three body-lengths long, it looks like it will float thirteen people. The wood has just begun to weather a silver-gray.

I turn to look at Gitchi. He stands on the river terrace where I left him, his lean body silhouetted against the firelight. He will warn me when they are coming.

Whimpers and sniffling sound as the children, and the two women, gather around me. I stare hard into their terrified faces. Their wide eyes glisten in the orange gleam reflecting from the river. "You have to be absolutely quiet. Do you understand?"

Nods eddy through the group. One of the two women, the younger, maybe sixteen summers, asks, "Are we going into the river? It'll be freezing. Can't we run—?"

"No, Dekanawida is right," the other woman, gaunt, with the skeletal face and short black hair, says. "This is the best chance we have. We can stand it."

I say, "What's your name?"

"Sagoy."

"We have to hurry, Sagoy. Both of you, help me roll this tree into the water."

The two women brace their feet, and together we roll the log into the river. When it's floating, I say, "Stay in the river for as long as you can, until you're starting to turn blue. By then, you will be far enough away that you'll probably be safe."

When Sagoy looks up at me, she's shaking badly. "But aren't you coming with us?"

"No. I—"

"They'll kill you, Cousin. You must know that!"

I wave the children forward. "Come on! All of you, wade into the water. Divide up, six on one side of the log, five on the other. You—" I point to the young woman—"take the front of the log. Try to guide it around the snags. Now! Get going."

The children splash into the icy river and grab hold of whatever they can. In only moments, their teeth are chattering. All I see as the log rides the waves is small tear-streaked faces.

Sagoy looks at me as though she's on the verge of blind panic. "They'll come after us, won't they?" She wrings her hands. "They'll chase us down!"

"Just be sure to put the river between you and them. Step out on the opposite shore and head straight for Wild River Village. It's the closest Flint Village." I cast a glance over my shoulder. Gitchi still stands looking at the camp. But I know I don't have long.

I shove Sagoy toward the log. "Hurry."

"But what about you? Where will you—?"

"I'm going to lead them on a wild chase. Now leave, before we're all dead!"

She splashes into the water and swims for the log. When it gets caught by the waves and pulled into the current, the log bucks wildly and water splashes around them. No one makes a sound. Then they are swept around the bend in the river, and I lose sight of them.

A soft bark draws my attention. Gitchi has one foot lifted.

I wave to him, and he runs like the wind, his muscular body stretching out, eating the distance between us. When he's close, I break into the run of my life.

Three

When Deru rushed into the forest, he found only two women sitting on the ground with their chins up, glaring at him defiantly. "What is this?"

He strode forward and kicked one of them in the chest, toppling her. "What are you doing here? Who are you? Survivors of the village?"

The gloating expression on the elder woman's face struck him like a blow to the belly. She was proud. Of what? He whirled to stare at where the captives were being held, certain she'd been one of them, and found them gone, along with Sky Messenger. As the slow burn of understanding began to sear Deru's chest, he gripped his war club in a hard fist.

"Utz, where are captives? Take six men and find them. Now!"

Utz ran, tapping men on the shoulder as he passed.

Through gritted teeth, Deru ordered. "Wampa, rope these two together and guard them. Hannock? Follow me."

Deru dashed back to examine the place where the captives had been held. Utz and his men were scouring the area, following out the trails through the leaves. Dredged by short legs, they headed to the water.

Hannock whispered, "They escaped down the river! Where's Sky Messenger? Did they kill him?" He immediately rushed to search the deep leaves for his friend's body.

Deru stalked down the slick riverbank, toward where Utz stood with an ugly expression on his face, examining Sky Messenger's distinctive moccasin prints. They lined the bank beside the children's.

Deru took his time walking the bank, reading the tracks. Sky Messenger and the two women had rolled a log into the water. Its path was clear. The children had been running when they'd followed the log into the water.

Deru clutched his war club tighter. A painful mixture of shock and rage surged through him. He continued walking. A short distance away, Sky Messenger had stood surrounded by the women and children . . . as though they'd been listening to him. Had he been giving instructions? Telling them what? How to avoid being recaptured by Deru?

Deru looked up. Utz's mouth was hanging open. The gap left by his rotted-out front teeth created a dark hole.

"Utz? Come here."

The warrior trotted to Deru. "Yes, War Chief?"

Deru ordered, "Take your men. Follow the riverbank south. Find Sky Messenger."

Utz glanced down at the moccasin prints and swallowed hard. "But, Deru, I don't care what it looks like, I—I don't believe it. He must have been taken hostage!"

Sky Messenger's mother, Koracoo, was Deru's closest friend, and his former war chief. She'd nominated Deru to replace her when she'd been elected as Speaker for the Women of Yellowtail Village. *Blessed Spirits, please let Sky Messenger be a hostage; then he'll only have to live down the jeers and taunts of friends asking how a bunch of women and children managed to subdue him.* He'd be the butt of jokes for a time, but he'd be alive. Unless the Flint women killed him before he could escape. On the other hand, if he had not been taken hostage . . .

"Do you believe it?" Utz asked. "That he betrayed—"

"If you keep standing here flapping your jaws, we'll never know, will we?"

"But War Chief, he's as loyal as I am. He couldn't—"

Deru gripped his arm hard. "If it looks like he's a hostage, give him the benefit of the doubt. If it's clear he's leading them . . . or running from us . . ." He didn't finish the sentence.

Utz nervously licked his lips. "I understand."

The punishment for treason was death.

Out in the river, water splashed over rocks, kicking up spray. Streamers of white foam frosted the waves as they rushed downstream toward the lands of the Flint People.

"Be back by tomorrow at noon," Deru ordered. "We will wait for you until then. Now move."

Utz backed away, calling to his search party, "Follow me! We're heading down the river."

With narrowed eyes, Deru watched the seven men trot away. On the opposite shore maples swayed in the icy breeze. Snowflakes had started to fall, featherlike, softly alighting on the branches. A crystalline sparkle lit the air.

"He's not a hostage," Deru whispered as he looked down at the clear tracks in the mud. "Why did he do it? He must have known the consequences."

Deru gripped his war club. He would rather face an entire Flint war party than call Koracoo's son a traitor.

He trudged back up the bank and out into the firelit meadow. His men stood in a semicircle waiting for him. Snow had already begun to frost their shoulders and heads. Their hushed voices sounded like the low hiss of a snake.

"Are all the captives gone?" one man called. "Two were mine!"

"Four belonged to my clan!" another man called.

"Where's Sky Messenger? Is he dead?"

Deru held up his hands to still the assault. "We know nothing yet. Go back to your suppers. Eat and sleep. We will remain here until Utz and his search party return. We won't have any answers until then."

Deru strode through the mumbling crowd and straight back to where Wampa held the two women. When she saw him coming, Wampa rose, clutching her war club. "War Chief, they say they are not from this village. They saw the smoke at dusk and came to find out what had happened."

He grunted. Wrinkles carved lines around the older woman's mouth and furrowed her forehead. Gray-streaked black hair clung damply to her sunken cheeks.

Deru crouched before her. "Who are you?"

The old woman chuckled. She'd seen perhaps forty summers and had an air of authority about her. She was accustomed to respect, which meant she had wielded power in her village.

He said, "Don't lie to me. I know you were one of our captives."

Her lips curled into a contemptuous smile. "That means nothing to me."

"It will. Soon. I plan to question your friend first." He gestured to the second, younger, woman, who had seen perhaps twenty-five summers. "Is that what you wish? Your silence will cause her great pain."

The old woman's nostrils trembled with loathing. "You can't hurt us now. Those we love are safe."

"For a while. But my search party will recapture them. How did you escape?"

Silence.

"Did my deputy, Sky Messenger, help you?"

Wampa sucked in air, startled by the suggestion, but she said nothing.

Wind Woman shrieked through the forest. When she hit the meadow, she tossed up autumn leaves like a playing child, and they fluttered away on the gust.

The old woman closed her eyes and began Singing her death Song. She had a deep, quavering voice that sent a chill through Deru's blood. The other woman joined her, and together their voices drifted over the camp. Every warrior quieted to listen.

Deru rose to his feet.

Wampa walked closer to him and softly said, "War Chief, it's not possible. Sky Messenger would never—"

"That's what I would have said one finger of time ago. But that was before I saw the tracks on the riverbank."

Wampa's face slackened. "Then . . . there's proof?"

"Not proof. Not yet." He waved a hand at the two women. "Wampa, take the captives to my fire, and shove some large branches into the coals. Fiery brands always hasten answers."

Four

Long before dawn, my lungs feel like they're on fire. I'm so exhausted I can barely concentrate. The storm has worsened. Icy wind whips my cape about my legs, hindering me as I climb through the deep snow, trying to reach the trail that runs along the ridgetop. If I can make it to the windswept highlands where the snow isn't so deep, the running will be easier. But this steep slope is slick and difficult. Towering hickory trees thrash above me, their dark limbs flailing against the faintly brighter sky.

Somewhere ahead, Gitchi climbs. I don't see him, but I hear his paws scratching for purchase. The sound makes me work harder.

I cast a glance over my shoulder. Wavering sheets of snow obscure the landscape. But they're back there. Seven warriors. One of them is Utz. I heard him calling orders when they almost caught me around midnight.

I grab hold of an exposed root and pull myself over a ledge where I can look down on my backtrail. Nothing. I see no one. I slump to the snow, trying to catch my breath. They're probably reeling on their feet, too.

They know, however, that they can't let me get too far ahead or the snow will cover my trail and they'll never find it again.

I scoop a handful of snow and shove it into my mouth. It goes down cold and seems to become a block of ice in my belly. My stomach knots. I eat more snow and contemplate what orders my friends carry. I have known Deru my entire life. Many times, he has treated me like a son.

Despite his affection for me, however, he is war chief. If he believes me guilty of treason, he must make an example of me.

Which means they have orders to kill me on sight.

Gitchi trots back and stands at my shoulder, panting. Even in the darkness, his eyes glint when he turns to look at me. I stroke his throat, and he whimpers, as though to say, *"Get up. We have to keep moving."*

I say, "I know," and force myself to stand. Wavering veils of white blow across the ridgetop. The trail is a vague serpentine slash through the forest, rising and falling with the terrain. Deer have kept it open, their hooves churning the snow away, their legs dredging it back.

Gitchi trots out ahead and vanishes into the falling snow. I pound the trail behind him.

It quickly becomes routine: just run, don't think about the future. Instead, I fall into the past. . . .

. . . She runs at my side, her perfect face streaked with sweat, her long hair dusted with summer pollen. . . .

How can these memories be so clear? Her footsteps are there. It's unnatural. A spike driven into the heart.

. . . Occasional touches, a bare brush of skin inflaming the world . . . Breathing hard because we know what we want of each other, but it must wait . . . Messages passing between us, directly through lips, eyes, carried on the sweltering, dogwood-perfumed, air . . .

Unconsciously, I reach for her, like a man in danger would reach for his war club. My fist closes on snowflakes. She is not here. She is not.

Behind me, twigs crack.

A voice. Utz.

I do not stop to look. I force my burning muscles to charge ahead. Like a madman, I dash around boulders and leap trees that have fallen across the path. Gitchi's sleek body flashes on the trail ahead of me, dark gray against the white snow.

"There he is!" Utz calls.

"I see him."

I do not recognize the second voice, and for a brief instant I try to determine why not. Has the man's voice gone hoarse from running? Perhaps he's turned away from me and his words are being blunted by the trees? Or maybe emotion has strangled it—because he knows what comes next?

As I pound into a dense grove of maples, the darkness closes in. Owls huddle on the branches, their feathers fluffed out for warmth, watching me with glistening eyes.

When I emerge from the grove, I enter a clearing ringed by short witch-hazel trees covered with straggly yellow blossoms. Winter solstice is only two moons away, and they are blossoming. Though these are the last flowers, for the fruit pods have already popped their seeds and sent them flying. The husks blow across the snow.

Momentarily, I am confused. I look around for Gitchi, or his tracks. I see neither. Which way did he go?

Utz calls, "I told you . . . south . . . Hannock, you go . . ."

They're spreading out, surrounding the meadow.

Suddenly, Wind Mother dies down to a soft purl. The branches stop clattering, and a lethal silence possesses the world. If I make a single move, they'll hear me. As though the Cloud People have sliced open their own bellies to hide me, torrents of snow flood from the dark sky. Wet snow, heavy. I can no longer see the trees, or anything more than two paces away. I swing around to look behind me. They could be right there and I'd never . . .

Yes. There.

A man walks through the heavy snow toward me. Soundless. His silhouette is faint, but definitely there. Swaying. Every instinct I have is urging me to pull my war club from my belt and strike him down before he sees me. As my heartbeat thrums, I start asking questions. Just because he is a friend, is his life worth more than mine? Besides, I don't have to kill him. Just disable him. Knock him unconscious so he can't call out. But if he does call out . . .

Subtly, I draw my club and brace my feet.

The snow has become a solid wall, pouring out of the darkness. It is so quiet I hear the flakes alighting on my shoulders. I blink to clear my eyelashes.

I've lost sight of him. Did he turn? Is he walking away from me? How is it possible that I hear nothing? His feet should be crunching snow.

As my fingers tighten around the shaft of my war club, my shoulder aches with fiery intensity. It is an old injury, broken by an enemy warrior when I'd seen eleven summers. On cold nights, it always hurts.

Another glimpse. Movement.

My heart beats harder, pounding against the large False Face gorget—a shell pendant that covers half my chest—resting beneath my war shirt. When Father gave it to me, he told me it would protect me. It is a Power object. Alive. Its soul is always present with me, but especially when . . .

The Voice is barely audible, *"Bahna is right. It's about forgiveness. All of it."*

The creature seems to ooze from the storm. Like an amorphous black cloud, he takes shape less than eight hand-lengths from me. My arms go weak. I lower my weapon. Old Bahna is a Healer in my home village, Yel-lowtail Village, but I have no notion what he's talking about.

He steps closer. His black cape has no snow upon it, but gleams as though enameled with the night. As always, I wonder if he's really here, or stands bathed in moonlight in the Land of the Dead, and only appears to be here in this meadow. He's never come this close to me before. My skin tingles as though I'm covered with biting ants. He's turned slightly away, watching the warriors who almost certainly surround us.

I've never known his real name. My sister, Tutelo, gave him a name twelve summers ago: Shago-niyoh. I so often only hear his voice seeping from the air that I generally call him "the Voice."

Barely audible, I breathe, "Why are you here?"

The earthiness of wet bark suffuses the darkness. The creature takes a step closer and stops with his black cape swinging around his tall body. I gaze into the utter darkness inside his hood. He leans toward me until his face—if he had one—would be almost touching mine, and says, *"Drop all of your weapons."*

I stiffen as though I've been slapped. Does he want me dead? Even if I do not plan to use them on my friends, I will surely need them later. "Why?"

"You are no longer a warrior."

Stunned, I say, "That won't matter to the Mountain People, or the—"

"Head north into the country of the Island People. I have one task to take care of; then I'll find you. Remember what I said."

"About forgiveness or the fact that I am no longer . . ."

There is only cascading snow in front of me now. I blink. Look around. It takes a few moments to catch my breath. My soul must be loose. The meadow is silent. Where are my pursuers? Where is Gitchi? He's proba-bly bedded down in the snow, hiding, as I taught him to do when enemy warriors approach.

I listen for any sound.

Wet flakes quietly pat upon my cape.

Finally, I look at the war club in my fist, heft its familiar weight. My life may well depend upon this single act. Still . . . I have never disobeyed Shago-niyoh before, but every instinct I have is telling me that this is suicide.

I force my hand to lay the club down. As I do, my fingers sting. Have I been clutching it so tightly? I scan the snow again, searching for move-ment, ready to grab the club if necessary.

Somewhere above me, beyond the snow, the Cloud People must be thinning, for paler gray stains the darkness. If I'm still here, in this open meadow, when my pursuers have enough light to see, I won't have to worry about anything ever again.

One by one, I strip my weapons belt, dropping stilettos, knives, anything else that might conceivably be considered a weapon. Each lands in the deep snow with barely a sound.

My empty hands flex at my sides. I've been a warrior for twelve summers. If I am no longer a warrior, what am I? *Who* am I?

I look around, trying to get my bearings. Which way is north?

In warrior's practice, when we are children, our parents blindfold us, lead us around in circles for half the day, and then lock us in a hole in the ground. From within the blackness, we must be able to identify the directions.

When I'm on the war trail, it's easy. The position of Elder Brother Sun, or the slant of sunlight, gives away the directions. Even at night, the positions of the campfires of the dead mark them. But at night in a storm? I have only my internal sense of place.

I close my eyes and try to feel the land. *What direction am I facing?* The faintest breeze blows. It's fall. Wind Mother usually comes from the west or north. The wettest snows, like this one, are born out over Skanodario Lake . . .

After several moments, I turn to the right, and start walking.

Five

War Chief Hiyawento's gaze drifted over the Wolf Clan longhouse in Coldspring Village. Four hundred hands long, the house spread forty hands wide, and forty-four tall. Twenty families lived here, their personal space arranged in ten compartments on either side of the house. Longhouses were basically one gigantic room with each family's compartment screened from its neighbor's by a bark wall on each side, and a curtain in front that could be drawn closed. However, for warmth, the curtain was generally left open facing the fire pit. That meant that Hiyawento could see across the house to the compartment on the opposite side. They shared the fire that stood between their compartments. Pedeza and her husband lay beneath thick hides on the wide sleeping bench attached to the wall and suspended six hands off the floor. Just like his own family's compartment, a long storage shelf hung above them, filled with pots of dried herbs, folded clothing, hides, tools, and several bark baskets containing dried corn kernels, beans, and nuts. A bundle of arrows was propped upright, the sharp chert points aimed at the roof. He thought that young Pedeza might be watching them, perhaps listening in the hope of learning his wife's plans. He'd heard that the council meeting today had been long and intense. So far, his wife, Matron Zateri, had told him nothing of what had happened, but he knew from her tone that the meeting had been deathly important.

"He needs me," Hiyawento murmured, lying in the warm nest of bearskins with his arms around Zateri. He gently stroked her long black hair. She felt so fragile, her bones small and thin. "I may be the only man in the world who truly understands what Sky Messenger did and why."

"Then you believe the Trader's story that he freed Flint captives and fled into the forest?"

"Yes."

Zateri shifted to look up at him. There were people who would say she was not a great beauty. Her two front teeth stuck out slightly, and she had a flat face with a wide nose and brown eyes that could melt a man's soul . . . at least his soul. He considered her to be the most amazing and beautiful woman in the world. But he saw more than others. Or perhaps it was that he'd known her since she'd seen ten summers, and understood her better than they ever could.

"What makes you think he's alive?" She always spoke slowly, as though considering each word before she uttered it.

"A feeling. And if he is, he needs a refuge and a friend."

Ordinarily she would have hugged him and wished him well, perhaps even decided to go with him. Instead, Zateri seemed to be staring at the dried cornstalks, bean vines, and sunflowers. They hung from the roof poles, drying in the warm sooty air that rose from the fire pits. Her breathing had gone shallow. Whatever she was tracking in her thoughts, it was dangerous.

He said, "Rumor says the council meeting in Atotarho Village this morning was grim. What happened?"

She shook her head lightly. "I need to think more on the consequences before I speak of it."

"What consequences?"

She reached out to twine her fingers with his, but did not answer.

Someone coughed at the far end of the longhouse; then a baby started crying. It seemed to awaken Zateri from her thoughts. "When are you going after him?"

"After tomorrow's War Council."

For a time, the silence was broken only by the whistling of Wind Mother as she scurried around the house chasing her two wayward twins, Gaha and Hadui. Even if he had not known his wife would be upset by his intentions, he could feel her muscles go tight with the uneasy knowledge that enemy warriors filled the trails.

"I love him, too," she said. "You know I do. But if you are killed while searching for Sky Messenger, what of our daughters then?"

He propped himself up on one elbow to gaze down into her eyes. His shoulder-length black hair caught a thread of light from the fire and gleamed with an amber brilliance. "I could be killed by your father tomorrow or War Chief Yenda from the Mountain People the day after. I could even be stupid enough to fall into the icy river and be swept downstream so that you'd never find me." He added, "I am not so easily killed, my wife. I'll be back. I give you my oath."

Beneath his hand, he felt her suck in a deep breath. "Who will serve as war chief while you are away?"

"Kallen has been an excellent deputy to me. She will guard our people well." He tenderly kissed her forehead and saw lines of worry etch the skin at the corners of her dark eyes. "Why won't you tell me what happened in the council meeting today? Was it that bad?"

She rolled away from him onto her back and stared up at the thick smoke that eddied along the ceiling. Drawn to the smokeholes above the fire pits, it would be sucked out into the night. "Grandmother is ill."

Her grandmother, High Matron Tila, had ruled the nation for thirty-three summers. "How ill?"

"Father says she will cross the bridge to the afterlife soon." She paused as though not wishing to say the next sentence. "Grandmother asked me to return to Atotarho Village and fulfill my responsibilities to the Wolf Clan."

Hiyawento's shoulder muscles hardened. He waited a full sixty heartbeats before he asked, "Will you?"

The day she'd become a woman at the age of fourteen summers, she'd left her father's village and moved a short distance away to establish this village, Coldspring Village. Many people had followed her, depleting Atotarho's ranks of warriors, potters, hunters, and builders, as well as the most powerful holy people, the shamans who called the rains from clear blue skies, and Healed the sick. While the Wolf Clan had refused to condemn her, the ruling matrons had relegated Zateri to the lowest status possible in the Women's Council. She was the matron of Coldspring Village, deserving of respect, but her words were always ignored. This would change everything. If she accepted the high matron's offer, she would step into the role of her dead mother and become the next woman in line for the position of high matron of the Wolf Clan, the most powerful woman in the Hills nation.

"Do you think Father is telling the truth?" she asked. "Do you think Grandmother is that ill?"

Hiyawento tightened his arms around her. "I think your father is a liar and a murderer. But my opinion doesn't matter. What do you think?"

She swiveled her head to gaze at their sleeping daughters, and her long black hair drew across his muscular arm like an ermine blanket. Aged three, five, and eight, the girls slept beneath one large elkhide, their sweet firelit faces in a row, breathing deep. Above their bedding, attached to the longhouse wall, yellow pond lily roots hung like the legs of a gigantic spider. In the flickering light, they seemed to wiggle and jerk. Yellow pond lily was a powerful Spirit plant. It blinded witches. If a witch looked toward this house, they would see only a pond. The roots kept their precious daughters safe. "I'm not sure I wish to lay such a burden upon our eldest daughter. Kahn-Tineta has a gentle soul."

Hiyawento's eyes were abruptly drawn to the opposite side of the house. Blessed Spirits, now he understood Pedeza's attention. If Zateri refused to return to Atotarho Village, then Pedeza's mother might be in line for the rulership, and after her, Pedeza herself.

He whispered in Zateri's ear, "Don't take too long. Pedeza's mother might decide to take fate into her own hands by getting rid of you."

Zateri did not laugh. "That possibility has already occurred to me, my war chief. Perhaps you should remain here, close at hand, to protect me."

"You can take care of yourself. I've seen you swing a war club." When her brow furrowed, he drew her closer and kissed her hair. "Forgive me. I know how serious this is."

The idea of moving his family to Atotarho Village left him in shock. He'd always hated her father. The high chief of the People of the Hills was a twisted monster. He acted only for his own gain—which was the definition of witchery. No one in the nation dared call him a witch, though, for fear his entire family would disappear mysteriously.

Alarm must have been clear on his lean face, for Zateri whispered, "I am the only daughter of my dead mother, the heir to the rulership of Atotarho Village and the entire nation. I cannot just refuse. Such selfishness and apparent disregard for the well-being of my People might cause them to accuse me of witchcraft."

He fumbled with a lock of her long hair. "You will be young for that position—twenty-two summers. Will the older women listen to you?"

Zateri wet her lips, and her protruding front teeth flashed with firelight. "They'll have to. As the leader of the Matrons' Council, I could directly influence the outcome of decisions. Now I am but one very small voice in the din."

He hesitated, afraid to ask the question that was making his throat ache. "Then, you're leaning toward agreeing to the high matron's request?"

After a long time, she said, "Maybe."

She turned her face away to stare at their daughters again, and her eyes tightened with the weight of the decision. "When is the War Council tomorrow?"

"Just after dawn."

"Dawn," she repeated in a forlorn voice and squeezed her eyes closed. "You're leaving tomorrow afternoon. No one has seen Sky Messenger in over one-half moon. What makes you think you can find him?"

"If he truly wants to hide, I won't. I'm just hoping he needs a friend."

"Well," she said with authority, "you know he does. The news has been running the trails like wildfire. Every Trader who enters our village says that Matron Kittle has accused him of treason and made him Outcast. Do you think he really helped the Flint captives escape?"

"I do . . . and you and I both know why. None of us can tolerate taking child captives."

"Yes, but declaring him Outcast without hearing his side of the story seems extreme to me."

"He also abandoned his war party, Zateri. That's not in question. He was deputy. No high matron could condone such a breach."

"I pray he went back to Baji. Perhaps they married, as they intended, and all is well."

"Perhaps, but I think such news would have reached us by now. His desertion of the Standing Stone nation would be a great coup for the Flint People. They would be paying every passing Trader to carry the news far and wide."

She filled her lungs and expelled the words, "If anything happens to him, it will crush my heart, too."

Hadui thrashed the leather curtain that covered the longhouse entry and blasted his way down the central corridor, throwing ashes high into the smoky air. Dogs leaped up barking, searching for the intruder, while people cursed and rolled over to go back to sleep.

"What if you don't find him?"

Hiyawento tilted his head and shrugged. "I'll return home."

"How long?"

"You mean how long will I give myself to search? One moon. No more."

She flipped over, threw her arms around his neck, and hugged him fiercely. "One moon. One entire moon. So much can happen in that amount of time. Be careful. Promise me you'll take no foolish chances. You are my heart and my strength. I couldn't stand to lose you."

"I will be careful. Now," he said and pulled slightly away from her to face her, "promise me something."

"What is it?"

"Promise me you will not make your decision about the high matron's offer until I return."

Her delicate brows drew together over her wide nose. "Grandmother has scheduled another Wolf Clan meeting three days from now. I promise you I will try to stall them, but I may not be able to. Why did you ask that?"

Barely above a whisper, he said, "Your father."

Zateri rolled onto her elbows, her dark hair hanging in a torrent to the bedding hides. Her voice was thoughtful, but not surprised. "So you think he's behind this, too?"

"Chief Atotarho always has hidden motives." Across the fire, he saw Pedeza cock an ear. Had he spoken so loudly? He lowered his voice, "I suspect he wants you in his village for another reason."

"Perhaps because if grandmother dies, and I do not return home to take up my rightful position as high matron, our clan may lose its right to rule, and the next clan, undoubtedly the Bear Clan, will replace him as chief?"

A hard smile edged his lips. That was something few people noticed about Zateri. Beneath her slow words lurked a stiletto-sharp mind with an almost supernatural sensitivity to tones of voice or the slightest shift of posture. There was not much she missed. *That's why, may my daughters and granddaughters forgive me, she will make a truly great high matron of the People of the Hills.*

He touched her cheek. "If you need help while I am away, you can go to Sindak. You know that, don't you?"

"He is my father's war chief, Hiyawento." She reached up, took his hand, and pressed it to her lips for a long moment before answering, "But, yes, I know I can trust him. I have trusted him since I was ten summers."

Many hands of time later, lying awake listening to the wind shiver the bones of the longhouse, memories taunted Hiyawento. They were not the thoughts of daylight, but the nagging images that come only in the dead of night and will not leave a man in peace. Jumbled, events out of order, he heard the distant chaos of screams and shouts, glimpsed the old woman's wrinkled face, and found himself lying hurt in a long-ago meadow so afraid he couldn't stop shivering. Snowflakes fell from the moonlit sky and perched upon the bare branches like fallen stars. The black bulk of the evil warrior Dakion loomed over him like Grandfather Bear standing on his hind legs. As the man lifted his war club to crush Hiyawento's skull, a hoarse shriek broke from the lips of Hiyawento's best friend, Odion, barely eleven summers. Then Odion stepped into the space below Dakion's uplifted arms, and the stiletto flashed in his hands. Odion repeatedly plunged it into the man's chest, belly, arms, anything he could reach.

He saved me.

An odd silence descended over the memory. Dakion's cries drifted slowly away in icy puffs. Odion's wavering scream faded like a dancing slip of foxfire.

Why had the sound died? Was it because he could no longer bear those voices? Or because he had relived this moment so many times that the shrieks had disfigured his souls? Like thick scars they wormed through his entire life. He could trace them with his hands; he didn't need to hear them.

In the drifting mist behind his eyes, the huge man-shaped blackness continued to writhe, heaving its bulk sideways to avoid the stiletto, trying to throw off the small boy on top of him, the boy who would not give up until the blackness stopped moving.

Though Hiyawento knew he lay in a warm longhouse surrounded by people who loved and respected him, he could not help but relive the terror of that final instant.

After an eternity, his gaze drifted over the few things arrayed in baskets lining the northern partition wall. They did not own much—no one did—but these simple things were precious to Zateri: a mussel shell bracelet that had belonged to her mother, an oddly shaped pot he'd brought her from his last battle walk against the People of the Mountain, a handful of quartz crystals that shone like shattered stars. Though deeply asleep, Zateri had one hand twined in the sleeve of his shirt, as though she couldn't bear to have him move too far away from her. The chill of her fingers penetrated the hide and cooled his arm. Gently, so as not to wake her, he drew the bearskin up over her hand to keep it warm.

His movements must have awakened his eight-summers-old daughter. Kahn-Tineta rolled to her back and yawned a wide deep yawn that revealed her missing front teeth. She blinked around the longhouse. When her gaze finally turned to him and she found him smiling at her, she slipped from her bedding hides and tiptoed across the floor to crawl beneath the bearskin beside him.

"Why aren't you asleep, my daughter?" He put his arm around her and kissed the top of her tangled hair.

She nuzzled her cheek against his shoulder. "I woke and saw you staring at Mother. You looked like you needed someone to hold you." She slipped her small arm over his chest and hugged him hard.

As though all the horrors he'd been reliving were nothing more than shreds of mist in bright sun, they evaporated. He stroked Kahn-Tineta's hair and whispered, "What took you so long?"

She giggled against his shoulder and yawned again. Within heartbeats she was asleep with her arm still around him.

He sighed and closed his eyes.

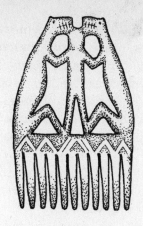

Six

From the dark recesses of the morning forest, a child's sobs echoed.

Sonon flipped up his black hood and continued along the icy riverbank, placing his sandals with care. To his left, the river roared over rocks, sending splashes leaping ten hands high. A misty halo of sparkling droplets fell in the wake.

He took his time. At dawn the snow had turned to freezing rain. Everything was sheathed with ice: the weathered driftwood along the shore, the tangled piles of freshly broken branches. Many trees had split down the middle. Others drooped mournfully, their heavy limbs bent and dragging the ground. Across the forest, a symphony of snaps, loud cracks, and thumps rang out as branches succumbed to the burden and came crashing down.

A whimper. Just ahead.

He hurried as much as the ice allowed.

When he reached the little girl, Sonon crouched beside her. She'd lost her grip on the log. The others had tried desperately to grab her as she was swept past. One of the women, the older one, had shoved away from the log and jumped in after the child.

He studied the body. The river had been brutal, raking her over rocks, dragging her across shallows—until she'd washed ashore here. Coated with ice, her naked body lay curled on its side—as though about to be born. She'd seen perhaps six summers, and bruises and cuts mangled her face, but it was also ethereally beautiful. The ice had turned her starved features into shimmering otherworldly sculptures. Frozen black hair slicked down around her face. Through the thin veil of ice, her shrunken opaque eyes stared up at him.

Another whimper.

He didn't turn. Instead, he looked out across the river where branches rolled in the waves, turning over and over as they were dragged downstream.

He caught a yellow twinkle at the edge of his vision.

Mildly, Sonon called, "Are you afraid?"

The cries stopped.

"It's confusing, isn't it?"

Stillness now. Observing.

Sonon had no idea how she saw him. Did he appear to be a man? An Earth Spirit? Perhaps one of the Flying Heads that thrashed through the trees?

"I'll make sure you get home," he said gently. "Don't worry about that. Please, come out of the shadows."

No movement.

As Elder Brother Sun climbed into the morning sky, the ice-coated trees resembled a translucent quartz forest. Every twig caught the sunlight and held it. When the breeze stirred them, the branches tinkled like seashell bells.

As he shifted, his shadow fell over the girl's frozen body. For a long moment, it held his attention.

Before he and his twin sister were sold into slavery at the age of eight summers, he used to go out of his way not to step on people's shadows, and was horrified if anyone stepped on his. It was strange to think of now. Even as a boy, he'd known shadows were more than darkness.

A carefully placed foot crackled the ice. Coming toward him.

Sonon vented a breath and watched the water splash over the rocks. People tended to dwell on the last moments, reliving them, trying not to die. This little girl must still be seeing the snow fall through the waves above her. Her heart must be fluttering as her lungs go cold. She may be struggling to call out to someone, a parent probably.

Flickers . . . at the edge of his vision. Trying not to frighten her, he turned slowly.

The small golden light swayed in the air. Beneath it, a pale shadow mirrored its movements. Most people could not see soul shadows, but they were always there. Everything that existed cast a shadow.

He gestured to her body. "I'm going to carry you to a place where you can see your home. You will need to visit your relatives in their dreams and guide them to the place where your body rests."

"Why?"

"So they can find you and prepare you to cross the bridge to the after-life."

The light flared, then faded to near nothingness, and trembled. *"Am I dead?"*

"Do you see your shadow?"

"Yes."

"It is the connection point between light and dark, between this world and the next. Once you've been prepared for the journey, it will lead you across the bridge to the afterlife, where your new life will begin."

He slipped his hands beneath her body and lifted it into his arms. She was feather-light. As he walked toward a high point overlooking the river, her crooked broken legs shook limply. He glanced over his shoulder to make certain the Spirit light was following. It was not easy to look upon your own death.

The light bobbed a few paces behind.

He climbed the low hill and placed her on top in the middle of a sunlit crystalline forest. The iced branches cast lacy patterns over her. He did his best to straighten her arms and legs and arrange her head so that she could watch the sky turn. "They'll be coming for you very soon. You must remain close to your body, though, so you don't get lost. Do you understand?"

As he rose and walked down the hill, heading back toward the river, the small bright light moved to hover over the little girl's body. Both cast shadows—the dead body and the soul light.

That was all that mattered now. It was all that ever mattered.

Sonon headed west, taking shelter in his own shadow, letting it guide his steps.

Seven

Elder Brother Sun had long ago crested the forest canopy, but the council house had not yet given up its deep cold. Hiyawento rubbed his arms beneath his heavy moosehide cape. Sunlight streaming down from the smoke hole forty hands above the central fire created swirling patterns in the thick bluish gray smoke that filled the house. He watched them for a time, as the representatives from the other villages entered. They all tried to arrive at the same time, so as not to force any village to suffer the indignity of waiting for others, but delays occurred. Today, the contingent from Riverbank Village came in last. Many were exhausted warriors, their capes still coated with the dust of the trail. Wearing grim expressions, they stripped off their weapons belts, unslung their bows and quivers, and placed them along the south wall near the entry. After the brilliance of the autumn dawn, it took time for their eyes to adjust to the dim council house. Finally, they proceeded sunwise around the fire to take up their proper positions. Before they sat, they turned, and each gave a respectful nod to the matrons sitting together on the east wall.

The six old women were the true decision makers. As the leaders of the Wolf, Bear, Deer, Snipe, Hawk, and Turtle clans, they would listen until all was said and done here today; then they would take the issues back to the other village matrons, who would in turn discuss them with every member of their clans before rendering a decision as to how to proceed. Each wore a cape painted with the sacred symbols of her clan.

Hiyawento and his deputy, Kallen, sat on the log on the north side of the fire. To his right were the Riverbank Village representatives, and to his left sat the people of Turtleback Village. Directly across the fire, the council members from Atotarho Village, including the evil chief himself, continued to stand together whispering. As the leader of the entire nation of the People of the Hills, Atotarho would be the last to take his seat, which was difficult for him since he suffered from the joint-stiffening disease that had so twisted his fingers and legs they appeared malformed. He had seen sixty-four summers pass, each more difficult than the last.

Hiyawento's gaze lingered on the council members from Riverbank Village. Towa should have been here. He wasn't. Originally from Atotarho Village, Towa had married and moved to Riverbank Village eight summers ago. He was a Trader and usually off on some wild expedition. Only recently had he returned home, when the violence grew too destabilizing. Hiyawento had been hoping to see him.

"Where is War Chief Sindak?" Kallen whispered from his right.

"I've been wondering the same thing. I suspect the chief will explain his absence. At least Negano is here."

Negano was Sindak's deputy war chief, but he was also the head of the chief's personal guards. He stood a short distance away, speaking softly to a grizzled old warrior. Negano had seen thirty-two summers and wore his long black hair in a single braid that draped the shoulder of his buckskin cape. It was strange to see a man with long hair these days, when so many had cut their hair in mourning.

Across the house, warriors studied each other. Everyone looked hungry. Cheeks were sunken, eyes squinted, mouths set into hard lines. Hushed voices were weary, but resolute, congratulating each other on the latest victory against the Flint People.

Hiyawento listened to them. The last battle had been brutal, costly, a waste of lives that gained many captives, but little food. In his opinion the only thing it had accomplished was to drain their slim food rations even more. With forty new captives to feed, everyone would have less.

Atotarho looked around, watching as the last of the Riverbank Village representatives was seated. As a symbol of his dedication to war, Atotarho always braided rattlesnake skins into his gray hair, then coiled it into a bun at the base of his head. The style gave his gaunt face a skeletal look. His beautiful black ritual cape, covered with circlets cut from human skulls, flashed with his movements.

Finally, Atotarho said, "Let us begin," and gingerly lowered his body to one of the logs on the south side of the fire. For several heartbeats, he sat with his head down and his eyes closed, as though contemplating the gravity of the issues that faced the council today. He rubbed his knee, and his wrinkled face tensed. His joints must ache from the long walk across the village to get here.

Atotarho lifted his hands. "Council members, the issues before us today are grave. Though united in our war against the other nations south of Skanodario Lake, we have profoundly different notions of how to win this struggle. I urge you to put such differences aside here, and allow every member to speak his heart. Lastly, please excuse the fact that my War Chief, Sindak, is absent. He is away on a crucial mission."

Kallen whispered, "What mission?"

"I know nothing of it."

As Atotarho leaned forward to retrieve the cup of plum tea that had been prepared for him, his gorget—a shell pendant that covered half his chest—fell from his cape. Everyone went silent. A sacred artifact of leadership, it was not a thing for ordinary eyes. Twelve summers ago it had been broken, the bottom half lost on a snowy hillside in the distant country of the People Who Separated. Though Atotarho had sent warriors to search for the bottom half, it had never been found, and he'd been forced to hire an artist to replicate the missing piece as best he could. A black line zigzagged through the center of the pendant where it had been glued together with pine pitch.

The pendant was ancient and chronicled the most sacred story of all: the great battle between human beings and Horned Serpent at the dawn of creation. Horned Serpent had crawled out of Skanodario Lake and attacked the People. His poisonous breath, like a black cloud, had swept over the land, killing almost everyone.

In terror, the People had cried out to the Great Spirit, and he had sent Thunder to help them. A vicious battle had ensued, and Thunder had thrown the greatest lightning bolt ever seen. The flash was so bright many of the People were instantly blinded. Then the concussion struck. The mountains shook, and the stars broke loose from the skies.

Legend said that at the time of the cataclysm, two pendants had been carved by the breath of Horned Serpent. One belonged to the chief, the other to the human False Face who would don a cape of white clouds and ride the winds of destruction across the face of the world.

Everyone felt the pendant's Power, as evidenced by the fact that they could not take their eyes from it. When Atotarho noticed, he tucked it back into his cape, and Hiyawento's gaze clung to the snake eyes tattooed on the chief's fingertips. The man wore bracelets of human finger bones.

The tallest, most heavily scarred man, Thona, a war chief renowned for his skill with a war ax, rose to his feet. "If it please the council, I would speak first."

Atotarho nodded. "War Chief Thona of Riverbank Village, please continue."

Hiyawento took a deep breath, preparing himself, and as he exhaled his breath hung before him in the cold air like a shimmering creature.

Thona rubbed a hand over his scarred face before he said, "The fever has come to Riverbank Village, brought in the bodies of the captives we took after our last battle with the Flint People."

The mood of the group changed abruptly. Perhaps all of them, Hiyawento included, had assumed that today's meeting would be about the destruction of Sedge Marsh Village, and the fearful prospect that the Standing Stone nation would continue to form more alliances with rogue Hills' villages. That's what had every clan matron enraged.

Thona propped his hands on his hips, and his cape flared outward, then fell into soft firelit folds around him. "Our Healers have removed many witch pellets from the captives' bodies, but the things are alive. Once removed they leap into another body, and another. Matron Kwahseti asks that, for the moment, we all forget about Sedge Marsh Village and their treachery, and agree to a new priority."

"And that is?"

"Our people are dying like leaves in the first heavy frost. We must find the witches and force them to remove their spells or kill them. If we don't, all of your villages are at risk, too."

A rumble of voices ran through the council house as people discussed this new development.

Kallen leaned sideways to say, "War Chief, I think we should leave. What if a witch pellet jumped into Thona's body, or another of his contingent? We could all run home carrying the fever with us. Is it worth the risk to remain? Atotarho will not listen to us anyway."

Hiyawento turned to her. Kallen had seen twenty-nine summers pass. Short black hair, cut in mourning, framed her triangular face, making her dark eyes appear huge, like polished mahogany moons riding over her thin nose. She shifted, and the soft fur of her cape, made from twisted strips of weasel hide, caught the sunlight falling through the smoke hole.

Hiyawento replied softly, "No, but perhaps the matrons will care what we have to say."

He glanced at the six old women who sat like silent white-haired statues. Their wrinkled faces might have been carved from stone, but their eyes were alert, listening to every word, and he thought he saw fear on

Tila's face. Was she dying? Or was this just a ruse to get Zateri to return to Atotarho Village?

"How many people have the fever?" Atotarho asked.

"When we left Riverbank Village three days ago," Thona said, and the white scars that crisscrossed his face tensed, "fifty-seven."

After a brief stunned silence, War Chief Joondoh of Turtleback Village stood to be recognized. Short, muscular, and loud, he said, "The Flint People did this on purpose. The cowards!"

"What are you saying?" Thona asked.

"I mean that when they heard that our warriors were on the trails, they witched their own people. They wanted us to attack and carry the sickness home."

Hiyawento opened his mouth to reply, but Thona cut him off. "They would not *dare* to do such a thing. They know we would slaughter them to the last person."

Atotarho rubbed his right knee and winced before saying, "I think they would dare. They would do anything to kill us."

"If I may comment?" Hiyawento rose to his feet, and Thona sat down. Eyes turned to Hiyawento—not all of them respectfully, for he was an adopted member of the Hills People. He had been born and raised among the Standing Stone People, and some here believed that's where his allegiance remained.

"Proceed," Atotarho said, but his eyes narrowed suspiciously. The other representatives noticed and cast distrustful looks Hiyawento's way.

"With deference to this assembly, I must say that I doubt the Flint People would witch their own families. It would be too dangerous. The disease might—"

War Chief Joondoh rose to shout, "That is *exactly* the sort of thing they would do! It would be a devastatingly effective method of killing us. After the battle, they could just have their witches remove the pellets from those who survived. Any who were captured would then become the greatest warriors, carrying the witch pellets into the very hearts of their enemy's longhouses."

"If you will allow me to finish, Chief?"

Atotarho stared at Hiyawento for a long moment before saying, "Please."

"I'm sure many of you have heard a different story from your own Flint captives." He paused to see heads nodding before cautiously continuing, "Though I'm sure none of us believes it, I think we should consider their side of this issue, for they say that the sickness comes from Chief Atotarho."

As a few outraged voices rose, Atotarho lifted a hand to silence them. "Go on, War Chief."

Hiyawento said, "Our captives say Atotarho has hired armies of witches to sicken his enemies, and that it is we who are to blame for the fever. In fact, the few survivors of the Sedge Marsh attack are adamant that their village grew ill and died in less than two days. They say that by the time the warriors from Atotarho Village arrived to punish them for allying with the Standing Stone nation, nearly everyone was already dead. That's why the chief lost not a single warrior in the fight." He looked around at the assembly. "It does sound like witchery."

Several warriors leaped to their feet with murderous expressions on their faces. He suspected they would have carried out those impulses if their weapons had not been stacked along the far wall. Hiyawento calmly sat down.

"That is a disgraceful accusation," Thona said in a seething voice. "Our chief does not consort with witches."

"Nonetheless," Hiyawento replied, "that is what they believe, and that is why they hate us so much. Perhaps if we made some effort to disprove this notion, if we sent some of our Healers to the Flint People, for instance, it might save the lives of many of our own villagers."

Joondoh roared, "The Flint People accuse our chief to cover their own witchery! It is ridiculous to pander to them."

Atotarho leaned forward and stared thoughtfully at the fire. Hiyawento scanned the faces of the warriors, assessing the impact of his words. No one looked at him, and whenever they, by chance, happened to meet his eyes, they quickly glanced away. That told him a great deal. Not only had they heard the same rumor from their Flint captives or, perhaps, the Sedge Marsh survivors, they believed them. Even if they wished to agree with him, they could not, at least not publicly, out of fear that their own families might be witched next.

Atotarho finally looked up. He stared straight at Hiyawento. "I, of course, have not heard this rumor. But now that Hiyawento has brought it in front of the council, it makes me wonder if the story is not to our advantage?" Eyes widened. People whispered behind their hands. "I do not object to being greatly feared. If the Sedge Marsh elders had feared me more, perhaps they would not have committed treason by allying themselves with the Standing Stone nation. Isn't fear the most effective weapon we have?"

A gust of wind flapped the leather door covering, and streamers of blue smoke swirled through the shafts of sunlight lancing through the smoke holes. People coughed and squinted against the onslaught while they considered the chief's question.

Joondoh rose. When Atotarho nodded, he said, "I confess that I believe this rumor may well be to our advantage. It's fear that causes the Flint People to abandon their villages when they hear we are on the trails. They leave so fast they abandon everything they have, including their meager food stores, for us to claim. Fear, it seems to me, will save far more lives than sending them Healers." He cast a disgusted look at Hiyawento.

When Joondoh sat down, Hiyawento and Thona leapt up at the same time. Atotarho nodded to Thona, and Hiyawento reluctantly reseated himself.

Thona said, "I agree with Joondoh, and respectfully submit to this council that we should make no attempt to disprove this notion."

Hiyawento stood again, but Atotarho silenced him by saying, "I think this matter has been adequately considered. Let us move on to discuss the next issue: the treachery of Sedge Marsh Village."

The change of subject had the force of a war club's impact. Warriors went silent. Many were obviously uncomfortable with dropping either the discussion of the fever, or the heinous accusation of witchcraft. On the east side of the longhouse, High Matron Tila of the Wolf Clan whispered to Matron Kelek of the Bear Clan. She nodded. Both women turned to speak to the other matrons. Moments later, they all turned to statues again.

Atotarho quietly said, "What have you all heard?"

"Treasonous dogs," Joondoh spat the last word. "We hear they allied themselves with Bur Oak and Yellowtail Villages for a few baskets of corn."

"It is obscene," Thona agreed. "They deserved to die. They had no honor, no pride in the war we fight against our enemies."

Hiyawento rose, and this time received the chief's approval. "So you all believe it?" Nods went round. Warriors leaning along the walls hissed threats in voices that brooked no disagreement. "And does anyone have proof?"

"We've heard the same story from a dozen Traders," Thona replied.

"And from Sedge Marsh captives!" Joondoh's deputy war chief, Dahana, a tall wiry man, insisted. "Why would they lie about such a thing?"

"They have no reason to lie about it." Joondoh squinted against the shifting smoke.

A chorus of soft voices went round.

At his side, Kallen expelled a breath and rose to her feet. "May I speak, Chief?"

Atotarho nodded, and Kallen said, "Coldspring Village has taken in five Sedge Marsh survivors. They have a different explanation of why they allied with the Standing Stone nation. They acknowledge that they accepted baskets of corn, but only after High Matron Tila refused to help them. They also say the alliance was one of mutual defense. They were afraid of the Flint People, and High Matron Kittle guaranteed them that she would place Standing Stone warriors on the southern trails to keep Flint war parties at bay." She sat down again.

Thona sneered. "They should have asked her to place warriors on the northern trails as well, to protect them from the wrath of their own people."

Joondoh added, "It might be wise for us to dispatch a runner to High Matron Kittle to inform her that she is responsible for the destruction of Sedge Marsh Village."

Atotarho shifted to ease the pain in his hip, and the circlets of skull on his black cape flashed. "Is Turtleback Village suggesting that we dispatch an emissary to High Matron Kittle to warn her not to interfere with any other Hills villages or she will face the consequences?"

"We are," Joondoh said.

"Riverbank Village sees no harm in this." Thona's scars gleamed whitely when he cast a respectful glance at the matrons, whose ancient faces remained impassive.

Atotarho rubbed his knee for a time before saying, "What message would the emissary carry?"

Joondoh replied, "We should tell her straightly that if she attempts to establish another alliance with a Hills Village we will attack Bur Oak Village and kill every last person."

Thona blinked thoughtfully. "Yes, but who will carry the message?"

Joondoh nodded. "They will recognize any Hills warrior who tries to approach their border. They know us just by the way we move, as we do them. Even if traveling with a white arrow, I suspect our emissary will be dead in less than a heartbeat. Perhaps a Trader?"

The white arrow signified that the traveler was on a special diplomatic mission. Most people respected it, but some did not. Kittle had been known to return white arrows soaked in the emissary's blood.

Almost too soft to hear, Atotarho said, "I agree. It must be someone they know."

While the warriors standing along the walls muttered darkly to each other, Hiyawento studied Atotarho. The chief's deeply wrinkled face had an odd expression. His eyes were downcast, apparently staring at the flames, but in the blue swirls of wood smoke that filled the sunlit air between them, Hiyawento thought he appeared almost triumphant.

Thona said, "Do you have someone in mind?"

Atotarho lifted his eyes, and his gaze fixed on Hiyawento. A faint smile touched his lips.

It took a moment for the realization to sink in, and when it did, the earth seemed to shake beneath Hiyawento. Every gaze stuck to him like boiled pine pitch.

"War Chief Hiyawento was born among the Standing Stone People. He moves as they do."

"I won't consider it!" Thona fumed and glowered at Hiyawento. "We can't trust him. It's unconscionable."

Atotarho said, "He's the best choice."

"Maybe, but what if they turn him? He may return as a spy. It's not worth it."

As a cacophony of dissenting voices erupted, Hiyawento slowly rose to his feet. "May I speak?"

"Go on."

"I am a man of the Hills People. Though I was not born among you, my wife is the chief's daughter. Our children are of the Wolf Clan. I will defend this village to my last breath, as I have done for the past eight summers." He paused to allow people to quiet down. "As all of you are aware, by allowing myself to be adopted into your people I committed treason. Rather than hearing the message I carry, I believe Matron Kittle will have me killed on sight."

Atotarho's lips pressed into a tight white line. Is that what the old witch had in mind? He could kill two birds with one arrow? He could threaten High Matron Kittle, and get Hiyawento out of the way? Or perhaps this was about Zateri? With Hiyawento out of the way would she be more inclined to return to Atotarho village?

"I think Hiyawento is far more likely to make it to the gates of Bur Oak Village than anyone born among the Hills People. Whether or not he is allowed inside the gates, I cannot say. But I believe he is still the best choice for this undertaking."

Kallen, astonished, said, "But, my chief, he will be murdered long before he has a chance to speak!" Kallen seated herself and whispered to Hiyawento, "Matron Zateri will surely vote no in the Women's Council. She—"

"No," Hiyawento cut her off. "She will vote to send me. As she should." He exhaled hard. All eyes were upon him. "Allow me to take back my objections. Chief Atotarho is right. I'm the best man for this mission."

A faint knowing smile touched Atotarho's face.

When Coldspring Village joined the Hills alliance eight summers before, every clan matron agreed to support the decisions of the Ruling Council of Matrons. If Zateri refused to accept one of the council's decisions, she would be breaking that agreement, and thereby separating Coldspring Village from the alliance. They would be on their own, a lone village vulnerable to attack by anyone. Their paltry three hundred warriors would be no match for a heavily armed party of Mountain or Flint warriors. Not only that, once the news reached their enemies, Coldspring Village would become a prime target.

On the eastern bench, Tila's frail hand lifted, and all eyes turned to her. As she leaned forward, short white hair, cut in mourning, fell around her deeply sunken cheeks. "How long will it take to prepare War Chief Hiyawento?"

Atotarho shrugged. "A day. No more. We need to carefully word our message, and make sure he can repeat it exactly."

Tila's neck trembled as she nodded. "We will discuss the issue with our clans, and return with our decision as soon as everyone's voice has been heard."

Such negotiations often took days, perhaps even moons. Hiyawento felt slightly ill. Atotarho's action had obligated him to remain close at hand until the matrons returned with their decision. And if they approved sending him to Bur Oak Village, Hiyawento would have no choice but to go. *Sky Messenger, forgive me, old friend. . . .*

"Thank you, High Matron." To the assembled warriors, Atotarho said, "This council meeting is dismissed until the matrons call a new meeting."

No one said a word as the old women rose and filed out of the house. They walked unsteadily, their white heads tottering above their capes. Tila was last in line. She used a walking stick to slowly make her way toward the leather door hanging. Once the matrons were gone, hostile voices rose, and the gazes that locked on Hiyawento were like lance thrusts. Knots of warriors began to form near the stacked weapons.

Kallen said, "I don't think you will be leaving on your journey to search for your friend today, War Chief."

"No."

Kallen's eyes slitted as she looked around. Men had started shifting their weight to the balls of their feet, moving like warriors on a blood trail. "Perhaps it would be best if we go home before this gets out of hand?"

He rose to his feet. "The sooner the better."

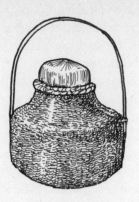

Eight

Sky Messenger

I jerk upright and try to force air into my starving lungs. The musty fragrance of fallen leaves carries on the night breeze. All around me the autumn forest is still and quiet, wrapped in a cool cloak of darkness. The campfires of the dead blaze through the swaying maple branches. I rub my hands over my face and fight to shove away the Dream images.

Gitchi whimpers. When I turn, I find the old wolf staring at me with luminous eyes.

"I'm all right." I reach out to gently stroke his side. His bushy tail wags.

After several deep soothing breaths, I heave a sigh and drag myself to my feet. Gitchi expectantly lifts his big head. The wolf has seen twelve summers pass. Though the thick fur on his lean body is still dark gray, his face has gone almost totally white. He gazes steadily at me, waiting. He has traveled the war trail with me since he was a puppy and I was a child. He knows my strange ways. This isn't the first time the Dream has awakened both of us like a clap of thunder.

Through a long, difficult exhalation, I whisper, "We have to go home, old friend. I have to tell them what I've seen."

Gitchi stretches, groans softly, and walks to my side. I know he will follow me anywhere, no matter the danger or disgrace. And there is no doubt in my heart that when I reach home my clan will heap mountains of humiliation upon me. I don't even wish to imagine the expression on Mother's face. Though she is now the Speaker for the Women of Yellowtail Village, a village of the Standing Stone People, she spent ten summers of her life as a war chief. Regaining her respect, and the respect of my clan, may well take the rest of my life.

"If it is even possible." The words echo through the dark trees, coming back sounding more desperate and forlorn than I imagined.

A deputy war chief who betrays his people after a particularly brutal battle and vanishes into the wilderness is a marked man. I pray I can make them understand why I did it, but I will probably be chased from the village as a traitor. I dare not imagine what my warriors, or my war chief, have said about me in my absence. They have, perhaps, declared me an Outcast. In that case, I am dead. When I walk through the gates, the whispering will begin, and I fear it will be like the hurricane that sweeps away my world.

I pat Gitchi's head, and he gazes up at me with loving eyes. "We may not have a home, my friend. Are you ready for that?"

He wags his tail, telling me he can stand anything so long as I am there with him.

Gitchi has always been at my side, fighting for me with blind loyalty, warming me with his body when I was freezing cold.

I have few other true friends. Four: Hiyawento; Zateri; my sister, Tutelo; and Baji. Our friendships were forged in the white-hot flames of slavery. Even when we are far apart, I feel them breathing inside me, and it gives me strength. Despite distance, or disagreements, or even death, I know they will come to find me if I need them. As I would if they needed me.

That's one of the reasons my clan considers me an oddity. I am a loner. I have never married, never produced children. To my clan this verges on being criminal. I've always managed to keep them at bay by excelling in the skills of diplomacy and warfare. Now, even that is gone.

Gitchi's luminous eyes stare off to the south. He cocks his head, as though wondering about something. I say, "I think the Flint children made it. By now, hopefully, they've found relatives in other Flint villages, and are being cared for and loved."

I reach for my pouch and tie it to my belt; then I take a few moments to study the night. Twenty paces away, a marshy bottom stretches to the east. The powerful scents of moss and wet vegetation waft on the cool fragrant air.

Gitchi stretches again, as though limbering up his stiff joints for the journey home.

Involuntarily, my gaze searches the trees for my Spirit Helper. He was just here . . . wasn't he?

Time has shifted. I don't know how long I've been here. Days? Weeks? Perhaps only moments.

Spirit Dreams, I think, do not really take place in the here and now, but in some otherworldly realm where the sky cycles have ceased. Perhaps it is the Land of the Dead. Or just a frozen future. I cannot say. "Come on, Gitchi. Let's go face Grandmother Jigonsaseh. And then . . ." I vent a deep halting breath. "Mother."

Her face appears on the fabric of my souls, and the darkness seems to close in.

As I turn toward the southern trail and begin placing one moccasin in front of the other, sweat melts down my face like tears.

Nine

Hiyawento and Zateri walked hand in hand through the cold morning. It was as if, during the night, the Spirits had frosted the forest with pearl dust, for every shrub, fallen log, and leaf that lay upon the ground glittered whitely.

When Zateri finally released his hand and stopped, they were far out into the trees, a long way from Coldspring Village. "I wanted to vote no, you understand that, don't you?" she asked with slow precision. "I know you long to be out hunting for Sky Messenger." She was so short and slender she looked childlike standing in the striped forest shadows. Her long black braid fell over the right shoulder of her white cape. Tipped up to him, her eyes wet, her face was as pretty as ever.

Hiyawento spread his hands. "You had to vote yes. I'm just surprised the decision came so quickly."

"No one objected. You were clearly the best choice."

Maples created a laced canopy over their heads, their remaining leaves like drops of blood against the blue sky. "I'm glad they think so. I'm just hoping I make it across the border into Standing Stone country. I'll be traveling under the white arrow and not allowed to carry weapons. A lone man makes for good target practice."

"Don't joke. If Kittle has you executed, it will give Father an excuse to attack the Standing Stone alliance, which will be a catastrophe. The matrons have consistently voted against it for eight summers." Worry filled her soft brown eyes. Her cape rustled as she folded her arms.

"Attacking Kittle's allied villages would be a lethal error. While they cannot muster the number of warriors we can, each village is ringed by three circles of palisades. Our losses will be very heavy."

Zateri reached down and picked up a fallen leaf. The red was still veined with pale green. She stroked it gently as she spoke. "Which means we will have to mount even larger war parties to capture children to replace our losses, and that will cost more lives, and then the whole thing will begin over again. I hate this."

"As I do. I just don't see any way out. We must protect ourselves."

On the fabric of his souls, like a faint brushstroke, flashed the moment yesterday in the war council when her father had smiled at him, and he'd felt the earth shake. To his warrior's eyes, the gesture had been larger than life, filled with unimaginable malice. After he and Kallen returned to Coldspring Village, he'd shoved it away, but he hadn't forgotten. The gesture lay like a coiled serpent sleeping in the darkness, ready to rear its ugly head and strike.

Zateri crumpled the leaf in her hand. "Don't go directly to Kittle."

His brows drew together. "But those are my orders."

"And these are mine." She spun around to stare at him. "Go to Koracoo. She is the Speaker for the Women of Yellowtail Village now. You will have a far better chance of actually meeting with Kittle if you plead your case before Koracoo first."

"Yes . . . but will she risk it?"

"I think she will."

He shifted his weight to his other foot. "Disobeying the council's orders—"

"May save your life, and the lives of many warriors who will die if your mission fails. How many relatives do you still have in Yellowtail Village?"

"Well, to my mind I have dozens of Bear Clan aunts, uncles, and cousins there. But I am Outcast. To them I do not exist."

She shook the crumpled leaf in her fist. "The Koracoo I know will at least hear you out. No matter what you've done."

"And then kill me," he said with certainty, and grinned at the irony in his own voice. Koracoo held a special place in his heart, as she did in Zateri's. It had been Koracoo—Sky Messenger's mother—who had organized the search party to find them when they'd been stolen as children. Koracoo; her former husband, Gonda; as well as Sindak and Towa had risked everything to rescue them. She would always be one of their greatest heroes. But the world had changed in the past decade, and Koracoo with it. He had no idea what pressures she might be facing or what decisions she might make when she saw him standing at the gates of Yellowtail Village.

Zateri gave him a perturbed look. "Go to Koracoo first."

"All right."

Relief slackened her face. She walked to him and slipped her arms around his waist. They stood together in the morning gleam. As Elder Brother Sun warmed the world, his light sparkled through the branches, falling around them in a dusty golden veil. On the forest floor, the golden rays resembled scattered fragments of amber. Here and there the last beetles scampered through the leaf mat.

"I've been ordered to leave at nightfall."

"I know," she whispered against his throat and hugged him tighter. When she backed away, she pulled a necklace over her head. "Traders say the fever has come to Bur Oak Village. I made this for you. It's wood nettle and white oak. It will counteract even the most powerful witchcraft. Don't take it off." She slipped it over his head.

Hiyawento tucked it into his cape. "Zateri, I want you to listen to me. Don't argue. Just listen. If anything happens to me, and it won't, but if it does, I want you to take our girls and go to Baji or Tutelo. Don't stay here. I'm afraid of what your father might do without me around to—"

"Enough, my husband," she said with tears in her voice. "I don't even wish to think of life without you. You're coming back."

He nodded firmly. "Yes. I'll be back."

"In less than half a moon."

"Thirteen days at most. Five days there, five days back, and three days to deliver the message and wrangle a way of keeping my head attached to my body." He crushed her thin body against him and kissed the top of her head.

Zateri nuzzled her cheek against his chest, and her hands slipped beneath his cape, smoothing her fingers over his chest, then venturing lower. A sensation like warm water flooded his veins.

"Zateri, we don't have much time."

"Then let's not waste it talking." She kissed him as she worked to lift his cape over his head.

Hiyawento pulled it off and spread it upon the soft leaves. Zateri sank down and extended a hand to him. "Come, let me hold you for just a short while."

He stretched out beside her and hastily worked to remove her cape and unlace the front of her soft dress.

They loved each other in the frosty meadow with Wind Mother playing through the branches above them. Each gust showered them with cascades of bright leaves.

Afterward, Hiyawento tenderly kissed the tears from her cheeks and held her tightly. "I love you, my wife. I love you so much."

"Don't take any unnecessary chances."

"You have my word."

They rose and dressed. As they walked back along the deer trail with their arms around each other, they talked and laughed, knowing full well that today might be all they would ever have.

Late that night Zateri lay in her bedding hides. Her sleeping girls snuggled beside her, as they always did when Hiyawento was gone. Every now and then laughter and soft voices eddied down the house. Somewhere, people gambled. She could hear the painted stones rattling in the cup before the gamblers tossed them out across the hide. Occasionally, a soft curse rose.

Memories filled her. Summer solstice, nine summers ago. She hadn't seen Wrass in four summers. She was a newly made woman with a woman's heart and needs, longing for children and a home . . . but unable to get over the scars left long ago by the terrifying days after she'd been sold into slavery. Every time a boy touched her, her heart seemed to shrivel in her chest. She couldn't breathe. She had the overwhelming urge to run away. Grandmother had told her to get over it. Plain and simple. *Just get over it. You are Wolf Clan. You have duties.*

Despite Zateri's objections, Grandmother had decided to negotiate her marriage to a youth from the Snipe Clan. Marriage was an obligation. Providing children for the clan a responsibility. She had little choice.

Lying here with her girls, she remembered Wrass the night she'd first seen him as a man. The summer solstice celebration that cycle had been huge. Over four thousand people had come. She'd been shouldering through the gathering, heading for the Wolf longhouse, when her breath had suddenly caught. He'd been standing at the edge of the firelight talking to three Traders. Despite the intervening summers, she would have known Wrass anywhere. He'd had the same eagle face, sharp dark eyes, and beaked nose that she'd loved when she was ten summers old—though he'd grown much taller than she'd ever imagined he would. He'd always had a special skill with languages, and had sneaked into the crowds enjoying the solstice feasting just to see her. Dear blessed gods, what a wonderful moment that had been.

When he'd finally seen her running across the plaza toward him, he'd smiled—as though seeing her again was the best thing that had ever happened to him. He'd moved away from the Traders just in time for Zateri to throw herself into his arms.

Three moons later, she had left her father's village among a flurry of accusations and threats, and formed her own village less than one-half hand of time away. Wrass was an enemy warrior, Grandmother had warned. She was a fool. Marrying beneath her. Father had been furious when she'd adopted Wrass into the Hills nation and requickened in him the legendary soul of her ancestor, Hiyawento, also known as He-Who-Combs-Away-Evil. She hadn't cared. Of all men, Hiyawento knew what she'd been through. In his arms, she found shelter and understanding. She longed for nothing more than to spend the rest of her life with him.

Kahn-Tineta shifted, rolling over, and Zateri looked at her eldest daughter. The girl's mouth was slightly open, showing her missing front teeth. If all went well, in five or six summers she would be married with her first child on the way. Zateri had already begun thinking about the boys in the village, sorting them, watching the ones who seemed to be brave, honest, loyal.

Pedeza's dog, Little Boy, got to his feet, stretched, and peered down the length of the house, as though curious about something he saw. A few instants later, Sindak, the war chief of her father's village, appeared standing at her fire, warming his hands. His black cape bore a coating of dust, as did his buckskin leggings. He had seen thirty-one difficult summers of almost constant warfare, and the trials had left their mark on his lean face, etching lines around his hooked nose and deeply sunken eyes. He wore his shoulder-length hair pulled back and tied with a cord.

Very softly, he whispered, "Are you awake?"

She nodded and eased out of the bedding hides so as not to wake her daughters, then reached for her cape, slipping it on as she walked toward him. "What's wrong?"

He gave her a smile, easing her fears. For her ears alone, he said, "I sent two men with him. No one knows. I told your father I'd sent them out to scout the trails."

Zateri threw her arms around his neck and hugged him hard. "Thank you, Sindak. Thank you. I was so afraid."

"You must tell no one." He gently shoved away from her, and his sharp gaze scanned the nearby compartments before he whispered, "It'll mean my head if Atotarho finds out."

"I understand."

He smiled at her again, but he made no move to leave. Instead, he looked away and frowned.

"When did you get back?" she whispered. "I heard you were gone."

"I was. I returned two hands of time ago. I haven't even reported to the chief yet."

Uneasily, she asked, "Where were you?"

Little Boy trotted across the floor and stood looking up at Sindak. The war chief absently patted the dog's head. "I have something more important to discuss with you. Something you probably haven't thought about in many summers."

"What is it?"

"Do you know what happened to Hehaka?"

A cold sensation, like ice forming in her veins, went through her. Her brother had disappeared long ago. "I heard rumors, that's all."

"What rumors?"

Zateri shrugged. She didn't like remembering; the images were stilettos lodged in her heart. "You . . . you remember. He ran away from Atotarho Village after only three days. I thought he would find another village. Another home. He'd only seen eleven summers. I convinced myself that someone would want to adopt him. But he was . . . He . . ."

"His soul was loose, Zateri. Out wandering the forest."

"Yes." She pulled her cape more tightly around her shoulders. "One rumor said that he'd found and joined a group of Outcast warriors who were hiding in the forest. Another said he went searching . . ." She paused to expel a breath.

How curious that even now as a grown woman with a family, the memories struck terror into her souls. As though the images were stored in every muscle, every sinew in her body, she found herself flinching, tensing to run from a horror that no longer existed in this world. "Apparently, the old woman had many stashes of rare Trade goods, worth a fortune, and he went back to Dawnland country to search for them."

It was forbidden to say the name of the evil old woman who'd captured her as a child. After the deaths of evil people, names were retired forever and forgotten by their people. But she didn't have to say it. Sindak had seen the old woman's dead body after Zateri, Baji, and Odion had killed her.

Snow and darkness. Bone stilettos slinging blood. A dripping ax.

She flinched and momentarily closed her eyes. When she opened them, she found Sindak staring at her sympathetically.

"Forgive me. I wouldn't have made you remember if I didn't need to know."

"Why? What's going on?"

Sindak continued rubbing Little Boy's ears while he thought. The dog tilted his head in pleasure. "You've heard nothing about him as an adult? Not where he might live? What he's doing?"

She shook her head. "No."

"I may have."

She folded her arms beneath her cape, protecting her heart. "Do I wish to know?"

Sindak frowned and blinked at the fire several times, as though considering what he should or should not say. "If I'm right, you will, but I'm not going to tell you anything until I'm sure. Except to say that it has to do with Ohsinoh."

"He's allied himself with the Bluebird Witch?"

"I promise I'll answer that question when I'm sure."

He leaned forward, kissed her lightly on the forehead, and left the longhouse as silently as he'd come.

Ten

Sky Messenger

South of Yellowtail Village the predawn forest rests as though under some terrible enchantment. I stop on the crest of the trail to survey the rolling hills. Sunrise is at least one hand of time away. The sky is so blue it's almost black.

My people rarely make war at night, but the scent of burning bark rides the breeze, and ash continually sifts down from the high branches, turning my black hair and cape a powdery gray. Gitchi shakes often to rid himself of the annoyance.

In the distance, I see Sedge Marsh Village, though I can't make out what happened to it. This is a Hills People village.

"Tell me it's still there," I murmur to myself, and Gitchi looks up. "They were our friends when I left."

For seven days now, I've been marching through burned villages and empty country. Trees have often been felled to block the trails into the village, or perhaps to close the trails behind those who fled. It's clear that someone wanted these paths closed.

My progress down the hill becomes a torment. The larger rock slides force me to scramble over them on my hands and knees, and the trip is agonizing for Gitchi's aching joints. He groans behind me. When at last we make it down to the trail again, the sky is a little brighter. Pale blue lights the forest floor and streams through the branches. Where it strikes the ground, steam rises into the air. The lack of people frightens me. I have seen no dead bodies. No injured. No orphaned children hiding in the trees. Yet every village I know is gone.

I stop just outside Sedge Marsh Village and study the charred palisade. This has been a wet autumn. Nothing burns easily, but the upright logs here have burned through at regular intervals, indicating that someone had the time to set fires purposefully, turning the palisade into a sieve impossible to defend.

"Easy now," I whisper to Gitchi, who's started to growl every time Elder Sister Gaha—the soft wind—whistles through the blackened husks of longhouses. It unnerves me, too, sounding so much like weeping that I keep spinning around, expecting to see someone following us.

My searching gaze finds only heaps of smoldering bark that, not so long ago, were walls and roofs.

For days I've deliberately avoided entering such villages, fearing lurking enemy warriors, but not today. Cautiously, I duck through one of the holes in the palisade and proceed across the ash-coated plaza. All that remains of the eight longhouses are blackened pole skeletons.

The air is smoky, difficult to breathe. I look around the destroyed village for any living creature—even the dogs have vanished—then I step inside a house that once stretched over six hundred hands in length. The gleam of dawn falling through the burned frame scatters the ground with rectangular squares of pale lavender. As I search, Gitchi's paws shish in the ash behind me. Pots, baskets, and weapons are missing. No shreds of burned bedding hides cling to the sleeping benches.

This is not war. Warriors ransack longhouses. They throw things around and take only what they most value. This house is empty. That can only mean that people packed up and walked away. Then the men must have set fire to the village to deny the enemy a refuge. Or perhaps the enemy burned it to prevent the villagers from returning to their homes.

I slip out through the palisade and head north again. I keep anticipating warriors. Either Hills warriors or Standing Stone. If the Standing Stone People attacked this village, someone should have been left to watch the trails. On the other hand, there may be Hills warriors hidden in the shadows, waiting for the enemy to return.

I do not see a single sentry.

There are, however, people. At every high point on the trail, I see fires winking across the forest, and sounds carry in the stillness: the ringing of an ax chopping wood, children crying, pots clacking, dogs barking. Ordinarily people leave their villages in the summertime to go hunting and fishing in distant parts of the country. Only a handful remain to tend the fields until their relatives return for harvest in the autumn. But this is something far more sinister.

The trail enters a dark section of the forest, and I slow my pace. Footprints mark the mud. I silently kneel to touch them. The edges of the tracks are not hard. Fresh. Two people. Probably a man and a woman.

I give Gitchi the hand sign to be quiet and creep forward with ghostly skill until I see them sitting on a log to the right of the trail. They sit alone in a pile of human bones, strips of jerky in their hands. Every now and then they rip off a hunk and chew it, but it is a curiously leisurely activity, as though they have not a care in the world, as though the sunbleached skulls, shoulder blades, and skeletal hands that surround their moccasins are a mirage.

Just loud enough for them to hear, I call, "Hello, I'm a friend. May I continue on the trail?"

The man leaps to his feet and squints at the darkness where Gitchi and I stand. "I can tell by your accent that you are Standing Stone, as we are. Yes, join us, friend!"

I walk forward with my arms spread, showing them I have no weapons. The man searches me with his gaze. He's seen around twenty-five summers and wears his long hair in a single braid down his back. His pug nose and small black-bead eyes give him a mean look, but his smile eases first impressions. He waves for me to come closer.

"Are you hungry, friend? We don't have much, but we do have good venison jerky."

"I would be grateful to join you. Thank you." I count skulls as I walk. Eight.

The woman, perhaps twenty summers, takes another bite of her jerky and chews. She appears exhausted, or disheartened. The cheeks of her narrow face sink in over her bones, making her eyes seem larger and more deeply set. As she watches me, her pointed nose casts a shadow upon her cheek.

I lower my arms as I approach, and the man digs around in his belt pouch until he draws out a strip of jerky, respectfully steps around the boneyard, and extends it to me.

I take it with a grateful nod. "You are very kind to share with me. I know these are starving times."

Neither of them mentions the human bones, partially covered with newly fallen leaves.

The man says, "We share with everyone we see. If you can't share with others, you have no right to expect others to share with you. Sit down, friend. There's plenty of room on this old log." He drops onto the log beside the woman and continues smiling at me.

The difference in their expressions makes me uneasy. The man seems happy and careless, while the woman is carrying the weight of the world on her narrow shoulders. Even in the cool air before dawn, I can smell her fear sweat.

The man says, "I am Kanadesego, and this is my wife, Pandurata. We are the Snipe Clan, Watha's lineage, from Cornstalk Village."

"Were," the woman corrects him.

I note the man's suddenly downcast eyes and say, "I've been traveling for a time and seen nothing but empty villages. Do you know what happened?"

"Are you deaf or stupid?" Pandurata asks sharply.

I look at their clothing, at the holes in their moccasins, the worn spots in their capes, their lack of jewelry. They probably Traded everything they had for food.

"Diatdagwut," Pandurata whispers, as though frightened to say his name out loud.

Diatdagwut is the transformed son of a great witch, a white beaver who lives in magic waters. He rarely appears to humans, but when he does, it means disaster.

"He's been appearing everywhere, in every Standing Stone village."

Kanadesego smiles brightly. "Yes. The world is coming to an end."

My gaze flicks from one to the other. "Was your village attacked?"

"No, I just told you," Pandurata says. "It's Diatdagwut."

When I say nothing, the two villagers return to eating their jerky. The bones at their feet shine. In a matter of moments, the color of the air changes, bleeding pink with sunrise, and the forest slowly goes from gray velvet to a soft reddish hue. Wind Mother rustles the brittle autumn leaves.

I tear off a chunk of jerky with my teeth and hand it to Gitchi, who swallows it in one bite and wags his tail.

As I rip off a bite for myself, I examine the bones. Surely the clan matrons would not have ordered the abandonment of their villages based upon a few sightings of Diatdagwut. Something else must have happened.

I chew and swallow before I say, "I don't understand."

The woman jerks around to stare at me suspiciously. "Why? Have you been witched? Is your afterlife soul loose?"

I am stunned by the charge. If a person is fortunate, one of his souls travels to the afterlife at death, while the other remains with the body forever. Sometimes, however, a person's afterlife soul gets shaken loose, often by a blow to the head, and wanders aimlessly into the forest until it becomes irretrievably lost. That's what causes insanity.

"My souls are fine," I insist.

Kanadesego examines me carefully before he whispers to her, "What do you think?"

"I don't know. It doesn't always show right away." She leans toward me to stare into my eyes, then pulls back. "Sorcerers fill the skies. Ohsinoh has been spotted in many places at once."

Ohsinoh is the most powerful witch in our country, an evil man who wears a beautiful cloak of bluebird feathers. He is also known as the Bluebird Witch.

"If you haven't been witched, what are you doing out here?" Pandurata asks abruptly. "The Standing Stone People long ago left these hills. Where are you from?"

Kanadesego seems to be holding his breath, waiting for my answer. I see his hand slowly edging toward his belted stiletto.

"I'm from Yellowtail Village."

"Yes, but how did you get out here?"

Their fears are growing, but I don't know why. I glance at the bones again. Kanadesego's hand now rests on his stiletto.

"I've spent the past twenty days on a vision hunt and am headed home."

"A vision hunt? Way out here? You should have gone seeking a Spirit Helper closer to your village. These hills are cursed."

Kanadesego nods. "The end is upon us, friend. It's only a matter of time before the human False Face dons a cape of white clouds and rides the winds of destruction across the face of the world."

Our people have a legend that foretells the coming of a half-man half-Spirit False Face. It is prophesied that he will don a cape of white clouds and ride the winds of destruction across the land, wiping evil from the face of Great Grandmother Earth. We have to memorize the story by the time we've seen eight summers.

"Yes, I'm sure that's true."

I reach up to touch the sacred shell gorget my father gave me twelve summers ago. It is hidden beneath my cape, but its image appears clearly on the canvas of my souls, the twisted face with buffalo horns and serpent eyes, falling stars tumbling down. . . . They must think I'm touching my heart to emphasize my beliefs.

Pandurata hisses, "This is a dark time. A time of despair. After the human False Face rides, the world will be reborn, fresh and clean. All lost souls will be found and shown the way to the Land of the Dead."

I take another bite of jerky. All my life I've heard stories of the One

Who Is to Come. They still stir my blood. My heart beats faster; my
lungs work. But my interpretation is different. As the warfare has grown
more brutal and desperate, I've become more and more certain that the
human False Face is already here, already riding the legendary winds of
destruction. There have, in fact, been times when I have wished for it.
Anything to end the struggle and the suffering. To blot out the hopelessness I see in the eyes of children.

I swallow my last bite of jerky and heave a sigh.

"We are on the road to find him, you know," Kanadesego says. "You
should join us."

"To find whom?"

They blink, glance at each other, and stare at me as though I'm stupid.
"The human False Face. Some say he's already in the forest battling the
sorcerers, as is prophesied. We are going to seek him out and help him."
Kanadesego seems pleased with this mission.

Pandurata scowls at me. "You really don't understand, do you? The
whole country north and south of Skanodario Lake is like this." She gestures to the empty smoldering village visible through the trees. "We are
not content to wait for the end. We're going forward to meet it. To help
bring it about. And we're taking our dearest ancestors with us." She
reaches down to stroke a skull.

As the forest brightens, the birds begin to sing and hop from branch to
branch over our heads. The musty scent of moist leaves fills the air. I take
some time to appreciate the beauty before I say, "I have felt that way myself, especially when the battles were most terrible."

Kanadesego sits up straighter. "You were a warrior, then? I thought
perhaps you were a shaman, a holy man."

A sensation of emptiness swells my chest, as though desert walks in
my heart and my souls are becoming wastelands of hope. "I was a warrior for twelve summers."

"Then you must have seen the signs," Pandurata insists. "Have you
not seen Diatdagwut, or witnessed the flocks of *gahai* that filter through
the forest? I have a friend who saw the Forks River turn to blood."

I dare not state my opinion for fear that they will attack me, or worse,
stop talking to me. I need to hear their stories. But I'm thinking that I
myself have seen rivers turn to blood—rivers swollen with the bodies of
the slain—and if the Forks River turned to blood, the Hills People and
their mad chief, Atotarho, are more likely to blame. I silently offer a
prayer for the dead and turn my attention to her words about the gahai.

Gahai are not Spirits of the first order, but lights that guide sorcerers
as they fly through the air on their evil journeys. Sometimes gahai lead

their masters to victims, other times to places where they can find charms. Her question, of course, goes along with her impression that the forest is filled with sorcerers, like Ohsinoh.

I reply, "Maybe it is the end."

"Oh, it is," Pandurata says fervently. "Last summer was like winter. The crops wouldn't grow." Tears catch her voice. She swallows before continuing, "And now this sickness."

My gaze rivets on her lean face. "What sickness?"

"Have you not heard? The witchery is more powerful than anything we've ever known. Even the old stories do not speak of such as this. As soon as the witches shoot their charms into your body your afterlife soul flees, and no Healer can find it and bring it back. It is lost, doomed to forever walk the earth."

That's why they wanted to know if I'd been witched. They fear I carry the sickness.

Kanadesego whispers, "The pain is excruciating. Eventually the body wastes away. As soon as it does, the charm is released and it leaps into another body. Death is everywhere. We were Trading in Canassatego Village when it struck our own village. Traders brought word. That was one moon ago. We waited until ten days ago to go home and gather our loved ones." He glances at the bones. "Now that the curse has swept Standing Stone country clean, it is striking at the heart of the People of the Flint."

Terror rises like a hot storm in my veins. "Twenty days ago, I was with a war party that attacked a Flint village. The people there were sick. Which Flint villages are affected today?"

"I don't know. They've suffered from the witchery for perhaps two moons. Long enough that most of them are gone. The Hills People have barely been touched. That makes everyone suspect that Atotarho and his witches loosed the sickness."

As I stare at Kanadesego, my souls seem to rise above me in the dawn-drenched air, and when they do, I am back with her, back to summer afternoons and a thousand blessed moments. . . . *Breezes laden with the kicked dust of warriors on the move . . . her fingers trailing down my face . . .*

"Did you hear me?" Pandurata says.

"Forgive me? What did you say?"

"I said that one by one the nations are crumbling. There's no one to tend the fields, no one to fight off invaders. Even the women who survive have no milk to suckle their babies." She paused. "You don't believe me, do you?"

I run a hand through my long black hair. "Yes, I do."

"This war only makes it worse," Kanadesego says. "Are we all fools?"

I cannot find the will to respond. The answer seems obvious. Finally, I say, "Why don't the clan matrons stop it? The easy answer is to end the war, pool our food, and give our Healers everything they need to fight the witchery."

Pandurata laughs out loud. Her eyes blaze when she looks at me. "Don't be silly. They don't wish to stop it. They want to destroy their enemies. Vengeance has become life. That's all. We are like packs of lost souls, forever seeking revenge. Little more than half-human beasts." She lifts a hand to her trembling lips.

Kanadesego slips his arm around her shoulders and pulls her close. "That's why we're here. We're going to help end it."

I have witnessed many horrors, more than I will ever be able to silence, including unexplained diseases that maraud through starving villages leaving husks of human beings behind to Sing death Songs over their own children. But witchery on the scale they describe seems impossible. Our people recognize three types of illness. Illness from natural causes can be cured by herbs, incisions, poultices, and profuse sweating. Illness caused by unfulfilled desires of the soul—of which the patient might not even be aware—can be cured by ascertaining and fulfilling the soul's desires. The third cause is the most insidious: witchcraft. Witchery can only be cured if the Healer discovers and removes all the spells or charms that have been shot into a person's body.

"Where are the Healers?" I ask.

"Oh, they died first. They ran from village to village with their Healing bags, tending the sick, until they, too, were overpowered by the witchery. There's no one left to Heal."

I don't believe it. Especially if the illness is racing across the nations, many Healers would rise to take the places of those who'd perished. She can't be right.

"It was all foretold," Kanadesego said, smiling again. "It's coming true. The world will be left clean and new. Humans will be better, smarter, next time. We won't destroy ourselves ever again."

A crow flaps overhead, cawing. I flinch. We all look up to watch its black body sailing through the trees. When it disappears amid the shadows an eerie feeling of clarity steals through me. I understand at last the petals of light that fall through my Dream.

I rise. "I thank you for your kindness. I was hungry and you fed me, though I know you must have very little left for yourselves. I won't forget you."

"You should stay here with us," Kanadesego calls. "You should wait, just wait. It will all be over soon."

"Thank you, but I must get home." I gesture to the bones. "To collect the remains of my own loved ones."

They seem to understand this. They both nod approvingly.

"Good luck, then!"

I start up the trail with Gitchi at my heel, and they both lift their hands. Pandurata calls, "May you find the end before it finds you, friend."

Just before I climb the next rise in the trail, I hear Pandurata Singing. I look back. Kanadesego's deep voice joins hers. They are sitting alone on the log Singing the death Song over their ancestors' bones.

I stare.

The human False Face is riding the winds of destruction. Nations are crumbling. Starvation stalks the land, and sorcerers have loosed a mysterious evil that is laying waste to one village after another. It's all crashing down.

Yet they sound so happy.

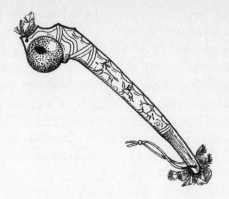

Eleven

Sky Messenger

Brilliant sunlight strikes my eyes as I walk the main trail toward the Yellowtail Village palisade, built of upright logs that stand forty hands tall. Sentries move along the catwalk at the top, just their heads and shoulders showing. By now they have seen me and notified War Chief Deru that a lone man is approaching.

As I pass the large marsh, Reed Marsh, that swings around the northern and western sides of the sister villages, Yellowtail and Bur Oak, I study the dense stands of cattails. Those closest to the shore, the easiest to gather, have been harvested. My people weave the leaves into mats and pound the roots to jelly to use as poultices on wounds, sores, and burns. The soft downy fuzz from the mature flowers is used to prevent chafing in babies, and absorb menstrual blood. The young flower heads stop diarrhea. We also eat the shoots, pollen, roots, and stamens. The entire plant is so useful I am puzzled that thousands of stalks in the middle of the marsh remain standing tall and straight. Has the fever struck here? Is that why the harvest is not yet completed? Soon the seedpods will burst and be carried away in the wind. They will be lost.

I continue walking. Blood begins to pound in my ears.

Ice skims the surface of the marsh. An empty muskrat house sits in the middle, the occupant long ago thrown into some stew pot. Soon the stems will be scavenged for firewood. Given the cold, I'm surprised it hasn't already been collected. I—

A shout goes up, and my gaze returns to the catwalk. Warriors are running, calling to each other. The commotion increases when I stride directly for the closed palisade gates.

"It's him and his wolf!" a man shouts. *"I'd know his walk anywhere!"*

"It can't be. There's a death sentence on his head. No man wishes to be executed by his own relatives."

I keep walking. When I stand before the gates, I look up at the warriors on the catwalk. Their eyes are wide with surprise. Some aim arrows down at me, debating whether or not to shoot me on sight. I know every face. I call, "Wampa, please inform Matron Jigonsaseh that her grandson wishes to address the Matron's Council."

Twelve

Koracoo dipped the soft hide into the water bowl again and wrung it out. All down the Bear Clan longhouse people muttered darkly or thrashed in their sleep, tended by exhausted relatives. The fever had come to Yellowtail Village seven days ago and swept through the longhouses like wildfire. The nauseating smell of vomit and loose bowels permeated the smoky air.

Two compartments away, the great Healer, old Bahna, sprinkled a man with water, then used a turkey tail to fan him. Healers had been working nonstop, but half the village was down. Forty-two dead. Bahna Sang softly. The lilting words of the Healing Song rose into the air like golden wings, soothing every person who could hear them.

Koracoo bent over and washed her mother's fiery face with the cool cloth. "Mother, try to sleep."

Matron Jigonsaseh, leader of the Matron's Council of Yellowtail Village, whispered, "Too much . . . to think about . . . fever . . . all the refugees. We're . . . vulnerable."

"Our warriors are prepared, Mother. Don't worry. I spoke with Kittle only yesterday. Every person able to carry a weapon knows he or she may be called at any moment to defend the five allied villages."

Koracoo smoothed the cloth over her mother's forehead. Long gray hair streamed around Jigonsaseh's face and looked stark against the black bear hide that covered her frail body. Sickness rattled in her lungs. In the past two days, her breathing had grown labored, as though there weren't enough air in the world. Koracoo dipped the hide again, wrung it out. Her heart ached.

When Mother closed her eyes, Koracoo leaned back and took a deep breath. A commotion had risen outside. Warriors called to each other on the catwalks. Feet pounded the plaza.

The instincts of ten summers as a war chief kicked in. Koracoo reached for her war club: CorpseEye. Firelight gilded the copper inlay in club, giving it an edge of flame. She smoothed her fingers over the dark, dense wood. He was old, very old. He had been passed down through her family for generations, each new warrior entrusted with the task of caring for the club's soul. Legend said that CorpseEye had once belonged to Sky Woman herself. Strange images were carved on the shaft: antlered wolves, winged tortoises, and prancing buffalo. A red quartzite cobble was tied to the top of the club, making it a very deadly weapon—one Koracoo wielded with great expertise.

She shoved to her feet just as her daughter, Tutelo, burst through the leather hanging and stood breathing hard, her eyes wide, as though with shock.

Koracoo said, "What is it? What's happened?"

"Mother . . ." Tutelo wet her lips. She was a pretty young woman with an oval face and long black hair that hung to the middle of her back. Sweat beaded on her small nose. She'd run hard to get here. "He's alive."

"Who's alive?

"Sky Messenger, he—"

Koracoo reached out, and her fingers sank into her daughter's shoulder. "Where is he? Tell me quickly." Blood roared in her ears.

"At the gates. He asked to speak with Grandmother and the Matron's Council."

"Blessed Spirits, he must not know that Kittle has—"

"Koracoo," Jigonsaseh whispered.

Koracoo spun around to look at her mother. Jigonsaseh lifted a clawlike hand. "Send a runner to Kittle. . . . Ask her to give us . . . one day to . . ." Her words were cut short by a violent coughing fit that racked her body.

Koracoo turned back to Tutelo. "Go to Kittle, ask her to give us one day to hear Sky Messenger's story before she carries out her execution order. Hurry."

Tutelo threw back the entry curtain and ran, vanishing into the daylight. Koracoo swung her foxhide cape around her shoulders and ducked outside carrying CorpseEye. People crowded the plaza, most of them refugees from devastated villages. Many carried baskets. Others raced around collecting things: rocks, potsherds, anything they could throw.

Koracoo stalked toward the gates like a hunting lynx, her muscles rippling, ready to do battle if necessary. He might be a traitor. No one knew for certain, but even if he was, he was still her son. Tomorrow she may have to club him to death herself, but it would not happen today. Not if she could stop it.

When War Chief Deru saw her approaching, he shoved a man aside. "Make room for the Speaker for the Women."

Like a school of fish at a thrown rock, people scattered, leaving a path for her. Ahead, she saw her son standing with his hands tied behind his back, surrounded by eight burly warriors. They looked as stunned as she probably did. Like everyone else, she'd assumed he was dead.

Koracoo strode up to stand less than six hands from him, and Sky Messenger clamped his jaw. "Mother, just give me one hand of time. You must hear what I have to say."

Gitchi, who stood at his heels, let out a low growl and bared his fangs, warning her to come no closer. When a warrior lifted his club to kill the dog, Koracoo said, "No." The man instantly lowered his weapon.

She stared at her son. Facing her was not easy for him, she could tell, but he did it unflinchingly. They gazed at each other eye to eye. The soot of many campfires streaked his round face. His breathing was shallow, his lips pressed into a tight line, but his brown eyes blazed with defiance.

In a powerful voice, he called to the crowd, "I know how the world dies! Do you care to know? Does anyone in this village want to hear my vision? Does anyone want to help me stop it?"

The crowd went silent, waiting for Koracoo's response. But an eddy of awed whispers moved across the plaza.

She studied Sky Messenger's blazing eyes. She'd seen that look for the first time twelve summers ago. He'd just become a man. The body of his enemy lay upon the snow-covered ground before him. That look was a kind of righteous terror. The look of a man who'd just accepted a mission that would lay waste to his world.

She said only, "Bring him."

As she strode back for the Bear Clan longhouse, villagers lined up to shout curses and pelt Sky Messenger with potsherds, rocks, dog feces—anything they'd collected. He grunted when the largest stones struck him, but said nothing.

One hand of time later, I sit before the fire in the middle of the Bear Clan longhouse. My hands and feet are bound. Mother sits to my right, with her war club, CorpseEye, resting across her lap. The red chert cobble hafted to the tip has two black spots, glistening eyes that stare at me. If the council so decides, it will be Mother's responsibility to kill me.

I gaze around. Dozens of my relatives stand at the edge of the firelight. Their backs are to me. They will have the opportunity later, if the matrons take the issue back to their clans for a vote, to express their opinions. For now, they may listen, but no interference will be tolerated.

All of the children are gone. The leather privacy curtains of the living chambers have been drawn closed so that I cannot gaze into the sacred eyes of the False Face masks that hang upon the walls. For now, even the Spirits of my clan have turned their backs to me. Despite the curtains, the moans and cries of the sick inside the chambers carry.

I scan the matrons around the fire. Mother is allowed to be here only because she is standing in for my ill grandmother, Matron Jigonsaseh.

"Go ahead," Matron Washais of the Wolf Clan says. Her elderly face has a shriveled appearance, like a winter-dried plum. She's pulled her red-and-black cape tightly around her frail body.

I shift on the floor mat, trying to find a comfortable position. With my hands and feet bound, it is difficult.

"The Dream always begins the same way," I say. "I can't feel my body, just the air cooling as the color leaches from the forest, leaving the land gray and shimmering. Then Brother Sky goes leaden, and the patches of light falling through the trees curve into bladelike crescents. Finally, I begin to sense my skin. My fingers work, clenching to hard fists, unclenching. Beneath me, a great cloud-sea moves, rising and falling like waves. The sea is punctured by a great tree whose roots sink deep into the water world far below. As though the birds know the unthinkable is about to happen, they tuck their beaks beneath their wings and close their eyes, roosting in the middle of the day. Insects that only moments ago twisted through the air like tiny tornadoes vanish. Butterflies settle upon the clouds at my feet and hide themselves in the mist. An eerie silence descends. A . . . a voice calls my name, and it is as though my heart has crumbled to dust and sifted through the cracks in my soul, leaving my chest hollow as a drum. Then Morning Star suddenly flares in the darkening sky, and fantastic shadow-bands, rapidly moving strips of light and dark, flicker across the cloud-sea."

Matron Washais whispers to Mother, who nods and says something to Matron Agwidi of the Turtle Clan.

Morning Star's appearance is always an omen. She is very powerful and rescues starving villages in times of famine.

Matron Washais says, "Continue."

Fires blaze down the length of the house, keeping the sick warm, cooking food. For a man who has spent the past moon sleeping in the open forest, it's hot. Very hot. "I become aware that I am not alone. I see the gray shades drifting through the air, surrounding me, and from a great distance I hear voices echo. I suddenly understand that I stand with the last congregation. The dead who still wait."

Washais's old eyes tighten, but no one speaks.

"As I look down through holes in the cloud-sea, an amorphous darkness rises from the watery depths and slithers along the horizon. Strange curls of black, like gigantic antlers, spin from the darkness and rake the bellies of the Cloud People."

"Horned Serpent," Matron Agwidi whispers.

My bound hands tremble. Horned Serpent tried to destroy the world in the Beginning Time. They must all be wondering if he's coming to try again.

I squeeze my eyes for a moment. The images are as powerful now as the last time I Dreamed them. "Elder Brother Sun's blazing face begins to darken. After an eternity, his last flash forms into a brilliant diamond, and blindingly white feathers sprout from his body. Elder Brother Sun is flying. Flying away into a black hole in the sky. Despair fills me. It is the end of all life . . . unless I do something. I know this. I don't know how, but it is up to me to stop the death of the world."

Mother turns slightly. She has not looked directly at me during the entire council meeting. Firelight reflects in the black depths of her eyes, but there is something else there, too: belief vying with disbelief.

I clench my jaw. My voice comes out too strong, sounding urgent. "Like an animal struck in the head with a rock, I stagger as my body wakes, then comes to life in a raging flood. Just as I turn to speak to the Shades . . . a child cries out. The sound is muffled and wavering, seeping through the ocean of other voices. It sounds like the little boy is suffocating, his mouth covered with a hand or hide. Fear freezes the air in my lungs. As though he has his lips pressed to my ear, a man orders, 'Lie down, boy. Stop crying or I'll cut your heart out.' The Dream bursts, like shards of ice striking a rock. For a time, there is only splintered brilliance. Then I—"

"Do you know this man?" Washais interrupts.

"I do. He hurt me. A long time ago. Twelve summers."

Washais does not blink; she just stares, evaluating, perhaps wondering why I do not tell her more. I honestly don't recall most of it. Only one other person knows the fragments that I do, and she is one of the four people on earth that I would willingly, without a second thought, die to protect.

"What happens next?" Mother asks. Her expression is stoic.

I exhale hard. I can't tell what Mother's thinking or feeling. "I see the flowers of the World Tree, made of pure light, fluttering down, disappearing into utter darkness. The last thing, the most recent addition to the Dream—" I expel a halting breath before I finish—"is that a great hole opens in the cloud-sea beneath my feet, and I fall. Wisps of cloud trail behind me as though I've snagged them with my feet. I fall and fall, plunging through eternal darkness surrounded by flowers of pure light."

"Do you ever strike the earth?" Mother asks.

"I just keep falling . . . as though Great Grandmother Earth is fleeing away from me."

I meet each woman's gaze. My eyes must be frightening, for several shrink away from me. Every moment a man lives is inexorably and deeply bound to the instant of his death. Every breath. Every heartbeat leads him up that shining path. I see that now. I see the path in their eyes. Perhaps when all is said and done learning to die is more important than fighting to stay alive.

Washais murmurs, "You understand that our village must pay a price for what you have done?"

"Yes, Matron."

"And you must pay a price to your own clan."

"I will do whatever the Bear Clan asks of me."

Washais waves a hand. Mother rises to her feet and signals to the four warriors waiting before the entry curtain. "Take him outside while the council deliberates."

Two men, men I have known since I was a child, stalk forward, roughly haul me to my feet, and drag me through the entry out into the cold afternoon wind. Storm clouds have massed over the treetops. Rain is falling. Gitchi quietly trots at my side, looking up. His yellow eyes are filled with love, as if he knows my souls are struggling to stay alive.

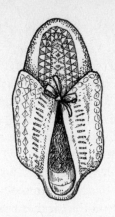

Thirteen

The crack of a palm against flesh pierced the slippery elm bark of the longhouse. Taya jumped as if it were she who had been slapped, and not Sky Messenger.

Grandmother Kittle's seething voice seemed to shiver the air: "I will not rescind the death sentence on his head! You should have already killed him. It is your responsibility, Koracoo. Instead, you dare to bring a traitor into my presence!"

"The Women's Council asks only that you hear his vision; then you may . . ." The voice faded until it was too low to hear.

Breathing hard, Taya slid through the narrow gap between the rear wall and the inner palisade. She needed to find a place where she could hear, but not be heard or seen. If Grandmother Kittle, the High Matron of the Ruling Council of allied villages, discovered Taya eavesdropping, Taya would be pounding corn with a wooden pestle until her arms fell off.

Taya took her time and continued easing along the wall toward Grandmother's compartment at the far end of the Deer Clan longhouse. She had just enough space between the wall and the palisade to walk, and thank the Spirits the ground was wet after the rain. Quiet. It felt spongy beneath her moccasins.

As she moved, she stroked the wall tenderly. She had seen fourteen summers. This was the only longhouse she remembered. It stretched five hundred hands long, forty hands wide, and fifty hands tall. Porches roofed the curtained entries on either end of the longhouse. Inside, a line of twenty-five hearths glittered down the length of the house like a strand of amber beads. Each hearth was shared by two related families, whose compartments stood on either side of the hearth. In total, there were fifty compartments, twenty-five on each side of the longhouse, which housed two-hundred and sixty-two people. And the Deer Clan longhouse was only one of four houses in Bur Oak Village. The entire village contained over one thousand people. Taya loved it. She knew every dip in the plaza where water pooled, every piece of bark that stuck out from the palisade walls and snagged her soft doeskin sleeves, every gap in the longhouse walls where a girl could secretly peer inside to watch, or listen. Though she was no longer a girl, she still cherished such childish activities.

"I cannot believe your impudence!" Grandmother's enraged voice carried. "Do you think me a fool that I would listen to his pathetic tale of woe? Sky Messenger released thirteen Flint captives. We needed those captives to replace our own dead relatives."

"He did it out of concern—"

"Concern? Don't be ridiculous. He has never cared for this nation. Has he ever added to your clan? No. By all rights, he should be forced to bring home twice as many captives as a warrior with children. Your son doesn't even know what that hard shaft between his legs is for!"

Grandmother's contemptuous voice shocked like a hammerstone to the skull. If the blood in Taya's veins stung, she could only imagine how Sky Messenger must be feeling.

"He realizes his failure in that regard and with your permission is willing to . . ."

Koracoo, Speaker for the Women of Yellowtail Village, murmured something else, but Taya couldn't hear it at all. She picked up her pace. She needed to get closer, to hear better. When in council, Koracoo always spoke in soft tones, which made it hard to hear her if a person stood more than a few hands distant.

Taya stopped just outside Grandmother Kittle's compartment, glanced through the tiny slit between the bark slabs that made up the wall, and surveyed the chamber. Grandmother must have ordered the area around her chamber cleared, because Taya couldn't see any of her Deer Clan relatives standing close by. Speaker Koracoo sat across the fire from Grandmother, while Sky Messenger stood in the rear. He was tall, and his shoulder-length black hair was longer than was proper for a warrior, given the constant state of mourning in Bur Oak and Yellowtail villages. He'd clenched his teeth so hard his jaw was off center. He clearly did not wish to be here.

Carefully, Taya pressed her ear to the wall. The damp elm had a sweet tangy scent.

Grandmother said, "Your son is guilty of treason. I don't care what story he invented to cover his cowardice. How dare you even suggest a marriage between Sky Messenger and Taya? It's ludicrous. I would never consent to such a thing!"

Taya's heart thumped so loudly it drowned out the voices in the longhouse. She'd been a woman for four moons. She'd had many suitors, all of them very high status, as befitted the granddaughter of the high matron, but no one, including grandmother, had yet suggested a mate to her. Sky Messenger was much older than Taya, twenty-three summers. Not only that, since he'd been back a flurry of activity had ensued—council meetings, arguments, violent clashes in the plaza, more council meetings. He was an Outcast! Taya's thoughts raced, trying to figure out what she might have done to so offend Grandmother that she would consider marrying her to a traitor?

Speaker Koracoo responded, "Sky Messenger is not a coward. He freed the captives and left the war party because the Spirits of the dead *demanded* it of him. After the captives were free, his Spirit Helper came to him and led him out into the wilderness, where he was tested and afflicted with Spirit Dreams. Dreams of our future, Kittle. And believe me, his visions were not pleasant, his sojourn not easy. There is a great darkness coming. We must heed his visions, or we will all be destro—"

"Your son, a Dreamer? Ha! But then, Odion was never a normal boy."

Taya quickly ducked to look through the slit. The sight of Grandmother's beautiful oval face, her dark eyes glittering savagely, made her go cold inside. Many summers ago, before the birth of Taya's mother, Grandmother Kittle was renowned as the most beautiful woman in the entire Standing Stone nation. Though she had now seen forty-four summers pass, men still cast admiring glances at her, and she brought many of these men to her bed. Grandmother's indiscretions were wonderfully legendary.

Sky Messenger said something she couldn't hear. His tone of voice, however, was insolent.

Grandmother laughed. "Finally, the deputy war chief shows his face again. I must say, I like this much better than the holy man charade."

"I never claimed to be a holy—"

"Enough!" Koracoo sharply turned to Sky Messenger and ordered, "You will not use that tone with the high matron of our nation. Do you understand?"

Sky Messenger didn't reply for a time; then his head dipped in a nod.

Speaker Koracoo continued, "Besides, there is no fault here. Any man who refuses to answer his Spirit Helper's call endangers not only himself, but his people."

"Well, you have the right to your sad opinion, Koracoo. He is, after all, of your clan and your village. But it is extremely unlikely that he will ever regain the respect of this village." Grandmother paused for effect before she added, "It would take a miracle. He would have to distinguish himself in war as no other man has ever done in the entire history of our people! Then, and only then, would he be worthy of siring children for the Deer Clan. Though I'm not certain your son even knows how to accomplish that."

Each venom-laced word had a clear ring of finality, as though the discussion were over.

Sky Messenger straightened to his full height, and his eyes focused on the longhouse wall, but he looked like an inferno was raging inside him.

Taya held her breath and strained to hear. Rain had started to patter on the roof and splat on her head. The noise made it even harder to hear.

"I will not fight again," Sky Messenger said defiantly.

Astonished, Grandmother said, "The Standing Stone People have been struck a devastating blow by the warfare and the fever. We are more vulnerable now than we have ever been. Are you saying openly that you refuse to protect your relatives?"

"I must protect them in a different way. My Dreams warn—"

"Bah!" Grandmother spat the word, and Taya saw her wave a slender heavily ringed hand through the firelight. Her numerous shell bracelets rattled. "A man who will not fight for his people should be condemned and chased from the village. Though I doubt your relatives have the stomach to do it."

Taya saw Speaker Koracoo's face go rigid. "Your ears seem to be filled with pine resin, Kittle." She stood up. "When you are ready to listen to Sky Messenger's visions, we will return. Until then, please think about this: in exchange for your approval of the marriage, the Bear Clan is willing to offer half its walnut harvest."

"Half?" Grandmother scoffed. "I want it all! And your hickory nut and plum harvests, as well!"

Grandmother had just subtly told Koracoo that *if* the Bear Clan offered enough, the marriage would happen. Taya felt like she'd been struck in the head with a rock. As a child, she had worshipped Sky Messenger. Back then, it had never seemed possible that she, the fifth granddaughter of the high matron, forever doomed to live in the shadows cast by her older sisters, would ever have a chance to marry the greatly esteemed grandson of the matron of the Bear Clan.

But she didn't want to marry him now! Horned Serpent's teeth! No matter what he did in the future, his disgrace would forever condemn their children to ignominy. Disgust churned her belly.

Koracoo replied, "Our Women's Council will consider your offer."

Grandmother must have been taken aback. She laughed out loud. "Yellowtail Village must truly be desperate for this alliance."

"I only said that I would present it. Nothing more."

Grandmother gave her a knowing smile. It was dangerous to show any weakness before Grandmother. She would use it like a fine chert knife to cut your heart out. "For the moment, I will rescind the death sentence on his head. But do not come back to me until you're prepared to pay the full price of Sky Messenger's actions. I will only meet with you one more time."

"That is acceptable."

Taya eased to the end of the wall to peer around the corner.

Koracoo and Sky Messenger ducked beneath the door curtain and stepped outside, followed by the old gray wolf that never left Sky Messenger's side. They stood beneath the porch for a time, murmuring to each other, apparently examining the makeshift refugee houses that leaned precariously along the palisade walls. In the past moon, Grandmother had welcomed almost five hundred refugees, far more than they had the food to feed. But what else could she do?

"She asks too much, Mother," Sky Messenger said. When he finally turned to face Koracoo, Taya saw his angry expression. "I know marriage is my penance, but this is preposterous. Choose another clan."

"We must be patient." Koracoo gazed out at the village plaza, mostly empty due to the rain, and her eyes seemed to linger on each of the longhouses, as though contemplating her chances for an alliance with the Wolf or Turtle clans.

Sky Messenger had turned away. Taya couldn't see his face, but he had his fists clenched tightly. "Maybe I should just leave."

"And abandon your vision?" Koracoo had seen thirty-nine summers pass. She was still a handsome woman. Though she kept her gray-streaked black hair cut short in mourning, it framed her small narrow nose and full lips.

Sky Messenger exhaled hard. "My vision is all I have. I'll never abandon it. But this alliance . . ." Frustrated, he slapped his arms against his sides. "Tell me what to do?"

He didn't look like he'd been sleeping. Dark puffy half-moons swelled beneath his brown eyes, and tiny lines etched the corners of his wide mouth. Despite that, his tanned round face was striking with its high cheekbones and slender nose. At twelve hands, he was taller than most men in the village, and the muscles of his shoulders, accustomed to wielding a war club, bulged through the leather of his belted knee-length shirt.

Koracoo said, "If we are to accomplish the things your Dreams say we must, we need this alliance."

He laughed softly and shook his head. "Very well, Mother, but I don't like it."

Koracoo flipped up the hood of her cape, adjusted it around her face, and said, "I must speak with our council again. Hear their thoughts. Then we'll arrange another meeting with Kittle. She'll be expecting us tonight. So we'll wait until tomorrow morning."

As Koracoo started to walk away, Sky Messenger caught her arm. "Mother, if . . . *if*. I will need you to approach Chief Cord of Wild River Village. I . . ." He released her arm. "We will need them on our side."

Taya stiffened. Wild River Village was of the Flint People, their enemies! Was this some plot?

Koracoo watched the rain for a time. "Is *she* still there?"

Sky Messenger squinted and looked away. "That's not the reason I asked you to go. I'm not afraid to see her. I just know that Cord will listen to you."

Taya wondered who *she* was.

"I see." Koracoo pulled her cape closed beneath her chin. When she exhaled, her breath condensed and drifted away. "I can't leave while the fever rages."

"No, of course not."

"When I can, I will discuss it with . . ."

As they walked away across the rainy plaza, Taya lost their voices. She leaned back against the longhouse wall and hugged herself. She didn't know how to feel about any of this. Why had no one consulted her about this marriage? Not that it was any of her business. Marriages were arranged by the prospective couple's mothers or grandmothers, in consultation with their respective clans. The man and woman involved had little say in the outcome of such negotiations, though if either party seriously objected his or her desires were taken into consideration. Taya had to make her objections known immediately!

She ran back the way she'd come, heedless of the number of times her elbows banged the wall.

Fourteen

Kittle gracefully paced through the firelight of the Deer Clan long-house, refusing to look at her granddaughter, her withering gaze instead upon her daughter, Yosha. How such an ugly child had come from her womb never ceased to annoy her. Yosha's nickname as a child had been Rodent-face, which aptly described her. She had small beady eyes, a long pointed nose and a bad overbite, as though her teeth were too big for her jaw. The thin mousy hair that hung to her chin added to the rodent im-age. Worse, she constantly pawed at things in a ratlike manner, and had the minuscule intelligence to match.

A young slave girl, recently captured from the Flint People, fluttered around Yosha and Taya, setting a platter of cornbread and cups of walnut milk before them. Yosha sniffed and looked away, taking no more notice of the girl than she would of a mosquito. Taya, to her credit, stared fixedly at the floor mats. She wore an elkhide cape with the hair turned in for warmth. The exterior leather was painted with a curious, fanciful pattern of flowers and finches. Petals and feathers—yellow, red, blue—scrolled across the shoulders. A girl's cape. Not a woman's. Leave it to Yosha to be oblivious.

Kittle folded her arms and glared. "Well?"

"Mother, you already know what I'm going to say. Please sit down so that we might discuss it in a civil manner."

Kittle turned to the slave girl. "Leave."

The girl bowed. "Yes, High Matron."

When she was gone, Kittle grudgingly sank onto the bear hides across the fire and propped her moccasins on one of the hearthstones to warm her feet. The night had been damp and bitter, and despite the morning's excitement, she remained cold to the bone. Kittle pulled her magnificent blue cape more closely around her and examined her daughter. Yosha selected a piece of cornbread filled with hickory nuts and dried mint and bit into it slowly, as though relishing the flavor. Sitting to Kittle's right, Taya was so still she might not have been there at all.

"Do you think I have all day to listen to your drivel? Get to the matter."

Yosha continued to chew at her leisure, then swallowed the bite and wiped the crumbs onto her knee-high legging. "Taya objects to the marriage. She says it will disgrace her children and the entire Deer Clan."

"She has seen fourteen summers. What does she know of disgrace? Ask me about her father. Now he was a disgrace. I should never have let you have your way on that one. From the instant I saw him I knew he was worthless. I'll never forget the day I sent him running for his home village. It's one of the high moments of my life."

The muscles in Yosha's jaw clenched a few times before she responded. "My choice of husbands is not at issue. Taya—"

"No, what is at issue is how silly a young woman can be about such things. One day she's frantic to have a man, and the next she hates him. That's why they should have no say whatsoever in the men chosen for them."

"But Sky Messenger is a traitor! You said so yourself."

Kittle lounged back on the warm bearhides and gave her daughter a half-lidded stare. "It's almost inconceivable that you are one of my daughters. How is it possible that I could have produced a woman this stupid?"

"Insulting me will not help, Mother. We need to—"

"You, of all people, should understand that this has nothing to do with either Taya or Sky Messenger."

Taya, who still had her eyes downcast, shifted slightly. Thank the gods that the girl had Kittle's face, from her large dark eyes and long eyelashes, to her sweet full lips and perfect nose. Taya's waist-length hair, glossy and jet black, fell over her narrow shoulders like a shining blanket. Hopefully she did not have her mother's rodent intelligence.

"So, Granddaughter," Kittle said to Taya, and the girl could not suppress the shudder that went through her. "What do you have to say to me?"

Taya's eyes instantly filled with tears. When she choked back a whimper, Kittle grabbed her wrist, and squeezed until her nails bit into the girl's flesh. Taya let out a pained yelp. "If you cry I will pick up that piece of firewood and beat you across the back."

Taya struggled to control herself. Kittle released her and leaned back. Her female descendants had to learn very early that displays of emotion were unacceptable. Tears, especially, made them appear to be weak fools, and women who might one day hold power in the Standing Stone nation could not afford such indulgences.

Taya wiped her eyes on her cape. "Grandmother, I know my obligations. I will obediently marry whomever you choose. But why Sky Messenger? Am I being punished?"

"If I were punishing you, you would not have to ask. You would feel it in your broken bones."

"Then . . . why?"

"Why? You are such a spoiled child!" Kittle waved a hand through the smoky air. "You used to swoon over him every time he returned from a war walk. Only last summer you flew in here clutching some trinket he'd brought you and danced around shouting that you loved him. Can true love die so quickly?"

Yosha said, "It always has for you, Mother. Stories of your whoring filled my youth. I recall once—"

"Recall later. Right now we're talking about your overprotected daughter. Or did you forget that?"

Taya glanced between them. "Grandmother, that was before he betrayed us! I don't wish to marry him now."

"My dear girl, you must have been standing right outside listening when his relatives were here or you would not yet know about the marriage plans." Taya's face flushed in a silent admission of guilt. "Did you not also hear his mother say that he'd had a great vision that could save this nation?"

"Well . . . yes, Grandmother."

"Then you did not believe it?" Kittle picked up her cup of walnut milk and sipped it, watching her granddaughter over the polished wooden rim.

Taya sat impassively. She appeared to be studying Kittle's expressions and gestures, which made Kittle smile to herself. The girl, thank the gods, was smarter than her mother. Already she had learned that revealing her true feelings to Kittle was like baring her breast to a stiletto. Better to study your opponent for a time before responding. You wouldn't get wounded nearly so often. Kittle took another drink of milk and waited to see what conclusion her granddaughter arrived at.

"I wasn't sure what to believe, Grandmother."

Kittle set her cup down on one of the hearthstones. "Nor was I. That's why I rescinded the death sentence."

Taya's delicate black brows pinched. She was thinking, assessing the implications. Remarkable.

Yosha said, "Mother, stop taunting her and just tell her why you—"

"Close your mouth while you still have teeth."

Yosha's jaw hung open like a clubbed dog's before she clamped it tight.

Kittle's attention returned to her granddaughter. Taya's eyes moved over the rear longhouse wall that stretched like a dark leather blanket. The scent of wet elm bark was fragrant, suffusing the fire-warmed air. Painted suits of wooden body armor, woven from slats of hardwood, leaned against the wall on the top shelf. Constructed by a master woodworker, they were strong enough to deflect an arrow. Above the armor hung an enormous False Face mask. Shagodyoweh gowah, the great Protector, cured sickness. His massive bent nose and wide mouth were both expertly carved. Long black hair framed the oiled face. Tied to the top of the mask was a tiny medicine bag filled with tobacco from Kittle's own sacred garden, dried over a basswood fire, then pulverized. Before rituals, she removed a pinch and burned the tobacco as an offering. Such masks required constant care and frequent use or they could cause illness. She'd known one woman whose mouth had started to grow crooked because of an unhappy mask that had not been danced in in a long while. Kittle listened to the cries and coughs that spanned the longhouse, then glared at the Great Protector. Half the village was sick, many dying. Refugees from decimated villages crowded her plaza. Shagodyoweh seemed powerless to fight the witchery that afflicted the world.

"But Grandmother, you told Speaker Koracoo that you didn't want to hear his tale of woe. Why? Did you already know the story?"

"Very good."

Taya hesitated. "From someone in Yellowtail Village?"

"A good high matron has spies everywhere. I need to know what happens in every longhouse in our nation."

Taya's chin lifted as though in understanding. "Then you believe his vision is true?"

"As soon as I heard that he'd returned I could have had him killed. I'm the one who placed the death sentence upon his head. It was an offense to our Ruling Council and a challenge to my authority when his clan did not immediately carry out the council's order. Why do you think I didn't have him killed?"

Taya's sharp gaze did not leave Kittle's face. "Speaker Koracoo?"

Kittle smiled knowingly. "Indeed. The Speaker for the Women may be soft-spoken these days, but she has a warrior's heart. She is no one's fool. Even if he is her son, if Koracoo had possessed any proof of treason, she would have killed him herself in a heartbeat. Just to set an example." Kittle tossed another branch on the fire, and sparks drifted lazily toward the smoke hole in the roof.

"Then, if Koracoo did not carry out the sentence of death, it was because she, too, believes Sky Messenger's vision?"

"I'm not sure yet. But she must think the fate of our nation may depend upon her son staying alive—and that gives me pause. Of all the women in the world, girl, never, ever underestimate Koracoo."

As the flames blazed higher, Taya shifted to move away from the heat. The painted finches on her cape swayed as though taking wing. "What is his vision, Grandmother? The bits I have heard sound like nonsense."

Kittle laughed softly, pleased by her granddaughter. Despite living a protected, privileged life, Taya was at least curious. Of course, she would never rule the nation, not with seven aunts and four older sisters, but it was rewarding to know that the intelligence that marked Kittle's maternal line had not died with Yosha. She watched morosely as her daughter pawed another chunk of cornbread from the platter and began to chomp it, totally unaware that an important discussion was taking place. Crumbs dropped into her lap and perched there like red insects.

More gently, Kittle said, "Do not say no to this marriage just yet, Taya. In some way I do not yet grasp, this alliance is critical to Yellowtail Village. Our village needs many things. Let us see what they offer first."

An ugly stubborn expression came over her granddaughter. She pulled her shoulders back and stared dry-eyed at Kittle. "Very well. But I wish you to know that I do not wish this alliance. Dadjo has as much as asked to marry me, and I—"

"Dadjo's wishes mean nothing to me."

"But Grandmother! He's the man I—"

"Stop sniveling. I have a job for you."

Taya sniffed. "What is it?"

"If you have the chance, I want you to convince Sky Messenger to return to the war trail. We—"

"How am I supposed to do that?" she asked in an aggrieved voice.

"You're a woman now. Think of something. We need every warrior we can get. Hug me now, and go away." Kittle opened her arms, and Taya grudgingly rose to hug her. It felt like nothing more than bones were encased in her cape. The harvests had been particularly bad this autumn. Hunger stalked every village, but so long as Kittle had breath in her body, Bur Oak Village would be the last to starve—even if she had to raid every village of the Flint or Mountain People to do it. "Leave us. I need to speak with your dimwitted mother."

Taya rose and walked to the other end of the longhouse toward her mother's compartment. Many young women and girls stopped her to ask her questions, but she just shook her head and continued on her way.

Yosha held a half-eaten chunk of bread in her hand. "She wishes to marry Dadjo, you know."

"I could not care less. At least I didn't have to beat her for being as ignorant and unconcerned about the welfare of her clan as you are. Give me the rest of that bread."

"No. It's mine." Yosha pulled it away.

Kittle held out her hand. "You've had enough food for the day. The rest of that could feed one of the refugee children in the plaza."

Yosha shoved the bread into her mouth and tried to swallow it whole before Kittle could take it away. She and Yosha had been engaged in a struggle of wills most of their lives. At this late date, Kittle had no intention of letting her daughter win. She reached across the fire and slapped the rest of the cornbread out of Yosha's mouth. It bounced across the floor mats, cracking into pieces as it cartwheeled. "That was for the 'whoring' comment."

Yosha cried, "Mother!"

"Now get down on your hands and knees and pick up every crumb. Do you hear me? If I find anything larger than a gnat's toe on that floor mat when you're done, you'll be licking it up with your tongue. When you're finished, I want you to personally take the bread outside and give it to one of the refugee children."

"But that's demeaning!" Yosha burst into tears and dropped to her knees to begin collecting the morsels.

"Feeding a hungry child is demeaning?"

Kittle glowered at her daughter. It galled her almost beyond bearing that one of her daughters could care so little about the needs of others. All those summers that Kittle had spent in loyal service to the clan, and for what? Her children and grandchildren to act like spoiled vermin? Neither Yosha nor her daughter knew anything of sacrifice or loyalty.

Kittle rose, walked to the entry, and shoved aside the leather curtain. She stepped out beneath the porch to survey Bur Oak Village. The rainy plaza stood empty, but for a few dogs that loped through the downpour. If the storm kept up, the rain would soon turn to snow.

Despite Kittle's hopes, Koracoo would not be back today. She would wait, let Kittle worry, then she would return and offer almost nothing. Kittle chuckled. It was the way of things.

Tomorrow would be an interesting day.

A young Trader, a man she had not seen before, ducked out of the Bear Clan longhouse and trotted across the plaza toward her. His Trader's pack bounced upon his back. He was tall, unusually tall, and had a very pleasant square-jawed face. As he approached, he said, "Good day, High Matron. Would you mind if I enter your longhouse to Trade?"

Kittle smiled for such a long time that the man blushed. "What is your name?"

"I am Hiyade, of the Hawk Clan in White Dog Village." He smiled back, but it was a shy, uncertain gesture.

"Of course you may Trade. After you are finished serving the rest of my kinsmen, return to me."

He bowed. "I'll be happy to, Matron." He darted into the longhouse like a frightened rabbit.

Kittle smiled to herself and stood for a time longer, watching the rain fall, before she returned to the warmth.

Fifteen

Storm winds buffeted the forest, sending showers of red and gold leaves gusting down the trail toward the two men who walked ahead of Hiyawento. The sharp gazes of his guards constantly roved the trees, searching for hidden enemies. Both men carried bows, quivers, and war clubs. They dressed in warrior garb, their capes painted with clan symbols. The red spirals of the Hawk Clan coiled around the bottom of Disu's cape. Saponi's bore a series of interlocking green-and-blue rectangles across the middle, marking him as a member of the Snipe Clan. Disu stood two heads taller than Saponi, but what Saponi lost in height, he made up for in muscles. His burly shoulders spread twice as wide as Disu's. When War Chief Sindak had met him on the trail two hands of time from Coldspring Village, he'd said, "These are good men. I would trust my life to either of them. They will guard you well on your journey." Then he'd pulled Hiyawento aside and softly added, "Listen to them. Believe them," and trotted back for Atotarho Village.

A fierce gust of rain struck Hiyawento, shoving his hood back. He pulled it up again and held it tightly beneath his chin while he studied the two warriors. They'd barely spoken all day, apparently concentrating on their duty instead.

When they reached the fork in the trail, rain pounded down, and the rocky trail ran with water. Disu and Saponi took the right fork.

Hiyawento frowned and called into the wind, "That's the wrong trail.

That leads to Sedge Marsh Village. We need to take the left fork to get to Bur Oak Village."

Disu propped his hands on his hips and said something soft to Saponi. Saponi pointed to his own chest, and walked back to face Hiyawento. The man had a pockmarked face with brown eyes and a nose like a flattened beetle. He halted two paces away and adjusted his hood, pulling it lower over his face. "Do you trust War Chief Sindak?"

Hiyawento stared at him. Sindak had been one of the people who had rescued him after he'd been stolen away from Yellowtail Village as a child. "Yes. Why?"

"Because our instructions are to take you to Sedge Marsh Village first. Then, if you wish to proceed on to Bur Oak Village, we will escort you there." His hood flapped around his face.

Hiyawento looked from Saponi to Disu and back. Both men wore stern expressions. "Why wouldn't I wish to continue on to Bur Oak Village?"

Neither answered. They appeared to be waiting for him to figure this out by himself. "What's going on? You know very well that the Ruling Council of Matrons ordered me to head straight to Bur Oak Village without delay."

Saponi nodded. "At most, this will delay your arrival by a few hands of time." He gestured to the left fork. "If we go now."

"Why don't you just give me the answer, so we won't have to delay our journey at all?"

Water ran around Saponi's moccasins. Freshly fallen autumn leaves and twigs filled the stream. "War Chief Sindak said we had to show you, not tell you."

Hiyawento expelled a breath—and took the right fork. As he headed down the trail to Sedge Marsh Village, he fretted over what Sindak wanted him to see. One destroyed village looked pretty much like another.

The guards had changed positions. Rather than both men walking in front of him to protect him from a frontal assault, as they had been, Disu now strode out in front, while Saponi walked behind Hiyawento. He wasn't sure he liked this, and he cast an uneasy glance over his shoulder. Probably they were just taking better care of him . . . but he felt like a caged packrat. If they were attacked, he could neither advance, nor retreat. He'd have to strike out through the brush.

As they continued down the trail, wind-tormented branches clattered and slashed the air above them. He bowed his head against the downpour and concentrated on plodding through the storm.

———

Two hands of time later, the water in the trail turned black, filled with ash or soot, and dread quickened his pulse. He twisted around to stare up at the beech trees that lined the trail. Gray streaks trickled down the trunks, as though not so long ago they had been coated with ash. When they reached the crest of the hill that looked down upon Sedge Marsh Village, he went numb.

Below, eight blackened pole skeletons stood where there had once been longhouses. The charred palisade had been breached in so many places he couldn't count them. The souls of the warriors that abided in the trees must be straining to keep it standing.

Disu and Saponi walked to stand on either side of him, and followed his gaze to the ruins below.

"I see a destroyed village," Hiyawento said. "A place where my relatives lived. It saddens me . . . but I don't know why I'm here."

"Come," Saponi said. He started down the hill.

Hiyawento expelled an annoyed breath, but followed. When Saponi scrambled through one of the gaping holes in the palisade and trotted out into the plaza, Hiyawento felt a strange sense of foreboding—and it was more than just the ghostly screams of rage that must fill the air. He turned round and round, searching for dead bodies, stray dogs, orphaned children. He didn't even see scattered baskets or broken pots lying on the ground, dropped by fleeing people when the attack came.

He shouted at Saponi, "This village was burned three days ago. Where are the dead bodies?"

Saponi slung his bow and folded his muscular arms. "Didn't you wonder why War Chief Sindak wasn't present at the War Council?"

"Yes. Everyone did."

"He wasn't there because he was here."

"Why? What was he doing?"

"We were ordered to care for the bodies."

Confused, Hiyawento shook his head. "We . . . then, you and Disu were with Sindak's party?"

"Yes."

"But their relatives, those that survived the attack, should have returned to take care of that."

Saponi's lips smiled, but there was no humor there. "Atotarho told them he'd kill them if they tried to bury their relatives. He said they were traitors who deserved to wander the earth forever."

"But . . . then he ordered Sindak to form a burial party?"

"Yes."

He wiped the rain from his eyes with the back of his hand. "You are, I sense, about to get to the point of why you brought me here."

Saponi put a hand on Hiyawento's shoulder. "Walk with me. There's more to this story. Something more interesting."

Saponi strode northward with his cape billowing around his legs.

"Interesting? That's a strange word to use, given the circumstances," he said as he followed.

"You'll see."

As they marched across the muddy plaza, Hiyawento's gaze searched the skeletons of each longhouse. They were empty, as though the people had just packed up and moved, then fired the village behind them. The whole scene was so odd.

They stepped through the palisade, and Saponi slogged out across the wet leaves, then led him down into a narrow trough between two low hills. Leaves filled the trough. The drenched branches of towering sycamores and chestnuts flailed high over their heads. Occasionally twigs snapped off and pattered the ground like hailstones.

Reverently, Saponi said, "The people are here. We stacked them seven high in a row two hundred hands long; then we burned them. We buried them as best we could, given that we were all terrified and anxious to get home."

"Burned them?" he said in shock. "Why?"

"Those were our orders."

Hiyawento swung around to stare back at the village. "Did you burn all of their belongings, too?"

Saponi lifted his arm and pointed to the east. "That charred pile over there? That's where we piled and burned the blankets, children's toys, bedding hides, and everything else."

Disu silently climbed the rise and surveyed the stormy forest before adding, "Sindak suspects we were doing more than assuring that traitors never reached the Land of the Dead."

The cold wind shifted, blowing directly into Hiyawento's face. He turned away and found himself glaring at withered leaves that cupped the falling rain like small colorful bowls. The storm noise made it difficult to think. Branches smashed into each other; leaves rattled; Wind Mother's son, *Hadui*, shrieked and whimpered as he beat his way through the trees—and the rain sounded like a siege, the far-off staccato of arrows slapping walls. "What do you mean?"

"He thinks we were sent to destroy evidence."

"Evidence of what?"

Saponi folded his arms and glared at the trough. "Don't you find it strange that none of us even knew they were ill, much less . . ."

The truth struck him like a blow. "Oh, dear gods, the stories our captives tell." He searched Saponi's and Disu's hard faces. "They were witched? You were ordered here to destroy the evidence of Atotarho's witchery?"

Saponi tilted his head uncertainly. "I doubt anyone will ever be able to prove it, but War Chief Sindak wonders. That's all."

"Did you find evidence of witchery?"

Disu answered, "For many moons we've heard rumors from passing Traders, and more from captives. No one believed them, except War Chief Sindak."

"What rumors?"

"Strange stories. Unbelievable. About the Bluebird Witch."

"There are thousands of stories about the Bluebird Witch, most of them silly. Which one did you have in mind?"

Saponi's eyes narrowed to slits. "The one about him being Chief Atotarho's son."

The shiver started deep down in Hiyawento's core and radiated outward until it shook his entire body. Across a gulf of twelve summers, he could hear Zateri crying far out in the warrior's camp, and Tutelo's little girl voice saying, *"But where's Odion? I can't leave without Odion! Where's my brother?"* His own childish voice answered, *"I'll wait for Odion. You have to go, Tutelo. Hurry. I'll take care of Gannajero and her men, kill them all, right down to the last breath in my body. But you have to save yourselves or it will mean nothing. Do you understand? My life for yours. That's the Trade. Now, please, get out of here before I lose my nerve."* Faintly, as though seeping up from even deeper inside him, Baji said, *"I'm coming back for you, Wrass. And I'm bringing a war party with me. Come on, Tutelo. Hehaka? Move!"*

"War Chief Hiyawento?"

Saponi's voice broke the memory, for which he was grateful. "Forgive me, I . . . I was remembering . . . his son."

"Perhaps you should think of this, too. If a very Powerful witch can sicken a village first, all a war party has to do is wait outside the gates until most of the enemy is sick or dead; then it can go in and kill the rest with little effort."

"And Sindak thinks that's what happened here? The Bluebird Witch sickened them first?"

"Maybe. We didn't lose a single warrior in the battle."

Hiyawento rubbed his hands over his face. "I need time to think. To consider the ramifications of such a strategy."

"Perhaps you should do that on the way back to Coldspring Village?"

"Coldspring Village? I'm not going home. I'm going on to Bur Oak Village."

Saponi scowled out at the storm-tormented trees. "Are you certain that's the wise course? Wouldn't it be better to return home, convene the Coldspring's council, and confront Atotarho about this? Every person who hears what we were ordered to do here will suspect we were covering up the truth."

Hiyawento spread his hands. "I understand that Sindak, as the War Chief of Atotarho Village, cannot bring such a claim before his own council. Sindak would be driven from the village with arrows flying around his head. But he should at least broach the subject with Matron Tila. Tell him I said that as soon as you get home."

"Home?"

"Yes, I'll be going on alone from here. I don't wish to risk your lives. But I'm grateful you guarded me to the boundary of Standing Stone country. Tell Sindak that is a kindness I will not forget."

"Sindak said you'd probably dismiss us," Disu replied. "He said you've never known what's good for you."

Despite the circumstances, Hiyawento laughed. "What else did he say?"

Saponi took a few instants to look up into the falling rain. It coated his hood and face. Oddly, his wet pockmarks shone more brightly than the rest of his skin. "He said that he feared this was just the beginning."

Sixteen

Sky Messenger

Istand beneath the porch of the Deer Clan longhouse, huddling against the wind. The storm is wild today, with an icy flush of wind that batters the forest and sends colorful leaves tumbling across the wet plaza. Every small depression shimmers, filled with water. Gitchi lies at my feet curled into a ball with his tail over his white muzzle.

From inside the house, I hear Mother say, "The most we will agree to is half of our walnut crop and one-quarter of our hickory nuts. But in exchange, we expect Sky Messenger to be allowed to freely pursue his calling as a Dreamer."

These negotiations are torture. My clan is giving up almost everything for my vision. If only I . . .

"We already have fifteen Dreamers in the surrounding five villages. Why do we need another?"

Exasperated, Mother says, "None of our other holy people have seen this coming darkness. Clearly the Spirits have chosen to speak through Sky Messenger about our future."

"Really? It suggests something far different to me. He's always been an imaginative boy. I think his visions are just so much wind." Matron Kittle's voice is scornful. "This one thing is not negotiable. By his actions he has forfeited his position as deputy war chief, but he must take up his weapons again and be prepared for the war trail."

My fists clench.

In a cold voice, Mother replies, "The way he serves the clan is not your affair, Kittle. The Yellowtail Village council has already decided that he will serve as apprentice to Old Bahna. Sky Messenger is skilled in his understanding of *Uki* and *Otkon*, the two halves of Spirit Power that inhabit the world, but Bahna says he needs training to understand how to use them to best benefit the People."

"If he wishes to marry my granddaughter, he will . . ."

I force my thoughts away from the anger and political maneuverings to the Spirit Power that inhabits all things. I feel it. It breathes all around me, passing through me, to Gitchi, and spreading out, inhabiting everything at once, tying me to the vision like an invisible net. All things are inextricably connected, though most of us have little awareness of the fact. Uki is a serene, hopeful power, never harmful to human beings, while Otkon is as unpredictable as a Trickster; it can either be beneficial or lethal. Though each half contains the same amount of light and darkness, Uki's half of the day runs from midnight to noon, while Otkon's operates from noon to midnight. When combined, the halves are potent portals to spiritual awareness, but new Dreamers must be careful with Otkon. I know this from personal experience. My Dream awakens me most often before midnight, during Otkon time, and I can never predict what I will do when I lurch to my feet. One night I grabbed my club and frantically raced through the forest like a madman. Another time, I woke and couldn't move. I was paralyzed until midnight, when my muscles started working again.

Instinctively, I reach down to touch the four Power bundles tied to my belt. Each is painted a different color—representing the sacred directions—and contains precious items given to me by my Spirit Helper while I wandered the forest. Old Bahna is right. I have only the vaguest notion of how to properly use Uki and Otkon. If I do not learn how to balance the powers, I may harm my People, rather than help them.

An old woman with white hair and a severely pointed chin approaches. She grumbles, "Traitor!" spits at my feet, and ducks beneath the leather curtain into the Deer Clan longhouse.

Shame courses through me. When most people look at me, all they see is a disgraced deputy war chief with no weapons, a man of some previous renown who betrayed his war party and ran away. Despite the fact that different versions of my vision are being circulated through the village, many do not believe. For now, I have only one responsibility: to help Mother and the council secure this marriage with the Deer Clan. Kittle is the most powerful matron in the nation. I understand now, after many discussions with the Yellowtail Council, that I must have her support to have any chance of building the alliances we will need in the future. Alliances with peoples who currently hate us and want to destroy us . . . as we do them.

"My granddaughter"—Matron Kittle's voice seems to explode between my souls—"may one day lead all the clans of the Standing Stone nation. She deserves better than your pathetic son, Koracoo."

"That's ridiculous, Kittle. After your seven daughters, and her four older sisters, Taya is *twelfth* in line for the matronship. It is unlikely—"

"Eleventh," Kittle said. "My daughter Yosha is unsuitable."

"Nonetheless, it is unlikely Taya will ever have a chance to rule, and you know it. Taya is a pampered and protected child with almost no useful skills, while Sky Messenger may well be the greatest Dreamer our people have ever known."

Kittle's low laugh chills my blood. "You have fanciful notions of your son's worth, Koracoo. He's always been curious. From the day he returned after being captured during the destruction of Yellowtail Village, he's been a loner. He's like a turtle with its head pulled into its shell. I don't know how he managed to rise to the position of deputy war chief. He must have—"

"Valor." Mother's voice cuts to the bone. "He distinguished himself in battle over and over. If you need proof, perhaps you should consult with your own war chief. Skenandoah gave Sky Messenger his name because of his ability to call sunlight from cloudy skies on the war trail. Skenandoah believed that Elder Brother Sun spoke directly to Sky Messenger."

There is silence for a long time. Kittle, of course, knows this.

Twenty heartbeats later, Taya pulls the door curtain aside and steps out carrying a steaming bowl of cornmeal mush with a wooden spoon stuck in it. She is a newly made woman with large brown eyes, and waist-length black hair that sways across the front of her cape as she walks. Her expression is stony.

She lifts the bowl to me. "It's cold today. Grandmother says you should eat."

For many summers, whenever I returned from a war walk and came to report to Matron Kittle, I brought Taya and her four sisters presents. Every warrior in the nation brought them gifts. It is part of our tradition, a way of honoring the high matron's lineage. Taya's needs have always been met. Slaves cook her meals, wash her clothing, run her errands. She has never known pain or real hunger. Because her lineage is so precious, she's rarely allowed to travel. She's never been more than a few days' walk from Bur Oak Village. Even if I tried to explain to her what I see coming, she has no framework for understanding such horror and loneliness.

I take the bowl. "Thank you for your kindness."

She tucks her hands beneath her cape and nervously wets her lips. She seems to be mustering her courage to speak to me.

"It's all right, Taya. You can ask me anything."

After swallowing hard, she says, "I've been thinking about this. I'm worried about our children. What your dishonor will do to them." She cautiously looks up at me from beneath long eyelashes. "It may stain them forever."

"In a few summers, our people will realize that what I did was for the good of all."

She tilts her head, not certain she believes this. Then she says, "I don't wish to marry you, do you know that? Did your clan tell you that I objected?"

I stop eating. "Yes. This is just a political alliance, Taya. Nothing more."

She flaps her arms at her sides, very much like a frustrated child. "I can see how being married to me will strengthen your clan, but how does such an arrangement benefit mine? You may or may not be a Dreamer. What if it turns out your Dream is all fantasy? Where will that leave me and our children?"

I take another bite and chew. Finally, I answer, "If it turns out that my Dream is false, and I disgrace you, then you may set my belongings outside the Deer Clan longhouse, and I will return to my own clan. Divorce is a simple matter."

"Yes, divorce may be, but the shame I will bear from your grandiose lies—"

"They are *not* lies," I reply sternly.

As though to cast the final insult, she tosses her head and adds, "Well, I don't love you."

I don't know what to make of this. Of course she doesn't. Why does she think she must tell me this? I try to think back to what I felt when I'd seen fourteen summers, but the analogy doesn't work. My childhood was rudely stripped from me when I'd seen eleven summers. I never had the chance to go through this awkward half-child and half-adult stage.

I force my thoughts back. "Taya, this has nothing to do with love. It's a political arrangement. That's all."

She wets her lips again. "Grandmother says you are a coward. A traitor. Are you?"

"If I were a coward, I would not be here. I would have lived out my life as an Outcast in the forest."

"Some people—mostly ignorant outsiders—are saying that you are the prophesied human False Face."

It isn't a question. She cocks her head, waiting for me to comment, probably to deny it. Claiming to be the prophesied human False Face is like saying you are Elder Brother Sun, or the good hero twin, Sapling.

I answer, "I don't know what I am. But I know what I must do, and it will take every ounce of strength I have to accomplish it. If you become my wife, your clan will expect you to help me stop the coming darkness. Can you do that?"

Taya lifts her chin in a superior manner. "Probably not. No. What you do about your *Dreams* is no affair of mine."

My heart suddenly tastes like dust, dry as a bone, struggling to beat in the shadows of a circling flock of vultures.

"Well," I say through a long exhalation, "at least we know where we stand."

Taya draws herself up. "You were an excellent deputy war chief. I've heard War Chief Deru tell stories about you . . ." She says all this while her gaze bores holes into me. "Even yesterday he told Grandmother that if he had just two dozen men like you he could conquer the world. If you really wanted to be useful, you would return to the war trail."

"Deru . . . defended me?" The warm bowl in my hands lowers, and the rain on the roof sounds suddenly loud.

"Yes. He said he didn't blame you for following your Spirit Helper. He told Grandmother he would have done the same if he'd been called into the forest by his Helper."

My heart transforms into a tight fist that makes it difficult to breathe. The night I vanished, he must have known in less than one hand of time that I'd betrayed him. How can he forgive me so easily?

I have been purposefully avoiding Deru, hiding from the accusations in his eyes. Now I know I must seek him out. "I am ashamed of myself," I say. "I should have gone to him immediately."

"Why?" She looks truly confused.

I stare at her. Her inability to grasp honor is especially disheartening. I eat more of the warm mush.

Taya watches me. Her eyes are deep dark pools. "If we marry, you will work very hard, won't you, to make certain your disgrace does not taint our children?"

There's so much more at stake than children. I hesitate.

The elders of the Bear Clan say marriage is the price I must pay for my actions on the war trail. I no longer have the luxury of being an "oddity." I must be a productive member of the clan. As must Taya. Even if we are betrothed, we cannot actually marry until she is carrying my child. That's how she proves her worth to my clan. Soon, perhaps before these negotiations are finished, I may be asked to begin sleeping in her bed, in her longhouse, and obeying the orders of her clan matron—as is the way of our people, where, after marriage, a man moves to his wife's village. I will do my duty to my clan, but . . . *Baji's smile appears just behind my eyes, filled with the candor of one who knows my darkest secrets and needs, and is unafraid.* . . .

A stunning sense of loss paralyzes me for an instant. I can't move or think. I stare unblinking at the far palisade. All I see is Baji.

"You haven't answered me. Why not?" Taya says in an annoyed voice.

I force myself to eat the last bites of mush and hand the empty bowl and spoon to her. Rain pounds the plaza, creating a drumlike cadence. A lone puppy trots through the downpour with his tail between his legs.

My clan believes this alliance is crucial.

Bluntly, I say, "If either of us survives to have children, then we'll talk about it. And, now, excuse me. I must see Old Bahna."

I bow to her and stride across the plaza for the Turtle Clan longhouse.

"But I'm not finished speaking with you!" she calls after me. "Come back here this instant!"

I walk faster. . . .

Seventeen

Koracoo ducked into the Turtle Clan longhouse in Yellowtail Village. While she let her eyes adjust to the darkness, she listened to the voices. She might not be able to see the people, but they saw her. Whispers ran the three-hundred-hand length of the house. Koracoo shivered in the warmth and began walking down the center aisle, past ten compartments and five fire hearths, before she reached Old Bahna's compartment in the middle of the house.

Sky Messenger and Bahna looked up at her expectantly as she removed her wet cape and dropped it beside the hearth where they sat with tea cups in their hands. Clearly, they'd been having a serious discussion. Firelight shadowed the deep furrows in Bahna's elderly face. He had seen fifty-three summers pass. Thin gray hair lay like spiderwebs across his leathery cheeks. He looked up at her with kind eyes. "What is the news, Speaker?"

Sky Messenger's jaw clenched, preparing himself for the worst.

Koracoo knelt on the far side of the fire. "Matron Kittle accepts our offer and will prepare a chamber for her granddaughter and her betrothed. Sky Messenger will sleep in the Deer Clan longhouse tonight."

Sky Messenger's head dropped, and he closed his eyes. Koracoo couldn't tell if it was in relief or dread. She extended her icy hands to the warmth of the flames.

"Marriage is a small price, my son."

"Yes, I know." He exhaled the words, and when Sky Messenger looked at her, pain shone in his dark eyes.

Koracoo knew about his relationship with Baji last summer when they'd briefly been allied with the Flint People, but she'd assumed their togetherness would be fleeting, a battle-walk romance over as soon as the alliance shifted . . . and alliances always shifted. Apparently, it had not ended, at least not to her son.

"Will you have a cup of tea, Speaker?" Bahna asked, and reached for one of the clay cups resting by the pot that nestled in the ashes at the edge of the fire.

"Yes, thank you. It's a wintry day out there."

Bahna dipped the cup into the pot, and the scent of raspberries wafted up with the steam. He extended it. Koracoo gratefully clutched the cup in her cold fingers. As she sipped the tea the delicious tartness of dried raspberries, lightly accented with mint leaves, coated her tongue. "This is good, Bahna."

"On days like this, it helps to drink fruity teas. They cleanse the blood and open the heart." Bahna leaned back on the woven floor mats and gave her a small troubled smile.

Koracoo frowned at the men. "What have you been discussing? Your expressions are dire."

"Many things," Bahna said with a deep sigh, "but mostly Sky Messenger's Dream. One part is very troubling."

Sky Messenger braced his elbows on his knees and gazed at her across the fire. The flame-light fluttered over his high cheekbones and blunt chin. It pleased her that he'd grown into a handsome man, though she feared for his future. If his Dream was true—and she believed it was—before next summer solstice he would be tested a thousand times. He might also be dead.

Sky Messenger said, "Bahna is concerned about the way my Dream ends."

Bahna nodded and waved crooked fingers through the firelight. The joint-stiffening disease had turned them into claws. He hadn't been able to fully open his fist for many summers. "Sky Messenger tells me there is a black hole in his afterlife soul, a place where he fears memories live, but he cannot find them. I believe that's where the man's voice comes from. The ghost is calling to him."

"Why?"

"Because, Speaker, the dead always wish to be buried so that they may travel to the afterlife."

As images from twelve summers ago appeared behind her eyes, rage filled Koracoo. She unconsciously gripped CorpseEye where he was slipped into her belt, and leaned forward. The gesture must have been threatening, for Bahna pulled away. "This man was evil, Bahna. He hurt many children. Believe me when I tell you that I *want* his soul to wander the earth alone for eternity. We deliberately mutilated his body and scattered the pieces so that no one would ever be able to recognize him and send his soul to the Land of the Dead. He is a condemned man, and that is what he deserves." Her voice had gone low.

"Yes," Bahna said with a tottering nod. "Sky Messenger told me. But you must understand, Speaker, that that is the problem."

"You mean that's why Sky Messenger hears his voice at the end of the Dream? The dead man wants someone to collect his bones and Sing his afterlife soul to the Land of the Dead?"

"Of course."

"This is a soul sickness, then? How do we cure it?"

Bahna frowned at her, then placed another branch on the fire. As sparks crackled and spat, he continued, "The ghosts of those killed by our hands or in our names must be mourned and cared for. The beginning for Sky Messenger is to remember the event that caused his sickness."

Sky Messenger did not look at Koracoo, but his jaw ground as though he'd rather die than do that. She did not know exactly what had happened to him that long-ago day. No one did. And if that little boy had felt it necessary to bury the memory deep down in the darkness between his souls, was it wise for anyone to dredge it up again?

As though reading the tracks of her souls, Bahna smiled faintly. The wrinkles around his mouth resembled sunlit rings on a dark pond. "Please try to understand, Speaker. Each of us can put ourselves in the place of another, but your son is called upon to do more. He must put himself in the place of many. In the next moons, the Spirits will demand much of him. He will not have the strength to endure unless he stares into the blackness inside him, and releases the man he has caged there."

Koracoo swirled the tea in her cup, perhaps a little too violently. The purple liquid sloshed out onto her hand. She wiped it on her red leather legging. "I think the entire matter is best left alone."

Sky Messenger seemed to be frowning at the blue smoke rising toward the smoke hole in the roof. He blinked, then lowered his gaze to the fire. "Bahna is right, Mother."

"How do you know that? Have you seen it in a Dr—"

"No, but Bahna has."

Her gaze flicked to the old man. Bahna said, "I am told that your son's life must be a life of flames, consuming itself as it illuminates the darkness. He understands that."

"He may, but I do not. What are you saying?"

Bahna placed a gnarled hand upon Sky Messenger's shoulder. "He must return to the place it happened. The man is waiting. He's been waiting for Sky Messenger for many summers."

Koracoo set her cup down hard. "It's a long way, and though the fighting should decrease as winter deepens, it will still be extremely dangerous. I don't see the point, at this time, in undertaking such a journey."

"The point?" Bahna asked with a gentle smile. His wrinkles rearranged into kind lines. "The point is forgiveness, Speaker. A man who hates has no eyes. He is a prisoner of darkness."

Sky Messenger stiffened. His head turned slowly, and he looked at Bahna with glowing eyes. He seemed to be holding his breath. Listening for more.

Bahna didn't seem to notice. He continued, "All of Sky Messenger's life, he's been hiding from a memory. He may not know it, but he's been afraid for so long, he doesn't know how to stop. He lives in a prison. Every day he repairs the chinking, adds new logs, seals himself in. He must stop, or he'll never be able to truly see the ghosts of grief and desperation that haunt this land."

Sky Messenger said, "You mean I'm protecting myself from a dead man?"

"He's not dead, Grandson. Just as you breathe soul into every arrow you create, a man can breathe soul into a memory. You have given him life. And he is just as much a prisoner as you are." Bahna leaned toward Sky Messenger. "You must set him free."

A strange almost euphoric expression tensed Sky Messenger's face, as though at last he understood. "Set him free," he repeated softly.

Bahna reached out and touched Sky Messenger's chest with a gnarled hand. "Forgiveness is not born through an act of will, or thought, but in the tears of a single human being. Your tears."

Sky Messenger appeared to be contemplating the words, struggling with the ramifications, but he said, "I will need the council's approval, Mother. Can you see to that?"

She gazed into his tormented eyes. He was her son, and she knew him well. While he had accepted the necessity of undertaking this journey, he didn't relish the idea. But she could also tell that he longed to get out of the village. "I will arrange it."

Bahna said, "Good." He reached over to draw a thick cedar splinter from the woodpile by the hearth, then handed it to Sky Messenger.

Sky Messenger turned it over in the light, examining the deep red wood. "What is this?"

"A stiletto to puncture your heart. Some wounds never Heal, but their blood gives life to the world. Remember that."

Sky Messenger stared at the splinter for a long time before he tugged open the laces of the red Power bundle on his belt and gently tucked the splinter inside. Afterward, he petted the bundle, as though soothing its pain.

"What about his new wife-to-be?" Koracoo asked. "If Sky Messenger must leave on this journey immediately—"

"I am told he must take her with him."

Simultaneously, Koracoo and Sky Messenger blurted, *"What!"*

Sky Messenger threw up his hands. "No, no. I am *not* taking Taya with me. It's too dangerous. She's barely more than a child. I will be madly paddling down the river, moving like lightning. Then, when I reach the Dawnland country, I will have to stow my canoe and run overland as fast as my legs can carry me, praying the entire time that I'm not discovered by Dawnland warriors, or Flint warriors in Dawnland country. I'm willing to risk my own life, but not hers."

Koracoo added, "He's right, Bahna. Taya has never traveled beyond the boundaries of Standing Stone country. She knows nothing of the war trail. Perhaps—"

"She must go with him." Bahna stared at Sky Messenger, but his old eyes seemed to be focused on the far distances, seeing something heartrending. "Grandson," he said gently. "The Spirits of your ancestors tell me she must be there. She is part of the Dream."

Sky Messenger massaged his forehead. "All right. I'll be leaving right after the betrothal ceremony. Who will inform High Matron Kittle?"

Bahna smiled. "I will, Grandson."

Eighteen

Sky Messenger

A hoarse cry rips from my lungs. I jerk upright in the bedding hides, panting. My sweat-drenched bare skin shimmers in the firelight reflecting from the walls of an unfamiliar longhouse. I don't know where I am. I . . . This is the Deer Clan longhouse. *Yes, I'm betrothed.*

All down the length of the house, dogs bark, while people grab for weapons. Gitchi, who sleeps beside me, softly licks my hand.

"What's happening?" a man shouts.

"Nothing," I respond. "Forgive me. My soul was walking in a f-fog." It's the only way I can describe the gray shimmering world I've just left. In my heart, I'm still falling, falling. . . .

"Well go back to sleep!"

Weapons clatter softly as they are returned to their places within reach of the owners, and warriors crawl beneath their hides again.

Taya braces herself on one elbow to stare at me. Long black hair frames her oval face. Her large dark eyes and straight nose glow faintly orange in the light of the dying fires.

"Are you going to wake me every night while we're on our journey to the Dawnland?" she whispers.

"I certainly hope not." I blink at the longhouse for a few moments longer, studying the bark walls, the corn, beans, and squash plants hanging from the roof poles . . . convincing myself this is the real world, not the cloud-sea or the eerie darkness. Then I lie down and pull the hides up over my bare chest.

Gitchi props his head across my stomach, just letting me know he's close. His yellow eyes blink sleepily at me. I stroke his soft neck.

Taya whispers, "Your screeching is probably going to get us killed on the trail." She flops over, turning her back to me.

The words make me long to say something unkind. I do not, of course. She's probably just beginning to realize that she's going to be alone with me for many days. She may be worried sick that her grandmother has gotten her into more than she can handle.

As her relatives begin to slumber again, I inhale the smoky air and listen to the dogs circling until they flop down and heave deep sighs.

Since I returned, the Dream has started coming more often. Two or three times a night. Why?

There's something I've forgotten. I have to remember.

With my hand still on Gitchi, I shift to study the back of Taya's head. Her long black hair spreads over the deer hides in a glossy wealth. The time is coming when all shadows die. How can I ever explain that horror to her?

Nineteen

High Matron Tila clung tightly to her granddaughter's arm. She propped her walking stick, took two steps, breathed, then took two more, forcing herself to keep moving across the cold plaza.

"We're almost there, Grandmother," Zateri said as she guided Tila around small rocks and indentations. Short and skinny, her granddaughter had a flat face with a wide nose. She'd twisted her long black hair into a bun at the back of her head and secured it with a polished tortoiseshell comb.

"This will be a hard day for you," Tila said weakly. "But it will be an important day."

"Grandmother, please tell me. What did you see in your Dream when the False Faces came to you?"

Tila leaned on her walking stick while she wheezed. She could never seem to get enough air these days. Elder Brother Sun had just awakened. A faint blue gleam painted the eastern horizon. High above them, the brightest campfires of the dead continued to sparkle. "You wore the same white cape you have on today." Blue wolf paw prints encircled the bottom of Zateri's cape. "You looked pretty. Calm. You made the right decision."

"Which was?"

Tila smiled and gingerly took another step toward the Women's Council house, a round structure less than twenty paces from the Wolf longhouse. This morning those twenty paces seemed to encompass the entire world. Tila made soft pained sounds as she moved. The cool morning breeze didn't help. It fluttered the hood of her wolfhide cape and blew thin strands of short white hair into her eyes. She didn't have the strength to shove them away.

"Wait just a moment while I pull back the leather door hanging, Grandmother."

Tila braced both hands on her walking stick and took the moment to survey the village. They'd moved to a new location, as they did every ten or twelve summers, just six moons ago. The four longhouses looked fresh and clean, their bark walls still brown, not gray with age. Arranged in an oval around the plaza were the smaller clan houses, which served as a meeting place for the individual clans: Bear, Wolf, Turtle, Hawk, Deer, and Snipe. Three other houses nestled to the north, the large village council house, the slightly smaller Women's Council house, and the prisoner's house.

The palisade, forty hands tall, and made of upright pine logs, had an imposing presence. Before Tila had become too ill, she'd personally selected each log by touch. The afterlife soul of those who died violently could not find the Sky Road that led to the Land of the Dead. They were excluded from joining their ancestors in the afterlife and doomed to spend eternity wandering the earth. The souls of such men and women moved into trees. It was these trees with indwelling warrior spirits, that the People cut to serve as palisade logs, thereby surrounding the village with Standing Warriors. When she'd run her fingers over the wood, she'd felt the souls of the warriors that inhabited the logs, and knew each had been very powerful and dedicated to protecting his or her people. There were no better guardians in any world than such men and women.

"Are you ready, Grandmother?" Zateri asked as she held aside the leather curtain.

"Yes, child."

Zateri steadied Tila's arm as she ducked beneath the curtain and entered the firelit warmth. Fifty women, or so, were already here, standing about talking softly beneath the great hollow-eyed False Face masks that lined the walls. Each had recently been rubbed with sunflower oil. Their crooked noses and wide mouths shone, framed by long hair.

"Thank you, Granddaughter. You may go to your proper place now."

"Are you sure you don't need me to help you—?"

"I must walk the last steps by myself. A high matron can't afford to look weak before the other matrons, or they will crush her bones with their teeth. Do you understand?"

"Yes, Grandmother."

Zateri hesitantly released Tila's arm and walked straight ahead to join the group of "little clan matrons"—village clan leaders who had not risen to the status of village matron, the woman who led all the clans in the village. Most cast vaguely hostile looks in her direction. Zateri was young and too strong-willed for their tastes. They thought her impulsive. Which she was. Only a recklessly impulsive young woman would, after an argument with the chief, strike out to form her own village at the age of fourteen summers. And that, of course, would be today's main topic. But Tila was prepared for it.

She blinked her dim eyes at the darkness. The sweet tang of hickory smoke filled the house. She was trembling as she propped her walking stick and carefully made the last five steps to the central fire. The other great-grandmothers, Inawa and Yi, respectfully dipped their heads to her. She nodded in return. As she lowered herself to the bench, a slave girl rushed to dunk a tea cup, made from the skull of an enemy warrior, into the boiling bag that hung on the tripod near the fire, and bring it to her.

"This will help warm you, Matron."

Tila took it, said, "Thank you, girl," and placed the cup on the bench before her fingers shook it empty.

Now that the great-grandmothers—the leaders of the Wolf Clan *ohwachiras*—were all settled, conversations hushed. Every eye turned to Tila, matron of the Wolf Clan, and high matron of the Ruling Council of the People of the Hills. She quietly scanned the assembly.

The world had a hierarchy. Great Grandmother Earth stood at the top, followed by Grandmother Moon, Wind Mother, Elder Sister Gaha, Elder Brother Sun, and many others. The ohwachira, the basic family unit, was patterned in the same way. An ohwachira was a kinship group that traced its descent from a common mother, and the members were bound together by the strongest tie known: blood. The ohwachira had great power, for it possessed and bestowed chieftainship titles and held the names of the great people of the past. It bestowed those names by raising up the souls of the dead and requickening them in the bodies of newly elected chiefs, adoptees, or other people. In the same way, if a new chief disappointed the ohwachira, after consultation with the clan, it could take back the name, remove the soul, and depose the chief. It was also the sisterhood of ohwachiras that decided when to go to war and when to make peace.

All three ohwachiras of the Wolf Clan were represented today. Tila's ohwachira was the largest and most powerful; then came Inawa's ohwachira, and lastly Yi's ohwachira.

The titles in the ohwachira were logical, beginning with the status of the eldest "mother," usually great-grandmother, but in rare cases in the past there had been great-great-grandmothers. After great grandmother, came grandmother, then mother. *Mother* had a much deeper meaning than just the woman who gave you birth. It was applied to all of her sisters and to all women of her generation in her sisters' lines of descent. This often confused members of other nations, for they called these same women *cousins.*

After *mother* came *uncle,* meaning only the mother's brother. The hierarchy continued to *elder sister, elder brother, younger sister, younger brother, granddaughter, grandson.* Only uncles used the terms *niece* and *nephew.* A person's title, such as *eldest daughter,* defined her duties and responsibilities to the clan.

The thing that tied the sisterhood of Wolf Clan ohwachiras together was a distant common female ancestor. In this case, their lines all originated with a long-ago ancestor named Dancing Fox. Dancing Fox's life story had been lost in the mists of time, though legend said she had bravely led the People through a Long Dark filled with monsters and into Elder Brother Sun's light.

Tila smoothed white hair away from her wrinkled face and softly called, "Come. Let us bring order to the world."

As the clan mothers seated themselves, Tila looked across the fire at Inawa. Inawa would be her main opponent today, since her ohwachira was next in line to lead the Wolf Clan, and by extension, the nation. Provided, that is, that the Bear Clan didn't squash Inawa like a bug after Tila's death, and take over the leadership.

Zateri shifted where she sat on the bench with the other village matrons, clearly uneasy. In a council house filled with great-grandmothers and grandmothers, she must feel very small and insignificant. As she should. Since the deaths of Tila's two daughters, Zateri was the only female left in Tila's direct line. She would lead Tila's ohwachira in the near future—if she chose to, and if the other mothers of the Wolf Clan did not seriously oppose her. She had disgraced herself eight summers before when she'd established Coldspring Village without the approval of the clan. Only Tila's political maneuvering, calling in every favor she'd ever earned in her sixty-five summers, had saved Zateri from being declared an Outcast.

Tila lifted one hand and said, "May Great Grandmother Earth hear our voices and guide us in our decisions for the good of all things, great and small. I would speak first, if there are no objections."

The house went still, waiting. The blue gleam falling through the smoke hole in the roof illuminated Inawa's and Yi's elderly faces. Inawa, who had seen fifty summers pass, had plump cheeks and a red nose.

Gray-streaked black hair hung limply over her shoulders. Her failing was that she talked too much and had a tendency to veer away from the subject at hand and start relating long disconnected stories. Yi, on the other hand, said little, and each careful word went to the heart of the matter. She had seen forty-eight summers. She sat to Tila's right, her back straight, her bearing stately, commanding attention. A few silver strands glittered in her short black hair, but deep wrinkles cut around her mouth and across her forehead. Tila heartily wished that Yi's ohwachira was next in line.

"I have little time left," Tila began. "Our Healers have done their best for me, but there is no earthly Spirit plant that will cure my illness. They say there is a witch's charm lodged inside me, but they cannot find it." She touched her sunken chest and moved her fingers over the swollen lumps. "I have perhaps a few moons. Nothing more."

A din of whispers began, several heartrending. A pained cry of "no," rose from the back, but Tila couldn't identify the speaker. Tila had been a good and fair clan matron. She was, for the most part, greatly loved.

Inawa said, "Then we must work harder to find the witch and force her to remove the charm! And maybe it isn't a charm, but an ordinary spell. Spells can be killed by killing the witch. It's a simple matter. I once knew a woman who'd been witched and her blood turned black. By the time anyone realized what was happening one of her feet had rotted and had to be cut off. The next thing—"

"We have the best Healers in the nation, Inawa. I'm sure they've correctly assessed my problem."

Indeed, the Healers had first tried a variety of Spirit Plants, herbs, grasses, and barks; then they'd rubbed her body with ashes to cleanse it. Afterward, they'd attempted to wash away the disease by performing the going-to-water ritual, taking her down to purify in the frigid river while they Sang and shook rattles. It was powerful magic, symbolically submerging her in the river of Great Grandmother Earth's blood that ran beneath the ground. After each battle, weapons were symbolically cast into that river to cleanse them of the taint of death. It could also cure the taint of witchery. When nothing had worked, her Healers prepared a pot of False Face pudding, burned sacred tobacco, and called upon the Faces of the Forest to aid them. Three of the masks spoke to Healer Towana, telling her a great wind was coming that would flatten the People of the Hills, and all of the Peoples south of Skanodario Lake, but the masks had promised to help the Hills People as much as they could. After relating her Dream, Towana brewed a tea from parched white sunflower seeds and manroot. As the masks had instructed, they'd drunk it together.

Which was why the fever had not struck here yet. They were being protected.

"How can the Healers know you are dying?" Yi asked.

"After the going-to-water ritual, Towana saw Sodowego pull the hides from my sleeping body to peer at my face."

Someone sobbed. No one could mistake the message. Sodowego—the great faceless harbinger of death—had seen her. She could not escape now. Soon, he would come for her.

Inawa wrung her hands and cast an unpleasant glance at Zateri. "Who will succeed you as matron? I notice your granddaughter sitting there, but surely you don't expect the other ohwachiras to approve of her? She is a divider by nature. How will she ever be able to unify the nation? Don't you recall when High Matron Dyo of the Snipe Clan nominated her silly daughter to take her place? The girl ruined the entire clan! She couldn't keep her hands off Traders. That's why the Snipe Clan lost power and the Wolf Clan took over the nation. We can't allow—"

Yi said, "Matron Tila is not Dyo. She would not so embarrass the Wolf Clan."

For a long time, only the crackling of the flames filled the council house. Zateri sat with her chin up, her eyes on Tila, looking totally unaffected by the criticism.

Tila extended a hand to her. "I would have my granddaughter come before the great-grandmothers."

Zateri's white cape swayed around her slender body as she slowly walked across the house to stand between Yi and Inawa. They both swiveled on their benches to look up at her.

"I present to the council, my granddaughter, Zateri, matron of Coldspring Village, and the next in line after me to lead the Wolf Clan. I would hear discussion on this matter. Yes, Matron Ganon of Turtleback Village."

The stocky old woman had stood up instantly, as though she couldn't bear to hold her tongue another moment. "Your wisdom has been the light of this clan for thirty-three summers, Tila. Not once in all that time have I cast my voice against you in council." Her arm lifted and swung dramatically to point at Zateri. "But if you select this—this *person*, Turtleback Village will refuse to hear her! Please, I beg you to choose another."

Inawa quipped, "Ganon's right. No one will support her. It will be like that time—"

"I will," a soft voice said from the far corner of the house, followed by another, "I will." Each woman who'd answered stood up.

Eyes strained to make out faces across the firelit distance. Tila said, "I ask that both of you come forward."

The matrons walked to stand shoulder to shoulder with Zateri. Only Kwahseti, from Riverbank Village, had moved beyond the level of a little clan matron to serve as the village matron, the leader of all the clans in the village. Though, if rumor was right, old Yana, the current village matron in Canassatego Village, was on her death bed, and Gwinodje was next in line to ascend to that position. Tila recognized Kwahseti first. "Matron Kwahseti of Riverbank Village, please state your reasons."

Kwahseti smoothed the folds from her buckskin cape and squared her shoulders. She had seen thirty-five summers pass, but looked far older. Her hair had gone almost completely gray. "I know arguments may be made against Matron Zateri. In her youth, she was brash. Since then, I believe she has led her village well. The other clans in Coldspring Village respect her and say she is thoughtful and wise. They follow her without question. Which of us would not love to have that sort of relationship with the other clans in our own villages? And, well, the truth is, the final decision is yours, Tila. We all know that. Your granddaughter has the right to rule, if you so decide. I just wish you to know that I believe, if given a chance, Matron Zateri will lead us with strength and honor."

Zateri bowed her head and blinked at the fire, as was appropriate.

Tila said, "I recognize Little Matron Gwinodje of Canassatego Village."

Gwinodje was short and so thin she appeared girlish. From behind, she was often mistaken for a child, as was Zateri. She had her black hair twisted into a tight bun on top of her head. A rabbit-bone skewer secured it. Nervous, she licked her lips. "I have heard Matron Zateri's warriors tell tales of her courage when dealing with enemy chiefs, and her generosity with captives. Perhaps more importantly, her villagers speak of her with deep respect, and that is the true measure of any matron. I think Matron Zateri would be firm but fair, as you are, Tila. I would embrace her as matron of the Wolf Clan."

Dissenting voices rose and seemed to boom from the walls. Tila stamped her walking stick on the ground to get their attention. "Would anyone else speak, or do you just wish to argue among yourselves?" No one stepped forward. Tila waited for a time longer before saying, "Then I would call for the casting of voices. Who would support Matron Zateri?"

She turned to Inawa first, who shook her head, and said, "No."

Yi said, "I ask that you pass me for the moment. I must consider for a time longer."

Tila smiled to herself. Yi was being smart, waiting to see how her ohwachira voted before she made her opinion known.

"Very well." Tila started along the eastern wall. "Little Matron Hooje?"

"No."

"Matron Wenta?"

"No."

By the time Tila had made it around the house, giving everyone a chance to speak, the pain in her chest was barely endurable. Her lungs did not want to breathe. More than anything, she longed to return to her soft hides and sleep. Instead, she gripped the head of her walking stick and grunted as she rose to her feet to stand before them. "The council is divided on this matter. I give you my oath that I will take every voice into consideration before making my decision. This council is dismissed." She lifted her chin to Zateri. "Granddaughter, will you walk with me?"

The vote had left Zateri stunned. Her face had gone snow white, her eyes blazing like crystals. She walked around the fire and took Tila's elbow, supporting her as she made her way across the council house and out into the dawn. The sky had turned opalescent, like the inside of a pink seashell tipped to reflect the sunlight.

When they were almost back to the Wolf longhouse, Zateri halted. She seemed to be staring at the two massive log pillars, the guardians of the longhouse. Carved with the Faces of the Forest and painted in rich shades of red, blue, black, and pure white, they stood on either side of the curtained entry. Each time they moved the village they dug up and moved the pillars, carrying them to the new location. Not even Tila knew for certain how old they were. They had stood since at least her great-grandmother's childhood. In a measured and peaceful voice, Zateri said, "I've made my decision, Grandmother."

Tila staggered as she turned to look at her. People moved about them, coming and going from the longhouse. "You should wait. Think about it more."

"I don't need to. I don't wish to lead them any more than they wish me to. My answer is no."

Tila vented a pained sigh. "Your father will not be pleased."

"No. I'm sure he won't." She gently took Tila's arm. "Let's get you into the warmth of the longhouse. I'm sorry I kept you outside any longer than necessary."

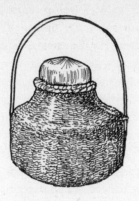

Twenty

High Matron Tila sat alone on the bench in her chamber at the northern end of the Wolf Clan longhouse. She had a cup of bear broth clutched in both hands. It took great effort to get the wooden cup to her lips without sloshing it all over her worn doeskin cape, but the broth was rich with fat and rested easy in her shrunken belly. There wasn't much she could eat these days that didn't come right back up, so she especially cherished this tasty treat.

She'd drawn the leather curtain at the front of her chamber closed, sealing out prying eyes so that she could think. She'd been going over and over the council meeting today, wondering, analyzing tones of voice and gestures. Not only that, she found the constant well-meant intentions of her relatives exhausting. With the curtain drawn, they would, perhaps, leave her alone.

Firelight from the longhouse fires outside coated the ceiling like amber resin and gave her chamber a soft yellow hue. The top of the chamber was open to the high roof, where whole cornstalks and sunflower plants hung. They'd been there for a full moon now, and had acquired a fuzzy coating of soot. As the winter deepened, she feared she would start getting requests for food from villages too weak to hunt or fish. In thirty-three summers, Tila had never refused to send food to any Hills village in need . . . until this summer. The harvests had been so bad, Atotarho Village simply could not spare a single kernel of corn. People had to fend for themselves as best they could. She prayed they all survived the winter. It was not going to be easy.

Tila clutched her cup and slowly, methodically, brought it to her lips. The warmth eased her pain a little. As she lowered the cup, a small amount shook out onto her cape. She just stared at it, too weak to even brush it away. The doeskin was little more than a rag anyway, worn through in too many places to count. What did it matter if it also bore a few stains? Tila heaved a sigh. She'd been fastidious her entire life. Everything had to be clean and polished, and in its proper place. She'd wanted her daughters to learn . . . Her daughters. All gone now. And her sisters, too.

As the pain in her chest throbbed, she squinted at the fragrant baskets of dried herbs, arranged according to size, nestled on the floor to her left. To her right, pots filled with corn kernels, beans, and squash seeds lined the wall. Heavy rocks served as lids to keep the pesky mice out.

On the shelf above her sleeping bench sat a special pot. Small and precious, it contained a lifetime of moments: a dried flower brought to her by her oldest daughter, eyes alight, when she'd seen five summers; a tiny, crudely carved finch, her youngest daughter's first attempt at woodcarving. And so many other things. She often took the pot down, especially of late, to handle each item, and remember those smiles and the love in those young voices.

She'd had a grand life, taken care of her people well, and made more than a few enemies. By and large, there would be more people who mourned her when she was gone than there would be people who celebrated her death. At least, she thought so. Perhaps more importantly, she had never been irrelevant. People still came to her for advice. They still listened to her every word. What more could an old woman ask?

A rush of cold wind swept inside as someone ducked through the longhouse entry. Her chamber curtain fluttered. Soft voices whispered.

Tila straightened and called, "Granddaughter? Did you come to see me?" Perhaps Zateri had changed her mind.

Zateri called back, "Yes, Grandmother, but we can wait. If you're in bed, we'll—"

"No, come in child. I'm just sitting here sipping broth."

Zateri pulled aside her chamber curtain and ducked inside, followed by War Chief Sindak. The sight of Sindak prickled her bones. He reported to Chief Atotarho, not Tila. Something had happened.

Tila gestured to the far end of the bench. "Sit down. Tell me what's wrong."

"Sindak came to me, Grandmother, and asked me to intercede on his behalf, to arrange a meeting with you."

Tila clutched her cup tighter, preparing herself. Over the past thirty-three summers, she'd become an expert in tones of voice. This was bad. "I am agreeable to meeting directly with the war chief. What happened?"

Zateri must have just bathed. Her long black hair and smooth skin gleamed. Sindak, however, appeared to have just come in off the trail. Dust coated his cape and hooked nose.

They seated themselves, and Zateri said, "Grandmother, Sindak received curious orders several days ago—orders regarding the Sedge Marsh Village. Were you aware of that?"

Tila frowned. "What do you mean? What orders? He was ordered to destroy the village and return home. That's all."

Sindak shoved dirty shoulder-length hair behind his ears. "The day after we returned home, Chief Atotarho told me to select a small party and return to take care of the dead."

"What do you mean? They were traitors. No one was to care for them."

Sindak's thin face hardened. "I know those were the council's orders, High Matron. However, the chief ordered us to return, gather all the bodies and belongings, and burn them; then he ordered us to bury them."

"Did he give you a reason?"

Sindak leaned forward and propped his elbows on his knees. "He said it would prevent the survivors from recognizing the bodies of their loved ones and Singing them to the Land of the Dead."

"But you think it was more."

"I do."

It was at times like this when her sickness took its greatest toll, for the pain made it hard to think rationally. In the old days, she'd have been two steps ahead of him, knowing before he did what he was going to say next. But tonight she could barely concentrate on his words.

"I'm feeble, War Chief. State your suspicions."

Sindak laced his hands before him. He had a thin face and dark brown eyes that always looked a little sad. "I think we may have been ordered to burn everything in an attempt to hide the truth."

Tila brought her shaking cup to her hands and sipped the warm broth to still her nerves. "Go on," she said, and took a long drink.

Zateri exchanged a glance with Sindak, and he nodded to her. Zateri said, "Grandmother, the survivors say that everyone in the village got sick and died in just two days. When Sindak's war party arrived, there was hardly anyone left alive to fight them. Doesn't that sound like witchery to you?"

Tila sat perfectly still, appraising the information. "We all agree that Sedge Marsh Village had been witched. The council even considered, as part of extenuating circumstances, that the elders may have had their souls stolen and that's why they betrayed us. Are you accusing someone of doing the witching?"

Zateri folded her arms beneath her cape and seemed to be hugging herself. "Grandmother? Is it possible that the fever is worse than we know?"

"Well, we've heard stories for moons. Every visitor brings a new version. Apparently it's been especially bad among the People of the Landing, but the Flint and Standing Stone peoples have been hit hard, too. But I don't see what that has to—"

"I'm wondering if perhaps Chief Atotarho hasn't decided to fight the war on two fronts at once," Sindak said.

Tila scowled and sat back on the bench. "I don't understand."

Sindak continued, "The Ruling Council of matrons has consistently forbidden attacking other nations unless we are attacked first. Which means that for many summers we've had a sort of undeclared truce with Bur Oak and Yellowtail villages. What if someone decided to use witchery, instead of warfare, to kill them, and their allies? Thereby circumventing the matrons altogether?"

"Let us be clear that by 'someone' you mean your chief. Is that correct?"

Sindak didn't drop his gaze. He bravely nodded. "Yes."

Accusing the chief of witchery could be construed as treason—and Sindak knew it—unless the accuser had evidence.

"That is a fanciful notion, War Chief. Do you have any proof?"

He lightly shook his head. "No, High Matron."

"Then, if you wish to pursue this line of thought, you had best find some." She extended a long skeletal finger to point at his heart. "And it had better be irrefutable. Do you know why?"

Zateri leaned forward and answered, "Yes, Grandmother. Because accusing our chief of witchcraft before the Ruling Council will split the nation."

Tila gave Zateri a sober look. Her granddaughter had a good political mind. It was too bad she refused to be high matron. "That is correct. The accusation will force people to take sides. Most of the nation will set themselves up against you, War Chief Sindak." Tila paused to see the effect her words had upon him. His level gaze never wavered.

"I understand, High Matron."

"Good. I don't want to hear another word about this until you have ample evidence. Now, leave me. I'm tired."

Zateri rose quickly, kissed her cheek, and said, "Good night, Grandmother."

"Good night, child. Kiss my great-granddaughters for me."

"I will."

Zateri and Sindak quietly ducked beneath the chamber curtain and vanished into the fluttering firelight.

Tila gulped the rest of her broth and set the cup aside. Gingerly, she stretched out on her side on the sleeping bench and watched the fire shadows dance upon her walls while she thought. She knew, as all the matrons did, that Chief Atotarho had often been accused of being a cannibal sorcerer. But he was a powerful man, hated by some for the strong positions he took on the war. And though she often disagreed with him, he had served their people well.

Though, as her eyes blessedly fell closed and the pain started to dim, she had to admit that she had, on occasion, wondered whether or not he had a hidden agenda . . . and if witchcraft was part of it.

Twenty-one

Sky Messenger

I stand beside Taya in the crowded plaza. Though it is cold, the storm has broken and sunlight pours down from the clean blue sky. Where it warms the bark walls of the four longhouses, or the shabby roofs of the refugee quarters, streamers of mist rise. People have been arriving all day, coming in from the allied Standing Stone villages to attend the betrothal feast for the granddaughter of High Matron Kittle. Jewelry sparkles around every throat and wrist, cut from shell or rare stones. A few priceless copper gorgets decorate the chests of the highest-status attendees, mostly the village matrons, chiefs, and wealthy Traders. Men and women mill around eating fish stew from bowls, or happily chewing cornmeal cakes, which is all the high matron can afford to serve and hope to feed the village for the remainder of the winter. The refugees are especially delighted by the feast. A welcome relief from the despair of losing their villages and loved ones, it also means that every person will have a full belly today.

I straighten my new cape. Made of finely tanned buckskin, it has a buttery appearance, like smoked amber. The symbols of my clan encircle the bottom of the cape: red bear claws, alternating with black bear tracks. While traditional, a betrothal cape was a lavish and unnecessary expense for my clan. I would far rather that they'd used the leather to make a cape for one of the ragged children running across the plaza.

Taya's new cape is even more luxurious. The doe hide has been painted sky blue and hung with figures carved from antler: tiny prancing fawns, bucks standing on their hind legs with their hooves flashing, a doe placidly grazing on invisible grass. Taya's mother twisted her long hair into a bun at the back of her head and secured it with a polished tortoiseshell comb. If it weren't for Taya's scowl, she'd be very pretty. I suspect she may be grieving. As I glance around the plaza, I study all of the young men who stare at Taya. Were any her suitors? Probably. Did she love one of them?

Taya greets an unending line of well-wishers with an extended hand. No matter her personal preferences, she knows her duty to her clan.

As I do to mine.

Nonetheless, all day long, I've been wondering what Baji will think when she discovers I am betrothed. Will she be sad? As I am? Or just feel betrayed?

An old woman, the matron of the Turtle Clan in White Dog Village, shoulders through the assembly with her two daughters and extends a parchment-like hand to Taya. "Dearest girl, I offer you my congratulations, and pray that you give the Deer Clan many strong daughters."

Taya takes the elder's hand and smiles. "Thank you for your wishes, Matron Daga. Are you well?"

"Well enough, child. The fever is rampaging through White Dog Village, but it has passed me by so far."

"We are grateful for that." She pats the elder's hand and releases it.

Before Matron Daga turns away, she casts a disgusted glance at me, and says, "Your father, Gonda, asked me to give you his regrets. His wife is ill with the fever, and he will not be able to attend this feast."

My heart sinks. I was hoping to see Father, to speak with him in private. "I appreciate you conveying his message, Matron."

Daga sniffs and leaves.

Taya whispers, "I don't know how many more of these false congratulations I can stand."

I don't respond. I don't know what to say. Of course she is smarting. After all, every person who approaches her sounds as if he or she is offering condolences, not congratulations. Obviously they think it unfortunate that Taya is being forced to marry a disgrace, a traitor.

She says, "Sky Messenger, go away for a while. I don't want you here."

It is an order. As though I am a servant.

I say, "Gladly."

As I walk away, I hear her exhale in relief.

I shoulder through the bright capes, defiantly meeting the scornful eyes, and duck into the Turtle Clan longhouse. As I walk down the center aisle past the fires, heading toward Bahna's chamber, the False Face masks on the rear wall seemed to glare hatefully at me. I don't see Bahna, but Kittle stands before Bahna's fire with her daughter, Yosha, speaking to an old man with dark, piercing eyes. Another man—the young Trader who'd been plying his wares around both Yellowtail and Bur Oak villages—stands beside the unknown elder. Each carries a bowl, and is leisurely dipping horn spoons into the steaming fish stew. Both men wear plain buckskin capes . . . which I find odd, especially on this day when displaying clan symbols is so important.

Yosha's eyes adopt a sleepy, half-lidded appearance as I approach. Sharply she asks, "What do you want? You should be outside escorting my daughter. Are you hiding?"

"I'm searching for Bahna."

"Don't tell me you're not hiding. It can't be agreeable to endure the scorn being heaped upon you. Just think how my daughter must feel. She's the victim, you know. Poor thing."

Kittle, who's overheard the conversation, gives her daughter a frosty look, and Yosha jerks up her chin like a pouting five-summers-old girl. So, Taya's mother disapproves of the marriage as much as her daughter does. How strange that no one told me this.

"Have you seen Bahna?" I say to the other people around the fire.

"Of course we've seen him," Yosha says. "He hasn't traveled the Sky Road yet. He was here not more than a few hundred heartbeats ago. I think he went to tend to the sick."

The old man with piercing eyes says, "Forgive me for interrupting, but aren't you Sky Messenger?"

"I am, Elder."

The man walks around the fire with his buckskin cape swaying and bows. "I am Tsani, of the Snipe Clan of the Flint People, a humble Trader. I know your father, Gonda. His speeches during the council meetings at White Dog Village are legendary–and biting for those with whom he disagrees. I appreciate his astringent presence. It keeps the council focused on the issues. Your father is well, I hope?"

Before I can answer, Yosha says, "Gonda does beautifully since he remarried and moved to White Dog Village eight summers ago. He needed to escape Koracoo."

Tsani purses his lips. He clearly disapproves of Yosha, and Yosha just as clearly does not care. He takes me by the arm and leads me around the fire toward where Kittle stands. The high matron is smiling at the young Trader with a great show of perfect teeth. In response, Hiyade leans slightly backward with his eyes squinted.

"Will you have tea?" Tsani asks. "I hope you do not mind, but I would speak with you for a time, if that's possible." Tsani dips a cup into the tea pot that nestles in the coals and hands it to me.

I take it, but say, "I must get back to my wife-to-be soon, but I'm happy to talk with you briefly."

"Excellent. I understand that you just came up from the south where you were on Dream quest. Is this so?"

It intrigues me that Tsani treats me as he would anyone in the village. Since it is impossible that he has missed the loathsome conversations about my cowardice and treason, there is more to this than is currently apparent. I watch him carefully.

"Yes."

The man sidles closer. In a low voice he says, "Then you have seen the devastation. The whole countryside is a wasteland, but no one here seems to know of it, and I have been hesitant to pass along the unbelievable stories I've heard. Perhaps you—"

"What do you mean no one's heard of it?" Kittle asks in disdain. "Sedge Marsh Village was just wiped off the face of Great Grandmother Earth, probably for allying themselves with us! People hiding in the brush claim they saw War Chief Sindak and a large party swarming through the burning village. I'm sure that despicable cannibal, Atotarho, is responsible for it."

Tsani regards her. "You have ears like a starving lynx. Go back to flirting and leave me to my conversation with Sky Messenger."

"Do not presume to give me orders, or before morning, your eyeballs will see nothing but the inside of a stew pot."

Tsani grins. "By the way, where's your husband? What's his name?"

"You very well know that his name is Yo-wige. . . . Oh, wait, that's not right. Kurath, yes, Kurath."

"Blessed gods, Mother!" Yosha blurts. "You can't even recall the name of your latest husband?"

"Well, what does it matter? He's off on some Trading expedition in the south country. Why do you care, Tsani?"

"I don't. I just thought Hiyade might wish to know Kurath's whereabouts in case he shows up unexpectedly."

"He won't. Traders are always gone."

"Which is, naturally, why you marry them."

Kittle smiles at Hiyade, and he blinks in terror.

"Mother," Yosha says. "Leave him alone. The boy looks like a cornered mouse."

"Mind your own affairs."

Tsani turns back. "Forgive me. Teasing her is more fun than bedding her. I know. I was young and stupid once. Now . . . what was I saying?"

"You asked about the stories traveling the trails. What stories?"

The man's black eyes glitter. "The plague survivors and the refugees from destroyed villages all recite the same words. They say the human False Face has come and is riding the winds of destruction across the land. Many claim to have seen him sailing across the sky with his white cape of clouds trailing behind him."

Fervently, I answer, "The human False Face *is* riding the winds of destruction. Who could doubt it? The war is worsening. Starvation stalks the land, and sorcerers have loosed a mysterious evil that is laying waste to one village after another. His ride *has* begun, and there's nothing we can do to stop it."

Tsani's eyes narrowed. "Then you believe the end is truly here?"

"Look around you, my friend. Our world is crumbling to dust before our eyes. I have—"

"Oh, I'm so clumsy," Matron Kittle says. "I've spilled stew on my skirt." Everyone looks. The glob of fish sticks to her skirt just above her "little canoe," where it is reputed men love to paddle. She bites her lip and her pupils grow larger and darker. Hiyade can't take his gaze from hers.

"It's in such an awkward place," Kittle says. "Will you see if your can brush it off?"

Hiyade swallows the lump in his throat, glances at Tsani and Sky Messenger, then lifts the hem of his cape and just stands there awkwardly.

Yosha's caustic voice rings out, "Why don't you let me call a slave to aid you in your distress, Mother? That way Hiyade can breathe again."

"That won't be necessary. Run out and see if your daughter has needs."

Yosha makes a low disgusted sound, spins, and tramps away.

"As I was saying . . ." A strange expression, almost too eager, creases Tsani's wrinkled face. "When you were on your Dream hunt, what did you Dream?"

Now I understand his expression. "Surely you've heard the story twenty times since you arrived."

"More like fifty, but each has been totally different. I'd really like to hear it from you. That way, when I tell it at the villages where I Trade, I can say I heard it from your own lips."

The images are alive inside me, always there, always urgent. Speaking of them brings back the dread. "There is a great darkness coming, Tsani. It will shake the World Tree. I pray that Elder Brother Sun survives."

Fear briefly crosses his expression. "You have foreseen the death of Elder Brother Sun?"

"I've seen a great black maw open behind him. Just before Elder Brother Sun is swallowed, there is a final blinding flash and a crack like the sky splitting."

Tsani has stopped breathing. He's standing motionless. His wide black eyes are focused unblinking on me. ". . . And then?"

"And then the World Tree shudders as though it's being uprooted by monstrous hands."

When I do not continue, he prompts, "Then you hear a man's voice. Isn't that right? That's what I heard—"

I unceremoniously hand him my tea cup. "I must return to my betrothed, Tsani. I've been away too long. Have a pleasant evening."

I bow and turn to leave.

"But wait!" Tsani implores. "Give me more that I can pass through the villages. It helps to pass the time while I Trade. Did you see the human False Face in your Dream? Did he come to you? Isn't that the voice—"

I shake my head. "No."

As I walk away down the length of the house, Tsani says, "Hiyade! Come over here. Kittle, why do you insist upon tormenting every young Trader who travels with me? Surely you can find someone your own age to play with?"

"Yes, but why would I when the world is filled with young men? And don't stand there glaring at me, you old fool. I could take on four like you. Hiyade, there's a rare pendant I wish to show you. Perhaps you can advise me on its value. It's in my chamber in the Deer Clan longhouse. . . ."

I shove aside the leather door curtain and step out into the sunlight. Taya stands in the same place by the central fire, talking with Chief Yellowtail and Chief Bur Oak. Other well-wishers surround them, waiting their chance to speak with the high matron's granddaughter. I pull my cape tightly around me. Rather than warming up, the day seems colder. As Taya speaks, her breath comes out in tiny puffs.

Soon, very soon, I must leave here on a journey I do not wish to take, with a spoiled child who does not wish to go. There is so little time left, and so many critical things that must be done. I do not understand why my ancestors would tell Bahna . . .

Taya turns. When she sees me, her smile fades.

My shoulder muscles contract. I fear that the next half moon is going to be worse than my exile in the forest. But this is how it must be.

I march toward her.

By the time darkness draped the land, Taya was exhausted—exhausted from smiling, from listening to the conversations whispered behind her back, from looking into the eyes of people who spoke of her bright future, but their tone was one of grief. Grieving for her because she was being forced to marry a man who, they believed, deserved to be executed. And it had grown bitterly cold. The air stung Taya's lungs when she inhaled. She moved closer to the bonfire and held her icy hands out to the flames. The exquisite antler carvings attached to her blue cape shimmered with her movements. People still roamed the plaza, but most had retreated to the warmth of the longhouses. Dutifully, Sky Messenger continued to stand at her side, as he had through almost the entire horrid affair. Tall, handsome, he'd bestowed small smiles upon each person who came forward, and all the while he'd looked like he would prefer execution to this torture.

"People are leaving," he said. "Perhaps it would be acceptable for us to return to the Deer Clan longhouse."

"Even if it's not acceptable, I'm leaving. I can't stand any more of this . . . this sham."

She tramped for her longhouse. Sky Messenger didn't follow right away; then she heard him running to catch up with her. Just before she ducked into the warmth of the house, he gripped her elbow and pulled her aside. "Speak with me for a moment, will you?"

Taya stared up into his dark intense eyes, where reflected firelight glimmered. "No. I don't wish to."

"Just for a moment."

"I said, no. Now leave me—"

He forcibly dragged her around behind the longhouse. Taya shook off his hand and stalked away down the narrow aisle between the house and the palisade, where, not so long ago, she'd first heard the possibility of their marriage mentioned. A few paces later, she stumbled upon two people grunting in the leaves, and Taya recognized the young Trader, Hiyade. He lay half on and half off a woman whose huge creamy breasts were exposed to the moonlight.

"What's happening? Why did you stop?" the woman said, and struggled to sit up, to see around the Trader's wide shoulders.

"Forgive us for intruding," Sky Messenger said. He gripped Taya's arm and pulled her backward, saying, "Let's continue our talk beneath the porch."

Embarrassed, and angry, Taya allowed him to shove her back down the aisle. When they emerged near the curtained entry, she was breathing hard. She said, "How dare you manhandle the granddaughter of the great—"

"She didn't appear all that great just now."

Then the truth dawned. "Blessed gods. I didn't recognize . . . That *was* her voice." Humiliation turned her face bright red. "Grandmother is such a disgrace!"

"She has needs, Taya, just like everyone else."

"Needs! She's—"

"Why do you think she's rutting out behind the longhouse in the dirt and leaves when she could be snuggled in her warm bedding hides? She's trying to be discreet."

"I hardly think—"

"I know you are angry with me. Let's discuss that."

"With . . . with you?" she said in confusion.

"At having to marry me."

Her breast was still heaving with indignation at her grandmother's indiscretions. It took her some time to refocus on what he was saying. "I didn't realize how much of an embarrassment this would be. Didn't you hear the scorn in the voices—?"

His grip on her arm tightened. "Try to understand. The small slights we suffered today will be nothing compared to what lies ahead. We stand on the verge of a great cataclysm. I don't know if I can stop it. You will need to be strong—"

"Why? Why do I have to be there? It has nothing to do with me!"

Sky Messenger's grip tightened even more, the hurtful grip of a careless stranger. He bent down to stare into her eyes. Like a man possessed by an evil Earth Spirit, his voice went strangely deep and guttural. "I don't know why. But you and I are about to embark on a long, dangerous journey that will not end until the vault of the sky splits wide open and Elder Brother Sun is swallowed by blackness. With your own eyes, you will see the World Tree ripped apart and her flowers fall like snow upon the barren earth. I guarantee you that you will feel utterly abandoned and alone. The weight of despair will crush your heart until you long to die. But you cannot turn away. You are part of the Dream now. It is your destiny. So . . ." He abruptly released her arm and straightened to his full height, towering over her. His dark eyes seemed to be backlit by a fire that burned inside him. "Are you brave enough to walk in the truth at my side?"

"Walk in the truth?"

His voice had affected her like a Spirit Plant in her veins. She felt lightheaded, her heart thundering. He'd never spoken to her this way. It was exhilarating. She leaned toward him, a sensual, instinctive movement, waiting for his next words, and his handsome face slackened. She could see desire in his eyes, but it was filled with such a deep aching sadness that it made her suddenly wish to weep.

"Who *was* she? You keep thinking about her!"

He blinked. "What?"

"The woman you loved. The one who left you? She's always between us, especially when we are beneath the hides together. Who was she?"

He didn't answer. Instead, he took her hand and led her to their chamber in the longhouse. He undressed her roughly. After they'd both slipped between the hides, he tenderly kissed her face and neck, the touch of his lips as soft as falling leaves. He was obviously trying to distract her from the question. His mouth moved to her slight breast, his warm tongue encircling her nipple, and she shivered. She had never experienced such sensations in her life. Not even when she'd been with the young warrior Dadjo. A trembling undercurrent of something akin to fear went through her, but it was delicious.

"Tell me," he said, "if I do anything that frightens you."

She whispered back, "I *want* you to frighten me," and arched her back against him.

Twenty-two

Grandmother Moon's gleam filled the midnight forest. The stark branches, mostly leafless now, shone with a dove-colored brilliance. A black filigree of twig shadows shifted in the slight breeze.

As Chief Atotarho wound around the rocky outcrops that jutted into the trail, he said, "This is where he said to meet him? A curious choice."

"Yes, my chief. I don't like it either. It's too far from the village." Negano, the leader of Atotarho's personal guards, had his war club clutched tightly in his fist. He was of medium height, muscular, wearing a black cape that blended with the darkness. He'd smeared his feral face with charcoal, as had the other four guards. It made them almost invisible on the trail behind Atotarho. "If he attacks you here—"

"I told him to come alone," Atotarho informed him.

"Let us hope he does so."

Atotarho looked at the dense oaks. Icicles hung from the branches. In the moonlight streaming across the forest, they resembled fangs, glimmering and still, waiting for careless prey to walk beneath them.

"He will. I pay him well."

Negano squinted at the clearing ahead. A small grassy area surrounded by massive boulders, it spread barely twenty hands across. The young people of the village called it "Lovers' Meadow." They came here to court and talk, and do the things they couldn't in the crowded longhouses.

"Let me go ahead, my chief, to make sure all is well."

"Yes, thank you." Atotarho propped his walking stick and leaned his crooked body against it while he watched Negano cautiously walk forward to search the moonlit meadow. The other guards moved up behind Atotarho to guard him while Negano was away.

The forest was utterly deserted, frigid, and smelled of fires long grown cold. Earlier in the evening, mist had curled across the ground. Hatho, the Frost Spirit, must have frozen it solid and sprinkled it over the piles of autumn leaves that leaned against every tree trunk, for they sparkled in the moonlight—which made the stillness seem all the more ominous.

Negano trotted back up the trail. "It's safe—at least as safe as it can be, given the circumstances."

"Good. Don't follow me. I want you and your men to stand twenty paces away."

"But, my chief, if he leaps for your throat, we'll never be able to get there in time."

"I will risk it." *To keep you out of hearing range.*

Negano bowed respectfully. "Of course. Qonde, you heard him. Circle the men around the meadow. Make sure each man can see the chief."

"Yes, Deputy."

The men silently moved away to take up their positions.

Atotarho's feet crackled in the frosty leaves as he placed his walking stick and slowly plodded toward the meadow. The circlets of human skull that decorated his black cape flashed as he walked.

When he entered the meadow he saw the time-smoothed rocks arranged around the fire pit like benches. The flecks of mica in the stone shimmered. He went to the closest rock and gingerly sat down. Every twisted joint in his body ached. He had to be careful. If he fell he'd be in excruciating pain for days.

While he waited, he rubbed his sore knees. Chunks of charcoal filled the fire pit before him. No one had been here for a while. The only things around the pit were a shattered tea cup and a rabbit rib cage. Mice had been chewing on it, leaving their distinctive teeth marks in the bone.

A faint sound, like a twig cracking, made him go still. He had the chill sensation of being watched, spied upon by a deadly predator too smart to allow itself to be seen until the time was right.

Through the gaps between the boulders, he spotted Negano standing on the trail with his war club propped on his shoulder, his eyes fixed on Atotarho, but he didn't see any of his other guards. Nonetheless, he knew they saw him, and that put him somewhat at ease.

Across the pit, directly in front of him, the darkness between two head-high boulders seemed to ripple. He stared at it. A cape blown by the wind? A hunting animal? A bar of pewter light lay across the ground like a polished sword carved from old rain-silvered wood. When the figure stepped into it, the bar slashed across his chest and flickered through the feathers of his cape as though they were aflame.

"You're afraid," a quiet voice said. "I can smell your fear sweat." He had painted his face pure white. That paleness, contrasting so sharply with the darkness, gave him an eerie, corpselike appearance. "Be at ease. I have no intention of doing you harm. Tonight."

"Did you come alone?"

"I abide by my agreements. Yes, I came alone."

A Hills People accent, but tinged with elements from the People of the Mountain, and a slight Flint drawl, the vowels rounded a little too much. As a boy, he had been around many different peoples. He continued standing in the bar of light, letting Atotarho see him, as if it were a momentary gift before he vanished like smoke.

"Come and sit down." Atotarho gestured to the stones around the dead fire pit.

"Sit? In your presence? Hardly."

The man had a starved face with upturned batlike nostrils and big ears. Oddly luminous, his obsidian eyes never blinked, or at least Atotarho had never seen it. Long black hair draped the front of his feathered cape. Ohsinoh lived off darkness like a nectar moth, moving from flower to flower, sucking it dry. On the rare occasions when they'd met in daylight, the bluebird feathers of his cape had gleamed an unearthly color. Tonight, however, they appeared washed with silver dust, each feather casting a tiny arc of shadow.

Ohsinoh must have moved, stepped closer, for the bar of light had moved from his chest to his face, where it glowed brilliantly off the white paint. The terrifying thing was that Atotarho had not seen him move. Shock froze his blood. To hide it, he clenched his fist on his walking stick. "If you will not sit, then let's get on with our discussion. You accomplished the task well."

"Have I ever failed?"

Atotarho reached beneath his cape, pulled open the ties on his belt pouch, and drew out a small bag of pearls. "Here is the remainder." He held it out.

Atotarho had the momentary impression of amusement dancing behind Ohsinoh's eyes. The man made no move to take the bag and was strangely immobile. Atotarho noticed for the first time the shell ring on one of Ohsinoh's thick fingers, and the fact that the man's earlobes had been stretched for earspools—though he wore none tonight.

Atotarho threw the bag at his feet. "There. I've kept my part of the bargain. Now, I wish to speak with you about another matter."

Ohsinoh looked down at the bag, as though some brief moral struggle was going on inside him. Then he bent to retrieve it and tucked it into his belt pouch. "What matter?"

"There is a war chief who's becoming a problem. Actually, he's been a problem for some time. I need the problem to go away."

The strange eyes held his. There was no movement in them, no expression at all, as though they were shiny obsidian beads. He regarded Atotarho with his head to one side. "Go away?"

"Yes."

"You want him dead?"

"Not necessarily, just . . . compliant."

The man's soft laughter was little more than the pushing of air. "But you have not ruled out murder."

"Not if he continues to be a problem, no. But *I* decide when that moment has arrived."

The long hair over Ohsinoh's cape snagged the bluebird feathers as he faintly shook his head, the gesture almost not there. "Then you just wish me to kill his heart, is that it? Take the fire from his words?"

"That would be acceptable."

"Killing a man's heart is more dangerous than destroying a village, and more difficult. What are you offering?"

"What do you want?"

The white painted lips smiled, but nothing else moved. "Who is this man?"

Atotarho shifted on the ice-cold rock, pulling his cape closed beneath his chin. He swore the air had grown colder. "War Chief Hiyawento. He's currently vulnerable, alone, out on the trail headed for Bur Oak Village. So you must act quickly."

Ohsinoh chucked. He didn't say anything for a time. "Do you care how I kill his heart?"

Atotarho waved a hand. "Just make certain it cannot be tied to me."

Ohsinoh walked forward, his stride oddly weightless. When less than two paces distant, he bent down, his white face glowing in the moonlight, and peered directly into Atotarho's eyes. His gaze was snakelike, almost hypnotic. Atotarho couldn't look away.

"The last Trader who was here, that filthy little beast from the Flint People, Tagosah, told me you Traded with him for many sheets of pounded copper from the Islanders' Confederacy. I want them all."

The Islanders lived north of Skanodario Lake. Their country was surrounded on three sides by huge lakes. The Islanders believed their world was an island floating in a vast primordial sea. Their confederacy was made up of four powerful nations, and they had Trade networks that spanned far greater distances than those of the People of the Hills. One of their networks brought them precious beautiful copper, which when properly worked, became magnificent pendants, bracelets, or breastplates. Each piece was worth a fortune.

"If you do the job well, what you ask is possible."

Ohsinoh's eyes narrowed. When he finally straightened up and turned away to gaze out into the dark trees, Atotarho subtly vented the breath he'd been holding.

"He is a skilled warrior. A very dangerous man. Getting close enough to shoot a charm into him will not be easy. I want half the plates in advance."

Atotarho propped a hand on the rock and used his walking stick to shove to his feet. Ohsinoh seemed to be studying his hunched back and crooked body; then his gaze shifted to where Atotarho's fingers clutched the head of his walking stick, perhaps studying the eyes tattooed on his fingertips . . . perhaps thinking they resembled knotted rawhide. "Shall I have it delivered to the usual place?"

Ohsinoh's head dipped in a nod. "And soon."

"Tomorrow morning?"

"Yes, before Elder Brother Sun wakes."

Atotarho lightly pounded his walking stick on the ground before he asked, "One last thing. What have you heard about Sky Messenger?"

"Why?"

"Do you know where he is?"

"Do you wish me to find him?"

Atotarho hated it when Ohsinoh answered a question with a question. It was irksome. "If you can, I will reward you well."

"Ah, I see. You've always been jealous of him. For most of your life the Hills People have believed that you were the human False Face, the Spirit-Man who would save them at the end of time. But now people are starting to whisper that Sky Messenger . . ."

Atotarho bravely turned his back on the man, and hobbled toward Negano. The warrior's sharp gaze remained focused behind Atotarho, on the Bluebird Witch, apparently cataloging the man's every movement until certain he wasn't going to attempt any evil tricks.

Finally, Negano said, "He's gone. Are you all right, my chief?"

"Yes. Call to your men. Let's get home. I have a task for you, and it will take you most of the night to complete it."

Negano, accustomed to such orders, nodded obediently. "Where am I going?"

"The same place."

Negano pursed his lips and made a sound like a pygmy owl. The call echoed softly through the trees, barely audible, but Qonde and the other guards immediately appeared out of the darkness and surrounded Atotarho.

The trail was slick. It took him time to find firm places to prop his walking stick. Getting back to the village in the streaming moonlight seemed to take forever.

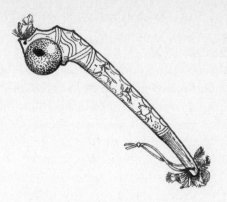

Twenty-three

As Sky Messenger stowed the last packs in the canoe, sleet began falling, creating a staccato among the tree branches and drumming on Taya's hood. She morosely folded her arms beneath her cape and let her gaze drift over the faces of the people who had come to see them off on their journey. Grandmother stood beside Speaker Koracoo, talking quietly. Around them, elders from both villages had gathered. In the distance, more people stood watching from just outside the dark palisades of Yellowtail Village and Bur Oak Village. Everyone had already said good-bye and wished them well, then had returned to their village.

They weren't even gone, and Taya was fiercely homesick. She didn't understand why she was being forced to leave her home with a man she barely knew, and travel into enemy country on a mission she did not understand. It was foolish! She had objected heartily when Grandmother ordered her to go, but to no avail. Even worse, as they'd packed and prepared to leave, she had, several times, caught Sky Messenger staring at her with a look of stunned surprise, as though he'd briefly forgotten she was going, and couldn't figure out why she was packing.

Angry tears swelled her throat. She had never imagined her marriage would begin this way. Through blurry eyes, she stared at the birds hopping from cattail to cattail in the marsh. Every instant she was not inside her safe, warm longhouse, her fear increased. Would they see war parties? Would they be chased? Her betrothed refused to carry weapons.

How would he defend her? What if she was captured by enemy warriors? All the horrifying images ever stirred by stories of rape, torture, and murder crowded her thoughts.

Sky Messenger straightened up. "Are you ready, Taya?"

She turned and blinked owlishly at him. He'd tied his black hair back with a cord. It made his dark eyes seem larger and more deeply set. Almost menacing. "No. But I don't have any choice, do I?"

"I don't like this any more than you do. Let's just make the best of it." He gestured to the canoe.

Taya turned to look back one last time. She longed to run as hard as she could to Bur Oak Village. Her heart seemed about to burst.

Grandmother frowned at Taya, broke away from the crowd, and walked over. Her beautiful face seemed the embodiment of malice and evil. "You are about to embark upon a Spirit journey. Few people ever have such an opportunity to distinguish themselves. You should be going."

"But, Grandmother—" Taya started object.

"Get in the canoe," Grandmother sternly ordered, and pointed to the boat.

Grudgingly, Taya climbed in and flopped to the bottom of the canoe, rattling the oars.

Sky Messenger respectfully dipped his head to Grandmother and said, "I'll take care of her, High Matron."

As Sky Messenger shoved the canoe into the river and leaped inside, Grandmother called, "She needs to learn to take care of herself! Did you hear me, Taya?"

A smoldering mixture of anger and embarrassment stung Taya's veins. Sky Messenger picked up his paddle and began guiding them out into the current.

When they hit the full force of the stream, the canoe jostled violently.

Sky Messenger looked over his shoulder and, as though taken aback, called, "Taya, you must help me paddle."

She grabbed her oar and violently stabbed it into the water.

Sky Messenger's brow furrowed. "Don't chop at the water. Dip and pull. It's a smooth motion. Has no one ever taught you how to use an oar?"

She shouted back at him, "Leave me alone! I'm rowing the best I can!"

The canoe plunged into a series of rough waves, and Sky Messenger instantly slid back to the middle of the canoe. To keep from being overturned, he was rowing as though he were the only occupant of the canoe.

If that's the way he wanted it, that was fine with her! Taya threw her oar onto the packs and folded her arms, glaring at his broad back. If it weren't for him and his foul Dream, she wouldn't be here.

When the river swept them downstream and she lost sight of the villages, a new emotion rose. It was like a hungry wolf chewing on her bones. She had no idea what dangers lay ahead. Every nerve in her body cried out for her to jump overboard and swim for home.

Grandmother will just drag me to another canoe and order some warrior to return me to Sky Messenger.

The angry sobs started deep down in her chest. She kept the sounds locked behind her gritted teeth and watched the trees pass.

Twenty-four

The scent of hickory dinner fires was strong, carried on the cold breeze that eddied through Yellowtail Village. Snow had been falling all day, but now, as dusk approached, it had slowed to a few flakes. The three longhouses inside the triple palisade appeared to be coated with pearl dust.

Koracoo gripped CorpseEye in her right fist and strode past the Turtle Clan longhouse toward the inner palisade gate. War Chief Deru strode beside her, his red cape flaring with each long step. When anyone came forward, as though to stop and speak with them, Deru's crushed face went hard, and they backed away, understanding that this was not a time for casual conversation.

"Who else knows he's here?" Koracoo asked softly.

"Just my son and I. He was very smart. He waited until he saw Heswe leave the village and walk down to the river. He approached Heswe while he was filling pots with water. My son brought me the message that Hiyawento wished to meet with you in private outside the village."

"Good. Tutelo is with Matron Jigonsaseh. Please have her meet me in the chestnut grove. Don't tell her why. As soon as I know his mission, I'll call for you. Is that agreeable?"

"Ordinarily I would insist that guards accompany you, Speaker, but I'll make an exception in your case. I warred with you long enough to know that if it comes to a fight, Hiyawento is in far more trouble than you are. However, I will be watching you from the catwalk with my bow nocked."

"That is acceptable, but just you, Deru. I don't want the word getting round."

"Understood."

As she approached, the guards shoved open the inner gate. There were gates at each of the three palisades. As she walked through the first, the locking planks clunked into position behind her—standard procedure these dangerous days, when leaving anything to chance might get your family killed. She marched through the second gate, and finally, at the third palisade, the men checked the trails outside before opening the gate, then slammed it closed behind her.

As she turned left and hurried down the narrow trail that ran along the palisade, Wind Mother flipped her short, graying-black hair around her face. She followed the trail out to the chestnut grove. The giant trees, almost leafless now, sheltered a small boulder-filled meadow. As she neared the meadow, she saw a tall man seated upon a rock with a white painted arrow. He kept fidgeting with the arrow. He'd grown up. He was a tall, broad-shouldered man now, but his eagle-like face was mostly the same.

She slowed to a walk, and just before she entered the clearing, she called, "I don't know how you managed to get this close to Yellowtail Village without our scouts seeing you. I'll have to speak with War Chief Deru about that."

A smile warmed Hiyawento's lean face. He'd tied his shoulder-length black hair back with a cord, and the style made his beaked nose seem longer. As he rose, his buckskin cape, painted with gray images of running wolves, fell into soft folds around him. He placed the arrow on the rock and lifted his empty hands, showing her he had no weapons. "It's Speaker Koracoo now, isn't it?"

"It is." Koracoo walked directly to him and spread her feet two paces away.

He smiled. "It's so good to see you."

"You were very foolish to come here, but it gladdens my heart to see you, as well. Is everything all right in Coldspring Village?"

He lowered his hands and propped them on his hips. His brow lined. "As well as it can be, given the insane world we live in."

"Tell me quickly why you're here."

Through a long exhalation, he said, "I bear a message for High Matron Kittle from the Ruling Council of the Hills nation."

Koracoo cocked her head, curious. "But you came to me first, why?"

He made a helpless gesture with one hand. "Zateri thought it was far more likely that you'd let me live long enough to deliver my message."

Koracoo nodded. "Your wife is wise. How is she? And your daughters? You have three, yes?"

Joy lit his face. "Yes, three. They are all well. My oldest, Kahn-Tineta, has seen eight summers now."

"The fever has not reached the Hills nation?"

"Despite what you may have heard, it has. Riverbank Village has been suffering greatly, but the evil Spirits have not entered our other villages. So far."

Koracoo's voice came out low and demanding. It was an order. "What is the message you carry."

He hesitated. He undoubtedly had specific instructions to relay it only to High Matron Kittle. Koracoo assessed his expression, waiting. A test of trust. Would he tell her or not?

Their gazes held.

Finally, he said, "The Ruling Council of the Hills nation would like to know if the Ruling Council of the Standing Stone People is prepared to have all of its villages destroyed? As Sedge Marsh Village was."

Koracoo laughed softly. "A threat? They're warning us not to attempt to make alliances with any more Hills villages."

"Yes. Sedge Marsh was destroyed because the council ruled that their alliance with you was treason."

As the breeze swayed the forest, clumps of snow shook loose from the chestnut branches and thumped the ground around them.

Koracoo said, "They were hungry, Hiyawento. They were on the very edge of your country, vulnerable to attacks from the Flint nation. They came to us for help after your own high matron refused to help them. We could not turn our backs on starving people, even if they were not of our nation."

Wind rustled the chestnuts, and old leaves twirled down around them. Several briefly alighted on the shoulders of his cape before continuing their journey to Great Grandmother Earth.

Hiyawento's brows drew together. "How do you think High Matron Kittle will respond to the message?"

"Well, to start with, she'll shout at you, and call threats back. After you leave, she'll start preparing our villages for a siege. By the time your war parties arrive, we'll have enough arrows, spears, clubs, and water stored in the villages to hold out for moons." While confidence filled her voice, she knew the words were not true. They'd be lucky to hold out for several days. "Tell High Matron Tila that we may fall in the end, but not before she's lost many fine young men and women to our arrows."

"That is not the message our Ruling Council is hoping for."

"No? They want us to say that we will never again try to form an alliance with a Hills village? We won't say it. We can't. You know as well as I do that every nation is in trouble. I fear the only way any of us will survive is if we agree to band together and share what we have."

Hiyawento's lean face slackened. In his dark eyes, she saw memories passing. "You've always been a peacemaker, Koracoo. I respect that, but I doubt our Ruling Council—"

"I doubt it, too," she interrupted. "We have all been reduced to acting like ravening wolves. We shred each other over scraps." In the distance, geese honked as they winged southward. She listened to the lonely sounds before she continued, "Hiyawento, there is a great darkness coming. Tell your people that Elder Brother Sun is going to turn his back on Great Grandmother Earth and flee, leaving us in darkness, unless we find a way to end this war."

Hiyawento slowly lifted his head. A somber expression creased his face. "I heard about his vision from a passing Trader named Tsani—though I'm sure many elements had been embellished. Is Sky Messenger well?"

"Well enough."

"Then Matron Kittle lifted her death sentence?"

Koracoo was only mildly surprised that he'd been keeping such close track of Sky Messenger's life. She knew they had not seen each other in five summers. "Even Kittle realizes that his vision is strong, and we dare not ignore it. Yes, she lifted the sentence."

"Is he here, Speaker?" Warmth and longing touched the words. "I would see him, if possible?"

"He's not here. He left four days ago on a journey to the Dawnland country. He had a fast canoe. He should return in ten days or so. Now, tell me what the Traders are saying about Sky Messenger's vision, and more importantly, how you know many elements have been embellished?"

"I . . ." He shifted his weight to his opposite foot. "Speaker, your son and I have had a pact since we were boys. I do not repeat the things he tells me. Not even to his mother. But the Traders are saying that Sky Messenger has foreseen the end of the world. They say Elder Brother Sun will burn to a blackened husk and his ashes will fall from the sky."

She waited to see if he'd tell her which parts he knew were embellished, but he did not.

She said, "If you do not object, War Chief, I'd like to speak with Kittle first, to prepare her for your arrival. You are traveling under a white arrow, but she's unpredictable. I'd like to be able to send you back to Zateri with your head still upon your shoulders."

"I'd like that myself. Kittle is reputed to—"

"*Wrass!*" Tutelo called when she reached the edge of the meadow and recognized him. She broke into a run, her long black hair flying out behind her as she thrashed through the leaves and threw her arms around him. "Wrass, blessed gods, what are you doing here? It's good to see you!"

Hiyawento clutched Tutelo to his chest, as though he never wished to let her go. "You're beautiful, Tutelo. I always knew you would be. Are you well? You have two children, yes?"

Tutelo pushed back with tears streaming down her cheeks. "Two girls. Little terrors."

Hiyawento laughed. "You married a man of the Hawk Clan, if the stories the Traders tell can be trusted."

"Yes, Idos. He's a good man."

"And a fine warrior," Koracoo praised with a smile. "Now, enough pleasantries. We are standing out in the open with an Outcast who has been assessed a traitor to our nation. We are all risking our lives. Tutelo, return to your longhouse and tell no one, not even Idos, that War Chief Hiyawento is here. Later, if there is time, we will all have a chance to speak together again."

"Yes, Mother." But she paused and gave Hiyawento a heartbreaking smile. "Just in case I don't see you before you go, I love you, Wrass. I always have. I want you to know that I'll never care what my people call you or Zateri. You'll always be two of my greatest heroes." She turned and walked away.

As she rounded the palisade wall, Wrass turned away, but not before Koracoo saw the sheen in his dark eyes. He stood for a moment with his head down, collecting himself, before he said, "I miss them so much."

It touched Koracoo's heart. "As they do you. I do not think a day has gone by in the past twelve summers that one of them hasn't mentioned your name. Yours or Zateri's."

The lines at the corners of his eyes deepened, as though wishing for things that could not be. "Where do you want me to wait while you speak with High Matron Kittle?"

"I'll leave that decision to my war chief." Koracoo turned. Through the weave of branches, she could see Deru standing on the catwalk, staring down at them. The crushed bones of his face cast odd shadows. She lifted a hand to him, then turned back to Hiyawento.

"As of this moment, you are under my protection. War Chief Deru will guard you until I return."

"Thank you, Speaker."

When Deru strode around the palisade and headed toward them,

Koracoo started back for the village. As they met on the trail, she told Deru, "He bears a message from the Ruling Council of the Hills nation. I've given him my word that no one will harm him. Protect him."

Deru nodded. "With my life, Speaker."

Twenty-five

The forest had gone silent. Snow fell out of the dusk sky, spiraling down, flecking the bare tips of the oak branches and frosting the pines. Out across the Forks River, the white veil wavered like a scarf blowing in the light breeze.

Taya winced, bent over, and cracked another branch from the base of a pine. As she placed the branch on the growing pile in her left arm, her shoulders ached with fiery intensity. For four days, they'd been paddling from before dawn until well after Elder Brother Sun journeyed into the underworlds to sleep—or rather, he'd been paddling. She'd paddled some, mostly when it seemed certain they'd overturn in the rapids if she didn't.

A foot rustled in the dry ferns to her right. She stole glances at her companions. Gitchi lay curled up a short distance from where Sky Messenger fished. The old white-faced wolf had covered his nose with his bushy tail and appeared to be sleeping, but every time she made a tiny sound the wolf opened his eyes and stared at her.

Sky Messenger cast out his net again. Every now and then, he'd pull it in, remove any fish he'd caught and drop them on the bank, then toss it back into the current. Their canoe rested four paces away from him, its white birch hull almost invisible in the snow. Her gaze returned to Sky Messenger. His eyes had gone dark and brooding. He'd barely touched her since that night in the longhouse when he'd loved her with such tenderness and passion, and she didn't understand why. Perhaps it was just that he was as tired as she at the end of the day, but it felt like more. Though she had little experience with such things, it felt like his souls were occupied with that other woman, the one he had loved and lost. That bothered her more than the fact that she was traveling through enemy country with a man who refused to carry weapons. After all, *she* was his betrothed.

Worse, perhaps, was the fact that he'd been treating her like a child on her first war walk. He insisted she learn the skills of stealth, how to make an almost invisible camp in the forest, how to hunt on the run. And he spent a good deal of time correcting her when she grew careless and made a mistake. Which was often. She'd never been away from her family for any length of time, and she was desperate to see her mother and sisters, even—Spirits forbid—Grandmother.

Taya carried her heavy load to their camp and thoughtlessly let it fall beside the firepit. At the clattering of branches, Gitchi's head shot up. Sky Messenger gave her an exasperated look.

She ignored him and wiped her forehead on her sleeve before she pulled her pack over and untied the laces. Inside, she found her firebox, a small stone container where she kept coals from the morning fire. It warmed her hand. First she made a bed of dry pine needles in the pit; then she opened the firebox, poured the coals on top of it, and added small twigs. When she leaned over to gently blow on the coals, she saw fish flopping in Sky Messenger's net as he dragged it to shore. He crouched and patiently disentangled them, placing them with the others he'd caught. Afterward, he just stared out at the falling snow, or perhaps the darkening river. He seemed to be thinking. He sat so still for so long that snow mounded on the shoulders of his cape and hood. When he finally rose to his feet, he had to brush them off. Gitchi stretched and stared up at him with loving, devoted eyes. Sky Messenger patted the wolf's head, collected the fish, and walked toward her.

She kept blowing on the coals, but her heart sank. Seeing the look in his eyes, she yearned to be home scooping up the moldering leaves that had collected against the palisade, or cleaning the fire pits and hauling ashes to the midden outside the village, even carrying water until she thought her arms would break. Of course, she'd never actually been forced to perform such menial duties, but she'd rather be a slave at home, than here with him!

When flames leaped through the tinder in the fire pit, she turned her attention to the tiny blaze, alternating more blowing with feeding it twigs until she had a decent fire going.

Sky Messenger plucked sticks from the woodpile, skewered each of their six fish, and propped them at the edge of the fire to cook. For a long time, he seemed to be watching the snow fall. She kept adding branches to build up the blaze. The longer he refused to look at her, the more difficult it was for Taya to catch her breath. She felt like she was smothering.

"I hate this," she said in a tight voice. "I want to go home." She stuffed another branch in the fire, and a cascade of sparks flitted into the air.

He gazed at her intently. "Then go."

"Alone? Someone will kill me!" She threw out her arms, as though to defend herself. "I don't know how any of this happened. One moment I was a happy child and the next I was betrothed to a crazy man." The last words turned into sobs.

Most men would have melted at the sight of her tears—at least that had been her experience—but not Sky Messenger.

Instead, he came around the fire, knelt in front of her, and unsympathetically said, "I can't take you home. Not now. We're too far from the village. I have to complete this task first. But after that, I will. If that's what you want."

It didn't matter in the slightest what she wanted. Grandmother had made it perfectly clear that the ancestors had personally spoken to Old Bahna. Taya had to accompany Sky Messenger on this Spirit journey. "But why do we have to do this? I know Bahna said—"

"Taya," he said sternly, "I'm going to explain this to you one more time, but that's all. So, listen. Something happened to me in the Dawnland country when I was a boy. I must face it . . . face him . . . before I can help our people."

She assessed his stony expression. "We're going to see a man? Who is he? Where does he live?"

Sky Messenger exhaled hard. "He's dead."

"What do you mean, dead?"

He stood up and went over to throw more branches on the fire. Snow had melted on his round face, making it shine.

"We're going to see a dead man?" she asked, confused. "You mean his burial place?"

His head waffled, as though trying to decide whether or not that was a good description. "That's a tougher question than you might suspect. He was never buried. You see, his severed head was burned, and his body was cut apart, and the pieces scattered far and wide—"

She sucked in a breath. "To immobilize his evil Spirit?"

"Partly, but mostly so no one could ever recognize him and Sing his afterlife soul to the Land of the Dead. Which, apparently, is what I must do."

Taya wiped her nose. Sky Messenger looked as though he resented being on this journey. She wondered if that gave her some kind of leverage. "But . . . if he was evil, why do you have to Sing him to afterlife? None of our ancestors will wish to have him there. He deserves to roam the earth alone forever. That is just."

He actually bowed his head and laughed. "Yes, well, apparently that changes nothing. I must do this."

She let her gaze drift over the river, watching the snow fall, before she said, "When will we arrive?"

"In two days. We've been making good time."

"And afterward, you'll take me home?"

"Yes."

"Thank the Spirits," she said through a long exhalation. "If I'd gone home alone, Grandmother would have killed me."

His brow furrowed. "I doubt—"

"No, believe me. I know her far better than you do. Once, when I'd seen seven summers, she told me to go find a pot of sunflower oil and oil the dinner bowls, which I hated to do. I sneaked off to play with my friends. One hand of time later, she appeared in the plaza, grabbed me by the hair, and dragged me into the forest, where she tied me to a tree." She sniffed at her clogged nose. "She left me there all night. I was certain I was going to be eaten by a Flying Head or a bear."

"But you survived."

"Barely."

He reached for the skewers and turned the fish around to cook on the other side. "I've never really liked your Grandmother . . . until now."

"What are you talking about? It was awful!"

"Yes, but she saw your weakness, and she took action. You're lucky."

She thought about that. Before that night, she'd been terrified of the dark. Afterward, she wasn't afraid of anything . . . well, except being away from home. Suddenly, she thought of all the things newly betrothed women did in Bur Oak Village, the new clothing they received, the jewelry, the things for their firstborn child, and harshly accused, "You're not going to give me a child, are you?"

"What?" He blurted. "Yes, of course, Taya."

"We cannot marry until I'm carrying your child. Is that why you won't touch me? You know it's your only way out?" Actually, she was hoping for that. She wanted to marry him less and less every day.

"Taya." The lines at the corners of his eyes were filled with soot and seemed to be etched there. "I know my duties to your clan. And to my own. I've been distracted. That's all."

Snowflakes stuck to her wet eyelashes, making it difficult to see him. "Tell me about her. Do it now. I can't stand wondering any longer."

His shoulder muscles contracted beneath his cape. When he half turned toward her, his hood shadowed most of his expression. "I don't wish to speak of her."

"What was her clan?"

Reluctantly, he replied, "She is Turtle Clan now."

"Now? That means she was adopted. And she's still alive."

His gaze, that could be so powerful, had taken on the alert brilliance of a wolf on a blood trail. "Were you hoping she wasn't?"

"Yes. Dead lovers are easier to fight than living ones. Did you love her very much?"

He stared at her. "I did."

"Why don't you go back to her? Didn't she wish to marry you? Or did your clan disapprove of her?"

"I never asked the Bear Clan to arrange a marriage with her."

Taya drew up her knees and wrapped her arms around them. "Well, if you never asked your clan's permission, you couldn't have loved her that much."

He didn't respond. Instead, he used a stick to scrape red coals up beneath the trout. As they heated, steam seeped from each fish and spiraled into the cold air. "Don't ask me anything else about her."

"But Sky Messenger, it's hard to trust you when you tell me so little about your life."

The howling of wolves filled the silence that followed. Their chorus drifted through the trees as though his old lover's relatives were calling to him, trying to convince him to come back to her. Gitchi lifted his head to listen and let out a low growl. Among their people, when a man married he moved to his wife's village, into her clan's longhouse, and was subject to the orders of her clan council. She wondered where he would be now if he'd married her. And if he'd still be afflicted with Dreams.

"Don't you want me to trust you? I have to know something about you before I can do that. Was this woman a warrior? Her name is Baji, isn't that right?"

The fish had started to drip fat into the flames; it sizzled and spat. The delicious scent of roasting trout rose. Sky Messenger slowly lowered himself to sit cross-legged on the ground. "If you know her name, you must know many things about her. What else have you heard?"

She made an airy gesture with her hand. "I know she is an enemy warrior from the Flint People. You're always comparing me to her, aren't you? She's supposed to be a great warrior. I'll bet she walked with the silence of a wolf. I'll bet she never spoke too loudly, or used her paddle improperly on the river, or—"

"No, she didn't. You're right," he said bluntly. "She was perfect in every way. She . . ." His face changed suddenly, softening, as though a memory had just caught him off guard. He shook his head as though angry with himself. "Taya, she is out of my life forever. I'll never see her again. You are going to be my wife. Why does it matter?"

Gitchi rose and trotted over to flop down beside Sky Messenger. As he propped his gray muzzle on his paws, his gaze went back and forth between them. The wolf seemed to have a preternatural ability to know the worst possible moment to intrude upon their conversations. Though, it occurred to her, Sky Messenger must think they were the best possible moments. When he reached over to scratch Gitchi's head, it gave him the opportunity to change the subject.

"I know you're frightened and don't wish to be here, Taya. There's a Dawnland village not far from here, a safe place. I know the village Healer, and the deputy war chief, Auma. Would you like me to take you there while I continue on? You'll be warm and well fed. I'll return for you as soon as I'm done."

Like a fish out of water, her mouth opened, then closed, struggling for breath. "The Dawnland People are our enemies! I don't want to go to any of their villages? Are you mad?"

His mouth quirked. "As far as I can tell? Almost certainly."

"That is *not* amusing."

She had seriously considered the possibility that his afterlife soul was out wandering the forest. He lurched upright in their bedding almost every night and stared out at the darkness as though he was searching for something, or someone, maybe even counting the eyes of the evil Spirits that had them surrounded. The prospect that he was mad? Not amusing in the slightest.

"I know what your clan says about me, Taya. They call me a fool. Try to understand, only a mad fool would accept the path I am on. I—"

"Then why don't you give it up?"

"Because madness is what is required." He spread his arms. "Look around you. What sane man would believe peace is possible?"

Sensing an opening, she leaned toward him and pressed her lips to his. Startled, he just sat there for a few instants; then he kissed her back, but there was no emotion in it. She might have been kissing a brother.

When she leaned away, she looked up at him somberly. "Why don't you ever hold me? Do you hate me so much?"

His smile faded. He heaved what sounded like an exasperated sigh and wrapped his arms around her. She propped her chin on his shoulder and watched the snow fall across the river. He held her like that until the skin on the fish started to peel and brown.

Finally, he pulled away. "Let's eat. You'll feel better."

He rose and walked around the fire. As he slid two fish from their sticks and into her bowl, Gitchi wagged his tail and licked his lips in anticipation. Sky Messenger handed Taya's bowl to her.

She took it and immediately pulled off small strips of white flesh and ate it. It stayed down.

Sky Messenger filled his bowl and set it aside. Then he removed the skewers from the last two fish and rolled them in the snow to cool them before calling, "Gitchi, come on."

The old wolf got up, shook off his coat, and trotted forward wagging his tail. He grabbed one of the fish and chewed it up. The second, he swallowed whole, though it took three tries to gulp it down.

Sky Messenger picked up his bowl and returned to sit beside Taya.

The phrases *mad fool* and *madness is what is required* kept circling around in her thoughts. The more she thought about them, the more ridiculous they sounded. "Can't you at least try to be sane?"

His hand, holding a piece of fish, stopped halfway to his mouth. He turned to look at her. His high cheekbones and slender nose caught snowflakes that melted and ran down his face like tears. "No."

Annoyed, she looked away. Across the fire, Gitchi's yellow eyes were fixed upon her, as though watching to see if, at last, she understood.

Taya said, "I hate that wolf. He always looks at me like I'm the one who's the fool."

Sky Messenger paused, seemed to think about it, then went on eating as though she hadn't spoken at all.

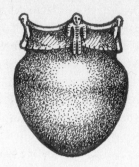

Twenty-six

Hiyawento clutched his white arrow in both hands and walked across the Bur Oak plaza behind Koracoo. Two guards flanked him, their eyes roving the mass of refugees who'd started to knot up to watch him pass. None of them knew who he was, thank the Spirits. To them, he appeared to be a man of the Standing Stone nation, which made the white arrow he carried all the more interesting. They whispered behind their hands and pointed, but no one made a hostile move toward him. Behind them, along the palisade, dead bodies were stacked like firewood, awaiting burial. The fever must be taking a great toll. Snow had collected on the gaunt faces, filling in the hollow cheeks and sunken eyes. In the growing darkness they seemed somehow unreal.

"Now, listen to me," Koracoo said when they stood beneath the porch of the Deer Clan longhouse. "To the matrons you are less than dirt, something to be scraped off their moccasins. They won't even meet with you in the council house. High Matron Kittle and two clan matrons have agreed to sit at the same fire with you. Three refused. That's the best you're going to get. You will do well to speak as little as necessary, and listen as much as possible."

"What about Chief Bur Oak?"

"He won't be there. Be happy you're still alive. The chief was not in favor of that."

He nodded. "I understand. Once again, I owe you more than I can ever repay."

Koracoo walked forward, pulled aside the entry curtain, and ordered, "Sit on the mat across the fire from our high matron."

She remained standing outside with the two guards while Hiyawento ducked beneath the curtain and into the firelit warmth of the Deer long-house. It was smaller than the longhouses in the Hills nation, stretching only five hundred or so hands long. Around twenty fires burned down the central aisle, and he could make out firelit faces watching him. Many were ill. Coughs and moans laced the air. He walked sunwise around the fire and seated himself on the empty floor mat between two elderly women. The woman to his left looked to have seen around forty-five summers. Short black-streaked gray hair fell around her gaunt face. The white wolf tracks on her blue cape marked her as the matron of the Wolf Clan in Bur Oak village. The woman to his right was Hawk clan. Interconnected red spirals encircled the top of her white cape. She was much older, perhaps sixty summers, with white hair and a deeply wrinkled face. He must know them. He'd grown up among the Standing Stone People, but he didn't recognize them.

He focused across the fire on High Matron Kittle. Despite her extraordinary beauty, her gaze was like a burning stick thrust in his vitals.

She opened her hand to the Hawk Clan matron. "This is Matron Sihata and"—her hand shifted to the matron of the Wolf Clan—"this is Matron Dehot. You, however, are dead to your people. You have no name here. If we refer to you at all, it will be as the 'nameless one.' Is that perfectly clear?"

"Yes, High Matron."

Kittle lifted her perfect chin and stared down her straight nose at him. "Deliver your message."

He placed the white arrow on the mat before him and braced himself. "The Ruling Council of the Hills nation would like to know if the Ruling Council of the Standing Stone People is prepared to have all of its villages destroyed. As Sedge Marsh Village was."

First, Kittle's large dark eyes blazed like sunlit jet; then her mouth contorted into a killing rage. She sprang to her feet with her breast heaving and shouted, "You can tell High Matron Tila and Chief Atotarho that if they ever threaten us again, we'll—"

In a very quiet voice, Matron Sihata broke in. "If it pleases the High Matron, I would ask a question."

Kittle clamped her jaw and glared. "Of course." She grudgingly sat back down.

Matron Sihata smoothed the red spirals on her cape for a few moments, clearly letting emotions settle, before she asked, "Why you? Why did they send you?"

Hiyawento tilted his head, reluctant to explain, but answered, "Because I was born among your people."

"Then they believed they were sending us one of our own, a man who might make it into our villages before we realized who and what he was?"

"Yes."

Kittle leaned back carelessly and gave him a cold smile. Her beautiful face was inscrutable, but there was a diabolical gleam in her eyes, as though something amused her greatly. "What a tragedy. They consider you to be one of our people, and we consider you to be dead. It seems you have no nation, Nameless One. How does a man live without a nation?"

He blushed as humiliation coursed through him, and prepared to say something, to tell her that his family was his nation, and it was none of her . . . But he stopped himself. Koracoo had told him to speak as little as necessary. He held his tongue and stared straight across the fire at her with no emotion whatsoever on his face. At least, he hoped the dim firelight hid his flush.

Matron Dehot softly said, "We sent Sedge Marsh Village baskets of freshly picked ears of corn. We didn't even shuck them first, though we could have used the husks for our own purposes, to make sacred masks, to weave into mats, to burn in our fires. You should tell the Ruling Council that the charity of the Standing Stone nation is not reserved strictly for our own people. If the hungry come to us, as both Sedge Marsh Village and White Dog Village recently did, we will feed them, no matter their nation. No matter our own needs. The Standing Stone People, especially Yellowtail Village, has fed more than a few of your war parties returning from attacks on the Flint People."

Hiyawento said, "And we are grateful, Matron. That is one of the reasons we have a sort of undeclared truce between us. Our warriors do not wish to attack you."

"Well, isn't that gracious of them?" Matron Kittle said in a mocking voice. "We can all sleep easier knowing that when they come to kill us, as their Ruling Council threatens, at least the Hills warriors will feel badly about cutting up our children and feeding them to their dogs."

Kittle's tone was like salt rubbed into an open wound. Hiyawento slowly asked, "Will you stop trying to make alliances with Hills villages?"

Kittle looked as if she was enjoying herself, and when she spoke there was odious ring to her voice. "No. We will not."

Matron Sihata's white head tottered on her neck. "This council has, many times, discussed the possible ramifications of feeding our enemies. It is our sovereign right to make alliances whenever and with whomever we please. Would the Hills Ruling Council wish us to tell them how to conduct their political affairs?"

Hiyawento didn't respond. They all knew the answer was a hearty no, and he was getting the feeling that his hold on life was becoming more tenuous with every breath. He just nodded and picked up his white arrow. "Then if the council has no more use for me—"

"Apparently, *no one* has any use for you," Kittle said with suave brutality. "Get out of our country as fast as you can."

He rose to his feet, bowed deeply, and ducked beneath the door curtain. Koracoo stood a few paces away, speaking with four warriors. Beyond them, light snow fell upon the roofs of the hastily constructed refugee houses—little more than lean-tos cramped against the palisade.

"Speaker?" Hiyawento called.

Koracoo turned and, instantly, she and the guards marched forward, closed ranks around him, and escorted him across the dark plaza.

In a confidential voice, she said, "The balance is precarious now. Tomorrow we will start preparing for a great battle with your people. I pray cooler tempers prevail and no one suggests that we take the fight to the Hills People first, before you can invade our country."

"Someone will, Speaker. Someone always does."

Koracoo swung CorpseEye up to rest on her shoulder. "Go home. Tell Tila she is courting disaster."

"I will."

She dismissed the guards and walked through the gates at Hiyawento's side. When they stood beneath the sheltering chestnut branches, she said, "I regret that we will not have a chance to speak more. Tutelo was very much looking forward to that."

"I was, too. I was hoping to see Tutelo's children and meet her husband. And I was especially looking forward to hearing about Sky Messenger's—"

"War Chief, if Sky Messenger were here, the first thing he would tell you is that this war must end. If it doesn't, he has foreseen catastrophe. So . . . in the future, we will either have a chance for many long discussions. Or we will all be dead."

Hiyawento absorbed her grim expression before he replied, "If it's the latter, I pray we have those long discussions in the Land of the Dead."

Koracoo tilted her head uncertainly. "We are warriors. That is unlikely."

"I will still hope, Speaker."

Hiyawento lifted a hand and trotted away. When he turned to look back, he saw Koracoo still standing there, her face faintly lavender in the deepening twilight. She watched him until he crested the ridge and plunged down the trail, heading home to Hills country.

Twenty-seven

Koracoo walked back through the first two gates, listening as each was locked behind her. When she passed through the last gate, she saw the large assembly of people who stood waiting for her. Most were curious refugees in tattered clothing. Their children wore starved, vaguely feral expressions.

One man, short with matted black hair, called as she walked by, "Speaker? Was he truly a messenger from the Hills People? What did he want?"

Another skinny woman shouted, "Are they planning to attack us? When?"

Koracoo answered, "We are all safe for now. The council is considering the messenger's words. As soon as their deliberations are concluded, you will all be notified."

Koracoo put her head down and bulled her way through the crowd. She needed to think before she said anything more.

Snow frosted the longhouses and the corpses piled near the palisade, along the walls, beneath the porches, anywhere their relatives could find space. Tomorrow at dawn, Bahna would hold a mass burial ritual. The bodies would be cleansed and Sung to the Land of the Dead.

But for now, the plague-stricken longhouses were so quiet, so dreadfully quiet. Which meant most of the suffering was over. The evil Spirits that had brought the fever were, at last, fleeing for other hunting grounds.

She had awakened at dawn and gone outside to help Tutelo and several other women bundle the fishing nets and cover them with hides. They had to be kept out of sight of the corpses. Each net had a soul, and it feared contact with the dead—as did fish. If they scented decaying flesh on the nets, they would not allow themselves to be caught. With so little food in the village already, they had to be especially cautious.

As she passed the Hawk longhouse, she lifted a hand to Deru, who stood giving orders to fifty warriors. He nodded back and went on with his nightly guard-duty assignments. The illness had left Yellowtail Village vulnerable. Many of their warriors were down with the fever. It would be strange, indeed, if all of their enemies missed such an opportunity.

One warrior, a man's whose face she couldn't see in the darkness, called, "Speaker? How is Matron Jigonsaseh?"

Koracoo shook her head. "Not well. I'm headed there now."

"I pray this ends soon."

"As do I. Be vigilant, warrior. You know the stakes."

She hurried across the plaza and ducked beneath the door curtain into the Bear Clan longhouse. The heat struck her like a fist in the face. The air was oppressive, scorching, and filled with the sickly sweet odor of death. Fires blazed down the length of the house, built up high to keep the sick warm. She untied her cape laces and pulled it away from her throat. Already sweat trickled beneath her armpits.

After days of weeping and agonized groans, the firelit silence was startling. It should have eased her frayed nerves, but it had the opposite effect. As she walked by the compartments, hollow-eyed people stared at her. Hopelessness pervaded the air. There were no sounds of supper being prepared. No children raised dust with their running feet. No dogs trotted by with tongues happily dangling and tails wagging. Somehow this evening's stillness felt even more sinister than the evenings filled with screams of grief and sobs.

No one spoke to her. They just watched her pass, as though they considered her to be just another ghost, one of many that roamed the house. The dishes that surrounded the fires sat dirty and in disarray, scattered, as though the owners had been too exhausted or disheartened to nest the cups or clean the pots. Children huddled in the rear of the compartments, their haunted eyes wide, staring at the empty places where mothers or fathers had once sat. When she looked at them, it was almost as though she could hear the loving voices behind their eyes: mothers telling them not to be afraid, fathers assuring them that everything was going to be all right. The voices of people they'd trusted, saying things they now knew to be untrue.

Tomorrow, after the burial ritual, they would all gather sticks and pots and walk through the longhouses beating them to chase away the ghosts so that they could not drag the living away into the Land of the Dead.

Koracoo's first glimpse of Tutelo caught her off guard. Her steps faltered. Tutelo was on her knees, hunched over her grandmother, gently wiping her face with a wet piece of hide. Tears ran down Tutelo's pretty face. "Mother? Please come quickly. She's been asking for you."

Koracoo knelt beside Tutelo. Unlike the compartments of most village matrons, this was the smallest in the longhouse, stretching just twelve hands long. The sleeping bench on the back wall, where her mother lay, brimmed with tattered hides and worn but neatly folded dresses. Jigonsaseh owned almost nothing. Each time a Trader brought her a gift to show his esteem, she gave it to the most needy family in the village. What she lacked in possessions, she made up for with the love of her people.

Matron Jigonsaseh lay on her back, pale and shrunken. She'd shoved the hides away from her fevered body. Two gray braids fell on either side of her wrinkled face, and her closed eyes were sunken in twin deep blue circles. Her shallow breaths rattled.

Koracoo smoothed her forehead. "Mother? It's me. I'm here."

Jigonsaseh's eyes fluttered open, then fell closed again. Her face had a yellow waxy sheen that Koracoo had seen many times on the war trail. It was drained of life's blood. She was dying. The idea transfixed Koracoo. Her mother had survived so much: the destruction of her village, the losses of three husbands, the deaths of many children, two just days old. She couldn't die, not when Yellowtail Village needed her so much. How would they survive without her wisdom and kindness?

Koracoo clasped her mother's limp hand, holding it between both of hers. The flesh was searing hot. Again, she said, "Mother, I'm here."

Jigonsaseh opened her eyes a slit, stared as though to make certain in was in fact Koracoo, then drew a phlegmy breath and whispered, "Tell me you'll accept. They'll be coming to you . . . soon. Promise me."

Koracoo exhaled a long slow breath before she replied, "There are others far more deserving."

"But none . . . more capable."

She gently squeezed her mother's hand. "Are you sure?"

There was the faintest hint of a smile on her pinched lips. "No . . . doubts. We talked about it . . . once. Remember?"

"Oh, yes, I do."

How could she ever forget that day twelve summers ago? Almost as clearly as if she were there again, she found herself standing in the smoldering ruins of the longhouse, frantically searching through the burned timbers for her family. She'd found her sister Tawi first, burned almost beyond recognition. Then she'd heard a barely audible sound, like a voice rising through layers of hide, and realized there was someone beneath Tawi. Her sister had died trying to protect their mother. Without Tawi's body to shield her from the roof-fall, Jigonsaseh would certainly have died that day. Amid the stifling heat and stench of burned flesh, Koracoo had dragged her mother free. As she'd carried her outside, her mother's voice had been crystal clear: *"Promise me. . . . Receive my name."*

Rattling breaths filled the silence, and Mother seemed to be fighting to gather enough strength to speak. "Your son . . ."

Koracoo frowned. "What about Sky Messenger?"

"He's . . . afraid. Told me—he'd done something."

Koracoo's brows drew together. "Something he couldn't tell me?"

"Anyone . . . close?"

Koracoo cast a glance over her shoulder. "Just Tutelo and me."

"Baji . . ." Her voice faded to a rattling like dry bones in the wind.

Tutelo looked at Koracoo with tear-filled eyes. "Why does she want to know about Baji?"

Koracoo shook her head. The time was almost at hand. Grief caught in her throat.

Jigonsaseh reached out to touch Koracoo's hair and feebly tugged at it. "Look . . . look at me."

Koracoo raised her head and gazed into her mother's loving eyes, drowsy with death. "What about Baji, Mother?"

". . . He . . . let her . . . adopt him."

As the truth of those words sank into Koracoo's souls, her heart seemed to stop. She clutched her mother's hand and leaned closer, so that no one could possibly overhear. "Are you saying he allowed the Flint People to adopt him?"

Jigonsaseh made a great effort to nod. "He wished to—marry. No other . . ."

Koracoo silently finished the sentence for her, *no other way*. In order to marry Baji, he would have had to become one of her people. Dear gods. If anyone found out, nothing else would matter, not his visions, not his former valor, nothing. He'd be dead in less than the time it took say the word *treason*. Even if he managed to escape and return to the Flint People, they had certainly "unadopted" him after he'd returned to take up his position as a Standing Stone deputy war chief. Which meant he would be a traitor to two nations, and he . . .

Jigonsaseh wheezed, "Protect . . . him."

Koracoo stared at her mother. Her breathing was coming in short desperate puffs. "Yes, of course. As best I can."

"His coming . . . was foretold."

Koracoo hesitated, uncertain what to say to that. "I'll look after him. I give you my oath."

". . . It will help."

Did she mean Koracoo's protection would help, or the fact that he'd allowed himself to be adopted into an enemy people would help? Surely, the former.

"I'm sure it will," she answered softly, and kissed her mother on the cheek.

As though Koracoo's promise had given her peace, the struggle seemed to go out of Matron Jigonsaseh's exhausted body. "You're . . . a leader—best leader—for our village."

At these words, pain constricted Koracoo's chest. She whispered, "I love you so much," and gently placed her mother's hand on the sleeping bench.

She heard moccasins rapidly coming down the longhouse but did not look up until Tutelo said, "Mother."

When she turned, Deru stood behind her with his war club in his fist, his massive shoulders heaving with swift breaths. He must have run to get here.

Koracoo lurched to her feet. "What is it? What's wrong?"

He clenched his jaw, and it set his caved-in left cheek at an odd angle. "Two scouts came in. We have a flood of refugees coming."

"What? How many? From where?"

"We won't know until they get here. Papon said hundreds, but you know how he is; he exaggerates."

"Did he have any other details? What village? Who attacked them?"

Deru shook his head, and short black hair flapped across his crushed cheek. "As soon as our scouts saw them on the trail in the distance, they climbed down from the sycamore where they were keeping watch and ran—"

Tutelo suddenly sobbed, "Oh, Mother!" She clapped a hand to her mouth to smother her cries. Her gaze fixed on her grandmother.

Koracoo turned. Jigonsaseh's eyes stared up blankly, peacefully, at the smoke hole in the roof, as though her afterlife soul saw the way out.

Deru said, "Oh, Speaker, I did not realize—"

"No one did. And I needed to hear your message, Deru. Thank you for bringing it swiftly. It gives me time to prepare."

Tears did not come easily to Koracoo. In her many summers as a warrior and then as war chief, she had seen dozens of friends perish. Sodowego, the harbinger of death, was an old familiar companion. Often, she'd been desperately glad to see him. As she was now. Yesterday had been the longest day of Koracoo's life, her mother's rattling lungs and whimpers unbearable. Now, the great matron's suffering was over, and for that, Koracoo was deeply grateful.

"I'll leave," Deru said. "I'm sorry to have disturbed—"

"How far away are the refugees?"

"A good distance. They were moving slowly. Papon suspected they'd make camp for the night, and come in tomorrow morning."

Koracoo expelled a breath. "Very well. Inform Chief Yellowtail. I'll inform the matrons."

"Yes, Speaker." Deru turned, and his steps pounded away.

Koracoo turned to her grief-stricken daughter. Tears blurred Tutelo's eyes. "Tutelo, please run to each longhouse and first inform the clan matrons that we have more hungry people coming in, probably tomorrow, but maybe tonight. They'll need places to sleep, and probably hides to keep them warm." She paused, then finished, "After all the deaths, they should have enough to share. Then tell them that the great Matron Jigonsaseh will need to travel to the afterlife tomorrow."

Tutelo dried her eyes on her cape and rose. "I miss her already."

Koracoo stroked her hair. "Thank you for staying with her."

"She was never alone, Mother. She always knew someone who loved her was close by. I'll be back to help you prepare her for the journey."

"No. Go home." She kissed Tutelo's forehead. "Your own daughter is ill. Take care of her. Eat. Spend time with your wonderful husband. Your family needs you. Your cousins will care for our matron."

Tutelo nodded. As she walked away, she wiped the tears from her cheeks with her hands.

Koracoo gazed down upon her dead mother. From long experience, she knew the pain would come, once the shock wore off. Once her duties and obligations were done. Once she'd tended to the new refugees, and stopped worrying about Hiyawento and the message from the Hills Ruling Council . . . once she had the luxury.

Twenty-eight

Sky Messenger

The sound of the rushing river fills the cool morning.

I turn to examine the faint lavender halo that swells over the eastern hills. As Elder Brother Sun nears the horizon, the old abandoned village seems to come alive, shadows stretching like dark fists from the overgrown piles of earth. Long ago, Bog Willow Village contained one hundred or more houses. All that remains are hillocks sprinkled with broken potsherds. Occasionally a charred log thrusts up through the leaf mat, saplings, and brush. There are many ghosts here. They roam the ruins as though still hunting for the bodies of lost loved ones.

To the west, dark blue mountains rise. I remember them. I remember everything about our rescue, and our flight from the battlefield. A desperate sense of guilt fills me when I think of that night. Baji, Tutelo, and I ran with all our hearts. We escaped, leaving Wrass and Zateri in the old woman's clutches. For days, while our party searched for them, I lived their horror in my souls.

At this point in my life, I realize there was nothing I could have done to save them, but strangely that truth doesn't alter the guilt. Sleeping deep inside me is the overwhelming sense that I should have tried to save them. Today, standing here, that desperate sensation returns to haunt me. My belly knots. My fists clench. I have to *do* something. Yet I am delaying marching into the meadow where the huge warrior camp sprawled.

Gusting up from the river, the cold breeze carries a mass of whirling leaves and smells sweetly of dew-soaked earth. I concentrate on the fragrance as I bend to grasp a potsherd, study it, and replace it in the exact location where I found it. Gitchi follows me with his ears pricked, listening to the morning.

Ten paces away, Taya sits on a rock with her knees hugged against her chest. Long black hair falls over the front of her cape, fluttering in the wind. When she catches me looking at her, she sucks in a breath, expels it in a disgusted rush.

I ignore her. Standing here . . . burns. My blood is aflame. Despite the cold, I'm roasting from the inside out. Gitchi feels it, too. He stays right at my heels, whimpering when he knows I'm on the verge of lashing out.

Like a knife in my heart, Taya calls, "I thought you said we were on an urgent mission to find a dead man. Why aren't you looking for him?"

My heartbeat begins to slam against my ribs. She's right. I force myself to turn to the meadow. *It's empty. Most of those men are long dead. Look around. They are not here. They're not hiding waiting to capture you again.*

But my ears ring with the hideous laughter that filled the night twelve summers ago. The celebration songs almost drown out the childish sobbing of the new captives . . . and Zateri's cries. Through the stench of burning longhouses, I smell clams boiling and dogs roasting.

Seeping up from inside me, Wrass orders, *"Hide in those leaves, Odion. If they find you, swing that club as hard as you can, and don't stop swinging. No matter what you hear or see, keep swinging. Do you hear me? I'm going to lead them away. I'll meet you . . ."*

My aching fingers go tight around a war club that rotted to dust long ago. I hear shouts, men calling to each other, chasing us down. . . .

"They are not here," I whisper to that terrified little boy who still huddles inside me. "Look. They are not here."

Taya cups a hand to her mouth and shouts, "When are we going home?"

"But Wrass, I'm scared. I want to go with you! Let me—"

"I told you to hide. Now do it!"

I shake myself. I have to force my cramping fingers to release the imaginary club I hold. My hand stings.

Dreams tormented me last night. I was back here. It was dark and cold, and I was sure Wrass was dying. They'd beaten him badly. He'd tried to protect me from the old woman's wrath. He shouldn't have. He . . .

When I jerked awake, I rose and went down to the river where I hurled rocks at the water until I killed it . . . or killed the reflection of me that I saw there.

I order my feet to move, to walk. My long cape slurs softly over the old leaves. Even now, upon the very ground where it happened . . . the black hole in my memory persists. *He took me by the hand, dragged me out into the forest . . .*

The rest is gone.

While I struggle to figure out why, I pick up a mud-caked arrow point, wipe it clean, turn it over, and gently put it down.

"What are you doing?" Taya demands to know.

I call, "I'm thinking."

I'm sure this isn't how she expected to spend the moons before her joining. She must long to be home putting the finishing touches on our place in the longhouse. Not out in the middle of the wilderness scrambling after winter-starved rodents and dodging war parties. Underlying her impatience and irritating demands, I realize she is on the verge of blind panic, and has been for days. I'm fairly certain she would bolt for home if she thought she could make it alone. I can't let her. She'll almost certainly be killed or captured.

There is a flash on the horizon. Gitchi's gray head turns, and he wags his tail. As Elder Brother Sun rises from his resting place in the branches of the celestial tree, an amber gleam spreads across the old village and hundreds of arrow points glisten. They are everywhere—testaments to the intensity of the long-ago battle that devastated Bog Willow Village.

Taya climbs down off the rock and trudges through the village ruins toward me.

I reach down and grasp a stone tool, an old scraper used to process corn husks, and hold it to my ear. I close my eyes, listening for the voices of people who might have seen what happened to me. The tool is quiet. I replace it in the exact spot in which I found it, and move on. Gitchi smells the stone before following.

Taya calls, "You are so *odd*."

As I open my mouth to respond . . .

"Odion?"

The Voice calls.

Blood freezes in my veins. Where is he? I turn, trying to find him.

He kneels in the meadow in the distance, his black hood blowing around dark emptiness. My senses become heightened, as always when he appears, and I smell old blood on the breeze. It infects his clothing like a foul miasma.

I stride straight through the ruins, headed north along the riverbank with Gitchi trotting at my heels.

In a childish whine, Taya says, "You never answer me!"

I've forgotten her question.

As I stride toward Shago-niyoh, the tangy smell of the river drifts up, displacing the taint of corruption. Bright autumn leaves pile along the shores, creating moldering borders that mingle with the fragrances of dead grass and moss. Birdsong fills the trees.

Taya trots through the meadow behind me, shouting, "What's wrong? Did I do something again?"

By the time she reaches my side, I am standing two paces from Shago-niyoh. He is not looking at me. His head is bent, and he seems to be study-ing something on the ground, something hidden in the colorful blanket of leaves.

I whisper to him, "There's one part . . . I don't . . . I can't remember. Do you know what happened to me?"

Taya stands breathing hard, staring at the place my eyes focus. Clearly she sees nothing. A thread of alarm enters her voice. "Who are you talk-ing to? Are you talking to me?"

Shago-niyoh looks toward the eastern horizon, where a honeyed glow arches into the sky. *"What is the first thing you recall about this place?"*

"The black blizzard. Swirling. Covering the trees and the ground."

"A black blizzard?" Taya asks. After several heartbeats without an an-swer, she turns to look back at the destroyed village. "You mean, from the burning village? Was ash falling?"

I prop my hands on my hips and turn to her. I do owe her answers. She is not here voluntarily. Of course, neither am I. But we are in this to-gether. "Yes, we arrived just after the attack."

"We? Who else was with you?"

Their faces appear just behind my eyes. And my anxiety lessens. I can breathe again. They're here with me. "Tutelo, Wrass, and others. My only friends." I don't wish to name the other children. They are from "enemy" peoples, and I don't wish to endure another lecture about my treasonous inclinations.

I gaze out at the wide river, where water burbles over rocks. Dark green spruces and pines dot the brilliant scarlet maples on the opposite bank. "I don't know why I can't remember everything. The images should be burned into my souls. Every other moment is."

"Maybe you were you struck in the head?" Taya suggests.

"Maybe. I recall beatings . . . and my flight through the forest with my Spirit Helper is perfectly clear."

Shago-niyoh shifts, but does not look up. His black cape waffles in the wind.

I add, "As is the instant when Mother and Father, and the two Hills warriors, Sindak and Towa, burst from the trees with their war clubs and killed the Outcast warriors who held us captive."

I realize my lapse too late.

Surprised, Taya says, "There were two Hills warriors with the party that rescued you? Two *enemy* warriors? Your mother allied herself with our enemies? How is it possible that I've never heard this part of the story?"

I lift a shoulder. I'm waiting for Shago-niyoh to speak to me. He called me here for a reason.

Taya says, "How did you make it home?"

Gitchi walks to my side and looks up at me with adoring yellow eyes. I stroke his warm throat. "My friends. They were just children, but they risked their lives to make sure we escaped." I gesture. "Three or four hundred warriors were camped here. The smell of roasting dogs and clams filled the night. There were hundreds of campfires. Sometimes, in my Dreams, I return here, and I . . . I hear that voice. The man's voice. That's where the gap is in my memory."

Shago-niyoh whispers, *"Gaps are thresholds. Step over."*

Taya tucks windblown long hair behind her ears. She's so young. I keep forgetting. "Who is he?"

For an instant, I'm confused about whom she means; then I rub my hands on my cape, cleaning them of the filth. Filth that has not existed, except in my souls, in a long time. "He was a war chief."

Taya's dark beautiful eyes seem larger. "What was his name?"

"He's dead. I cannot speak his name."

Taya flaps her arms against her sides. "Sky Messenger, think about this. You obviously have a ghost sickness and need to see a good Healer, not someone like old Bahna. In Bur Oak Village, Genonsgwa is the best. She says . . ."

It's hard to concentrate on what she's saying. Shago-niyoh is brushing away leaves, searching the ground. Absently, I murmur, "Healers can't help me now."

"There is a way through. A way out. The doorway to freedom is right here. Step through." Shago-niyoh's hood tilts to the side, waiting for me to understand.

"A way through?" I don't understand.

Taya stalks forward and brusquely says, "If we came here to find a dead man, let's do it! Tell me where to look. I want to get out of here as soon as possible."

I stare at Shago-niyoh. Is he speaking about the "prison" Old Bahna says I've constructed to protect myself? *There is a way out. . . .*

"Sky Messenger, talk to me!"

I tear my gaze away from Shago-niyoh to study Taya. Her expression is wild with barely suppressed terror. She gazes at me as though I am not human, but one of the monsters that stalked the primeval world of the creation.

I point to the ground. "He's here. I think."

Shago-niyoh rises in a sort of weightless drifting and turns to face me expectantly.

I lower my eyes to the ground, where the leaves are still parted, revealing dark black soil. Gitchi sniffs the grass, and a low growl rumbles his throat.

"What's the matter with your wolf?" To Taya it looks like dead grass and leaves.

"I think this is where . . . Her campfire was here. I'm sure of it."

I turn around in a complete circle, examining the trees, the location of the burned village, and the river. For a long time, I stare at Shago-niyoh, who stands no more than two paces distant, his hood absolutely still in the fierce gust of wind that sweeps the meadow.

"You said 'her' camp. But I thought you said the voice belongs to a man?"

"It does." I turn to her. Taya's eyes have started to dart about, as though expecting hideous creatures to emerge from the shadows and gobble her whole. "The old woman's name has been forgotten by our people. I thank the gods that no one will ever speak it again."

Taya's brows draw together over her straight nose. "Forgotten? Was she that evil?"

Names are clan property. Immediately after birth, a child is given a name that had belonged to a revered ancestor. After the deaths of evil people, names are retired forever and no one mentions them again.

"She was a witch. Powerful . . . incredibly Powerful. The things she did . . ."

Taya lowers her voice to a whisper. "As Powerful as the foul Bluebird Witch? I've heard he can kill with a glance or the wave of a hand. Just seeing him out in the forest can be a death sentence."

I crouch and begin parting the leaves and grass with my fingers, trying to see what Shago-niyoh wished me to. The leaves rustle with my motions.

Taya spreads her feet, as though preparing for a battle of wills. "Hurry, can you? We're in enemy country, vulnerable every instant." She pauses and adds, "I have no idea why your Spirit Helper told you to abandon your weapons. If I were you, I'd find a different Spirit Helper."

I continue searching. "I was called to something greater. That's all."

"What did he ask you to do—other than see visions?" The last word comes out sounding like a curse.

"His call is less a summons to *do* something than an invitation to *be* something."

Impatiently, she says, "You mean to be a hermit, to run away from life, as you did after that battle? Grandmother still wants you to return to the war trail, you know."

This refrain is becoming almost unbearable. She says almost these exact words to me at least once a day. Through gritted teeth, I respond, "I was called into life, Taya, into relationship with the Faces of the Forest, and Cloudland Eagle, even the grains of sand. I'll never return to my old life. So you might want to stop hoping for that."

Her mouth purses. "All right. Fine."

Gitchi moves forward to help me. He claws at the ground, tearing away the grass. Flecks of charcoal emerge. Gitchi sniffs the charcoal, licks his muzzle nervously, and pants.

"Did he find something?" Taya asks.

After I have cleared away more grass, I stare at it. The cries are barely audible at first, then gather strength, seeping up from the ground. Men wail and shout. I'm breathing as hard as Gitchi now.

Taya asks, "What's the matter? You're panting like a dog."

Hoarsely, I say, "Don't you hear them?"

"What?"

"The men, screaming."

"You mean men who died in the attack? Are their ghosts still here? You hear ghosts? What do they want?" She spins around searching for ghosts.

Shago-niyoh moves across the meadow, heading toward a small clearing surrounded by scrub bladdernut trees. I may not remember critical moments of that night . . . but I recall that clearing. That's where we were held. Warriors guarded us while the old woman plied her Trade, buying and selling children from the victorious warriors. Atotarho was here that night. . . . Amid the deep morning shadows, Shago-niyoh's black cape is almost invisible.

I brush at the charcoal. Large sherds from a big pot, probably a stew pot, thrust up through the dark gray soil. I reach for the largest sherd and tug it from the ground. A handful of earth comes up with it, filled with charred bones. One chunk appears to be from a human skull. My hand shakes when I try to touch it. I pull back. Every time I reach for it, my fingers go numb.

"Here, let me help you, I can get it out. Maybe if we pull out that big potsherd first, it will dislodge the bone, and we can leave." Taya kneels beside me and reaches for the sherd.

"Don't touch it!" I order. "The stew was poisoned. I'm sure it's all right now, but just . . . don't."

I don't want her tainted by what happened that night.

She jerks her hand back. "*Poisoned?* Who poisoned the stew? Why? Was this the evil witch's stew pot?"

In a voice almost too faint to hear, I say, "Yes."

I steady myself, pull the sherd out, and set it to the side. Then I return to digging through the old charcoal and debris. More charred bone emerges from the upturned dirt, including a palm-sized blackened fragment of human skull.

I swallow hard.

"What's wrong?" she asks.

I feel my eyes go enormous and shiny. Old rage, aged to horrific perfection, washes around inside me. "The next day, we returned here. I remember everything. The smell of death permeated the air. When we found his body, Father hacked it to pieces with his war ax. Everyone helped scatter the bloody pieces. Then . . ." I look at the pile of bone fragments. "Then Father cut off the man's head and forced me to carry it to this fire. He made me throw it in and watch it burn."

Violently, I wipe my hands on my cape.

"Why did your father do that? It sounds cruel. You were just a boy."

A low, bizarre laugh shakes me. Tears press against the inside of my skull, just as they did that day. "Father was not cruel. He did exactly the right thing. For that single instant I had power over this piece of filth."

I can't help it. I ball my fists and viciously slam them into the bone fragments, over and over, making small agonized sounds as I pulverize them. *I see his smile.* . . . I have to kill him. "You deserve to wander the earth forever. You deserve it!" I slam my fist into the skull fragment hard enough to send splinters flying in all directions.

"Who does?" Taya cries. "Is that the war chief's skull?"

I can't stop to answer. I have to keep killing him. I continue beating the bones. When my hands are torn and bloody, I jerk a rock from the ground, and pound the bones to dust. The sharp *crack! crack! CRACK!* rings through the meadow.

Taya backs away. Her expression tells me everything. My actions have terrified her. She knows for certain now that I am indeed a madman. Despite the danger, she's seriously considering running home alone.

The rock in my fist hovers in midair, suspended over the battered splinters. She'll never make it. I rise, draw my arm back, and hurl the rock as far as I can. The breeze blows loose black hair over my eyes. I'm surprised when strands stick to my cheeks as though they are wet.

"Sky Messenger, you're scaring me!"

I wipe my face on my sleeve. My eyes ache, but it is more than just the cries I've kept locked inside me all these summers. I suddenly *understand*.

"Blessed gods," I murmur. "This is not about *the way out*. The long summers of war made me forget a very important lesson."

"What lesson?" Taya fearfully glances over her shoulder and clenches her jaw. She's shaking.

As though the words are engraved on my soul, I say, "Our people have an amnesia of the heart. We've forgotten that we were once one people."

"We? Who is we?"

"All of us. All of the peoples south of Skanodario Lake."

The words seem to stun her. "Don't *ever* say that again. I refuse to believe that any part of me could come from Flint or Mountain blood. They are evil beasts who deserve to be destroyed. When I am clan matron, I will be brave enough to—"

"To what?" My voice comes out savage. "Kill more people? Burn more villages? Only the bravest dare to try to end the violence, Taya. You want to be brave? Make that your goal."

"Peacemaking is just another word for cowardice. It—"

"Peacemaking is the *best* quality of the brave, and the only thing to fight for!"

She clenches her fists at her sides. "I want to go home! This journey is making you even stranger."

"Taya . . ." I have to remind myself that she is terrified. I force calm into my voice. "I think, maybe, the way out is to dip with the river, not against it. I'm not sure I can do it. I am frail and more than a little frightened, but I must try."

"I don't care. I just want to go home!"

I blink at her, truly seeing her for the first time. She has left all of the camp duties to me: fishing, cooking, cleaning. I set up camp and take it down. She doesn't lift a finger to help. She acts very much as though she's home and I am just another of her slaves. On the war trail, every warrior cares for himself, so this is not a burden to me. . . . It's just—I had hoped this journey would help her grow up.

"I'm going to take you home. I've already promised you that. There's one stop I must make on the way. Then I'll take you straight home."

She wets her full lips and gazes at me suspiciously. Uneasily, she says, "Where do we have to stop? We are in enemy country surrounded by those who wish to kill us. We should go straight home."

"I have to see an old friend. He saved me once. I pray he can do it again."

Night is falling. . . . Wrass keeps glancing at me from where he walks at my side. . . . In a very soft voice, he says, "I will be there. I promise you on my life, I will be right at your side." When the end comes.

Sulking, Taya breaks the memory, saying, "We should never have come here. What can an old fire pit filled with bones teach you? We—"

"I had to. Bahna was right."

I bend, pick up a splinter of skull, and clutch it so hard my knuckles go white. Sickness tickles the back of my throat. The last thing on earth I wish to do is Sing him to the Land of the Dead.

As I walk away from Taya, she lets out a small frustrated cry. "Where are you taking that piece of skull? Put it down!"

Gitchi trails a few paces behind me, taking his time licking the morning dew off the blades of grass.

Taya does not follow.

She looked across the field of blowing leaves to where Sky Messenger stood at the edge of the forest, turning the splinter in his hands. As though hot, he'd thrown his cape back over his shoulders, revealing his tattered war shirt and the array of Power bundles dangling like cocoons around his waist. Taya was utterly convinced now that he'd lost his soul. Maybe he'd lost it here, and that's why he kept speaking to invisible things. Was his soul standing right here beside her? Is that who he was talking to? Cold and terrified, she desperately longed to run away. She looked around, judging which direction to go. She had no idea which way led home.

Sky Messenger tilted his head back. In the sky above him, Cloud People, scouts of the Thunderers, marched westward through the pink rays of dawn. The cool breeze tousled his shoulder-length hair around his face. His lips moved, but she couldn't hear his words. Was he calling to his loose soul? Or to the ghosts of those long dead, killed in this forgotten battle? He spread his arms, hesitated like a hovering kestrel, then whirled in the motions of the Thunder Dance. The seven Thunderers, very Powerful sky-dwellers, controlled the rains, and also kept the monsters of destruction, like Horned Serpent and Tawiscaro, the Evil-Minded One, locked beneath the earth.

Sky Messenger's muscles bulged through his shirt as he swayed and spun, his feet stamping the ground while he clutched the splinter of human skull and Sang as though his heart were bursting.

Taya's brows plunged down. "What's he doing? Calling the Cloud

People so the dead war chief can use them as stepping stones to reach the Path of Souls? But he said the man deserved to wander the earth. . . ."

Without warning, lightning flashed and the deep rumble of the coming Thunderers shook the morning. Rain drifted out of the sky in a glistening wind-borne mist. A hushed whisper filled the air as drops pattered on the grass and brittle leaves. Sky Messenger continued dancing, his moccasins cutting dark swaths across the wet meadow.

As though rubbed with fox fur, the hair on Taya's arms stood up. Her whole body seemed to be crawling with ants. With each stamp of his feet, she could feel the Power quickening. Gitchi must have felt it, too. He flopped down in the grass and laid his ears back.

Finally, Sky Messenger lifted the bone splinter straight over his head. As though they'd heard his pleas and opened their eternal eyes, the Thunderers roared so loudly Great Grandmother Earth shuddered.

Taya cried, "The Thunderers are getting closer! We should run for cover!"

He didn't hear her, or he was ignoring her, which she suspected he often did. Rain drenched his upturned face and ratty war shirt.

"You fool! You're going to get blasted by lightning!" *Then how will I make it home?*

When he still didn't answer, she ran for the riverbank, slipping and sliding her way down to the bottom. This seemed to be a canoe landing, for almost no brush grew here. She could just peer at Sky Messenger over the lip of the drainage. He was spinning like a mad fool.

Suddenly, as though Elder Brother Sun had waited for this exact moment, a brilliant lance of sunlight shot through the clouds and cleaved a bright path through the leaves at Sky Messenger's feet. It resembled a pointing finger. He stopped spinning, and his gaze traced the light as it moved westward across the forest; then he wiped the rain from his cheeks with the back of his hand. Just as he turned toward her, lightning split the morning and the blaze turned his body into a pillar of pure white.

Sky Messenger lifted the skull splinter up to the shower again. Only after it had been washed clean did he tuck it into the red Power bundle that hung from his belt. For more than one hundred heartbeats, he stood with his eyes closed, letting the rain drench his upturned face. Finally, he turned and plodded toward her.

She scrambled up the bank and trotted to meet him. "Are we finished here? Can we go?"

He turned to look at the small clearing surrounded by bladdernut trees. He seemed to be watching something move. "No, not yet."

"Why did you keep that blackened piece of skull?"

He put his hand on the red Power bundle, and his bushy brows drew together. "I'm collecting wounds."

What does that mean? "And now that you have it, why do we have to stay here?"

He turned to gaze back at the edge of the forest. "A . . . a threshold."

He walked away, following the path illuminated earlier by Elder Brother Sun.

She miserably glowered at the rain that drifted around his tall body like smoke-colored veils of silk. In the distance, towering hickories swayed through the gray haze.

He kept walking, his gaze focused on the small clearing as though his life depended upon it.

She trudged through the thick leaves after him.

He stopped at the edge of the bladdernut trees and stared out into the deep forest shadows. His gaze focused on something she could not see. She, again, had the feeling he was talking to a ghost that stood barely a hand's breadth away.

As though answering a question, Sky Messenger whispered, "I can't welcome the serpent's poison as it pours into my ears. I . . ." As though listening, he paused before finishing, "Well, suffering certainly feels evil."

Taya glanced around the forest with her heart skipping. She saw nothing but autumn trees and dead grass. Here and there deadfall created dark heaps in the depths of the forest. He *was* talking with something!

Sky Messenger heaved a breath and bowed his head. "I don't understand. If the *way through* is right here, why don't I see it?" Another pause. He shook his head. "I do *not* have my hands over my eyes."

"Who are you talking to? Tell me!"

Sky Messenger turned and at first didn't seem to see her; then he blinked, and his eyes cleared. "Do you . . . ? Taya, do you think there is a child inside you who forever keeps his hands clapped over his eyes?"

His expression was pleading. She tried to piece together the fragments of conversation she'd been listening to for over one hand of time. "I think that's gibberish. I have no idea what you're talking about."

But she wondered . . . If the child removed its hands would it see *the way through*?

Sky Messenger suddenly went rigid, staring into the forest shadows as though a monster had just appeared. After a time, he turned to Taya and softly said, "I have to go in there. But you can remain out here, if you wish."

"I'm not staying here alone! There are ghosts everywhere!"

He balled his fists and swallowed hard. She followed him into the cold morning shadows. Twigs snapped beneath her feet, but he didn't seem to notice.

He'd taken only ten steps before he faltered. His brows drew together. "This is the place."

"What place?"

He moved around as though his feet were weighted with rocks. Gitchi padded at his heels, but his yellow eyes had narrowed, and his ears lay flat against his skull. Sky Messenger placed a hand against an enormous pine and searched the snow-tipped needles. After several moments, he said, "This is where it happened," and looked up at the sky. "The tree branches are different. I was looking up at them . . . part of the time."

"Well, walk around, think about it. Just hurry."

Gitchi let out a low growl and froze, his muzzle pointing at a scrubby grove of prickly ash trees. Leafless, they resembled a cluster of spikes.

Sky Messenger followed the wolf's gaze, and his expression changed completely. He froze like a big cat spotting a mouse. His eyes went wide and alert. Barely above a whisper, he said, "Taya, don't move. Don't even breathe."

"But, why? I don't—"

He grabbed her wrist in a death grip to silence her.

The six men ghosted through the trees. They were far enough away that she could not tell their nation, just floating glimpses of clothing and glints of arrow points. When they'd passed out of sight, Sky Messenger said, "We have to get out of here *now*."

He ducked low and led the way with Gitchi trotting in his footsteps. Taya brought up the rear with her heart in her throat. The mosaic of sunlight, barred with indigo shadows, seemed to stretch across the broken land forever.

Twenty-nine

Sleet pattered on the roof of the longhouse, creating a faint chatter that competed with the crackling fire and the whispers in the Council House at Bur Oak Village. Fires blazed down the length of the house, lighting the faces of the people who'd assembled to hear Gonda's story.

"Give me just a—a moment." Gonda, Speaker for the Warriors of White Dog Village, lifted his hands to massage his temples. He was a thin, wiry man with a moonish face and brown eyes. He'd seen thirty-eight summers pass, most of them in Yellowtail Village. Never, in all that time, had he felt this weary. Evil Spirits had been cavorting in his head since the attack two days ago, plunging stilettos behind his eyes as though trying to puncture a way to freedom.

When the pain had eased a little, he lowered his hands and prepared to finish the telling. He stood beside the central fire examining the faces of the Ruling Council of the People of the Standing Stone. Concentric rings of benches encircled the fire. Each person had his or her place. The six clan matrons and High Matron Kittle sat on the innermost ring of benches closest to the fire. Behind them, on the middle ring, sat the village chiefs and village matrons. The outermost ring was crowded with the Speakers. Each of the five villages had four Speakers, elected representatives who conveyed various group decisions and asked questions on the group's behalf. The Speakers for the Warriors sat on the outermost northern benches, including the War Chief of Bur Oak Village,

Skenandoah, and War Chief Deru of Yellowtail Village. The Speakers for the Women sat on the eastern benches. The Speakers for the Men occupied the western benches, and the Speakers for the Shamans filled the southern benches.

Gonda responded, "The sickness began the same day the baskets of corn arrived. Our village was deeply grateful for the food sent by the Ruling Council. Portions were divided for each longhouse. By nightfall most people were so ill they could barely stand. The attack came at dawn the next morning." As he spoke, the whispers quieted and expressions went somber. "Those who could carry a weapon did so, but we couldn't defend all three palisades. Our war chief, whose name I cannot speak for he is traveling the Path of Souls, ordered all of our fighters to stand on the outermost palisade. As each palisade was overwhelmed, we moved to the next. We were simply too weak to defend the village. The battle was over in less than two hands of time."

Matron Kittle stood. Still an extremely handsome woman, the firm contours of her oval face had just begun to sag. He could see it in the slight wrinkles at her throat and the lines at the corners of her deeply set dark eyes. She wore her black hair pulled back and twisted into a knot at the base of her skull and fastened with a tortoiseshell comb. Her beautiful white cape, reserved for council meetings, glimmered with circlets of seashells. "Forgive us for keeping you here, Speaker. We realize you are tired, but we must understand what happened so that we can immediately begin planning a response."

Gonda nodded. "I understand."

Kittle continued, "Are you suggesting that it was the baskets of corn that sickened White Dog Village and made them vulnerable to attack?"

"Yes, but we cannot say for certain that the corn was to blame. If we'd had more time, High Matron, we could have verified our suspicions. As it was, we barely had time enough to escape with our lives."

"High Matron," a deep voice called from the eastern benches, and a very tall woman rose to her feet.

Gonda's gaze fixed on her. She'd cut her gray-streaked black hair short in mourning, and it made her small narrow nose and full lips seem all the more beautiful to him. Despite all the unpleasantness that had gone between them over the twelve long summers since she'd divorced him, his heart gladdened. Just the sight of her was like the feel of a war club in his hand; it gave him confidence that he could face anything.

"Koracoo, Speaker for the Women of Yellowtail Village, proceed," Matron Kittle said.

Koracoo folded her arms, and firelight played through the reddish fur

of her woven foxhide cape. "In recent days, we have all heard similar stories from the survivors of Sedge Marsh Village. It must be obvious to this
council now that someone is poisoning the baskets of corn that we send
to needy villages."

"High Matron?" War Chief Deru said from the northern benches. His
massive bearlike body rose and loomed in the murky shadows. Oddly,
firelight pooled in his caved-in cheek, turning it amber while the rest of
his features remained dim.

"Proceed, War Chief," Kittle acknowledged him.

"If Speaker Koracoo is right, someone is trying to make it look as
though we are poisoning these villages. Which of our enemies is clever
enough to accomplish this?"

"It must be a man or woman who can freely walk through both Hills
and Standing Stone villages," Koracoo said. "A Trader? Or a messenger
traveling under the white arrow?"

Kittle lifted her pointed chin and surveyed the council. "Since both
Sedge Marsh Village and White Dog Village were attacked by Atotarho's
warriors, the man behind it seems clear. The question is, who is Atotarho's poisoner?"

Daga, Matron of the Turtle Clan in White Dog Village, braced a hand
on the bench and grunted as she rose to her feet on spindly legs. Her fifty-
six summers showed in her snowy hair and the deep wrinkles around her
toothless mouth. "As you all know, I was here attending the betrothal feast
of the high matron's granddaughter when the attack came on my home.
Because of that, there are many things I do not know about what went on
in White Dog Village. Speaker Gonda, what is your opinion about the poisoner?"

He ran a hand through his black hair. "I cannot even offer a guess,
Matron Daga. The day the corn arrived was a day of joy for us. Every
longhouse feasted. Many people honored the gift by wearing their best
clothing, jewelry, and painting their faces. Identifying a stranger would
have been difficult."

Chief Yellowtail lifted a hand. He stood right behind Kittle. As he
rose, his shoulder-length dark gray hair swayed around his wrinkled
face. "If the Ruling Council of the People of the Hills is to blame, is it
trying to provoke us into attacking Atotarho Village?"

"Blessed gods, I pray not," Gonda said. "They have four times as
many warriors as we do. Such an assault would be doomed to failure and
a foolish waste of our young warriors' lives."

Murmuring filled the council house. Gonda spread his feet and waited.
He needed to get back to his sick wife, Pawen, who lay in the Bear Clan

longhouse being tended by his daughter, Tutelo. Pawen had been very ill before the attack, but after the poisoned corn and the long journey here . . .

"High Matron, how can we be sure it was the corn, and not some other evil? Perhaps a spell was cast upon White Dog Village by Atotarho's army of witches?" War Chief Skenandoah asked. He had seen around thirty-four summers, and had a square chin and thin lips. He was of medium height, and his short black hair had started to gray at the temples.

Gonda replied, "We aren't sure, War Chief. I apologize if I gave that impression. We suspect the corn was poisoned, but the illness may have been witchery. Who can say?"

The phrase "army of witches" was whispered throughout the council as nods went round. Gonda stumbled and righted himself.

High Matron Kittle noticed. "If there are no objections, perhaps we should dismiss this council and reconvene tomorrow. Speaker Gonda needs to rest, and it will give us all time to consider his words. Do I hear any objections?"

There were none.

Kittle called, "We will reconvene this council tomorrow morning just after dawn. Go in peace."

People began to file out of the council house. Gonda didn't wish to be jostled by the crowd, so he continued standing by the fire, biding his time. When most of the councilors had gone, he saw Koracoo looking at him. She excused herself from the group of Yellowtail matrons that had her surrounded and made her way through the benches to get to him.

He gave her a tired smile. "You look well."

"And you look like you can barely stay on your feet. How is Pawen?"

He shook his head and looked away. "Tutelo is with her. I—I don't know."

Koracoo put a gentle hand on his shoulder. "She's young and strong. She'll get well."

He jerked a nod and changed the subject. "You must tell me about Sky Messenger's Dream. I've already heard five different versions."

She looked around at the few people still standing nearby, then slipped her arm through his. "Let us speak in private. I have much to tell you."

"Are the Yellowtail matrons finished with you? They look like they're still waiting to talk more."

"They have my answer. They're just discussing the timing."

She tightened her hold on his arm. At her touch he realized that, without being conscious of it, he'd needed her closeness. This was the first time they'd seen each other in two summers. Not so long ago, even a glance from her would have fired his veins. Now her touch was as warm and comfortable as a worn pair of moccasins. She looked down at him, for she was taller than he, and smiled in the old way he loved—smiling as though they'd never said hateful things to each other.

"I swear I'm getting old and decrepit," she said.

"Well, the good thing about being a legendary former war chief is that few men will ever be brave enough to suggest it."

She smothered a chuckle. "Then I am more fortunate than I deserve."

He clutched her arm as they made their way out of the council house and across the plaza through the cold sleet. When they stood beneath the porch of the Bear Clan longhouse, Koracoo stopped.

"Let's speak of the important things out here."

He nodded. "Of course."

Her warm smile turned into a bleak tight-lipped expression. "First, I want you to know that I believe battle with Atotarho Village is a certainty."

"Why?"

"War Chief Hiyawento was just here. He came to deliver a message from the Hills Ruling Council."

"A threat, no doubt."

"Yes. They told us not to attempt to make any other alliances with Hills villages or they would destroy us. Many members of our Ruling Council believe that it is foolish to live in fear that they will carry out their threat, and wiser to attack them first."

Gonda bowed his head. "That would be a grave error. They will cut us up and lay us down like a summer hailstorm does the corn. Are you trying to talk sense into them?"

"Trying without much success."

"Is this just pride or—?"

"No, it's Sky Messenger's Dream."

For a long quiet moment, they gazed at each other. Between them lay many summers of warring side by side, of mad desperate passion, of two beloved children stolen and rescued and now grown to adulthood . . . so many intimate moments unthinkingly shared. And he could tell from the way she ground her teeth that she needed someone to talk to, someone she trusted.

Gonda said, "He Dreamed the end of the world, or so I've heard."

"He says that we must end this war, and if we do not, there is a great darkness coming."

With a touch of irony, he said, "You, naturally, believe that means making peace with our enemies. Matron Kittle, however, thinks it means annihilating them. Is that pretty much it?"

A small hard-edged smile curved her lips. "Pretty much."

Gonda squinted out across the plaza, watching the sleet fall. It bounced from the frozen ground as though alive. "With your mother gone, you will soon be the Yellowtail Village matron, won't you?"

"I have agreed to the Requickening Ceremony, yes. That's what the matrons were discussing in the council house."

"When will the ritual take place?"

"Tomorrow, midmorning."

He sighed. "Then this is the last day of our lives when I will be able to call you Koracoo. Tomorrow, you will become Matron Jigonsaseh. The following day you will have considerably more power to direct the future course of the nation."

Her expression tightened. "Village matrons have power in their own villages. In the Ruling Council, however, each voice is just one of many."

He remembered all the times he'd called her a "peacemaker" with loathing in his voice. Apparently, so did she. She had a guarded expression on her face, as though preparing to hear the same words she'd always heard from him.

Instead, he said, "Let me speak with what's left of the White Dog Village council. Perhaps I can convince them to back your peace efforts. The Spirits know we cannot win a war against the Hills People. There simply aren't enough of us to wage the fight."

When he looked back at her, he saw an unsettling mixture of relief and old love in her eyes. "I would like to have Bahna present Sky Messenger's vision to your council, if you think that would be acceptable."

"I'm sure they'd rather hear it from your lips, but I'll ask."

She walked forward and drew aside the entry curtain. Warm air rushed out, and when it struck his face, he shivered.

She said, "Let's tend to those who need us. Perhaps, if you are not too tired, we can speak more later."

"I'd like that."

Just before Gonda ducked through, Koracoo said, "Gonda, immediately after the Requickening, I'm leaving."

"Leaving? This is hardly the time for the new matron of Yellowtail Village to be away."

She gazed at him without blinking, as though worried how he was going to respond to what she was about to say. "Sky Messenger asked me to carry his vision to Chief Cord."

A tiny thread of old jealousy went through him, which amused him. It had been twelve long summers since she'd removed Gonda as her deputy war chief and installed Cord in his place. What did it matter now?

"Well," he said, "we need more warriors. If you can convince Cord to join us, even just for this battle, it will help."

She gave him a grateful smile, and Gonda ducked beneath the curtain and headed for Tutelo's chamber, where his ill wife rested.

Cord. Why did it have to be Cord?

Thirty

Four nights later, Taya and Sky Messenger made camp in the hollow of a toppled pine. The deep hole had been gouged when the old giant had blown over in a windstorm; it was filled with rocks and gravel and, in her opinion, created the worst place possible to try to sleep. They'd stowed their canoe, hidden it in a pile of brush along the river, and now were traveling on foot through the trackless wilderness of enemy territory.

As she arranged the kindling on the small island of dirt at the rear of the hole, she morosely glanced around. The hole, deeper than she was tall, didn't give her much to look at. High above, crooked pine roots zigzagged over her head, and beyond them, the campfires of the dead filled the sky and sparkled through the treetops. Her gaze drifted over the brush that fringed the rim of the hole—a mixture of ironwood saplings and dense holly. The forest canopy was luminous. Moonlight streamed between the sycamores, bleaching the bark where it struck or draping inky weblike shadows through the forest.

She couldn't see him, but she knew Sky Messenger was gathering wood. At night, he moved with the stealth of a cougar. Were it not for the occasional snapping of twigs, she wouldn't know he was out there. She couldn't hear Gitchi at all, but the wolf was at Sky Messenger's side. He always was.

Taya finished arranging the kindling, pulled her cape closely around her, and flopped back against the cold dirt wall. Rocks poked into her back. She shifted to avoid them.

When water starting soaking through her cape, Taya jerked forward and dragged the doeskin around to look at the wet spot. "Not only is this a rocky hole, it's oozing water!" She leaned forward and took a good look at the floor of the hole. All around the small island of dirt, water glistened.

"Wonderful. Just wonderful," she groaned. This was the most abominable place he'd yet chosen to camp. Was he trying to punish her for wanting to go home? This just made her long for the warmth of her longhouse even more.

The brush rattled softly as Sky Messenger shouldered through the holly and carefully worked his way down into the hole. The old gray-faced wolf came through behind him. Taya watched them with an annoyed expression on her face. Sky Messenger carried a small pile of branches in the crook of his left arm.

"That's not nearly enough wood," she complained. "There's water in this hole." She pointed to the puddles. "We'll have to build a really big fire to dry it out."

"We can't, Taya. We're in the middle of Hills country. Our fire will have to be very small. Even that is a risk. You can have my blanket tonight. I'll be plenty warm wrapped in my cape." Sky Messenger knelt and placed the wood beside her kindling. As he pulled his pack off and drew out the little pot where he kept coals from their morning fire, she frowned at him. Grandmother Moon cast a queer silvery sheen over his cape and hair, and threw the planes of his face into sharply contrasting arcs of gray and black. Sky Messenger carefully tucked the coals into her twig pile, added some dry leaves, and began blowing on the coals. It seemed to take forever before they reddened and flames licked through the tinder. She instantly extended her cold hands to the tiny blaze and sighed. "Thank the Spirits."

"Here, this will help." Sky Messenger reached into his pack and pulled out his carefully folded rabbit-fur blanket. Composed of worn, sewn-together rabbit pelts, it resembled a shabby patchwork. As he draped it over her shoulders, he said, "Why don't you also pull your blanket from your pack? Then you—"

"Please, do so."

He blinked as though annoyed about being ordered around like one of her slaves. He picked up her pack and tossed it at her. "I'm sure it's in there."

Indignant, she roughly rummaged through her pack and jerked out the wadded pine marten blanket. The thin strips of marten fur, woven tightly together, were beautiful, and kept her very warm. She tugged it over her shoulders.

Sky Messenger added twigs to build up the blaze, but it was barely a palm's width across.

"Why can't we make a bigger fire?"

As though irritated because he'd already explained, he said again, "We're in Hills country. A big fire will reflect from the trees and can be seen from a good distance. It will also produce a lot of smoke. The scent carries. On a dark night, billowing smoke wouldn't matter so much, but tonight there's a full moon. Streamers from a big fire would rise over the treetops and stretch out across the sky like a trail. Anyone could follow it to us."

"But a small fire will produce light and smoke, too."

"Yes, but not much, if it's built correctly. Down here in this hole, a small fire will be almost invisible to passersby, and what little smoke rises will be diffused by the breeze and the thick branches over our heads. If anyone gets close enough, they'll still smell the smoke. Every fire is a risk."

She cocked her head and thought about it. "That makes sense. I guess I'd rather be alive than warm."

"I'd rather you be alive, as well."

They sat in silence, listening to the crackling of the fire, while he set up the dinner pot. The size of two fists put together, the pot held barely enough to feed them both, but since he always cooked, she never complained. It was a little like being at home in the longhouse where the newly adopted war captives cooked for her family. She wondered if he realized that, and did it to make the nights easier for her, or if it was just his way. Because it was small, the pot did boil faster, which allowed them to get more sleep. She liked that.

Sky Messenger drew his chert knife from his belt and sliced up the squirrel they'd snared at dusk, letting pieces drop into the pot, occasionally tossing a piece to Gitchi. After he'd poured water over the top and set the pot at the edge of the flames to boil, he sat down cross-legged beside her. His black cape spread around him in sculpted folds.

"Are you certain you'll be warm enough without your blanket? I want you rested tomorrow."

He glanced up as though intrigued that she cared. "I'll be fine. I am accustomed to the cold."

He tossed another twig on the meager flames. Sparks sailed into the air. He frowned uneasily at them until they winked out amid the sycamore branches.

"Sky Messenger?" she said hesitantly. "This friend who saved you, the man we'll be stopping to see on the way home, who is he?"

Even pitched low, as it was tonight, his deep voice was startlingly beautiful. Gitchi eased down and propped his big muzzle in Sky Messenger's lap. Sky Messenger stroked his head. "He's a war chief. He taught me everything I know about honor and duty." More softly, he added, "And about self-sacrifice."

"Really?" She brightened. If he was a war chief, when they got there, they'd be feasted and showered with gifts. Her world was brightening. "I probably know him. Standing Stone war chiefs come to see Grandmother all the time. What's his name?"

"He's not Standing Stone, though he was born among our people."

It took a moment for her to digest this news. "You can't mean . . . Are you trying to tell me that we're going to walk into an enemy village without a war party at our backs?"

"I think we'll be all right."

"You *think?*"

He leaned against the dirt wall and worked to find a comfortable position before he replied, "I can't be sure. I haven't seen him in a long while. And it won't be easy getting close to his village. But if we make it, I think he will protect us."

"What nation is he?" Her eyes slitted.

"He was adopted by the People of the Hills. The woman he loved was there. He went to her. They have three beautiful daughters." While he scratched Gitchi's ears, he gazed at the moon-glittered water that pooled between the rocks in the bottom of the hole. "I am happy for them, though I miss them very much."

Indignantly, she said, "And is your mother happy that you are friends with an enemy war chief? She was once a great Standing Stone war chief. Doesn't it worry her?"

"I'm sure it does." Love and respect softened his voice. "Especially now that she is the Speaker for the Women."

"And she will soon be the Yellowtail Village matron."

"I suspect she will, yes."

When his grandmother, Jigonsaseh, journeyed to the afterlife, the matrons of the Bear Clan would almost certainly cast their voices to requicken Jigonsaseh's soul in her daughter, Koracoo.

"We will all mourn the loss of your grandmother," Taya said sincerely. "She is a great leader. Matron Jigonsaseh must have been distressed when you told her you were giving up your weapons for good, and—"

"I haven't told her. The one time I got to speak with Grandmother . . . I had more pressing concerns. I needed her advice."

He seemed to be concentrating on the twinkling campfires of the dead.

Or perhaps he was assessing how much smoke from their fire was escaping through the treetops into the sky beyond.

"Her advice about what?"

"My . . . treason."

"So this was before your clan heard your vision?" It must have been, since afterward they'd absolved him of the crime, but his expression appeared uncertain.

He pulled a horn spoon from his pack and bent over the cook pot, stirring it. The delicious smell of boiling squirrel wafted into the air. As the rising steam coated his tanned face, it seemed to flow into the lines at the corners of his eyes, making them appear deeper.

"It won't be long now," he said in a mild voice. "You must be starving. We've been canoeing hard, and we walked a long way today."

He kept staring down into the pot, stirring it, and she tried to fathom what he could possibly be thinking. He looked like he wanted to tell her something, but had decided against it. And she had the feeling it was more than just his discussion with Jigonsaseh about his treason. He was hiding something. His gaze had that haunted look that was becoming so familiar. He was no longer here with her, but traveling some war trail in the past. Perhaps, with *her*.

"You're dreaming about her again, aren't you? Do you wish she was here, instead of me?"

He looked up. The moonlight sheathed his eyes with such strength she could see her own reflection. "She *is* here. They all are." He touched his cape over his heart. "My friends never leave me."

"I don't understand what that means. I don't see them here."

His brows lifted, as though not surprised; then he drew wooden cups and another spoon from his pack. "Let's eat so that we can get some rest."

As he ladled soup into the cups, Gitchi watched him, perhaps hoping for the last dregs. Taya took the cup Sky Messenger handed her, and her gaze wandered as she blew on the hot stew to cool it. Just when she started to sip, she saw something in the branches overhead. Her cup halted halfway to her lips. "Did you see that?"

"Hmm? What?" he asked around a half-chewed a bite of squirrel.

An eerie chill prickled her spine. She went very still, as though her body sensed a predator nearby, even if her eyes didn't see one. The moonlit sycamore limbs seemed unusually bright against the night sky. Faint tendrils of smoke threaded the canopy, but nothing seemed amiss. Gitchi, however, silently rose to his feet and stared at the same place in the canopy.

Sky Messenger instantly set his cup down and followed Gitchi's gaze.

His brow furrowed as he examined the trees. Barely above a whisper, he repeated, "What did you see, Taya?"

"Probably just one of Grandmother Moon's tricks. A flicker of light, nothing more."

That didn't seem to soothe him. He stared at her fixedly, not blinking. "A flicker of light?"

"Well, yes." A breath of wind swirled around the hole, and the flames leaped, casting a gaudy gleam over his concerned face. "It was nothing, Sky Messenger. Just eat. I'm sorry I said anything." She took a drink of her squirrel soup, swallowing a chunk of squirrel whole, and forced a smile.

This time, he didn't smile back. "What color was the light?"

"I don't know, bluish, like a string of tarnished copper beads—"

In less than a heartbeat, he'd leaped to his feet and kicked dirt over the tiny blaze to smother it. Gitchi seemed to have turned to stone. Only his eyes moved as he watched Sky Messenger part the holly to stare out at the forest beyond.

Taya set her cup down, rose, and went to Sky Messenger's side, whispering, "Did you hear something?"

He patted his lips with his hand, instructing her to be silent.

She had to stand on her tiptoes to see through the dense brush. Out among the forest shadows, she thought she made out the dark looming shapes of deer running the trail. It was a small herd, perhaps six or seven animals. She squinted as one animal veered closer to their hiding place. It must be a large buck for it . . . Against the tracery of black shadows, the elusive wink of moonlight flashed on shell.

Her breathing died.

Sky Messenger used a hand to gesture for her to be perfectly still, but it was unnecessary. She'd already gone rigid.

The figure moved as though not tethered to the ground, drifting through the moonlight like one of the Flying Heads. Awful creatures, they were just heads with long trailing hair and huge paws that were continually grasping at things, for they were forever hungry. Or it might be one of the *oki,* Spirits who inhabited Powerful beings, including the seven Thunderers, rivers, certain rocks, valiant warriors, and sometimes lunatics. Even shamans, witches, or others who possessed supernatural Power had a companion oki that helped them.

Taya kept her eyes on the figure. The only sounds in the night were the soft hissing of her breathing and the panicked hammering of her heart.

Moonlight caught in the shell beads sewn to his cape, and there was a prolonged glimmer. Was he examining the brush where they hid?

The hair at the nape of her neck felt like it was on fire.

Warriors. Had they followed them from Bog Willow Village? Other shadows closed around the first. From the bristly ridge of hair down the center of their scalps, all but one were of the Flint People. The last man, the man with long black hair, hung at the rear. It was difficult to see him. The warriors hissed to each other and sniffed the breeze.

Taya turned to . . .

Sky Messenger hissed, *"Not one word."*

She had to lock her knees to keep standing. There was something horrifying about the sudden quiet. It was unnatural. The wind had stopped. The silvered branches resembled thousands of ancient knobby fingers reaching down to grab her, and Gitchi stood like a grass-stuffed dog skin, his unblinking yellow eyes on Sky Messenger.

The lead warrior said, "I don't see anything. I thought you said they'd be here. Isn't this the place your *hanehwa* told you about?"

Taya shuddered. Hanehwa were human skins that had been flayed whole by a witch and served as guards. These skin-beings never slept. They warned witches of danger by giving three shouts.

There was a pause; then the man with long black hair replied, "They're here. Somewhere close by."

Another warrior said, "You've been saying that for days. I was sure I smelled smoke, but I don't smell anything now."

"You imagined it," the lead man said, and swung his war club up to rest on his shoulder. "Come on. Let's keep searching. I want to get home before dawn."

Their words affected her bones like war clubs, striking and trembling them until she felt certain her skeleton would splinter to dust. A witch was hunting them, sending out his hanehwa to fly over the land and bring back information about their movements. That's the only thing it could mean. When she knew she was going to collapse from sheer terror, Sky Messenger slipped an arm around her shoulders and physically held her up. All she could do was squeeze her eyes closed and lean heavily against him.

Finally, she heard their steps moving away and held her breath, listening for voices. When they seemed to be gone, her fingernails dug into Sky Messenger's cape. He wrapped his arms around her and hugged her tightly.

"It's all right," he whispered. "They're gone. We're all right."

Terrified beyond rational thought, she stood dumbly, feeling the hard muscles of his thighs pressing against her and the large shell gorget he wore beneath his cape crushing her breasts. A strange sensation, bewildering and frightening, came over her. Her thin body rigid with fury, she wildly slammed her fists into his chest, and just above a whisper, wept, "If you'd had weapons, I wouldn't have been so afraid! At least you could have kept a few of them busy while I made a run for it! Let me go, you *coward*!"

Rage and hate flowed into her. She wrenched her body from his arms, and her quaking knees instantly buckled. She collapsed to the ground in tears and sat there with her shoulders heaving, not making a sound. Dear gods, she wanted to be home!

Sky Messenger took one last look out at the forest. When he seemed certain they were truly gone, he knelt before her and lightly touched her hair, stroking it comfortingly. "We're going to be all right."

"How can you say that? We're being hunted by a witch! Didn't you understand that?"

"I've been hunted by witches before. We're going to be fine."

She wiped her eyes on her cape. "How could you escape a witch? They have armies of hanehwa and gahai, and—"

"Just do as I say, and we'll make it home. Can you stand up?"

"Of course I can." She rose on shaky legs.

He whispered, "The last man in line, the one with long black hair and big ears, looked over his shoulder again as they left. He wasn't satisfied with the decision to move on. He may return to search this spot."

She scrambled for her pack. Sky Messenger kept watch while she hastily packed their things. His face was grim, and for the first time she saw the sweat pouring down his temples. It had glued his black hair to his cheeks.

"Why is a witch hunting us, Sky Messenger?"

With a warrior's deadly agility, he climbed out of the hole and extended a hand to her. Gitchi slid past her leg like warm smoke and eased through the holly. She reached for Sky Messenger's hand.

As he pulled her up, he whispered, "Evil needs no reason."

Thirty-one

Sky Messenger

I quietly examine the dark shapes that fill the forest. The warriors are gone, but there is still something out there. I catch glimpses of it as it moves between the trees, pale and flickering. One of the gahai?

"What are we waiting for?" Taya asks.

"There's something I need to look at more closely."

"What do you mean?" She grips my sleeve in terror.

"Just wait here for me. If you see anything suspicious, dive back in that hole. I won't be long."

As I trot for the place I saw the light, she calls, "Don't get out of my sight? Do you hear me? I want to be able to see you at all times!"

I lift a hand, showing that I've heard, and slow down to enter the thick trees. Gitchi moves at my side with ghostly stealth. When the wolf utters a barely audible growl, I subtly turn to look in the direction he's pointing.

As soon as my eyes adjust, I see them. Two small balls of light wander close to the ground. Prior to two moons ago, I'd never seen such things. Since then, I've seen more than I wish to, most floating aimlessly around destroyed villages.

"They aren't gahai," I whisper to Gitchi.

Gahai move purposely, in straight lines, because they always know where they are going. These lights float in one direction, then another, clearly confused.

I tiptoe forward and lean my shoulder against the trunk of a gigantic hickory to watch them. A herd of four deer emerge from the trees and keep watch on the lights, trailing them as they head into a narrow clearing surrounded by plum trees. The bucks are young. Their forked antlers blaze whitely when they pass through the thin bars of moonlight.

Gitchi has probably always seen lost souls roaming the forests, but it is relatively new to me. I am fascinated, still learning about them.

I shift against the hickory trunk, and the scent of wet bark rises. These lights are tiny, barely larger than my thumb. Are they the lost souls of children?

The two lights bob into the meadow with the deer trotting behind them. When the bucks can see the sky clearly, they playfully kick up their hooves and charge headlong for the glowing balls. The souls seem to understand. I sense a happiness in the air, or perhaps it is relief that someone has found them. They hover perfectly still, allowing the bucks to scoop them into their antlers and toss them into the air, high over the treetops.

In awe, I watch them climb into the night sky until they disappear among the glittering campfires of the dead that crowd the Path of Souls.

"They're on their way now."

Yes, as you should be.

The words are so soft I'm not sure whether I actually heard them, or if they exist only in my souls. When moccasins crunch the dry leaves to my right, I turn slowly.

He stands four paces away, with his gaze focused on the bucks in the meadow. There is an eerie quality to the man, a stillness so complete it is as though he has been standing beside me unnoticed all my life, just waiting for me to see him. His pale hands are folded in front of him. Against his black cape they appear pure white. He wears sandals, apparently immune to the cold, or perhaps it is warm where he stands. He seems to be looking around the forest, and sadness pervades the air.

"Why are you here?" I ask.

"The cold."

"I don't understand."

His cape waffles as though touched by wind, though I do not feel a breeze.

"The cold has worked its way into the hearts of all living creatures and twined around the roots of the sycamores and oaks. It's killing us all. Especially him."

"Who?"

The Voice is unsettlingly soft: *"He has no afterlife soul. She locked it in her soul pot."*

Deep inside me, memories flash. The tormented faces of children.

Terror congeals like the impact of an arrow. "Are you talking about Hehaka?"

Twelve summers ago, the old woman who held us captive used an eagle-bone sucking tube to suck out the boy's afterlife soul. Hehaka. Zateri's brother. He'd seen eleven summers. She blew Hehaka's soul into a pot where she imprisoned the souls of anyone who crossed her. The old woman used the pot to threaten Hehaka, telling him to do as she ordered, or when he died she'd take his soul far away and release it to wander among enemy ghosts for eternity.

Suddenly, I understand. "Are you saying that Hehaka is the witch who's hunting me? Was he the man with the Flint warriors?"

"You know where it is."

He says the words with a strange serenity far more frightening than a shout.

"The pot? Yes, I—"

"He needs it."

I shake my head. "Is that why he became a witch? Is that what you're telling me? His afterlife soul is still locked in that pot?"

The Voice moves its pale hands, reclasps them. It is an inhuman gesture, as quiet as the frost. *"Help him."*

"Help Hehaka?" I say angrily. "Why? Don't you recall that he betrayed us to the old woman? I hope I never see him again. For many summers, I prayed he was dead."

He turns toward me. Inside his hood is only darkness. Both Tutelo and Wrass have seen his face. Why won't he show it to me? Just empty blackness fills the space where eyes, nose, and mouth should be.

"If you are to find brothers in all human beings, you must start with the most abandoned. There's something you've forgotten. He has not."

I become acutely conscious of the blood pounding in my ears. Memories struggle to rise. Images burst in my mind like bubbles on a pond—I'm back in the clearing with the other children. . . .

Wrass asks, *"Do you know what they'll do to you if they catch you?"*

Zateri lowers her eyes, and her face flushes. "I'm not going to lie to you. I'm scared to death of what they'll do . . . mostly scared of what they'll do before they kill me. But I can stand it, Wrass. If I know you're all safe, I can stand anything."

A faint smile touches Wrass' lips. "What if one of us gets injured escaping? He will need you and your Healing knowledge. I think you're the only one of us who is not expendable, Zateri."

Zateri's mouth quivers. "But I—"

"You're too valuable. Not you, Zateri."

He does not look my way, but I feel Wrass thinking about me. Waiting for me to speak.

Baji sits up straighter, girding herself, and smooths long black hair away from her face. She knows from firsthand experience what the warriors will do to her before they kill her. How can she volunteer?

Baji says, "Me. I'm the one, Wrass. I'll do it."

"You?" I say in panic. "Why—"

Wrass grasps my arm to stop me from continuing. He nods at Baji. "Baji may be the only one of us who can get close enough."

"Why do you think that?" I demand to know.

With tears in her eyes, Baji answers, "Because, silly boy, I'm beautiful. I can make the men want me enough that they'll carry me right into their camp and sit me down by the stew pot. No matter what happens, by the end of the night, I will have dumped the Spirit plants in that pot." Her eyes are stony, resolved to do what must be done.

I . . .

The Voice intrudes: *"It wasn't your fault. You must stop blaming yourself because you did not volunteer. If you had, well . . . we wouldn't be standing here now."*

The emotion in the words never touches the glassy stillness of his tall body. He remains oddly motionless, as if eternity has taught him that, like the white hare hidden in the snow, survival rests in closing your eyes and freezing as solid as the drift.

When I do not respond, he turns and starts walking away through the trees.

I clench my fists. "If I can, I will help Hehaka."

He stops. His back is to me. His hood moves in a nod, which is at best a faint imitation of an earthly gesture.

As I watch him blend with the night, there is an instant of terrible certainty where I know my Spirit Helper is an evil monster in disguise, a deceiver biding its time, waiting to leap until its chosen prey grows careless. I don't believe I'm his prey . . . but I sense that I am important for his final kill.

Or perhaps I am just frightened. All men are bound in the swaddling clothes of their deepest fears, and the truth is that I am more afraid of the dead now than the living. Dancing soul lights, Spirit Helpers, ghosts— they are far more my world today than the land of the living.

Twigs crack, and I glance back over my shoulder at Taya. She has crouched down beside the toppled pine and is studying me. Waiting impatiently for me. She is certain I am mad. I can see it when she looks at me. Of course, she isn't alone. I heard many people at the betrothal feast whispering behind their hands that the last battle was too much for me. They said it had driven my afterlife soul from my body, leaving an empty husk of a man.

Taya stands up, obviously wondering what's taking me so long. My fingers lower to gently pet Gitchi's head. "Let's go back, old friend," I whisper, and the wolf trots for Taya.

I gaze longingly at the Path of Souls for a time, imagining what that brilliant glittering silence must be like. Like all men, sometimes I yearn for it.

"Come on!" Taya says.

I walk back.

Taya clutches my sleeve as though her life depends upon it. "Let's go." I say, "We must be very quiet."

"I will."

This time I think she finally understands.

Ohsinoh stepped from the cold shadows of the boulder, and the night breeze blew his long black hair around his triangular face. He smoothed the locks behind his oversized ears. The Flint warriors he'd been traveling with were long gone, headed home. The only other human sounds in the forest were the soft voices of the two people on the trail ahead of him. He knew Sky Messenger. He'd been watching him, dogging his path, since they were children, though he doubted Sky Messenger had the slightest idea.

They were only thirty paces in front of Ohsinoh. He had to be cautious. His enemies said he had ears like a bat, but Sky Messenger's hearing was even better. It had been honed by many summers on the war trail when missing a strange sound could have cost him his life.

He glanced around, wondering what had happened to his gahai. Had the deer and the lost souls scared them away?

With the stealth of a big cat, he moved from tree trunk to tree trunk, hiding long enough to listen to the forest. Finally, lights flickered to his right, out in the trees. When he turned to look at them, they sped away, heading straight for Sky Messenger.

He smiled and followed.

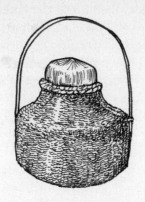

Thirty-two

As the two warriors dipped their paddles to steer around the bend in the river, the canoe rocked beneath Koracoo and water slapped the hull, shooting spray over her white hood and cape. She wiped the drops from her face and returned her gaze to the shoreline, searching the maples and red cedars, expecting to see a war party emerge at any instant. Despite the fact that she'd sent a runner ahead with a white arrow, she kept Corpse-Eye resting across her lap, just in case. She didn't trust the Flint People to honor the request. In fact, it would not surprise her to find her runner's body on display, lying gutted on the bank, when she arrived.

Pale pink shards of broken dusk light scattered over the river, twinkling and shifting as Wind Mother touched the branches that overhung the water. Koracoo—*no, I am Jigonsaseh now*—Jigonsaseh took a few moments to appreciate them before her thoughts returned to the Flint People.

After they started bickering last summer, their alliance dissolved, and the relationship between the Standing Stone and Flint peoples had gone from bad to worse. It had started with war parties clashing on the trails, then a few raids where warriors had attacked people harvesting crops and stolen their food, and finally they'd fallen upon each other like wolves. When the Ruling Council had ordered War Chief Deru and Deputy Sky Messenger to attack a Flint Village, there had been no going back.

The low harsh *kak-kak-kak* of a gyrfalcon sounded overhead. She looked up. Against the pastel evening sky, the bird's sleek body resembled an arrow in flight as it plummeted toward the ground. Every other bird in the forest launched itself heavenward, flocking together for protection. The air was suddenly filled with warning chirps and batting wings. When the gyrfalcon disappeared into a copse of oaks, the flocks of smaller birds seemed to calm down. In barely ten heartbeats the sky was empty again, except for three ducks circling over the glassy river ahead.

Deputy Wampa, kneeling in the bow, lifted her nose and scented the air. She wore a slate gray cape painted with brown spirals that blended with the leafless trees and brush. The morning dew had glued her shoulder-length black hair to her cheeks, making her nose seem wider and her lips more narrow. "Matron Jigonsaseh? Do you—?"

"Yes, Deputy. I smell the smoke." She could also hear the far-off sounds of the village: people chopping wood, dogs barking. Her fist went tight around the smooth wooden shaft of CorpseEye. He was cool in her hand, which made her nervous. CorpseEye always grew warm when there was danger or he was trying to show her something. How could there not be danger ahead?

A short while later, warriors appeared on the right bank and ran along the river trail, paralleling her canoe. They carried nocked bows, but the bows were not aimed at her. Instead, the warriors' gazes scanned the trees, as though searching for anyone who might wish to do Koracoo and her party harm.

"What do you make of that?" Wampa said.

From the rear of the canoe, Jonsoc replied, "It looks like they're here to protect us. I'm intrigued. Maybe my relatives won't have to requicken my soul in another body after all."

"Don't get overconfident," Koracoo warned. "It could be a ruse to make us feel safe."

"Yes," Wampa agreed. "It's a lot easier to hack people to pieces when they're inside your palisade than outside where they can run."

As they came around the curve in the river, Koracoo saw the crowd at the canoe landing. There had to be thirty people.

"What's this?" Wampa hissed, and her eyes narrowed.

"I don't know, but I don't like it," Jonsoc said.

"Wait," Koracoo breathed, and clutched CorpseEye tighter.

Standing near the front of the assembly was a tall man with a black roach of hair down the middle of his shaved head. As the canoe slid closer, she could see the snake tattoos on his cheeks. He'd seen forty-one summers now, and had moved up through the ranks from war chief to the Chief of Wild River Village. He wore a black cape decorated with turtle shell carvings, symbols of his clan.

When Jonsoc dragged his paddle, steering them toward the landing, Chief Cord walked out of the crowd and down to the water's edge. As the canoe came slapping in over the waves, Cord reached out, grasped the bow, and dragged it ashore.

Wampa leaped out first and stood beside Cord with her hand on her belted war club while she gave him threatening looks. "You are Chief Cord?" she asked.

"Yes, warrior."

Wampa extended a hand. "May I present the esteemed matron of Yellowtail Village, Matron Jigonsaseh."

Cord's gaze warmed when he looked at her. She gave him a small smile, for old times' sake, and he walked forward and extended a hand to help her from the canoe. Jigonsaseh took it and stepped onto the sand. He must have been standing outside waiting for her for a long time. His grip was iron and ice. The knife scar that cut across his jaw had puckered from the cold, and his long pointed nose was flushed.

In a deep voice, he greeted, "You are welcome in Wild River Village, Kor . . . Forgive me, Matron Jigonsaseh."

"It's all right, Chief. It is new to me as well."

He nodded. "My warriors have orders to protect you and your guards with their lives. We have prepared chambers for you, if you wish to spend the night here."

"That is gracious. We will consider it."

"Good. If you'll follow me, I'll escort you to the council house."

Jigonsaseh turned and handed CorpseEye to Wampa. "Please take care of him while I am gone."

Wampa took the legendary war club. Her eyes widened, as though she felt his Spirit tingling her fingertips; then her gaze shot back to Jigonsaseh. "Gone? What do you mean, gone?"

"I want you and Jonsoc to remain with the canoe until I return."

Wampa's mouth fell open. "But, Matron, you need a guard! What if they—?"

"I trust the chief," she said with soft, implacable precision, and started bravely walking through the enemy crowd toward the palisade gates.

The villagers pushed and shoved each other trying to get closer, to see her. No Standing Stone matron, least of all a member of the Ruling Council, had ever set foot in Wild River Village. Their expressions were mixtures of awe and suspicion, but there was an undercurrent she didn't quite grasp. They were too calm. Not a single stone had been hurled yet. If a Flint matron had suddenly appeared in Yellowtail Village asking to meet with the chief, Jigonsaseh would have had to order half her warriors to encircle the matron for protection and had the other half put down the violent protests.

Cord walked easily at her side. His voice was measured and peaceful, a little reproving. "If you'd come earlier, I doubt our alliance would have collapsed."

"I couldn't have done much, old friend. Four moons ago, I was not in a position to influence war policy. As Speaker for the Women, I only relayed decisions."

His gaze scanned the black bear paws on her white cape. "That has changed, I see. I was saddened to hear of your mother's death. She was a strong, courageous leader."

She turned. Very few men were as tall as she. It was strange to look at someone eye-to-eye. "You didn't have to say that. It was kind, especially given what happened at Flatwoods Village."

His bushy black brows drew together. "That is something we will speak of, I hope."

"Yes."

As they neared the upright log palisade, he lifted a hand and warriors scurried to pull back the heavy gates. The men and women on the catwalk watched her with tight eyes, but not a single weapon shifted in her direction. Koracoo nodded in admiration.

"Your warriors are well trained."

"I take that as a compliment to my war chief. She will be pleased to hear you said that."

Cord guided her across the plaza, where children stood staring at her with frightened eyes, but the women calmly continued pounding corn in hollow logs. A few old men reclined against the longhouse walls, enjoying the last warmth of the day, smiling as they talked. Jigonsaseh studied the four longhouses. They were around three hundred hands long, arranged in a square around the plaza. Covered with white birch bark, the longhouses had a pearlescent sheen in the evening glow. Several smaller houses dotted the edges of the plaza. Cord was leading her toward the circular house that stood straight across from the central fire. Two warriors waited outside, standing guard.

"Warn me," she said. "Who will I be meeting with?"

"Myself, Village Matron Buckshen, who is also the matron of the Turtle Clan, Wolf Clan matron Gahela, and Bear Clan matron Kiska. Others may be called in as necessary."

"Has Matron Buckshen given you any indication of whether she views my mission favorably or unfavorably?"

"I think our entire village council wishes to hear Sky Messenger's vision."

Jigonsaseh breathed a quiet sigh of relief. Often such councils turned into shouting matches where both sides hurled accusations. She prayed that would not be so tonight.

Cord halted. "Before we enter the council, may I ask you something?"

"Of course."

"Why did you choose Wild River Village? You could have gone to more prestigious and powerful Flint villages. Why here?"

"I didn't make the choice, Cord. Sky Messenger asked me to come here. But I believe he selected your village because of you. Despite the horrors between our peoples, he has trusted you since he was a child. He respects you a great deal."

"And I him." He drew back the leather door curtain and gestured for her to enter.

She ducked inside. For a time, all she could see was the shaft of light pouring through the smoke hole over the fire pit; then, as her eyes adjusted, she saw the three women sitting on benches around the fire. They all wore red capes, but each was uniquely painted with the clan images of turtles, wolves, and bears.

"Let me introduce you," Cord said.

As she followed him across the hard-packed floor, she looked at the sacred False Face masks on the walls. Their crooked noses and misshapen mouths were expertly carved and painted. She could sense their Spirits watching her, judging her. When she gazed into their empty eye sockets, she wondered what conclusions they'd come to.

Cord walked sunwise around the fire and halted between Matron Buckshen and Matron Kiska. "Allow me to present Matron Jigonsaseh of the Bear Clan in Yellowtail Village, and member of the Ruling Council of the Standing Stone nation."

She bowed deeply to the matrons. They dipped their heads in return. "Thank you for agreeing to meet with me."

Matron Buckshen stared at her. White turtles painted her red cape. Perhaps sixty summers old, a white haze covered her eyes. She must be half-blind, but she had a kind face, round and deeply wrinkled, framed by thin gray hair. Buckshen extended a hand to the empty bench to her right. "Please sit down, Matron Jigonsaseh. You have been on the water many days and must be very tired."

"Thank you. I am." She seated herself, and her white cape fell into soft folds around her feet. She took a few moments to study Gahela and Kiska.

Around forty summers, both had black hair, but silver threads shone in Gahela's. The matron of the Wolf clan, Gahela, had slitted brown eyes and a hard mouth. She looked at Koracoo with her jaw set. Kiska of the Bear clan, however, appeared relaxed, even happy to see Koracoo—which she doubted. It was probably just that Kiska's thin childlike face and soft brown eyes gave her a friendly appearance.

Cord seated himself across the fire from her, on the bench beside Kiska, and said, "Please tell us why you've come, Matron Jigonsaseh."

She took a deep breath, preparing herself. The fragrance of burning hickory encircled her. "My son, Sky Messenger, asked that I come to you. He—"

"You are his mother," Matron Buckshen softly said, "but we are his People."

Jigonsaseh's eyes narrowed, confused. "Forgive me. I assumed that after he returned to Yellowtail Village and became a deputy war chief for our nation that you would have considered him to be a traitor and un-adopted him."

"No," Kiska said. "In fact, many of our people consider him to be a hero."

Jigonsaseh sat back on the bench and looked to Cord for some sort of explanation.

He turned to Matron Buckshen. "If you will allow me, Matron?" When she nodded, he continued, "After the Flatwoods Village battle, your son shoved a log into the river, told our women and children to grab hold, and then he led the enemy warriors away. He risked his own life to save them. Many of the survivors came here, to Wild River Village. Those women and children speak his name with great reverence."

Matron Kiska added, "Without Dekanawida, the man you call Sky Messenger, they would be dead or serving as slaves in enemy nations."

Matron Buckshen shifted on the bench, and all eyes turned to her. "You see, after hearing their stories, we realized that he had never turned his back on his adopted nation. Instead, he'd been serving our people the entire time."

Koracoo felt a little bewildered. She wasn't sure she liked the idea that they believed her son had been acting as a spy in the Standing Stone nation. But if it helped her today . . .

"It was at that battle," she said respectfully, "that the Spirits of your relatives came to him." The matrons went silent, listening intently, and the crackling of the fire seemed louder. "Just before he released the women and children, the Spirits of the dead rose up from the battlefield and encircled him. Hundreds of bobbing soul lights followed him to where the captives were being held, and guarded him while he made sure they got away. After they were safe, Sky Messenger's Spirit Helper called him into the forest, where he was tormented with Spirit Dreams for many days. Visions of our future."

Almost breathlessly, Matron Buckshen said, "We have heard the stories the Traders tell, but did not know how much to believe. As you know, Traders are not always reliable. They like to embellish to make the stories more entertaining."

Koracoo smiled. "Yes. I know."

Her voice light and disinterested, Matron Gahela asked, "So is the world really going to end?"

A log in the fire split, and green flames erupted from the crack. Jigonsaseh watched them until they faded to amber again. "When Sky Messenger's Dream begins, he can't feel his body, just the air cooling as the color drains from the world, leaving it gray and shimmering. A great cloud-sea moves beneath his feet, a restless dark ocean punctured by a great tree with flowers of pure light—"

"The World Tree," Kiska whispered. Her eyes are bright and alert.

"Hush, Kiska," Matron Buckshen said. "Let her finish."

"Oh, forgive me."

Jigonsaseh waited a few instants before continuing, ". . . punctured by a great tree whose roots sink through Great Grandmother Earth and plant themselves upon the back of the Great Tortoise floating in the primeval ocean below. Suddenly, the birds in the trees tuck their beaks beneath their wings, roosting in broad daylight, and butterflies secret themselves in the clouds at his feet. A strange silence descends."

The matrons shifted. Kiska leaned forward, bracing her elbows on her knees, while Buckshen inhaled a deep breath. Gahela just stared at Koracoo with a sour expression.

"Dimly, Sky Messenger, Dekanawida, becomes aware that he is not alone. Gray shades drift through the air around him, and he knows they are the last congregation, the dead who still walk and breathe. A voice calls his name, and he turns. Beyond the cloud-sea a darkness rises and slithers along the horizon. Strange black curls, like gigantic antlers, spin from the darkness and rake—"

"Horned Serpent?" Kiska hissed, then clapped a hand to her mouth and looked apologetically at Buckshen. "Sorry."

"Please go on, Matron Jigonsaseh," Buckshen instructed.

Jigonsaseh focused on the fire. The red coals winked as the flames danced. "The antlers rake the bellies of the Cloud People, and Elder Brother Sun trembles in the sky. There is a brilliant flash, and white feathers sprout from his edges. As he flies away into a black hole in the sky, a crack sounds, and when Sky Messenger looks down, he sees a great pine tree pushing up through Great Grandmother Earth. As it grows, its white roots stretch out to the four directions, and a snowy blanket of thistledown rains upon the world." She hesitated, not sure she wished to tell them the whole Dream. "Then the Dream bursts, and for a time there is only blinding light. Finally, Sky Messenger sees the flowers of the World Tree fluttering down, down, and he falls through a hole in the cloud-sea, and keeps falling, tumbling through nothingness surrounded by petals of pure light. Wisps of cloud trail behind him."

When she stopped, she looked up and found Matron Buckshen's white-filmed eyes on something insubstantial, perhaps living the Dream. The other two matrons contemplatively stared at the fire. Then Matron Kiska closed her eyes with desperate effort, as though to blot out the images. Only Cord was looking at her, and he had a slight frown on his handsome face.

"That is his Dream."

"And what does Dekanawida make of this Dream?" Buckshen asked.

Jigonsaseh wasn't accustomed to his Flint name yet. It took her a moment to answer. "He thinks our war is killing Great Grandmother Earth and will cause Elder Brother Sun to turn his back on us. He wants the war to stop."

Matron Gahela's eyes went strange, almost accusatory. "Are you trying to talk us into another alliance? The last one didn't work out too well. Many of our people are dead. Ask the survivors of Flatwoods Village. They—"

"Gahela," Buckshen softly chastised. "We all grieve with you over the loss of your relatives, but—"

"*She* does not grieve with me." Gahela's eyes blazed at Jigonsaseh.

Jigonsaseh calmly returned her gaze. "I was not a member of the Ruling Council at the time, Matron Gahela. If I had been, I assure you I would have voted no. We had no cause to attack Flatwoods Village. It was a bad decision, and I grieve both for your losses and ours."

That seemed to somewhat mollify Gahela. She lowered her eyes but continued to grind her teeth.

Buckshen said, "What does Dekanawida wish us to do to end the war?"

"He said to tell you that there will come a time in the very near future when we must tie our people together again to fight for peace. He asks that you consider joining us, and if you agree, then you should prepare yourselves. He will send a messenger when he needs you to join the fight."

"When will that be?"

"I cannot say." She sat back on the bench and heaved a breath. "When I left Yellowtail Village we were preparing to attack Atotarho Village. I pray that is not the battle my son needs you for. I suspect it will be long and bloody."

Kiska blinked owlishly. "But what if it is? Atotarho is an evil sorcerer. His witchery has killed many of our children, and his warriors have killed the rest! If we band together to destroy him, will that stop Elder Brother Sun from turning his back on us?"

Matron Gahela snorted disdainfully. "You're not thinking, Kiska. Dekanawida's request makes no sense. He says he wants us join the Standing Stone nation to fight for peace. Does that mean he wishes to fight, or not to fight?"

Buckshen said, "That is a good question. Matron Jigonsaseh?"

Koracoo gestured uncertainly. "I'm no Dreamer, Matrons. Just a Dreamer's messenger. I leave all interpretations up to you. But I suspect, sooner than any of us wish, we will all know the answer to that question."

Buckshen tilted her head, and the firelight reflected from her white-filmed eyes, turning them into amber mirrors. "The council will need to deliberate on this matter; then we must seek the opinions of our clans."

"I understand. I will return to my own village and await your decision. I thank you with all my heart for agreeing to hear my son's Dream." She stood and bowed deeply to the council members.

Cord stood up. "Matron Jigonsaseh, if it would not delay your journey, I would offer you something to eat and drink. Our village makes an excellent walnut bread."

She dipped her head in gratitude. "I would very much enjoy that."

She and Cord walked across the council house to the door curtain.

When they stepped outside, the light had changed. A lavender veil had fallen over the land and with it, a hush. The village was calm, the warriors on the catwalk unconcerned.

"Well," Jigonsaseh asked. "What do you think?"

"I think they're worried this is a trick. But I also suspect they believe you."

She jerked a nod. "I wish Sky . . . Dekanawida . . . could have been here to present his vision himself. They would have had no doubts."

"Maybe."

There was an awkward moment where neither of them said anything.

Then Cord gestured to the closest longhouse. "I had hoped you could spend an extra hand of time here. My niece has already prepared supper for us, and carried food to your warriors. Will you join me?"

She smiled. "Yes, thank you."

The warmth in his eyes caught her off guard. How was it possible that the old attraction between them had not died in the past twelve summers of war?

The two of them, enemies, made a strange pair as they walked across the plaza—he dressed in black, she in white, talking like the old friends they were.

Thirty-three

Sky Messenger

Wind Mother rampages through the twilight forest, whipping my black cape so wildly that I can scarcely walk. Taya is having an even tougher time. She has her thin willowy body leaned into the gale, but is still stumbling. I walk back and take her hand, helping steady her steps as we plod toward White Dog Village. I need to see my father, Gonda, to hear the gossip. I especially need to know if War Chief Hiyawento is out on the war trail. If so, I needn't risk traveling to Coldspring Village.

Taya asks, "Do you smell that?" Despite the wind, she's been trying very hard to keep her voice low.

"Yes." The faintest hint of smoke rides the air.

I lead her off the main path and onto a narrow deer trail that slithers between trees and massive head-high boulders. All around us, the forest shrieks and branches crash together. A constant shower of leaves and twigs pelts our faces and capes. Taya has one arm up to protect her eyes.

"Sky Messenger?" Her voice is almost lost in the gale. "How much farther to White Dog Village?"

"By now we should see the firelight reflecting—" I stop suddenly and sniff the wind again. "Blessed gods," I say when the distinct scent of burning longhouses reaches me. "Stay here! Gitchi, don't let her follow me!"

I release her hand and break into a dead run.

As I round the curve in the trail, the dark bulk of the still-burning village, with its high log palisade and skeletons of charred longhouses, looms like a black wall. I feel as though I've just been kicked in the belly. Firelight halos the village, but the surrounding forest is uncommonly dark and blustery.

"No!" I run, duck through a charred hole in the palisade, and dash across the plaza toward the Snipe Clan longhouse, the clan my father married into. Discarded arrows cover the ground. Baskets, broken pots, and dropped capes are scattered everywhere. Hungry dogs lope through the devastation with their tongues hanging out, looking frantic, or in despair. Their masters are gone, probably dead, but they do not know that, and won't leave the chaos of charred ruins until they search every crevice and nook.

I can tell now that the village was attacked days ago. The longhouses are little more than piles of ash, the remaining poles and log benches fanned to flames by today's gale. If Father is alive, he is not here. He fled with the other survivors. I pray they made it to Bur Oak Village.

From outside the burned palisade, Gitchi barks, and I hear Taya shout, "Let me go!"

I trot back to the hole in the palisade and duck outside. Gitchi, still obeying me, has his teeth embedded in Taya's sleeve and is tugging her backward. She must have tried to follow me.

"Let me go!" Taya screams in rage, and shakes her arm, trying to dislodge the wolf's massive jaws.

"Gitchi, it's all right," I call. "Let her go."

Gitchi releases her and leaps back to avoid Taya's fists. "I *hate* this animal!" she shrieks.

Panicked by her loud cries, I dash back. "Are you trying to attract the attention of the attacking warriors?"

"No, I—"

I grab her hand and drag Taya into the shadows of nearby trees, pausing only long enough to examine the forest for hidden warriors, or desperate survivors who will kill anyone not from their village. Beneath the cacophony of wind and storm, the faint whining of village dogs rides the gusts.

With Gitchi at my side, I drag Taya to a small meadow ringed by black oaks. The shiny ridges of bark on the trunks glisten in the fading light. Swirling leaves and the pungent scent of the ferns crushed by our feet trail us to the fallen log.

"Sit down," I order. "I need time to think."

"I don't understand," Taya says. "Why are we stopping? We should keep moving. This is dangerous! Can't you think while we run?"

"No. I need to be here, Taya. Since the villagers are gone, my only choice is to wait until tomorrow morning to get the information I need. There's someone I have to meet." My thoughts race, thinking about the Trader's rounds, trying to figure out . . .

"But there must be enemy warriors and hundreds of angry ghosts roaming the forest!"

I close my eyes for a long moment, calming myself, then lift my gaze to the clearing. "I'll keep watch tonight, just in case either warriors or survivors return."

"What good will that do? You have no weapons to protect us." Taya jerks her cape more closely about her, pouting. "When did this happen?"

I clench my fists to keep from saying something that will hurt her. "Four or five days ago. There are no bodies along the main trail, and I don't see any scattered around the palisade, which means the survivors already collected the remains of their dead relatives."

"But if it happened five days ago, why are the flames still so high?"

"The wind kicked up this afternoon. It must have fanned the embers smoldering beneath the charred piles of bark and timber."

She grabs her flying hair when a particularly brutal gust sweeps the forest, cracking limbs together and hurling a barrage of acorns and twigs at us. When it passes, she asks, "Do you think your father is alive?"

I rub my hands over my stunned face. I can still feel Father's breath moving inside me, as I can my sister's and mother's, and a handful of friends. But hope often masquerades as truth. "I pray he is."

She studies me, notes my expression, and says, "Who do you think attacked the village?"

"In the morning I'll be able to tell by the decorations on the arrows, but tonight? My guess is Mountain People."

"But we're far from the lands of the Mountain People."

"Doesn't matter. A large enough war party makes territorial boundaries meaningless."

We ate supper earlier—at her insistence—and I am suddenly grateful. It would be impossible to get a fire going in this wind, and I have no appetite at all. As I look around, the scene takes on the wavering and misted edges of a Spirit Dream. Thoughts hang like raindrops caught in a spiderweb, shiny, fragile. I can make no sense of this. But I must. And I must face the possibility that Father and dozens of cousins are dead.

Taya's head moves, turning to examine the dark forest, as though afraid. "I don't like it here. Please, let's move on."

"We can't leave until after dawn tomorrow."

"Why not?"

"I need to meet someone."

"You never mentioned before—"

"If my father were here, we wouldn't have to stay. Since he's not, we must. I need more information before we head for Coldspring Village. There's a Trader who is always here on the last day of the moon. It's part of his regular rounds. He will know all the gossip."

As the stunned sensation begins to drain away, a cold new light illuminates the political ramifications. Whoever attacked White Dog Village has earned a swift and devastating response from Matron Kittle, and I—

"Sky Messenger?"

Curtly, I say, "Taya, there's a soft bed of leaves right over there. Why don't you try to sleep? I'm going to go stand guard beneath that oak." I point.

Panic trembles her voice. "But you'll stay in my sight, won't you? If I awake and look for you, I'll see you?"

"I told you. I'll be right there." Exasperated by this constant refrain, I turn my back and walk to the oak to take up my position.

Occasionally, when the wind shifts, ash and billows of black smoke completely obscure my view of the trail as it snakes down the hill and into the narrow dusk-cloaked valley beyond. A large pond fills part of the valley. Battered by the wind, it appears to be boiling, sloshing back and forth.

When the White Dog survivors arrive at Bur Oak or Yellowtail Village and ask for help, the matrons will be obliged to give it, and there is simply not enough food. At this very instant Grandmother must be calling in elders from all the surrounding villages, preparing them for the worst.

I glare at the tormented forest and think about the quagmire that is clan politics, of my own stake in it, and of matrons like Taya's grandmother, who scheme and lie and plot so her own kin will remain in power. For many summers High Matron Kittle has been amassing warriors, keeping them close. In the past, villages were widely separated, many days apart. They couldn't protect each other. So Kittle convinced the other Standing Stone villages to move closer to Bur Oak Village. That way, in time of need, they could pool their warriors and defend each other against attacks. It made sense. It also meant that she had five thousand warriors at her command—providing the individual village councils approved her schemes. And provided they had warning that an attack was imminent. White Dog Village must have been taken completely by surprise. Kittle's rage must be tearing the nation apart.

"Sky Messenger?"

Startled, I spin around. "What *is* it? I thought you were going to sleep?"

She stands three paces away with her blankets pulled tightly around her slender body. "No." It is almost a sob.

When I frown at her, she looks at the ground and nervously moves one moccasin back and forth through the fallen leaves. She looks very young and, though she probably doesn't know it, very beautiful. Her long hair blows about her pretty face.

"What's wrong, Taya?"

"Sky Messenger, I want you to come to the meadow. Please. Come and lie down with me? I'm cold and I'm afraid to be alone tonight."

"I'm only eight paces away. I need to keep watch on the main trail."

"You never try to understand how I feel!"

I suck in a breath and hold it to keep my temper in check. "Explain it to me, please."

"I'm lonely! At Bur Oak Village, my longhouse had almost three hundred people in it. There was always someone to talk to, or conversations to listen to as I fell asleep at night. Dogs to pet as they trotted by. Here . . ." She looked up at the violently flailing branches that filled the sky. "There's no one. No one but you and Gitchi. Please, I don't want to be alone."

When she lifts her gaze to look at me, I see desperation, and it occurs to me that my own qualms about this journey have made me impatient and callous. Seeing her first burned village has probably stirred up her fears.

"Yes. All right, Taya. I'll come—"

"Thank you." She runs forward and throws her arms around my waist. The setting . . . the smell of war . . . her arms . . . memories of the war trail overwhelm me, memories interlaced with pain.

I am with her . . . exhilarating, striking more deeply than anything else in my life. At the end, I'd known exactly what I wanted . . . and did not. Exactly who I was, and was not.

"Sky Messenger, if you need to watch the main trail, I can sleep right here beside you. That way, you won't have to sleep with me. But I'll be close to you. I'll be able to hear you when you move."

The empty wasteland inside me yawns wider. I ask, "Are you cold?"

"Freezing."

Against her hair, I say, "Perhaps I can find a way to warm us both up."

Thirty-four

Cord held the door curtain aside for Jigonsaseh to enter the Turtle Clan longhouse. When she ducked past him, he caught the scent of pine needles, and found it strangely powerful. On the war trail, he had spent many summers sleeping on soft beds of pine, spruce, or juniper needles. The fragrance brought back those days, and with them the odd comingled thrill of victory and the despair of friends lost on long-ago battlefields.

"My chamber is on the right," he said as he let the curtain fall closed behind him.

She politely waited for him to remove his black cape and hang it on a peg on the wall, then followed him into his chamber. The space was small, fifteen hands across. He hosted so many visitors that benches lined all three walls. His belongings were neatly stowed in baskets and pots beneath the benches. His niece had arranged the wooden trays of food and cups of tea in the center of the floor mats, then spread soft hides around them.

He extended a hand. "Please, sit."

Jigonsaseh gracefully removed her white cape and knelt on the deer hides. He couldn't help but stare at her. She wore no jewelry, just a simple tan doehide dress that conformed to her slender muscular body, and red knee-high moccasins. She had seen thirty-nine summers pass, and though a few silver threads glistened in her short black hair, she was as beautiful as he remembered. Her small narrow nose and full lips were perfectly balanced in her oval face, and her jet black eyes . . . a man could get lost in those eyes. A long time ago, he had considered it, but it hadn't been the right time for either of them. And now? Their peoples were at war.

Cord sat down across from her, removed the lid on the tea pot, and dipped a cup into the warm liquid. When he handed it to her, their fingers touched for a lot longer than he suspected either of them intended. She gave him a tight smile and drew the cup away.

As he divided the walnut bread between the two bowls, he said, "How were your harvests this year?"

"Poor. And with all of the attacks on our people, our remaining villages are flooded with refugees. I doubt our supplies will last the winter. Which, as you well know, means we will be forced to take what we need from our enemies."

He blinked. Revealing such vulnerabilities was not a wise military strategy. She knew better, so he wondered why she'd said it. "I had forgotten how frank you are."

She sipped her tea, and a shiver went through her. After many nights of camping in the open, the cold must have settled in her bones. He knew from experience that it would take a long time for her to get truly warm. Slowly, she replied, "I'm sorry, I did not intend—"

"Don't be. I'm sick to death of all the deception and political maneuvering. It's good to hear honest words."

She shifted positions, turning slightly away so that she could bring up her knees and prop her cup atop them. From this side view she looked even more slender, almost frail. It touched something inside him, some illogical masculine need to protect—as if legendary War Chief Koracoo needed anyone to protect her. He suspected many men before him had felt this same protective urge and were now dead because they had hesitated when they'd had the chance to kill her.

"I appreciate your willingness to hear honest words. May I ask you some questions?" The glimmering light from the longhouse fires reflected in her dark eyes.

"Certainly." He handed her the tray of walnut bread and dipped himself a cup of tea.

"How were your harvests? Will you need to attack us this spring?"

His brow furrowed. Thoughtfully, he set his tea cup down. "Matron, the fever took a great toll on our villages. We do not have the number of mouths to feed that you do. We have enough food, I think." In a low earnest voice, he added, "But understand that if we are attacked and our food stores taken, we will have no choice."

"Yes, that's how it works, isn't it? You strike us. We strike you. The Mountain People strike us both, and it goes on and on. Sky Messenger is right. This has to end before there's no one left to fight."

He studied her. She looked tired. He picked up his tea cup and let it warm his cold fingers before he said, "The question is, how? Every time my people move their villages to a new location and get settled, someone attacks us. We end up running for our lives. Our war strategy is based upon that fact. We don't want to run any longer. In fact, we won't. This is good bottom country. Our crops grow well here. We plan to keep it. That means we have to kill anyone who tries to take it away." The subtle question in his comment did not escape her notice.

"Chief, I assure you I will vote no if anyone in the Standing Stone nation suggests attacking a Flint village. I give you my oath."

That intrigued him. He pulled his head back in mock amazement. "It eases my souls to hear you say that, but we both know that food is the greatest of all tools for manipulation." He paused. "And High Matron Kittle is not a friend to the Flint People."

Jigonsaseh took a bite of her walnut bread and ate it slowly, apparently relishing the flavor. "This is excellent, Cord. Please give your niece my thanks."

"She will be delighted that she pleased you."

Cord bit into his chunk of walnut bread and took a moment to enjoy the sweet flavor. Made from a mixture of acorn meal, walnuts, and bear fat, with a pinch of wood ash for leavening, it tasted wonderful.

They ate in silence for a time. When she'd finished her second piece of bread, she dusted the crumbs from her hands and softly said, "These are not easy times. I pray people hear Sky Messenger's vision and heed it, for I fear we are on the verge of destroying our own world."

He lightly stroked the fine wood grain of his bread bowl. "The Flint People will lay down weapons two instants after the Standing Stone People do—which will be three instants after the Hills people do, five instants after the Landing People do, and one full day after the Mountain People do, since they are the least trustworthy."

She smiled at that and lifted her hand to cover a yawn.

"Shall we cut this short? You look very tired. We've prepared a chamber . . ." When he started to rise, she reached across to touch his sleeve. He could feel the chill of her tanned fingers through his shirt.

"I'd much rather talk with you, if you don't mind."

A tingle went through him. He lowered himself back to the hides. "I don't . . . but I'd appreciate it if we could abandon the war talk. I haven't seen you in so long there are many things I'd prefer to discuss."

"I am agreeable to that."

"May I ask about your family?"

"What do you wish to know?"

He paused for only an instant, but it was uncomfortable. "Have you remarried?"

She smiled. "No. After Gonda and I parted, I had two children to raise, and my duties as war chief, which entailed many nights on the trail. When I returned home I wanted to spend what few moments I had with Odion and Tutelo. And, truly, there was no man who interested me. Which perhaps says more about me than it does them. And you? Did you remarry?"

She sounded like she was genuinely interested. "I remarried ten summers ago. She gave me a strong son. But we divorced two summers ago. I have not had the strength to consider another marriage, though my clan keeps insisting. As I'm sure yours does."

"With regularity."

He laughed softly and saw the lines around her eyes crinkle in return. "And Gonda? A Trader once told me he remarried and moved to White Dog Village. Is that correct?"

Her smile faded. She looked away. "It was. White Dog Village was destroyed by the Hills People—"

Cord sat forward. "Blessed gods, when?"

"Five days ago."

Cord stared down the length of the longhouse, absently noting the movements of the people as they cooked supper or washed their children's faces. Two dogs wrestled three compartments down. "Is Yellowtail Village overrun with refugees?"

"Yes, and Bur Oak Village, too."

He turned his cup in his hands. Somehow, they had circled around each other and returned to talking about the war. They fell silent, gazing at each other, both of their faces lined with concern. A small connection of warmth grew between them, like hands reaching across time and clasping tentatively, then strengthening. When he started to feel it in all the wrong places, he dropped his gaze and frowned into his tea cup. In the pale green liquid, his black roach of hair appeared faintly purple.

"How is Baji?" Jigonsaseh asked, changing the subject. "I think of her often."

"She's still strong-willed and too confident for her own good, but my adopted daughter is well. Her warriors elected her war chief three moons ago."

"Well, that does not surprise me. Even as a child she had a powerful presence. She was a born leader." A tender smile came to her lips.

Cord tried to hide his pride, but his voice showed it: "Yes, she is. It will sadden her that she missed seeing you."

"She is away?"

"Yes, and won't be back for days."

She politely did not ask why, and it relieved him that he didn't have to hide the fact that Baji was out on the war trail.

Jigonsaseh sipped more tea. "I pray that Sodowego does not see her face. Has she married?"

Cord shook his head. "No. You know why, I suppose."

Her delicate black brows pulled down. "No, why?"

"I'm surprised Dekanawida didn't tell you. It's a lengthy story." Cord stretched out on his side on the mats, propping himself up on one elbow. As his sleeve slipped down, the tattoos covering his arms were revealed. She seemed to be studying them, perhaps remembering. "My grandmother has tried to marry Baji several times to good men. She has refused."

"Does she give you any reason?"

"Of course not. But the reason is clear. No man equals your son."

Something about the softness in her expression touched him, building a warmth below his heart. He longed to speak of more personal things, things between the two of them, but he couldn't let himself. He feared where it might lead.

"Why did they part, Cord? He's never told me." She drained her tea, set the cup on the floor, and laced her fingers over her knees. Her beautiful face had a pale yellow gleam.

"Oh," he said through a taut exhale. "I only know part of it. Baji is not one to openly speak of such matters. I heard they had a violent battlefield squabble over captives. There was an infant, a little boy, that Baji wished to bring home and adopt. Dekanawida objected. Apparently they had a pact that neither would ever take a child captive."

"Had she changed her mind?"

He lifted his shoulders in a shrug. "I think, perhaps, she wished to make an exception in the baby's case. I wonder if her lack of a child is not beginning to bother her. Every other woman in the village who has seen twenty-four summers has five or six children. Baji has none."

Jigonsaseh blinked thoughtfully at the floor. "I felt that way once after a raid. There was a baby boy crying in the midst of a collapsed house. I couldn't leave him there. Gonda and I brought him home and raised him as our own."

"Odion?"

"Yes."

"Does he know that?"

"Oh, yes, we told him the story as soon as he could understand, at four or five summers."

Cord watched the silver glints in her hair reflect the firelight that filled the longhouse. "Then I am especially surprised he didn't help Baji raise the child. They would have made good parents, I think."

"What happened to the infant boy?"

"I have no idea. I only know that no one brought him home."

Few warriors dared to adopt infants. Almost no one could afford the luxury of carrying and feeding a baby for days on the war trail. His lips pressed tightly together. "I regret that they parted. I looked forward to having Dekanawida here. Not only because I liked and respected him; but he was a very fine warrior. We could have used him."

Through a long exhalation, she said, "Well, he's decided that he will never touch a weapon again. So . . ." She tilted her head as though to say *who knows what the future will bring.* Then she exhaled, and her face suddenly appeared haggard.

"Will you spend the night, Matron?"

"No, but I thank you for the offer. We must get home. Our village councils are deliberating the issue of attacking Atotarho Village at this instant. When the vote comes—if it hasn't already—our war chiefs will begin planning the assault. I must be there."

"How many days until the battle?"

"Hard to say. At least six or seven. I pray we have more time."

As she started to rise, he said, "Perhaps . . ." She looked up, saw his expression, and sat back down. "Perhaps I should send a war party with you. If my people decide to join yours in the fight, there will be no time for us to ready ourselves and get there before the arrows start flying. At least you would have a few more warriors—"

"That is a kind offer, and I appreciate it. But that would be dangerous for you. If your people vote no, they will ask why Flint warriors were engaged in a fight they did not authorize. No, Cord. Wait. I will send a fast runner when the time comes."

"Very well."

She started to rise again, and he got to his feet and instinctively offered her a hand. She put her fingers into his and he helped her to her feet. When she looked up at him, time seemed to stop. Conflicting emotions danced across her beautiful face: a magnetic attraction to him, fear, desperation. They stood less than two hands apart, holding hands for so long that blood began to rush in his ears.

"I wish you would stay the night."

"I can't." She gently pulled her hand away. "I wish I could. Truly. But I must get home."

"At least allow me to walk you back to your canoe," he said. "That will give us a few more moments."

"I would welcome that."

She shrugged her white cape over her shoulders and ducked beneath the door curtain into the darkness. Cord, two steps behind her, thought, *Blessed gods, we haven't seen each other in twelve summers, and I'm still in love with her.*

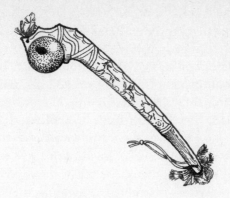

Thirty-five

Taya woke to the rich smell of cooking grouse. When she opened her eyes, she saw Sky Messenger crouched before a fire adjusting the roasting stick so the bird would cook on the other side. The faint gray rays of early morning outlined his muscular body. Last night, his tenderness had left her breathless. Her gaze moved from his shoulders to his narrow waist and legs, and it occurred to her that he wasn't wearing his cape, just his knee-length buckskin shirt and leggings. She looked down and saw that he'd draped his cape over the top of the blankets to keep her warmer through the night.

"Are you awake?" he called.

Taya dragged herself to a sitting position and rubbed her eyes. "Barely."

Gitchi's head turned from where he lay beside the fire, tearing a rabbit apart. Blood covered his gray muzzle. He gave Taya an unnerving appraisal, then went back to his rabbit.

The wind had died down. Only a few leaves cartwheeled across the trail. She reached for her pack and drew out her carved antler comb. Yesterday's gale had turned her hair into a snarled mess. While he cooked, she took her time, combed the waist-length strands smooth, and then plaited them into a long braid. She knew the style accented her perfect oval face and made her dark eyes seem larger, and she wanted to please him this morning.

He dipped a cup into the pot at the edge of the flames, then rose and brought it to her. "It's spruce needle tea. The grouse is almost ready."

"Thank you." She took a sip of the hot tea and let the tangy flavor filter through her waking body.

"You're beautiful this morning." He stroked her hair and went back to turn the bird again. As fat dripped onto the flames, they sputtered.

It was comforting sitting with the warm blankets coiled around her waist. She was hesitant to leave them. She drank more tea and studied the burned village. Smoke still scented the air, but there were no flames this morning, at least none she could see. The charred palisade—burned through in many places—resembled a gigantic mouth of rotted black teeth. Through the holes, collapsed houses were visible, standing in smoldering piles, but she saw no dead bodies, just a few roaming dogs.

Taya shoved her blankets aside and rose with her cup in her hand. "Did you see anyone in the night?"

Sky Messenger's brown eyes lifted and narrowed. He seemed to be watching someone right now, someone moving through the destroyed village. But he said, "No. Come and sit down. I'll fill our bowls."

As she walked toward him, he slid the grouse off the stick and into one bowl, then used his fingers to quickly rip it in half and deposited the larger portion in her bowl. Afterward, he sucked on his fingers as though he'd burned them.

She sat down beside him, placed her tea cup to the side, and picked up her bowl. As she blew on the grouse to cool it, she said, "You could have used my knife"—she touched the hafted chert knife on her belt—"to cut up the grouse."

"Yes, thank you. That would probably have been acceptable."

"Acceptable?" She pulled off a succulent strip of dark meat and put it in her mouth. The delicious flavor coated her tongue. "This is good. When did you have time to hunt? I didn't hear a thing."

"It wasn't much of a hunt," he said, and swallowed a bite of meat. "The bird fluttered up on that fallen log five paces away. I killed it with a rock, a lucky throw; then I skinned it and slid a hickory stick through the middle."

"Yes, the hickory flavor is wonderful."

As they ate, she smiled at him, and he seemed confused by it. She felt so happy this morning. When she'd eaten everything but the leg, she picked it up and placed it in his bowl. "You need more food than I do, Sky Messenger, though I appreciate you for taking care of me."

He glanced at the leg and suspiciously said, "Are you sure? I don't want you to get hungry on the trail."

"I'll be fine." She rubbed her greasy fingers in the dry leaves to clean them and reached for her tea cup again. As she sipped, she watched Gitchi. He was taking his time eating the rabbit. His tail wagged often. "You should have taken that rabbit away from him and cooked it for us. Then neither of us would have to worry about being hungry on the trail."

Sky Messenger replied, "It's his rabbit. He hunted it."

"You could give him a leg, or maybe even two, but he's a wolf. He doesn't need as much food as we do."

"The rabbit belongs to Gitchi."

Annoyed, she chastised, "You protect that old gray-faced wolf like he's a human being, Sky Messenger. He's not."

Sky Messenger reached out to pet the wolf's head, and the love in Gitchi's eyes touched even her. "He's my friend."

Taya frowned into her tea cup. She hated to admit it, but she was jealous of the affection he lavished on the decrepit wolf. She turned the cup in her hands and decided to change the subject. Anything to keep the morning filled with warmth and conversation.

"What did you mean when you said it would have been 'acceptable' to cut up the grouse with my knife?"

The wrinkles across his forehead deepened. He finished chewing the bite in his mouth before he replied, "I'm still finding my way, discovering what I can and cannot live with."

"I don't understand. What's wrong with cutting up a grouse with a fine chert blade?"

"I just need to think about it for a time longer."

This confused Taya, who tried to decipher what he meant. *A knife is unacceptable to him.* Why? She could understand, no matter how ridiculous, that he didn't want to carry a bow, spear, stiletto, or war club—he'd stopped fighting—but a knife?

"So," she said, "you consider a knife to be a weapon?"

His head waffled, as though uncertain. "I'm just at the foolish stage, Taya. Don't waste too much time trying to figure it out. I don't understand it myself yet."

"But, you mean you're at the stage of figuring out what is a weapon and what is not?"

"Yes." He picked up the leg she'd given him and concentrated on eating it. When he finished, he lowered the bone to his bowl and wiped his greasy hands on his leggings. Many people did that because the oil helped to keep water from soaking into the leather. Sky Messenger rose to his feet and extended a hand. "May I take your bones away?"

She gave him her bowl. It was considered disrespectful to the animal to throw its bones on the ground. He walked away to the sycamore and carefully placed the bones in the crook of the tree. Then he said a soft prayer, thanking the grouse for its life, and walked back to kneel in front of her. When he bowed his head, his heavy brow cast shadows over his brown eyes, and his black hair fell forward.

"A knife is a tool, Sky Messenger, not a weapon. A leather punch is a tool. An awl is a tool."

"Yes, in most hands. But in my hands"—he opened his palms and stared at them distastefully—"they have often been weapons. I can see the faces of each person I killed with a bone awl, a punch, or a fine chert blade."

"You were a warrior fighting for your people. Of course you used whatever you could find to defeat the enemy. You should be proud of it. Not ashamed."

The few brief moments of happiness between them vanished. The curtain closed over his eyes again. He rose and walked away to stare down the trail toward the distant pond, which shone a deep blue.

Taya drank her tea and frowned at his back. Was he going to start refusing to use tools? If he wouldn't touch an ax, how could he chop wood to keep them warm? If he wouldn't touch a knife, how could he skin animals for their food? What good was he if he wasn't willing to be a warrior, a hunter, or perform any other manly duty?

Blessed gods, does Grandmother know this?

Sky Messenger folded his arms and walked out into the trail, apparently waiting for the Trader.

Beyond the rolling tree-whiskered hills, dawn had begun to blush color into the day. A swath of deep purple limned the eastern horizon. High above it, the brightest campfires of the dead continued to gleam.

When she'd finished her tea, she silently gathered up their things and packed them—a menial duty she usually left to him. Then she set both packs beside the trail and went to grab his cape. It smelled of wood smoke and crushed grass. She held it to her nose for a time, just breathing in his scent, before she walked to him and draped it over his shoulders.

It must have startled him, for he jumped slightly and looked at her. "Thank you," he said softly. He pulled it forward and tied it beneath his chin.

Taya touched his arm. "I'm sorry. I know you'd like to thrash me for the things I just said."

"You exaggerate."

"I'm just trying to figure you out, probably as hard as you're trying to—"

He threw up a hand to silence her and squinted down the trail. "There he is."

An ugly little man with five pack dogs trotted toward them. He was humming a tune, watching his feet. When he lifted his head and saw Sky Messenger standing in the middle of the trail, he stopped suddenly. Greasy black hair framed his scarred face. "What are *you* doing here?"

Sky Messenger called, "I came to find you, Raloga."

"Me?" The man's hand flew to his chest. "Why? What did I do? Where's your war party?" His gaze darted across the forest.

As he walked forward, Sky Messenger pulled something from his belt pouch and handed it to the Trader. "White Dog Village was burned several days ago. There's no need for you to stop. I will pay you to deliver a message for me, but it must be done quickly."

The man took the exquisite pearl bracelet, turned it over in his hands, and eyed Sky Messenger suspiciously. "This is valuable. You must want me to do something dangerous. Where would you have me go?"

"To Coldspring Village."

Raloga glanced at Taya, then looked back at Sky Messenger. "And who am I to see?"

"I want my message delivered exactly, do you understand?"

The Trader nodded.

"Tell War Chief Hiyawento that Odion wants to meet him in the aspen meadow at midnight."

Taya's blood went cold. *Hiyawento?* He was one of the most feared war chiefs among the Hills People. *He* was Sky Messenger's old friend? The man who'd saved him? He was a monster!

"Umm," Raloga said. "Who is Odion?"

"Just tell him. He'll understand."

Raloga shrugged and grinned, revealing four yellow teeth in an otherwise toothless mouth. "You are paying me well for such a simple message. Is it risky?"

Sky Messenger's voice took on a timbre Taya had never heard before, low, threatening. "I'm not paying you to ask questions."

Raloga's smile drooped. "Fine. That's fine. I didn't mean to anger you. I'll deliver it exactly as you said."

"Then you will live a long and happy life, my friend." Sky Messenger slapped him on the back hard enough to make the Trader stumble.

"Er, yes, well . . . then, if you don't mind, I'll be on my way." He lifted a hand and quickly trotted away with his dogs surrounding him. He cast two backward glances, apparently to make certain he wasn't being followed, and vanished up the trail.

Taya walked to stand beside Sky Messenger. Her cape flapped around her legs. "What are you trying to do? Hiyawento is married to Chief Atotarho's daughter! We can't go see him. Atotarho is an evil cannibal sorcerer. If he captures us, he'll cut our hearts out and eat them for breakfast. Do you want to die?"

Sky Messenger's gaze remained on the point where the Trader had disappeared. "We should be there by midnight. I'll be able to answer your question then."

Thirty-six

Raloga scratched his itching armpit. He'd had to run hard to get here in time, and sweat drenched his shirt. It was almost midnight, yet people crowded the plaza of Atotarho Village. Everywhere he looked cook pots boiled near huge bonfires, and the scent of sweet corn cakes baking in ashes rose. Drum beats pounded the air. Arranged in a rough oval around the plaza were four longhouses, four smaller clan houses, and a prisoners' house. The magnificent longhouses—the biggest ever built—were constructed of pole frames and covered with elm bark. The Wolf Clan longhouse was truly stunning; it stretched over eight hundred hand-lengths long and forty wide. The others were shorter, two or three hundred hands long, but still impressive. The arched roofs soared fifty hands high. Was Hiyawento in council with the matrons? Or the elders? He might have just been meeting with War Chief Sindak, or various war deputies.

"There must be three thousand people here. What's happening?" His five dogs pricked their ears and looked at him. "Come on, we don't have much time."

As he shouldered through the crowd looking for War Chief Hiyawento, he passed people in brilliant capes, wearing elaborate shell, copper and carved wooden jewelry. Sounds of laughter and singing echoed from somewhere ahead.

He tapped a youth of perhaps sixteen summers on the shoulder. "What's happening?"

The young warrior's face was alight. He wore his hair pulled back and fastened in a tight bun. "We captured two hundred prisoners in our last raid. The matrons are deciding who will be adopted into the clans and who will be tortured to death." He clapped Raloga on the shoulder. "There's plenty of food. Fill a bowl and join the celebration."

"Actually, I'm trying to find War Chief Hiyawento. The guards at Coldspring Village told me he was here. Have you seen him?"

The youth craned his neck, spied what he was looking for, and pointed. "His personal guards are standing over in front of the Wolf Clan house. He's probably in council."

Raloga smiled. "Thank you. Have an enjoyable night."

He strode away with his dogs trailing behind him. Each time one growled at a village dog, he shouted stern words, and his dogs put their tails between their legs and fell into line again.

The guards standing at the southern end of the longhouse scowled at him as he approached. "A pleasant evening to you, brave warriors," he greeted. "I am Raloga, and I carry an urgent message for War Chief Hiyawento."

The tall woman sneered. Perhaps twenty-nine or thirty summers, she had short black hair and an oval face. "Who is the message from?"

Raloga wouldn't dare say Sky Messenger's name in this company. That would get him cut into tiny pieces and fed to the village dogs. "A man called Odion."

The guards looked at each other and exchanged annoyed glances. The shorter man with a broken nose and scars the width of a man's finger running across his right cheek, said, "I've never heard of him. Have you, Kallen?"

"No," the woman replied in a bored voice.

"Nonetheless, the message I carry is extremely important."

"Yes, yes," Kallen said as though she'd been hearing similar claims all day. "Sit down over there, and when the war chief is available, I'll let him know you're here."

"No, friend, you don't understand," Raloga pressed. "I must see him immediately."

Kallen said, "*Sit down* before I crack your skull with my club." She swung it to emphasize her point.

Raloga swallowed hard. "I have another solution. I will be perfectly content to give the message to you, his trusted guards, and have you relay it to him. That way, the responsibility for delivering it in a timely fashion rests with you."

"Very well," Kallen said, "what is the message?"

"Come closer. I don't wish anyone to overhear it."

Kallen bent down and let the ugly little Trader whisper the message in her ear. She straightened. "That doesn't sound urgent to me."

"Trust me, friend, the war chief will think it is." Raloga bowed slightly, gave them an ingratiating smile, and trotted away with his dogs at his heels.

As Raloga hurried across the village, Kallen shook her head. "He's an onerous character. I've never liked him."

Gosha stared after the Trader. "What did he say?"

"Just that Odion, whoever that is, wishes to meet the war chief in the aspen meadow at midnight, and he's traveling with a woman."

Gosha adjusted his weapons belt, shifting it on his hips. "Should you interrupt the war chief? Midnight is fast approaching, and if the aspen grove at issue is the one just outside of Coldspring Village, it's a hard run to get there in time."

Kallen jerked an irritated nod. "Hiyawento said he did not wish to be disturbed. Matron Tila has never called a council meeting in her chamber before. Everyone important is there."

"I know. If this is some sort of joke, I'd rather not be the one to pull the war chief out of the council."

"Stop looking at me. I don't want to do it," Kallen exclaimed.

Gosha distastefully examined the celebration. Atotarho had attacked White Dog Village six days ago, and his people considered him a hero. The fact that his actions might split the Hills nation in two did not seem to worry him. The attack had stunned Hiyawento and the Coldspring Village council, and at least two other villages had been forced to put down riots over the outrage. Whispers of civil war were running rampant across Hills country.

Given the stakes, who knew what "a message from Odion," might mean?

Kallen looked at the longhouse door curtain. Firelight glimmered around the edges, creating an enormous luminous square. Inside, she could hear Hiyawento's deep measured voice making some point.

"All right." Kallen straightened. "I'm going in. If he kills me, make sure my family finds my body."

"He won't dismember you. No one would allow it. You're an honored deputy war chief."

Gosha gave Kallen a confident nod, which slightly unnerved her. She took a deep breath, pulled back the curtain, and stepped into the firelit warmth of the longhouse. Forty fires burned down the length, lighting each family's compartment and reflecting from the faces of the council members. Matron Tila sat on the bench in the back wrapped in so many hides she resembled a fat furry animal, except for her pain-stricken face. Matron Kelek of the Bear Clan sat to Tila's left, apparently holding her up. The other council members—Hiyawento, Zateri, War Chief Sindak, Matron Ganon of Turtleback Village, and Matron Kwahseti of Riverbank Village—were seated on mats around the fire. Kwahseti's war chief, Thona, stood just behind her with his war ax shining on his belt. Next to him stood Negano, the chief's personal guard. The sight of Atotarho made Kallen's bowels go watery. A beautiful black ritual cape, covered with cir-clets of bone cut from human skulls, covered his twisted, deformed body. Gray hair, braided with rattlesnake skins, haloed his bony face. When he gestured at Hiyawento's wife, Zateri, his bracelets, made of human finger bones, rattled.

Atotarho said, "You seem to have forgotten you are my daughter. Have you lost all respect for the elders of this nation?"

Matron Zateri calmly stared him straight in the eyes. She was stately, but unattractive. Her face was too round, and her front teeth stuck out slightly, but she had a powerful presence. "I respect those who obey the will of the people, Father. You consulted no one before you and your vil-lage council decided to raid White Dog Village. It seems to me it is you who has shown disrespect. Did you think the other village councils would not care?"

Atotarho's eyes narrowed in anger, but his voice came out with deadly softness. "I expected them to be grateful. The destruction of White Dog Village has demonstrated to the Ruling Council of the Standing Stone nation that we will not be toyed with. Perhaps in the future they will not take our threats so lightly."

Hiyawento said, "They did not take our threat lightly, Chief. In fact, I'm sure from High Matron Kittle's response that they are already pre-paring for our attack. If we were wise, I think we would try to arrange a meeting to discuss the situation before it gets out of hand."

War Chief Sindak said, "I agree with Hiyawento. We are standing on a precipice. Any wrong move now and we will all fall into chaos. Many lives will be lost."

Matron Kwahseti tucked gray hair behind her ear and let out a sigh. "I am also forced to agree with Hiyawento. We should all take a step back. My village council is outraged by the attack on White Dog Village, and we will not stand by and be drawn into this conflict. We—"

Matron Kelek's raspy voice called, "You would take sides against your own people, Kwahseti? You would fight against your relatives? How many times have we sent our warriors to protect your village from Mountain war parties? Hmm? How many times?"

Matron Kwahseti lowered her eyes in shame. "Many times, Matron, but—"

"There are no *but*s. Either you are part of this alliance, or you are not. Choose."

Zateri softly said, "None of us should be forced to choose, Matron Kelek. But you are right. That is where we stand, as War Chief Sindak says, 'on a precipice.' Before we all push each other over the edge, let us calm our voices, and . . ."

While Zateri continued talking, Kallen eased up behind Hiyawento and knelt. The war chief was a tall man with sharp eyes and a hooked nose. Black hair brushed the collar of his buckskin shirt.

Without looking at her, Hiyawento asked, "This had better be critical, Kallen."

"A Trader came through. He said he had a message for you."

"Yes?" He still didn't look at her. His gaze moved back and forth between Zateri and the matrons, judging their expressions. "What is it?"

"Odion wishes to meet with you in the aspen meadow at midnight."

Hiyawento seemed to stop breathing. His eyes widened. He leaned closer to Kallen. "What do you mean? He's here?"

"Apparently."

"Dear gods, is he alone?"

"No, the Trader said there's a woman with him."

"A woman! Why wasn't I informed immediately! They need protection. Organize six guards and meet me at the aspen meadow. Hurry."

Hiyawento scrambled to his feet and strode for the door curtain. Everyone in the meeting stopped to stare. Leaving without the consent of the elders was considered a grievous insult to the council. Atotarho leaned back and glowered at Hiyawento's back. Matron Zateri just watched him, concerned.

Kallen apologized, "Forgive him. A minor emergency. He meant no disrespect." She bowed to the council and swiftly backed outside into the cold night.

Thirty-seven

Taya could not say what made the first sight of War Chief Hiyawento so impressive. He had no guards, no attendants, no extraordinary jewelry, none of the trappings of prestige and power; the man was not even armed. When he first glimpsed Taya and Sky Messenger in the forest, he stood alone, frozen, silent. A formidable man, tall, with a narrow beaked face and burning eyes, black hair blew around his shoulders. Dressed in a worn, knee-length buckskin shirt, he was dwarfed by the soaring height of the Coldspring Village palisade behind him. But if there had been hundreds of people assembled in this clearing, none of them would have had eyes for anything but this man. He was clearly a war chief to be reckoned with.

Sky Messenger's words were like pebbles striking at the silence. "Wrass, it does my heart good to see you."

The war chief strode forward and embraced Sky Messenger so hard his muscular arms shook. "Blessed gods, Odion, I have dreamed of this day a thousand times."

They should have long ago given up their childhood names, and perhaps they had with every other person in the world, but it struck Taya as strangely intimate.

They continued to hold each other, their muscles bulging through their shirts, until the war chief pushed back. "I can't believe you made it this far. Why are you alive?"

Taya noticed that Sky Messenger had tears in his eyes. "I know I'm placing you in danger, forgive me, but I had to see you."

"What's wrong?"

Sky Messenger extended a hand. "First, let me present Taya, granddaughter of High Matron Kittle. The woman to whom I am betrothed."

Hiyawento's mouth opened slightly, as though he didn't know what to say.

Taya stepped forward, uncertain how to act; then her Grandmother's training took over, and she extended her hand to the man who was the sworn enemy of her people. "I am honored to meet you, War Chief Hiyawento."

He took her hand, and when he felt the slight tremor in her grip, he said, "You are here under my protection. Don't be afraid."

Warriors emerged from the trees, six of them, carrying nocked bows and quivers bristling with arrows on their backs. Hiyawento instructed, "Fan out. I don't want anyone to get close enough to see my guests."

The warriors ghosted away into the shadows, and though she knew they had to be close, she could not see them.

Sky Messenger and Hiyawento walked into the small clearing in the middle of the aspen grove and sat down on the fallen log. Taya trailed behind them. It was very late, and she was exhausted from running all day. Despite Hiyawento's guarantee of safety, they were Hills People. They couldn't be trusted. She kept glancing around, trying to see if anyone was sneaking up on them.

Hiyawento and Sky Messenger just stared at each other for a time, smiling, as though memorizing the other's face.

Hiyawento finally said, "I returned from Bur Oak Village just last night. Were you aware of that?"

"No. Why were you there?"

"I delivered a message from our Ruling Council. Basically it was a threat to destroy the entire Standing Stone nation if it ever attempted to establish an alliance with a Hills village again. You can guess how High Matron Kittle responded."

Sky Messenger nodded, but before he spoke, Taya said, "She must have shouted and threatened back. Believe me, she meant every word."

"I did believe it," Hiyawento said.

Sky Messenger propped a fist in his lap. "Mother will try to ease the situation."

"Yes, Speaker Koracoo is a peacemaker at heart, but I'm not sure she can. We have a tidal wave of rage building here. I fear this next battle is going to be long and bloody. You heard the news?"

Sky Messenger's forehead wrinkled. "No. We've been on the trail. What news?"

"Blessed Spirits, I thought that's why you'd come."

Hiyawento leaned forward and braced his elbows on his knees. "Six days ago Chief Atotarho, without consulting any of the other village councils, decided to attack White Dog Village. He—"

"Yes." The rush of air behind the word made it sound like a gasp. "I know. We passed by it on the way here. How is the Hills nation reacting?"

Hiyawento hesitated. "Aren't you concerned about your father? I heard Gonda and his wife escaped, along with most of the elders."

"I'm greatly relieved to hear that, but right this instant I am more concerned about how your people are taking the news."

"Badly. It could mean civil war. The attack was not sanctioned by the Ruling Council. Coldspring Village is not the only Hills village upset by the outrage. Riverbank Village and Canassatego Village are both up in arms."

Sky Messenger let out a breath that fogged in the cold air; then he stared up at the firelight reflecting from the aspen leaves. As the golden leaves trembled in the breeze, the light fractured and flashed in hundreds of places at once. "After everything he did to us, I don't know how you can live here and not kill him."

"He's Zateri father. If I didn't love her so desperately, I assure you"—he glanced around to make certain his warriors could not overhear their words—"I'd have killed him when I first came here. His words are like an eel in your hand, slippery. You can never quite get hold of them."

In a warm voice, Sky Messenger asked, "How is Zateri?"

"She is well. But she's going to be devastated that she didn't get to see you."

"I was hoping to see her," Sky Messenger said, disappointed.

"You won't. She'll be in council for most of the night. And you, my friend, are going to have to leave here before either of us wishes it."

"How soon?"

"Very soon. Before anyone finds out you're here. We have, perhaps, one-half hand of time."

"Then I should get to the point." But he hesitated and wiped his palms on his cape.

Hiyawento noticed the action, and with great care said, "I was glad to hear that Matron Kittle reversed your death sentence." He cast a meaningful glance at Taya. "Your vision was on everyone's lips."

"Yes, it's a long story, and that's why I'm here." Sky Messenger massaged his forehead. "I've been having Spirit Dreams. I don't know what to make of some of them."

Hiyawento straightened. "Is there more than one, or is this the same Dream that started when you'd seen eleven summers?"

Taya's head jerked around to stare. He'd been having the *same* Spirit Dream for twelve summers? Did Grandmother know that? Or any of the Ruling Council? Blessed gods, if it were true . . .

"It's basically the same Dream." Blood flushed Sky Messenger's cheeks. Even in the pale light, Taya could see it. "It's changed slightly over the summers. Images get added, some are deleted, as though not even the Spirits know the final shape of the story."

"Does the Dream come every night?"

"Recently, it's afflicted me two or three times in a night. I just abruptly find myself walking in a strange glittering world where Elder Brother Sun—"

"Covers his face with the soot of the dying world?"

Taya's spine tingled. She glanced at Sky Messenger.

He shuddered as if he'd been doused with ice water. Just above a whisper, he said, "Blessed gods, those words are as powerful today as the day you first said them. They still strike at my heart."

Hiyawento leaned closer to Sky Messenger. "Mine, too. I remember the day I heard them as though it were this morning."

Sky Messenger hesitated. "Could you tell Taya the story of what happened to you that day, Wrass?"

Hiyawento was quiet for a time, as though preparing himself for the memories. "It was twelve summers ago, just before War Chief Koracoo and her search party found us. I was lying in the old witch's canoe. The beatings I'd taken the day before had left me badly fevered. I was lying with my cheek on the cold gunwale when a man walked through the water toward me. He had a bent nose, like one of the Faces of the Forest."

Sky Messenger whispered, "Shago-niyoh. The Voice."

Taya sat down hard in front of them. Her knees had gone weak. Sky Messenger's Spirit Helper had also come to Hiyawento? That meant Sky Messenger might not be a mad fool. "Then what happened?"

Hiyawento's dark eyes took on a troubled expression. "I was afraid. I asked him if he was one of the hanehwa."

Instinctively, Taya's gaze went to the forest, searching for flits of gray slipping between the trees. "What did he say?"

"He said, '*We are all husks, Wrass, flayed from the soil of fire and blood. This won't be over for any of us until the Great Face shakes the World Tree.*

Then, when Elder Brother Sun blackens his face with the soot of the dying world, the judgment will take place.' I swear the words are burned into my afterlife soul. I hear them in my sleep, on the war trail, when I'm playing with my daughters. I wish I knew what they mean."

The lines at the corners of Sky Messenger's eyes pinched. He shoved his cape aside and reached into the red Power pouch tied to his belt, where he drew out the splinter of charred skull. Attached to it was a tightly wound strand of black hair that had been tied with a cord—as though it were precious to him—and she wondered if it belonged to Baji.

Sky Messenger tenderly tucked the hair back into the Power pouch and held out the piece of skull. "This has something to do with the 'judgment.'"

Hiyawento frowned at it.

Sky Messenger flipped it in his hand. "This skull ties you and me to the Dream. I just . . . I'm not certain how yet. But I must find out."

Hiyawento extended his hand, and Sky Messenger placed the piece of skull in it. The war chief's black brows drew together over his hooked nose. He examined it carefully. "Where did you find this?"

"Just north of Bog Willow Village. It belongs to the . . . Do you . . . do you remember the Mountain war chief . . . the one who took me out into the forest?"

A swallow went down Hiyawento's throat. His voice came out filled with hatred. "Yes."

"What did he do to me, Wrass? What happened out in the trees?"

Hiyawento bowed his head and shook it, as though to ease the memories. "I didn't see it, Odion. I know he hurt you. You told me he did. But I don't know for sure. Something . . . something terrible. Why do you ask?" He handed the piece of skull back and rubbed his hands hard on his shirt as though to rid them of the taint.

Sky Messenger tucked it into the red pouch again and pulled the laces tight. "At the end of my Dream, I hear his voice."

Hiyawento paused. "What does he say?"

"It's as though he has his lips pressed to my ear. He orders, 'Lie down, boy. Stop crying or I'll cut your heart out.' Then a great hole opens in the cloud-sea beneath my feet, and I fall and fall. Wisps of cloud trail behind me as I tumble through nothingness surrounded by glittering petals shaken from the World Tree."

Taya sat stunned. Blood pounded in her ears. *Blessed gods, what did the war chief do to him?* A sensation of pained awe filled her. It was real. The Dream was true, and it was tied to whatever had happened to both Sky Messenger and Hiyawento twelve summers ago. She had thought his soul was loose. But if Sky Messenger and Hiyawento had the same Spirit Helper and both were having the same dream . . . great ancestors!

"Taya and I just came from the Dawnland country. I spent a day walking the old campsite and the forest, trying to remember that part. The last thing I recall is being taken by the hand and dragged into the forest. The rest . . . the rest is just gone."

Softly, Hiyawento asked, "Why is it so important to remember, Odion? There's nothing but pain there."

"Old Bahna says that before I can stop Elder Brother Sun from turning his back on the world, I have to remember." Sky Messenger clenched his fists. "Wrass, there's something I must ask of you."

Hiyawento said, "Long ago I promised you on my life that I would be there with you. At the end. I mean to keep that promise. So be careful what you ask, for I will do it without question."

For a time, Sky Messenger just stared into his friend's eyes. Finally, he said, "Great Grandmother Earth is dying. Our war is killing her. We have to stop it."

"I agree, but how? It's been going on for generations."

"Will you ask Zateri to speak to the matrons of the other Hills villages about establishing a truce so that I may tell them my Dream? I know Atotarho won't listen, but perhaps they will."

"I will ask her. And what do you wish me to do?"

Sky Messenger took a deep breath. "I hesitate to ask, because I know what it will cost you. Will you, War Chief Hiyawento, speak against war in your next council?"

Hiyawento straightened. The ramifications must be sinking in. A war chief who argued for peace was likely to find a stiletto between his ribs.

Finally, Hiyawento nodded. "Yes, I will. And you know Zateri will do everything necessary to support you. She . . ." Hiyawento's expression slackened, as though something dire had just occurred to him.

"What is it?"

"Nothing, it's just . . . nothing." He shook his head as though denying some inner warning. "I will speak with her. That's all."

He was holding something back. Sky Messenger said, "If there was any other way—"

"Don't get sentimental," Hiyawento replied. "We both know the price of your Dream. We've known it for more than a decade."

They smiled at each other, the smiles of men who've known each other since boyhood, fought side by side through the worst of times, and are ready to fight again. Men who share an unbreakable bond of trust.

Blood pounded in Taya's ears. *The price of the Dream.* For the first time, she considered the possibility that Sky Messenger might truly be the prophesied human False Face. Along with that shocking moment came the realization that his vision—the same vision of War Chief Hiyawento— might also save both of their peoples from the abyss that yawned before them. *It might save all of the peoples south of Skanodario Lake.*

She sat back and looked at the two men. She couldn't believe it. The man she was betrothed to might actually be a prophet. Taya had to concentrate to keep her stomach from rising into her throat.

Thirty-eight

Taya swallowed hard. "May I speak?"

Sky Messenger swiveled on the log to look at her and blinked as though he had forgotten she was there. "Yes, of course, Taya."

She wet her lips. War Chief Hiyawento seemed to be staring right through her. Fear and excitement had conjured the unthinkable in her heart, and she didn't know how to deal with it. But . . . but she was beginning, dimly, to understand why Bahna had said she had to go with Sky Messenger on this journey.

Shakily, she said, "I was wondering if perhaps more alliances like the one Grandmother established between the allied Standing Stone villages and Sedge Marsh Village might be possible?"

Hiyawento shifted. Set against the background of firelit palisade, he looked vaguely unreal, his hair dancing around his dark face. "Why do you ask?"

Taya gestured helplessly. "I have spent my life listening to Grandmother's political lectures, so I know something of what our people need and, perhaps, a little of what the Hills People need. If our two peoples could just agree to protect each other from Chief Atotarho"—she wet her lips again—"I mean, he's the problem, isn't he?"

"So far as I'm concerned, he is," the war chief responded.

Sky Messenger stared at her as if confused. And why wouldn't he be? Just a few days ago she'd argued that they had to kill all of their enemies to survive. "I was thinking that if we could agree on that one thing—that Chief Atotarho should be destroyed—and we could create an alliance to do that . . . Well, it would be a start."

Hiyawento's eyes narrowed enough to let Taya know he was suspicious of her motives. "Before the destruction of White Dog Village there might have been a chance, but why would High Matron Kittle agree to such an alliance now? I suspect that at this very instant she's engaged in whipping up a fervor to kill every Hills person alive."

"But your village was not involved in that attack."

"No. Most of our nation didn't even know about it until it was long over. Nonetheless, rage and pain tend to simplify the world, Taya. Your grandmother and the Ruling Council will see only that the Hills People just attacked a Standing Stone village. Such an act demands a response. Your people must be preparing for it as we speak. Our people certainly are."

"Even Sindak?" Affection laced Sky Messenger's voice.

"Of course, my friend. He is an excellent war chief. Protecting our people is his sole responsibility. He'll do whatever it takes to stop a Standing Stone attack. As you would, if the reverse were—"

Sky Messenger shook his head. "No. I've given up my weapons. For good. I'll never touch a bow, or club, again, never raise my hand in violence, not even to save my own life, or the lives of people I love."

Hiyawento appeared stunned. He hesitated, before quietly saying, "Odion, I'm not sure that this is the time for—"

Taya cried, "Yes, please, tell him how foolish it is! He should take up his weapons and return to being deputy war chief before it's too—"

Sky Messenger interrupted, "The *only* position I would accept now is that of *peace* chief." He gave Taya a disgruntled look.

"Peace chief?" Hiyawento leaned back and chuckled softly. "I like the sound of that. It implies something not of this earth."

Taya flapped her arms against her sides. "Let's get back to the subject. I'm telling you, if Grandmother knew the truth about what really happened to White Dog Village, the matrons would vote not to attack the Hills villages that weren't responsible. Grandmother hates Chief Atotarho—she says he's an evil cannibal sorcerer who deserves to die— but she can be reasonable. Perhaps, if Sky Messenger and I can get home quickly enough, we can redirect Grandmother's rage."

"What do you mean? Redirect it?" Hiyawento asked.

"Perhaps we can use it like pine pitch, to glue our peoples together for one purpose: to destroy Atotarho. Please listen to me. I'm sure Grandmother would like that idea, as would the other matrons. Even if it required an onerous alliance with you to achieve it, killing the enemy chief responsible for the deaths of so many Standing Stone women and children would be worth it."

In an ominous voice, Sky Messenger said, "We are all talking treason. Let us not forget that. If we do this, it will have to be done with the stealth of Cougar stalking Hare. Are we all prepared for that? Taya? Are you?"

Am I?

She took a deep breath and exhaled the words: "By the time we reach Bur Oak Village, I think I will be."

Sky Messenger and Hiyawento both nodded to her, as though understanding perfectly well that it took time to brace the body and souls for the possibility of being executed. But then, both men had already committed treason, at least in the eyes of some—Hiyawento for allowing himself to be adopted into the Hills nation, and Sky Messenger for releasing the Flint captives. They understood, as few men ever can, the price of loosing the whirlwind. Once released, its path was almost impossible to control.

"Then we will speak with our matrons about this," Sky Messenger said.

"And I will speak with Zateri about gathering the Women's Council to consider a truce to hear your vision. But don't get your hopes—"

A tall woman warrior, silent as a wolf on a blood trail, trotted out of the darkness, her short black hair flapping around her taut face. "War Chief? You must hurry. Several of Atotarho's warriors are coming. They mean to bring you back to the council meeting."

Hiyawento leaped to his feet. "Kallen, pick two warriors and take my guests to the Bur Oak Village trail. Be back by morning. I don't wish anyone to know you were gone."

"Yes, War Chief."

Hiyawento and Sky Messenger embraced one last time. Hiyawento whispered, "Before you go, tell me of Baji? Is she well?"

"I don't know. I've had no news from Wild River Village for moons. I pray she's safe."

Baji is from Wild River Village. . . .

"Be off, my friend. I'll send word as soon as I know if the matrons will hear your vision."

Sky Messenger gripped Taya's elbow and turned to Kallen. "We're ready."

"We must move quickly." Kallen took the lead, pointing to warriors as they emerged from the forest. Two men fell into line behind Taya.

As they trotted away, Taya said, "Why didn't you tell me that Shagoniyoh had come to both you and Hiyawento?"

Sky Messenger shoved her ahead of him and took up the rear. "We are not the only two people who have been visited by him."

"Others have seen the Spirit, as well? Blessed gods! If I'd known, it would have made a difference." She shook her head. "I'm still terrified, but—"

"You can still change your mind, Taya."

"No, not after tonight. Not after what I heard. I am with you, my future husband. To be against you is even more scary."

Thirty-nine

Ohsinoh followed the mob at a distance, lagging behind the others as they crossed the plaza of Atotarho Village and proceeded on to the sacred platform. Ten hands tall, three upright logs stood in the center of the platform. Some of the most impressive longhouses in the country formed a square around it. People crowded near the platform, their gazes fixed on the man who staggered in the midst of the warriors. He'd been captured seven days ago, and had managed to survive the torture until this moment. His two friends had not. Their bodies hung limply from the two poles on the sides. The crows and magpies had been at them for days. Their eyes were blood-blackened sockets, and the flesh had almost been completely stripped from their faces, leaving gape-mouthed skulls to stare down upon the people of Atotarho Village.

Ohsinoh stopped, allowing the party to continue without him, and knelt to dip a handful of water from a puddle. It tasted earthy and dank. He sang a little to himself as he drank, *"The crow comes, the crow comes, pity the little children, beat the drum . . ."*

The words had been stuck in his head since childhood. He heard the tune all day and all night, repeating over and over as though seeping up from a black door inside him. There were times when it drove him so mad he beat his head with rocks, trying to make it go away.

People glanced at him, wondering why he didn't simply help himself to the large pots of rainwater that stood near the houses. But he would never do that. He'd never share water with these people. The Wolf Clan had abandoned him to horror when he'd seen just four summers. Everything here was unclean, full of contagion. If a man stayed too long, he felt certain a part of his soul would remain behind, condemned to wander the village until the last timbers rotted to dust.

Two old women passed, pointed at him, and whispered behind their hands. He gave them a grim smile, and they made the sign against evil and hurried away.

When he dipped his hand again, he saw his reflection. He'd painted his face to hide his identity. His white face paint was decorated with black stripes. Though the paint did not hide his oversized ears, upturned nostrils, and small dark eyes, it obscured them, as the striped shadows of the forest did the deer. Few people ever recognized him when he wore face paint. Those who did didn't live long.

As he rose to his feet, his heavy moosehide cape waffled around his tall body. Powerfully built, he'd seen twenty-three summers pass. His thick eyebrows were obsidian black and formed a single line over his slitted eyes.

A flock of children veered wide around him, laughing, running to see the latest spectacle. Their dirty feet were bare and caked with mud.

Warriors marched the doomed man up the platform steps and tied him to the middle pole. Ohsinoh couldn't tear his gaze away. He had never even met the victim, but—like everyone else here—he yearned to watch him die. The prisoner was a warrior from White Dog Village, a village of the Standing Stone People. That was enough reason to hate him.

The man's head hung down, and he breathed heavily. His muscular body had endured much over the past few days. Slashes and punctures adorned his flesh. All had been cauterized with fiery brands. Even from this distance, Ohsinoh could smell the taint of burned skin and muscle.

The esteemed and powerful Atotarho emerged from the Wolf longhouse and with great ceremony marched toward the platform. Two holy men followed him. As he climbed the steps to stand before the doomed man, the circlets of human skull on Atotarho's black cape flashed. The prisoner had no strength left. His chest heaved, and he panted as he licked parched lips. With little ceremony, Atotarho drew out his flint knife and slit open the man's belly. When his entrails fell onto the platform, the man let out one final wail and slumped. As was his right, Atotarho cut the still-beating heart from the warrior's chest and presented it to the glorious war chief, Sindak, who'd won the battle. Sindak bowed and strode away to eat his prize in private.

Ohsinoh chuckled. The rest of the human carcass was soon cut up and distributed among the villagers. Three little girls ran by him carrying bloody pieces of meat, their faces alight.

When the crowd dispersed, Ohsinoh stood for a while gazing up at the three dead men. They'd gotten better than they deserved. The Standing Stone People were savage beasts, cowards not worthy of life. Even Wrass and Odion had chosen to be adopted by other nations.

He moved a little closer, standing in the rear, waiting to catch the great Atotarho's gaze. The chief stood atop the platform speaking with the holy men.

Finally, Atotarho turned, glimpsed Ohsinoh, and paled. His crooked body careened down the platform steps, his walking stick clacking. "I told you *never* to come here. You were supposed to send a messenger telling me where to meet you."

"But, Father, I wished to see my home. Surely I have that right. I've been away too many summers. I'm certain my relatives have missed me."

He smiled at the old man, and the chief's eyes narrowed. Atotarho looked around to see who was watching and whispered, "Give me your message and leave."

"I've accomplished both tasks."

Atotarho blinked. "Really? Because it isn't apparent. If anything, my daughter's husband is even more a problem now than before. Last night in council he urged peace. *Peace!* And after everything we've gone through, his words had power. Two clan matrons sided with him and the Coldspring Village council. It was a disgusting display of arrogance."

Ohsinoh leaned down to whisper in an amused voice, "Sky Messenger has pitied the little children, and soon, very soon, the Crow will come to sit upon Hiyawento's head."

"That's gibberish. Are you saying you've seen Sky Messenger?"

"Oh, yes." Ohsinoh chuckled. "Sky Messenger met with Hiyawento last night outside of Coldspring Village, just before Hiyawento rejoined your council meeting."

It took a few instants for the words to sink in; then rage twisted the old man's wrinkles into frightening lines. "Are you certain of this?"

"I personally followed him from Atotarho Village to Coldspring Village. I saw them sitting together in the aspen meadow."

Atotarho stamped his walking stick on the ground as though to punish Great Grandmother Earth for allowing such an abomination. "My own daughter's husband is conspiring with the Standing Stone People behind my back? What did they talk about?"

"I couldn't get close to hear, but given what he said in council, it isn't hard to figure out."

Enraged, Atotarho said, "Very well. You've brought your message. Now get out of my village before someone recognizes you. When it is clear to me, and it isn't yet, that you have accomplished both of the tasks I gave you, I'll send your payment to the usual place."

Ohsinoh laughed and gave him an exaggerated mocking bow. As he strode across Atotarho Village, he drew magical symbols in the air, cursing his relatives. When people noticed, they hastened to flee from him. Even the dogs trotted away growling.

Forty

That night Zateri knelt before the fire in the longhouse, stirring a pot of cornmeal mush filled with strips of venison jerky and pine nuts. The rich scent of the jerky mixed with the sweetness of the corn and scented the air. Hiyawento sat on the mat beside her, staring at the fire as though praying hard the flames would speak to him and tell him what to do next. The council meeting had not gone well. Hiyawento had been openly accused of cowardice and collaborating with the enemy. At the end, it had almost come to blows.

Across the fire, their three daughters played with a corn-husk doll, handing it back and forth, tousling its long corn-silk hair, rattling the beaded fringe on the doll's leather dress. It was a pretty thing. She wondered where Hiyawento had gotten it.

Barely above a whisper, Hiyawento asked, "What about the other matrons?"

She shook her head. "I don't know. Grandmother wishes to hear Sky Messenger's vision. She agreed to send messengers to the others. She'll inform us if there is a consensus that he should be heard. But this is the worst possible time to be asking such a thing. The turmoil in the nation is growing worse."

Early that morning she'd run to Grandmother's chamber in the Wolf longhouse and told her about Sky Messenger's visit. She'd also begged Grandmother not to tell Father for fear that he'd immediately dispatch a party to hunt down and kill Sky Messenger and Taya. Grandmother, who'd barely been able to lift her head from her bedding hides, had reluctantly agreed.

"What are you thinking about, my husband?"

He stretched out on his side on the mat and propped his head on his hand, watching the girls play. "About the Dream. He said it changes, as though not even the Spirits know the final shape of the story, but he's certain it has to do with what happened to him that last night in the old woman's camp. He asked me if I'd seen what happened."

Her heart twinged. "He doesn't remember?"

"No." Hiyawento grimaced at his tea cup. "Which I think is a blessing, but he says he must know."

"He's always been touched by Spirits. I wish I'd seen him. I would have so loved that." They had endured so much together as children. He was almost as much a part of her souls as Hiyawento was. "What did you think of his betrothed?"

"Hmm?" Hiyawento blinked as though just hearing her. "Oh, his wife-to-be? She's very young, fourteen summers. Pretty. Actually, she looks very much like her grandmother, High Matron Kittle."

"In that case, she's not pretty, she's stunningly beautiful."

He shrugged and fiddled with his empty tea cup, turning it where it rested upon the mat. She watched him closely. His thoughts seemed far away.

"What else did Sky Messenger say? The thing you haven't told me. Was it Sky Messenger who asked you to argue against war in the council?"

Hiyawento looked at each person who was close enough to hear them, then he lowered his voice. Barely audible, he said, "Yes, but he's right."

"But in a war council?" She felt slightly ill. "Urging peace in a village council meeting is one thing, but in a war council?"

"Zateri, someone has to stand up for peace. You know it as well as I do. I don't mind being the first."

She placed the horn spoon upon one of the hearth rocks and sat down beside him to stare into his worried eyes. "Peace, no matter the cause? Even if we are attacked by Mountain warriors?"

"Yes." He squinted at the flickering flames.

"He can't be suggesting you refuse to defend our village?"

"If we are attacked, I'm sure he knows I will fight to my last breath to protect our people. Just . . . I think he wants one war chief out there who always, in every case, counsels against war."

"He must know, however, that if the Ruling Council approves an attack, you will have no choice but to lead our warriors into the fight. He does understand that, doesn't he?"

"All he asked was that I vote no in council. He said nothing about what happened when everyone else voted yes."

She drew up her knees and propped her elbows atop them, trying to imagine how the council had gone. The other members of the war council must have been furious, especially if they'd just lost loved ones in the White Dog Village battle. Hiyawento had told her he'd been accused of both cowardice and treason, but she suspected a few people had also probably threatened his life. If anyone attempted to carry out that threat, it would be catastrophic. Murder was the worst crime. It placed an absolute obligation upon the relatives of the deceased. They had to seek revenge, or retribution. Often grieving family members claimed the life of a member of the murderer's clan—his mother, grandmother, even the clan matron—as was their right. Blood feuds could and did escalate into civil wars. And the nation was already on the verge of splitting down the middle.

She asked, "Does Sky Messenger realize that always voting no will make you appear to be a simpering weakling? Not to mention a fool?"

"He's thought it through, Zateri. He needs a symbol."

"A symbol?"

"A war chief who preaches peace. He needs me to become a *peace chief*. He says he will never pick up a weapon again, never raise his hand in violence, not even to save his own life, or the lives of people he loves."

Zateri frowned at the sooty shadows clinging in the corners. The firelight turned them into spectral dancers, their dark feet pounding out the sacred rhythms that had created the world. A strange, almost bizarre notion was forming in her heart. "He's trying to launch an unarmed revolt."

He lifted his head. "What do you mean?"

"I mean if village matrons followed his example and simply refused to cooperate—to attend council meetings—the Ruling Council could never vote to dispatch warriors."

"Any matron who refuses to attend a meeting of the Ruling Council will be labeled a traitor." As he thought about it, Hiyawento's brows drew together over his hooked nose. "For the renegade matrons to remain steadfast will require a great deal more bravery than swinging a war club at an enemy warrior."

Zateri considered the ramifications of refusing to attend the next council. Blunting the arrows of war through noncooperation would be very much like swinging an invisible war club at her own relatives. Could she, with her minimal influence, gather enough matrons together to accomplish anything meaningful? "Do you believe his vision?"

Hiyawento didn't even hesitate, "You know I do."

"Then you also believe you will be there when the World Tree shakes and Elder Brother Sun covers his face with the soot of the dying world?"

He answered in a sober voice. "Yes, and he'll need me more at that moment than at any other time in our lives."

When he looked up at her, his eyes were like night stars. Too bright. She had to look away. She prayed to all the ancestors who had ever lived to give her, and Hiyawento, the strength for the trials ahead. "When is the next war council?"

"Tomorrow. The war chiefs are afraid that Kittle's retribution will be swift. Every village is preparing to be attacked."

"What will you say to them when they suggest striking first?"

Firelight fluttered over his tense features. "I will counsel against war, as I did today."

"Then you had best take ten warriors with you to guard your back. I don't want you waylaid on the way home."

He smiled. "That would make me appear afraid. I can't afford such—"

Across the fire, a shrill, *"You're ruining it!"* erupted, and Zateri looked up in time to see Kahn-Tineta rip the corn-husk doll from her youngest sister's mouth. As she wiped the drool on her cape, she cried, "Look what you did, Jimer! Now it's going to fall apart!"

Three-summers-old Jimer let out a yowl and tried to grab it back.

"Here, give it to me." Zateri held out her hand.

Kahn-Tineta's lower lip quivered. She clutched the doll to her chest. "Mother, it's my turn to play with it. Jimer and Catta have been chewing on it for the past hand of time!"

"Give it to me *now*, Kahn-Tineta," Zateri ordered, and extended her hand farther.

Kahn-Tineta grudgingly handed it over, and Zateri placed it on the mat beside the hearth ring. When she turned back to Hiyawento, he was struggling to suppress a smile.

"The doll is a pretty thing," he said. "Where did you get it?"

"Me?" she asked in surprise. "I thought you brought it to them. I've never seen it before tonight."

They both turned to stare at their daughters. Jimer's gaze was still fixed on the doll, while Kahn-Tineta glared at Zateri, and Catta seemed to have found something fascinating on the bottom of her moccasin.

"Kahn-Tineta," Zateri asked, "where did you get the doll? You didn't take it from another child in the longhouse, did you?"

"No, Mother! I wouldn't take something from one of my relatives. Catta brought the doll to me this afternoon. She said a man gave it to her."

"A man? Catta, who gave you the doll?"

Catta's five-summers-old face took on a guilty expression. She licked her lips nervously. "I don't know his name. He was scary. He said the doll came from Sedge Marsh Village and he wanted me to have it—though he said it was really more of a gift for you, Father, than for me."

Hiyawento lifted his head slowly, his eyes unblinking. "What did the man look like, Catta?"

She drew lines across her young face. "He had his face painted white with black stripes. He said he was a friend of yours."

"A friend . . . to me?"

Someone from the war council.

Catta nodded vigorously. "And to Mother. He said he'd known you both since you were children."

When Zateri turned to meet Hiyawento's eyes, she found him staring not at her, but at the corn-husk doll. "Did the man say anything else?"

Catta swallowed hard. Her enormous eyes were shiny with tears. "No."

Zateri's gaze burned into Hiyawento's. "There's something I have to tell you. I—I've been meaning to. Sindak came to me. He said . . . he—he wasn't going to tell me anything until he was sure."

"What about?"

"Hehaka. And Ohsinoh."

With the swiftness of lightning striking, Hiyawento grabbed the doll and threw it in the fire. The dry corn husks instantly caught and burst into flame.

"Father!" Catta groaned. "No!"

Zateri glanced at her chastened daughters, then at the charred doll in the fire pit. It was little more than a human-shaped clump of ash now. The polished stone beads that had decorated the dress fringe had split apart and rolled across the logs. The holes in their centers, where the beads had been strung, resembled tiny glowing eyes.

Hiyawento dropped his face into his hands and massaged his temples. "Blessed gods, I pray Sindak is wrong. I . . ."

Kahn-Tineta screamed, *"Mother!"* just as Jimer toppled backward and went into convulsions. Her body flopped and jerked across the mats. Before Zateri could even get to her feet, Catta collapsed with her mouth foaming and her limbs twitching like a clubbed dog's.

Hiyawento lunged to his feet and grabbed Catta. "Zateri! What's happening?"

"I don't know!" She scrambled around the fire and stared down at

Jimer's face. The little girl's eyes rolled in her head as her jaws spasmodi-
cally clapped together. She lifted her head and shouted, "Pedeza, go find
Ahweyoh!"

Her cousin ran.

Zateri dropped to the floor and pulled Jimer into her lap, holding her
daughter, praying that the seizure would end soon, and she could . . .
Jimer's body suddenly went limp. Zateri lifted her up and pressed her ear
to her daughter's chest. She couldn't hear a heartbeat. She shook Jimer
until the girl's head flopped. "Jimer? Jimer, no!"

Hiyawento cried, "Blessed Spirits, this can't be . . . what's happening?"
Hiyawento clutched Catta tightly against his chest. He was rocking back
and forth with tears streaming down his face. Catta's head flopped with
his motions. Half the longhouse had crowded around them. A buzz of
hushed conversations rose.

"Hiyawento?" A sob caught Zateri's throat. "Is Catta . . . ? Is she . . . ?"

"She—she's not breathing."

Kahn-Tineta burst into tears. "Mother! Father!" The last word became
a wail.

Forty-one

Zateri gazed down at Ahweyoh while the old Healer examined Catta and Jimer. Ahweyoh had seen almost sixty summers and had thin, chin-length white hair and a face like a shriveled scrap of leather. He wore a tattered buckskin cape over his sleep shirt. Everyone in the longhouse had crowded close, whispering, shaking their heads as they watched.

The little girls rested on Zateri and Hiyawento's bedding hides. Their faces looked so peaceful. Their mouths were ajar, their eyes closed. Catta's head tilted to the left, spilling black hair across her right cheek. Jimer lay on her back with her arms over her head. Ahweyoh pressed Jimer's ribs; then his hands moved lower to prod her belly. A strange moldy scent issued from her mouth. Ahweyoh leaned forward to sniff her breath. Finally, the old Healer's somber expression slackened, and he stood. Ahweyoh glanced at the far corner of the chamber where Hiyawento sat holding Kahn-Tineta. Kahn-Tineta had her face buried against his shoulder, weeping softly. Hiyawento patted her back and spoke into her ear, but his face had gone deathly gray, wiped clean of all except the hideous realization that his two youngest daughters were dead.

Ahweyoh said, "It was musquash root, probably in the doll."

"In the doll?" Zateri asked.

"Yes, I suspect the powdered root had been folded between the corn husks."

At the expression on Hiyawento's face, Zateri's heart went cold. Three women nearby sobbed. Zateri kept her eyes on her husband, for he looked as though he longed to be dead himself. His expression had contorted. He couldn't take his gaze from his little girls.

"Are you certain? I need to know," Zateri asked. She felt numb, not really there. None of this seemed real. But she knew, all too soon, her world would come crashing down. As her gaze flicked to the people standing close by, her breathing went shallow. She was the village matron. No matter what personal loss she sustained, she could not appear weak or ineffective. She had enemies. Every matron did. Give them one small opening, and they would slit her throat politically.

Ahweyoh searched Hiyawento's face, clearly cataloging the extent of Hiyawento's strain, perhaps wondering what he might do next. "Yes, I'm sure."

Hiyawento lifted Kahn-Tineta's chin to look into her brimming eyes. "Your mother and I must speak. Could you stay with Pedeza for a time?"

"No, Father, don't leave me!" she wailed. "I'm afraid!"

"You'll be all right. Go on now. We won't be long."

Kahn-Tineta shrieked as she ran across the house and grabbed Pedeza around the legs. Pedeza petted her hair. "Come, let's make a cup of tea and talk."

Hiyawento wiped his nose on his sleeve and got to his feet. He was shaking badly. "Come with me, Zateri. Outside."

"Let me grab my cape."

She swung it around her shoulders and followed him out of the house into the icy night wind.

Hiyawento led her to the central village fire, where a bed of coals glowed. He kept his back to her, trying to hide his face. Her heart ached for him. He was on the verge of drastic actions, but she did not know whether they were based upon grief, or rage.

A strange, eerie clarity had come over Zateri. Unlike the people in the longhouse, Zateri did not make futile anxious gestures or sob. Her souls were busy, piecing things together. The instant she'd understood without a doubt that her daughters were dead, she'd started asking why, how, and who. As the truth took shape, it loomed over her like the shadow of a dark clawed beast.

Hiyawento sank down on one of the log benches that surrounded the fire and dropped his face into his hands. She saw his wide shoulders shake and heard the desperate choking sounds he made. When he raised his head and she glimpsed his face, she swiftly went to him and sat down on the log.

"Hiyawento," she began. His arms went suddenly around her waist, and he crushed her against his broad chest.

"Dear gods, what have I done?"

"You?" she said in confusion. She stroked his shoulder-length hair. "You're not to blame."

"It's the war council. I should never have . . ." His grip tightened around her waist, and he began speaking rapidly, babbling incoherent words while he pressed his cheek against hers. "I knew it would be dangerous . . . when I agreed . . . but I thought . . . Zateri, you know I'm right!"

He continued, speaking against her hair, words blurred, indistinct, saying things she could not decipher. "Stop this," she said. "There is something important I must speak with you about."

"Dear Gods," he wept, "they . . . can't be . . . can't be dead."

She shoved away and forced him to look at her. His face had contorted. "Listen to me. Try to concentrate."

"What is it?"

"I don't think this has anything to do with your peace initiatives in the war council."

"How can you say that? You know what they accused—"

"Listen to me. Just after Ahweyoh arrived, I heard a rumor that Ohsinoh was in Atotarho Village today."

He didn't seem to comprehend her implication. "The Bluebird Witch wouldn't dare walk into a village. He'd be killed on sight."

"Apparently, he wore elaborate face paint."

"Face paint . . ." Hiyawento's voice faded. "Like the man who . . . who gave our daughter the doll?"

"Pedeza heard that his face was painted white with black stripes. Think about this: He said he was a friend of ours, and that he'd known us since we were children. I think, maybe, Hehaka is Ohsinoh."

A frightening mixture of rage and fear creased his face. "Even if he is, why would Hehaka want to destroy our family? We never did anything to him—except free him from slavery."

"He may see things differently."

"What do you mean?"

Two people emerged from the Snipe Clan longhouse and proceeded across the plaza. They spoke in low ominous tones as they cast glances at Zateri and Hiyawento. Already, the news must have spread through every longhouse in Coldspring Village.

"He loved that old woman, Hiyawento. Our clan abandoned him when he'd seen four summers. For all practical purposes, she was the only mother he'd ever known. He probably also saw her Outcast warriors as his family—"

Hiyawento's bloodshot eyes fixed upon her face. "But they enslaved and tortured him!"

"Yes, but the old woman and her men were all he had."

". . . And we killed them."

A haunted sensation filtered through her. His words repeated in her head, spinning around, mixing with memories of Hehaka's facial expressions from twelve summers ago. After Koracoo's party had rescued him, Hehaka had fought like a caged bear to get back to the evil witch.

"You didn't kill the old woman, my husband. Baji, Odion, and I did."

Hiyawento seemed to wilt. He sagged against her, burying his face in her long hair. "I killed several of her men. He must blame all of us."

"So . . . this is the Law of Retribution? We killed the old witch and her guards, and he believes that gives him the right to—"

"Your father could just as easily be to blame. He consorts with witches! Do you think he's responsible?"

"I can't believe he would murder his own granddaughters. Even my father—"

"He's a monster, and you know it!" he replied. "He's capable of anything. Even this." Hiyawento suddenly swung around to look at the longhouse with blazing eyes. "They can't be dead!"

He leaped to his feet and marched away so swiftly, Zateri had to grab the log to keep from falling. She called, "Hiyawento, come back."

"No, I—I have to check them again. Maybe they're breathing now." He broke into a run.

Zateri rubbed her cold arms. The red coals in the fire pit flared when Wind Woman breathed upon them, shimmering and casting reddish light across the longhouses. Where had Ohsinoh gone after he'd left? He was her brother. Or at least, it seemed likely. Was he still here, perhaps watching her? They had no proof that it was Ohsinoh who'd poisoned the corn-husk doll. Many people painted their faces white with black stripes. It was common enough, but . . .

Did my father pay a witch to kill my daughters?

Somewhere in the quiet depths of her soul, details churned, some matching, some not. All relevant if she could just keep the overwhelming grief at bay long enough to figure them out.

Her gaze moved over the plaza. Blue smoke curled from the smoke holes in the roofs and hung over the village like ghostly serpents. They twined together and slithered upward, flying for the Sky World.

Memories seeped up from the deep recesses of her heart. In the background, Zateri could hear Baji screaming . . . then Hehaka's voice: *"Sometimes the men want boys. You should be ready. They're going to hurt you."*

"Tonight?" Wrass asks.

Hehaka shrugs. "I don't know. Maybe."

Wrass looks around, says to Odion, "Hehaka is just guessing. How could he know that?"

Hehaka crawls closer, his batlike face alight. He has seen eleven summers. "I know. Believe me. There are a few men who keep coming back just for me."

The horror of that memory snapped Zateri back to the plaza, but not before a thin wail started deep in her lungs. She had to shake herself to force it down. If she lived to see ten thousand summers pass, the pride in Hehaka's voice—his words spoken against a background of Baji's screams—would still ring in her ears.

Shouts rose in the Wolf longhouse. Hiyawento yelled, "They're my daughters! Give them to me!" A woman's shrill voice responded.

Zateri dragged herself to her feet.

For a few terrible moments she continued staring out at the firelit darkness, trying to imagine what life would be like without the running patter of their small feet, without the feel of their arms around her neck or the sound of their laughter in her ears. The shining eyes that had looked up at her with such love . . . gone.

Pedeza shouted, "Leave Kahn-Tineta alone! She doesn't know anything else!"

Zateri squared her narrow shoulders and started back.

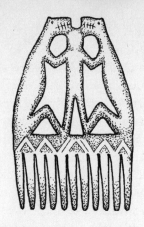

Forty-two

As Pedeza marched across the plaza of Atotarho Village, people raced around her, flying in and out of longhouses, carrying water and firewood, already preparing for the Standing Stone attack that everyone knew was coming. All, that is, except for the young men. Most of them huddled around the council house. Some had their ears pressed to the walls, listening. She wondered why they needed to, for she could hear the raised voices from here.

Two guards stood outside the council house door, their faces set into hard lines, war clubs braced upon their broad shoulders. She hated this village, hated Chief Atotarho: He had brought so much pain to the Wolf Clan. If her lineage achieved prominence, the first thing it would do would be to remove Atotarho.

She was dressed in a long buckskin cape without decorations. Her black braid bounced upon her back as she hurried through the cold wind.

When she halted before the guards, her voice sounded small, even to her. "Please. I need to see War Chief Sindak?"

"There's a war council going on, woman. Can't you hear the shouting?"

"I need to see him. It's urgent."

"Urgent?" The guard hooked a thumb over his shoulder. "They're talking about annihilating the entire Standing Stone nation before it can attack us, and you want me to disturb the discussion? Go away. Come back later."

Pedeza wrung her hands. "Please. If I don't see Sindak, someone he cares about is going to die."

The guard's expression changed. He looked at her from the corner of his eye, apparently thinking about the ramifications if Sindak's friend died because he'd refused to deliver a simple message. Finally, the guard pulled his war club off his shoulder, set it beside the door, and stabbed a finger at her. "All right. I'll tell him, but if you're wrong and Sindak slits my throat for this—"

"He won't. I swear. He'll reward you. Maybe even make you deputy war chief. It's *that* important."

The man scowled at her, ducked beneath the curtain, and vanished.

While Pedeza waited under the second guard's alert gaze, she paced. Last night had been the worst of her life. She'd loved those little girls. Watching them die, seeing them lying cold and still in the firelight, had been like dying herself. Then the parade of relatives and Healers had begun and hadn't ended until this morning. Pedeza was exhausted and heartbroken. Zateri had met each person, consoled their grief, and thanked them for coming. All the while, she'd watched Hiyawento disintegrating like a sand sculpture in a rainstorm.

Sindak ducked beneath the curtain. When he saw her, his narrow face creased with worry. He wore a pure black cape—the color of war and death—and had his hair tied back with a cord. The style made his lean face appear even more narrow. "What is it, Pedeza?"

"Hiyawento . . ."

Misunderstanding, he said, "He's not here. The war council is livid."

She hesitated, uncertain where to begin. "Then you haven't heard about Matron Zateri's daughters? They're dead."

His deeply sunken eyes were bloodshot and red-rimmed, as though he hadn't slept in days. "Blessed gods, forgive me. No one told me. When did it happen?"

"Last night. Please, I know this meeting is critical, but if I could just have a few moments to speak with you in private—"

"I don't have much time," he said as he took her by the arm and led her into the middle of the plaza, out of hearing range of the guards. "How did they die?"

"I don't know everything—just that an unknown man gave the girls a doll, and it was poisoned. Our Healers say it was filled with ground musquash root. You know how children are. They put the doll in their mouths."

Sindak bowed his head. "That's terrible, but how can I help?"

She braced herself. "It's Hiyawento."

"Is he all right? I can't even imagine how he must be feeling. Those little girls were beautiful."

Suddenly Pedeza's tears began to flow. She lifted her cape and dried her eyes. "You have to come, War Chief. Matron Zateri has done the best she can, but Hiyawento has become a madman. I swear he's lost his soul."

"What do you mean?"

"He's gone crazy! Last night after he knew they were dead, he charged around the longhouse smashing pots, tearing down the bark partition walls, screaming at the top of his lungs. You know how much he loved those little girls. This morning at dawn, he carried them out into the forest and won't come home. He says he's never coming back to Coldspring Village."

Earnestly, Sindak replied, "Tell me quickly what Zateri needs. I'll help if I can."

"She wants you to speak with him. She says he needs a friend, a man he trusts, and you're the only man in our entire nation that he'll listen to."

Shouts rang out from the council house. Sindak turned to look, and his jaw went hard. He took Pedeza's arm in a friendly grasp. "Where is Hiyawento?"

"Between the aspen grove and Mallard Marsh."

"Very well. Tell Matron Zateri I will come as soon as I can."

"Yes. I will. Thank you, War Chief."

Pedeza watched Sindak stride back to the council house, his long legs eating the distance; then she smothered her sobs and started back for Coldspring Village.

Forty-three

The scents of water and soggy leaves rode the evening breeze near the marsh.

Sindak halted at the edge of the aspen grove and stared out across the reeds and dead cattails. Golden leaves pirouetted through the frigid air around him, alighting on his shoulders and black hair. He paid them no notice. In the distance, a thin streamer of smoke spiraled into the dove-gray twilight. The thought of trying to talk sense into a man as grief-stricken as Hiyawento made him long to return to the insanity of the war council. What could he say? Nothing, nothing in the world, could lessen the pain of losing a loved one, especially an innocent child. Or worse, two. For a moment he hesitated, trying to imagine how the conversation might go; then he shook his head and tramped around the edge of the marsh toward the campfire. Somewhere out on the water, ducks quacked.

When he got close, Hiyawento shouted, "Go away or I'll kill you!"

Sindak suppressed the urge to pull his war club from his belt and called, "I'm a friend. At least I think I am. Correct me if I'm wrong about that?"

Hiyawento thrashed through the brush. When he stood no more than ten paces away, he looked at Sindak with bright glazed eyes. He held his nocked bow up, aimed at Sindak's heart. His jaw muscles trembled despite his efforts to clench his teeth—the action that of a man teetering on madness.

Sindak spread his arms. "I heard the doll was poisoned. Yesterday someone in Atotarho Village claimed he'd seen Ohsinoh talking with the chief. Have you heard this rumor?"

The bow lowered slightly, and Hiyawento's broad shoulders shook. In a choking voice, he said, "Yes."

"I need more information about your daughters' deaths. May I speak with you?"

Hiyawento relaxed and lowered the bow. "Come." He turned and walked back toward the campfire.

When Sindak made it through the brush, he found Hiyawento standing over the dead children. They'd been laid out on their backs, their clothing smoothed, their hair combed. Each stared up at the sky with shrunken death-gray eyes. Their white faces shone in the firelight. No matter how long he lived, that wrenching image would never leave Sindak.

He knelt on the opposite side of the fire and watched Hiyawento stroking Jimer's face.

Sindak said, "Ohsinoh would never have had the audacity to enter Atotarho Village unless he knew he'd be protected."

Hiyawento's eyes went shiny. In a lethal voice, he said, "The man who gave my daughter the doll he—he had painted his face white with black stripes."

Sindak nodded. "That matches the description of the man who spoke with Atotarho."

Hiyawento's grip tightened on the elk hide over Catta's heart, and words tumbled from his mouth, hoarse and broken. "He told her that . . . it . . . the doll. Was more a gift for me than for her."

Sindak quietly released the breath he'd been holding. If he could keep Hiyawento talking, everything might be all right. "Listen to me. For the past nine moons, I've had a man tracking Negano. The chief has met with the Bluebird Witch several times, and Negano has delivered many bags of payment to a clearing two days' run from here. I think Atotarho has been working with Ohsinoh for a long time, perhaps for many summers."

"Blessed gods, Sindak, if he's been working with Atotarho, then the chief paid him to do this! He—the old man—he wanted me to watch my daughters die. He's punishing me for speaking out against war in the council. I swear before my ancestors that I will *kill* him! I will cut his heart out—"

"And I will help you do it," Sindak said, and waited for Hiyawento to turn so he could stare directly into the man's wild eyes. "But I must have proof."

"Proof?" Hiyawento cried and sprang to his feet. "I'm not waiting for proof! I'll kill anyone who tries to stop me!"

Sindak remained kneeling before the fire, but his thoughts were on the war club tucked into his belt. Could he get to it faster than Hiyawento could shoot an arrow through his lungs? Just as Sindak's hand started to edge for his club, Hiyawento seemed to deflate. He hung his head, and tears filled his eyes. "This is my fault, Sindak. All . . . my fault."

"None of this is your fault."

Tears ran down his face as Hiyawento hugged himself and looked back at his daughters. "Yes, it is. I should never have come to Hills country. I should have left Zateri alone. I—I loved her so. I'd loved her since we were children. We'd endured so much together. I thought . . . maybe, if I just . . . I tried to obey my clan and marry another, but . . . oh, gods. I'm leaving, I tell you. I'm killing the chief, then I'm leaving and never coming back." He put his head in his hands and squeezed as though to crush the thoughts. "Blessed ancestors, what have I done?"

"You made a life for yourself, a good life, that's what. And a good life for Zateri, too."

"*If it weren't for me, none of this—*"

"That's foolish." Sindak rose to his feet to loom over Hiyawento.

Hiyawento blinked and gazed up at him with a stunned expression. "You haven't heard a word I've said. I've been trying to tell you—"

"You're moaning like a twelve-summers-old boy. You still have a loving wife and daughter who need you more than they ever have. I saw Zateri on my way here. Kahn-Tineta was lying curled in a ball with Zateri stroking her hair. If you think you're dying inside, how do you think they feel? Zateri and Pedeza have laid out clean clothes and all the ritual necessities to clean your daughters and send them on their journey. If you cared at all about them"—he waved his hand to the dead girls—"you would take them back so that their mother could prepare them. Instead, the great war chief, Hiyawento, is out hiding in the forest weeping like an infant."

Anger twisted Hiyawento's face. Sindak didn't budge as Hiyawento leaned close and growled, "You're asking for a stiletto in your heart."

Sindak stared into those blazing eyes for several moments, assessing, before he replied, "Do you want to twist my head off and kick it around for the village dogs?"

Through gritted teeth Hiyawento said, "Yes!"

"Then you're sounding more like your old self. You must be feeling better. So I'm leaving now." He turned his back on Hiyawento and walked away.

When he'd gone twenty paces without an arrow in his back, he dared to exhale.

In another ten paces, he heard Hiyawento call, "Sindak?"

"Yes?" He turned.

Hiyawento wiped his eyes with his hands. His voice was stronger, if hollow. "How did the war council vote today?"

Sindak waited as Hiyawento tipped his head back and stared at the first campfires of the dead that gleamed along the Path of Souls. He seemed to be gathering his strength to speak.

"The vote was unanimous to attack the allied Standing Stone villages before they can get organized to attack us. The matrons promised to return with their final decision as soon as possible. I expect a decision tomorrow."

"Did anyone speak for peace?"

Sindak frowned. "No."

Guilt ravaged his face. He looked back at his dead daughters. As evening deepened, their small white faces picked up the wavering gleam of the fire. "This is just what Atotarho wanted. I played right into his hands."

Sindak didn't respond. If the chief had been responsible for the deaths of the man's daughters, he was right. It was a calculated move designed to eliminate Hiyawento's influence. And it had worked. If Hiyawento had been there, Sindak suspected the vote would have been split and never referred to the Ruling Council.

To silence Hiyawento, Atotarho was willing to murder his own grand-daughters.

Hiyawento called, "War Chief?"

"Yes?"

Hiyawento wiped his face on his sleeve. "If you wouldn't mind, I'd appreciate it if you could help me carry my little girls home."

Sindak walked back. As Hiyawento scooped up Jimer and clutched her to his chest, Sindak gently lifted Catta into his arms. Her small body had grown stiff.

They silently walked around the marsh trail. Just before they reached the Coldspring palisade, Hiyawento halted and turned to gaze at Sindak with bloodshot eyes.

"I want you to answer a question. Do you believe Ohsinoh is Hehaka?"

Sindak tightened his hold on Catta's cold body. "I think so, yes."

Hiyawento didn't say a word. He just walked for the palisade gates.

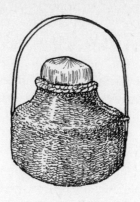

Forty-four

High Matron Tila sat wrapped in hides on her bench, her back propped against the wall of her compartment. Without that support, she would have dissolved like a fistful of earth in a thunderstorm. The excruciating pain in her chest had left her trembling. She did the best she could to hide it as she looked at the old man pacing before her. Atotarho's crooked body made his movements more of a careening than a simple placing of one foot in front of the other. His gray hair, braided with rattlesnake skins, shimmered.

She listened to his walking stick thump on the hard-packed dirt floor. She had known him his entire life, but she had never hated him more than at this moment. The emotion was so powerful it felt like a dark miasma enveloping the world, turning it into something monstrous. The expression on his gaunt skeletal face told her something had surprised him, and he didn't like it at all.

Tila whispered, "Don't bother to deny it. I don't have the strength for lies. Did you know he'd kill your granddaughters?"

Atotarho's wrinkled lips pursed. He didn't answer for a time. Finally, he shook his head, and the circlets of skull on his black cape flashed. "No."

His voice was genuinely troubled, but he'd perfected that tone over the long summers, so she had no idea if he truly regretted his actions or not. "You've turned your daughter against you for good. There's nothing you can do now, or ever, to redeem yourself in her eyes. Do you realize that? You've lost her completely."

"She doesn't know I was responsible. She must think it was witchery, or perhaps—"

"You're a fool." Tila watched him try to indignantly straighten his hunched back without success. "She is *my* granddaughter. I guarantee you she will concentrate all her efforts on destroying you. You don't have long to rule, Chief."

Atotarho leaned heavily on his walking stick. In the firelight, the snake eyes tattooed on his fingertips seemed to wink. "I'll find a way to make it up to her. Perhaps start placing suggestions that her husband should be promoted to a higher position on the Ruling Council—"

Tila let out a low disdainful laugh. "You can't 'make up' for killing a woman's daughters, even if it was accidental. Besides, you won't have the chance. If I were Hiyawento I'd be plotting your murder this instant. He just has to bide his time until the moment is right." She sucked in an agonized breath. When she let it out, she said, "If I had the strength, I'd save him the trouble."

Atotarho's wrinkled face twisted with anger. He'd always hated hearing blunt words. "I tell you I didn't know the witch would do this. It wasn't my fault."

"Well, that doesn't matter now, does it?"

Stubbornly, he said, "It matters to me. I would never have harmed my own granddaughters! They are my legacy. The future rulership of the Wolf Clan depends upon—"

"You should have thought of that before you gave a witch free rein to take care of 'your problem' however he saw fit."

Atotarho glared at the herb pots lining the wall to Tila's left. Softly, he answered, "I realize that now."

Tila sighed and let her chin fall to rest upon the bulky hides that wrapped her like a soft, many-layered cocoon. It was so hard to breathe. Her souls were itching to be released from the sick cage of her body. When all this was over, and she found herself walking the Path of Souls with her laughing daughters surrounding her, perhaps then she would be able to think clearly. But tonight it was almost impossible. Any subtlety she had ever learned in her life was gone.

Brutally, she said, "You are unfit to rule this nation, but the council cannot afford to remove you on the eve of battle."

He jerked around. "Are you saying the Ruling Council has reached a consensus?"

"Not yet, but it will. Even though the attack on White Dog Village has split this nation down the middle, the council members do not have the heart to wait until we are attacked. The alliance will hold long enough to take the fight to the enemy. After that, I cannot say." She shook her head. "Old Yana just walked the Path of Souls. Gwinodje is now the village matron in Canassatego Village, and she does not wish this war with the Standing Stone People. Nor, I've heard, does Matron Kwahseti."

"Will they fight?"

"I believe they will. But they will do it under protest."

His lockjawed expression gnawed at Tila.

In a voice that could make muscles flinch, he said, "Then I will prepare our war chief."

"Sindak already knows. I told him myself. After all, he spent half the day trying to control his warriors during the council. He had a right to know. But there is something you could do."

He gave her an askance look. "What is it?"

"When each village has made its decision, they will send warriors to join us. Within days, I expect Atotarho Village to be overrun with hungry men and women eager to do battle. We must ration our food even more conscientiously. I want you to oversee the feeding of the war parties."

"Of course, High Matron."

Atotarho repositioned himself, and his polished finger bone bracelets glimmered like frost. He seemed to be trying to decide how to ask her a question.

"Ask," she ordered.

"I'm just curious about something."

"Yes?"

"I know you sent runners to each of the village matrons asking them to call a truce to hear Sky Messenger's vision. Have the runners returned?"

Tila's eyes narrowed. At this point, it did not matter what he knew, but it irked her. It meant that someone among her trusted few was his spy, and she'd missed it. As she struggled to lift her chin, her head tottered on the slender stem of her neck. "They couldn't agree. Kwahseti and Gwinodje wished to hear it. The others did not. Without a consensus, there will be no truce. And I . . . ." She forced a breath into her burning lungs. "I must find a way to tell Zateri. It will be another blow to her heart, and it crushes my souls to have to do it."

Atotarho drew himself up and got that arrogant look on his face that she knew so well—he hated Sky Messenger and was preparing to scold her for sending the runners. Tila said, "What makes you think I care at all what you have to say? Two of my great-granddaughters are dead, and you killed them. Leave me so that I may hurt in private."

He careened toward the leather curtain, flung it aside, and stepped out to where his guards waited for him.

Tila stared at the swaying door curtain. Atotarho's reputation for vengeance was legendary. In the old days she wouldn't have pushed him, but she no longer cared what he might do to her.

Outside, Atotarho's petulant voice erupted, ordering men around, as he took out his frustration on his personal guards. As they moved away, she leaned her head back against the bark wall. She didn't have the strength to lie down. If she tried, she would only manage to collapse and perhaps topple off her sleeping bench—which would create a flurry of activity that she couldn't stand just now.

She closed her eyes and sought sleep. She had endured the deaths of so many loved ones, but somehow the loss of her precious great-granddaughters was unbearable. Perhaps it was just that she was dying and that made life all the more dear, but she also had the eerie sensation that their deaths presaged disaster. Perhaps the darkness foreseen by Sky Messenger truly was coming. She could sense it right over the next hill, rolling down upon them like a massive boulder loosed by an earthquake, and she had the feeling there was nothing anyone could do to stop it, least of all her. Which felt . . . peculiar.

For most of her life she had been the power behind the Ruling Council of the People of the Hills. No matter the threat, she'd always been able to do something to protect her people. But in her current condition, she was powerless. She could barely prop herself up and stay there without crumpling. Dying was such a disgrace.

And that, perhaps, hurt most of all.

One hand of time later, Atotarho stood beneath the porch of the Bear Clan longhouse, waiting for Matron Kelek to dress. In the ochre firelight streaming around the door curtain, frost glinted, outlining the undulations in the bark walls and glimmering down the shaft of his walking stick. He was frustrated and freezing, and his patience was wearing thin. He'd ordered his guards to stand twenty paces away, so that no one could overhear the conversation he was about to have.

He knew now that his lifelong alliance with the Wolf Clan was over. He had to make other . . .

Kelek stepped through the leather curtain with her chin elevated, regarding him as if he were a beggar. Her white hair and deeply wrinkled face appeared pale and drawn. She'd pulled a tattered bear hide over her shoulders to stave off the cold. "It's the middle of the night. What is it?"

He leaned on his walking stick. "I have a proposition I think you will appreciate."

Forty-five

"Will the Flint People join us?" Kittle asked.

As the Cloud People sailed southward, alternating splashes of darkness and brilliant sunlight covered Bur Oak Village, accentuating the worried expressions of the hundreds of people who had gathered to hear the news brought back by Matron Jigonsaseh. Jigonsaseh stood calmly beside Kittle, her hands held out to the warmth of the flames. She was so tall and slender, she looked statuesque. The long reddish hairs on her woven foxhide cape glistened. She remained still for so long that the silver threads in her short black hair caught the light and her head seemed to be covered with sunlit cobwebs.

In a strong voice, Jigonsaseh answered, "They did not say no. The matrons are consulting with their clans and will send a runner when they've made a decision."

A hum went through the crowd as people relayed her words to those farther in back who couldn't hear.

Kittle paced before the central plaza fire with her blue-painted cape flaring around her legs. Her shell rings and bracelets clicked with her impatient movements. Two of her spies had returned at dawn and told her they'd seen thousands of warriors at Atotarho Village. Worse, their capes and weapons indicated they'd come from all the surrounding Hills villages.

The news had left Kittle anxious and filled with dread. Of course Tila expected a response after the destruction of White Dog Village, but this could only mean one thing: The Hills People were preparing for a monumental attack. There was no going back. She had the uneasy sensation that the entire Standing Stone nation was little more than an autumn leaf balanced on Wind Mother's breath above a bloodbath. The instant she turned her head, they would be submerged, and she wasn't sure they could fight their way out—not without help.

"And what did your instincts tell you?" Kittle pressed. "Are the Flint People likely to agree to an alliance?"

Jigonsaseh quietly exhaled, and it trailed away in a thin white streamer. "I don't know. The Wolf Clan matron, Gahela, did not seem inclined to agree. Which means the other matrons will be hard-put to gain a consensus."

"Then you are saying your instincts tell you they will not join us?"

Jigonsaseh tilted her head uncertainly. "My guess, High Matron—and a guess is all it is—is no, they won't. I think we're on our own."

Another low hum, this one like a swarm of angry bees, rose. Facial expressions changed, going from worry to despair. Many people started to wander away, heading back to the warmth of their longhouses, perhaps to hug their children and stuff a few more belongings into hide bags. Already villagers had begun burying precious belongings in the forest, praying they survived and could return to dig them up after the Standing Stone nation had been wiped from the face of Great Grandmother Earth. As she looked around at the remaining people, the hopelessness seemed to congeal into a deadly creature of enormous proportions—a creature just as likely to kill them as the Hills nation.

Kittle announced, "Go home now. Nothing more is going to happen today. Prepare yourselves. We have the finest warriors in the world. We will triumph!"

Kittle took Jigonsaseh by the arm and dragged her away toward the Deer Clan longhouse. As they walked, she said, "We must attack soon."

"Agreed. We're going to need every man, woman, and child who can wield a bow. Atotarho can mount an eight-thousand-person army if he wishes to. How many warriors can we gather?"

Kittle subtly shook her head. "The sickness and all the recent battles have gutted us. If we're lucky, we'll muster three thousand. The odds are overwhelmingly against us. We *need* the Flint People."

"I know, Kittle, but what else can we do?"

"Did they look hungry? We could send them food."

Jigonsaseh stared down at her. Her jet black eyes had an odd tightness to them. "As it is, we don't have enough food to make it through the winter.

But even if we didn't need the food, it wouldn't help. The fever has also taken a heavy toll in Flint lands. Chief Cord told me flatly that they have more than enough food for the people who survived. I fear our only hope is Sky Messenger's vision. If they believe it, they will join us. If they do not . . ."

She didn't finish the sentence. She didn't have to.

Kittle released her arm and drew her cold hands beneath her cape. Her fingers had turned to ice. Several onlookers trailed after them, whispering, trying to overhear their conversation. She kept her voice low. "Where is Sky Messenger? We need him here."

Jigonsaseh lifted her head, and her gaze scanned the towering chestnuts beyond the palisades. Their leafless branches swayed in the frigid breeze. As though she could sense his presence out on the trail, she said, "He's coming. He'll be here."

"I pray you're right, because we are on the verge of a battle that will devastate this entire country and cost thousands of lives. The least he could do is to march around spouting his vision to rally our warriors."

Jigonsaseh nodded. "He will be here, Kittle. He's coming."

Forty-six

The sound of pebbles striking rocks woke Taya. The *click-clack* rang with such clarity that for a moment she thought it was someone chopping wood in the distance. She roused herself, sitting up in her blankets to listen. Sky Messenger and Gitchi were gone. When panic seized her heart, her gaze instantly searched the starlit forest for them. A storm must be moving in. The bitter night air nipped at her face with particular intensity. Taya threw aside her blanket and followed the sound of rocks being hurled.

She and Sky Messenger had both endured a terrible night. One Dream after another had awakened him. It was as if the Spirits were tormenting him. Often he'd cried out in his sleep. She didn't know him well enough, and doubted she ever would, to guess whether it was dreams of the future that woke him, or dreams of the past.

I'll bet Baji can tell the difference.

Jealousy stung her, but only for a moment. And that was a major achievement. For the first time in her life, she was learning to see the world through the eyes of others, and it had broadened her view considerably. What did it matter if he loved another woman? He was going to marry her. And they both knew the marriage was a political alliance, nothing more. Though, she had to admit, she couldn't help wishing he loved her. On the other hand, she did not love him. She had only just come to the conclusion that his soul was still in his body and not out roaming the forest. She needed time for all of this to sink into her souls. However, she knew one thing for certain: She had to give up her girlish dream of marrying a man she loved. For the sake of her clan and her nation, she could do it.

When it occurred to her that Grandmother would be proud of her, she felt a little better.

In the past few days, she'd come to other conclusions, as well. She might, truly, become the wife of the greatest Dreamer in the history of their nation. That was worth a lot more than love . . . at least if the Keepers of the Stories spoke well of Taya of the Deer Clan, granddaughter of High Matron Kittle and one of the leaders of the Standing Stone nation— for surely she would become a leader if her husband became a legend.

A small pond spread to her left, surreally bright in the gleam cast by the campfires of the dead. The trail wound around the water's edge. As she walked, she studied the owls sailing over the treetops, silent, deadly, hunting the darkness for mice or rabbits.

The clacking of rocks grew so loud she could almost feel them pounding against her skin. She followed the curving trail through a copse of maples and into a boulder-filled clearing. The rounded rocks appeared to have melted together, as though they'd spent thousands of summers conforming to each other's shape. Upon the top of the tallest boulder, Sky Messenger sat, his tall body limned in starlight. He had his handsome face tipped up, as though conversing with the ancestors who peered down upon him from the Path of Souls.

At the sight of him, a sensation of wonder came over her. He was right there. The prophet. As the truth filtered through her body, her muscles relaxed and her breathing slowed down.

For a timeless moment, she felt as though she'd crawled through a badger hole and emerged in a strange sanctuary nestled in the calm heart of the world. The fear that the Hills People would attack and kill everyone she loved had receded into nothingness. *I must be Dreaming. Soon, I'll wake and the terror will return.*

The savory odor of wet leaves met her nostrils. She inhaled deeply and hugged herself. Another rock clacked! Taya silently walked down the deer trail to the place where Sky Messenger must have climbed up, for the rounded stones resembled steps. The rocks were cold and damp as she ascended. She couldn't see him for a while. Then when she glimpsed him at the top, she felt almost euphoric.

He *was* the human False Face.

When she emerged three paces away from him, he turned to her. Bathed in starlight, with black hair dancing around his broad shoulders, his gaze made Taya's heart stand still. A gust flattened his cape across his muscular chest. She carefully stepped across the slick boulders to reach him. He smelled faintly of crushed grass and forest-scented winds.

Sky Messenger said, "You should be sleeping."

When she tried to sit down next to him, her moccasins slipped on the wet rocks and she grabbed for his arm to steady herself. The hard muscles beneath the soft buckskin felt comforting. "As you should. What are you doing up here?" She eased down beside him.

"Throwing rocks."

"That's what woke me. Why?"

He shrugged. "It seems to ease the Dreams."

She gazed out across the sparkling pond to where a flock of geese paddled. The white feathers on their throats flashed as they bobbed up and down on the waves. "I missed you. The blankets grew stone-cold after you left."

He hesitated for a while. "I was too anxious. I couldn't lie there any longer."

She squeezed his hand. "How strange. You're anxious, and I feel so happy. Too happy. I'm sure I'm Dreaming."

"Well, if you're happy, I suggest you don't wake. What I see coming will certainly ruin it for you."

Taya gazed up into his starlit eyes. "Tell me what you see. Please?"

Sky Messenger's eyes tightened. He kept staring at her, his gaze intense, searching. Probably measuring her sincerity.

Taya heaved a sigh and explained, "I believe you now. I didn't. I didn't believe any of it—until four days ago when you met with War Chief Hiyawento. I'm sorry. It's taken me a few days to come to grips with the truth that you're actually a great Dreamer and not a crazy man, but I think I have. I would like to know what you see coming. If you wish to tell me."

He looked out across the pond. As the trees swayed in the night breeze, the black limb shadows moved across the silver water.

Finally, Sky Messenger replied, "The beginning is almost upon us. In the depths of my souls, the air is cooling off, and the colors are leaching from the forest. My heart already sees that gray and shimmering world. And that world is the start of everything." He heaved a breath. "I feel like . . . like my heart is crumbling, sifting through the cracks in my soul a grain at a time, vanishing into eternal stillness."

His tone of voice, the lilt of the words, seemed to cast a spell upon her. Softly, she asked, "How long do we have before Elder Brother Sun covers his face with the soot of the dying world?"

The muscles in his arm went hard, as though straining against what was to come. "I don't know. The way the Dream plays out, I can't tell if the events occur over a single day, or several years. The images jump around, rearranging themselves in a different order. I—"

"'As though not even the Spirits know the final shape of the story,'" she repeated the words he'd said to Hiyawento.

The Power in his haunted eyes stunned her. "Yes, that's right."

The breeze that blew over the pond batted at Sky Messenger's hood where it rested upon his back. Taya nodded and said, "How may I help you?"

He inclined his head uncertainly, or perhaps it was suspiciously. "I don't wish to place you in danger."

"I'm already in danger. I'm with you, aren't I? You may as well let me help."

He hurled another rock, which splashed in the darkness. "As I get closer, I suspect I'll have a better idea of what each of us can do. But right now, I honestly don't."

"All right. I'll be ready."

He frowned at her from the corner of his eye. "I think, perhaps, you've grown up some."

Taya wet her lips. Wind Mother whispered through the trees. A wall of dark clouds had formed in the north, blotting out the campfires of the dead. "Sky Messenger, since our meeting with War Chief Hiyawento, I've been thinking a lot about the Beginning Time story. It was Sapling, the Good-Minded Twin, who brought order after the creation. He made lakes and rivers, brought good weather, ensured the corn grew, and released the animals from the great cave where they were being held. It was his brother Tawiscaro, the Evil-Minded Twin, who tried to undo everything good that Sapling had accomplished. He sent bad weather and brought chaos and death to the world." She took his one hand in both of hers and held it to her heart. "I think, one day, there will be stories told about you. Great stories of life and death, and good and evil. I truly believe that you are the human False Face."

He flinched and drew his hand away from her. "I am not."

"How do you know? You wear that gorget that matches the stories, and you—"

"My gorget is a copy; it's not the original. Chief Atotarho wears the original—or half of it."

Annoyed, Taya said, "The stories speak of two gorgets crafted just after the creation. One must have been made first. So the other is obviously a copy. No one knows whether the human False Face wears the original or the copy. Yours could be the sacred gorget, and the other is just a distraction."

He hurled another rock. He appeared uncomfortable with the entire discussion of legends. "I am *not* the human False Face."

Taya shrugged. "All right. But maybe you are the person who clears the path for the arrival of the human False Face. That's still critically important."

His head dipped once. "Yes, it is."

In the distance, the geese started flapping their wings and honking, as though preparing to take flight. Their beautiful calls serenaded the night. "My Spirit Helper told me something tonight that worries me."

Almost breathlessly, she said, "Shago-niyoh was here? What did he say?"

He watched her closely, as if trying to anticipate how she would respond to what he was about to say. "He told me that I must dive headfirst into the darkness and blood. If I do, others will follow."

Taya's breathing went shallow. "But . . . that sounds like . . . it sounds like you're talking about dying. I'm mistaken, aren't I? That's not what you meant?"

Sky Messenger didn't answer.

Taya slid away from him. "If you're planning on dying, tell me now."

"Why? So you can start looking for another husband?"

"No, so I can beat you senseless for being an idiot!"

"Taya, I'm not planning to die, but if it's the only way—"

"It's not the only way!" She leaped to her feet. "We're going home to convince Grandmother that it's possible to create an alliance with several Hills villages to destroy Atotarho. That's the way to end the war."

"Yes, I hope so. But Taya, I have this feeling that things have gone too far, and we can't—"

"We're going to form this alliance; then everything will be all right," she insisted.

"I hope so." Sky Messenger rose to his feet and stood uneasily before her. After several heartbeats, she felt his hand stroke the long hair that draped down her back. "Earlier, you asked if there was something you could do to help me. I've changed my mind. There is."

"I will *not* help you die!"

They stood for a long time, looking at each other. He lowered his hand. "I would never ask that of anyone. But there may come a moment in the storm when I need someone politically astute to act as a negotiator on my behalf. I know you are young, but—"

"I can do it," she said with utter confidence. "I have watched and listened to my grandmother all my life." She drew herself up and faced him squarely. "*But* . . ." She pointed a stern finger at him. "Not if I know that you're planning on sacrificing yourself for the greater good, or some other stupid notion. Do you understand?"

His gaze went over her angry face as though memorizing it. "Yes. I understand."

They stood for a time, just gazing out at the glimmers of starlight on the pond, until Sky Messenger said, "I'm going back to camp and try to sleep. Are you coming?"

"Not yet."

He looked around at the darkness and seemed to be wondering why she wasn't terrified to be more than a few paces from him. She was wondering that herself.

"Very well. I'll be waiting for you."

She listened to his steps as he climbed down the slippery boulders. A short while later, she saw him slowly walking the trail back to the camp. He was alone. Where was Gitchi?

Taya climbed down the boulders and found the wolf standing with his ears pricked. He did not wag his tail. He merely gazed at her with shining yellow eyes, as though waiting for a command.

"Leave," she ordered, and flung her arm to point back to camp.

Gitchi stood his ground. The old wolf's graying head had a curious sheen in the silver light.

"I don't want you here. Go home. Go find Sky Messenger."

Gitchi licked his muzzle and sat on his haunches.

"Did Sky Messenger tell you to stay and protect me?"

He stared up at her, and she threw up her hands. "Gods, that means I'll never get rid of you. All right, come on."

Taya marched along the shore with Gitchi at her heels. When she reached the far side of the pond, she stared across the shimmering surface to where their camp nestled in the maples. She couldn't see him, but she knew Sky Messenger was there; it tore her souls apart. "Do you really think he's planning on dying?"

She slumped down on the sand and put her head in her hands, trying to force sense into her worry-laced brain.

Gitchi eased forward, lay down, and rested his muzzle on top of her feet. When she looked at him, his tail thumped the ground as though he knew she was hurting, and he was trying to comfort her.

He was a curious animal, totally devoted to Sky Messenger. In all the world, the only person who really seemed to exist for Gitchi was Sky Messenger. Yet . . . here he was. Taya reached out and stroked his warm fur. "I don't really like you, and you know it, don't you?"

Gitchi wagged his tail.

Elder Sister Gaha pushed the air with a soft invisible hand, and Taya tugged her cape up beneath her chin. Gitchi watched her. When she shivered, the wolf got to his feet, walked around behind her, and curled his body warmly around hers.

Tears filled Taya's eyes. She slid a hand from beneath her cape to stroke his head. "We can't let him die, Gitchi. Even if he's foolish enough to think it's the only way. You'll protect him, won't you?"

The wolf's gaze suddenly shifted to the opposite side of the pond. A low growl rumbled his throat.

"What is it?"

Gitchi eased to his feet, his eyes still focused on the forest shadows across the pond. His muscles bunched as though ready to spring forward. She tried to see what he was looking at. By now Sky Messenger was wrapped in his cape and almost asleep—yet something moved near their camp. A black silhouette. It ghosted through the darkness.

Silent as the moonlight, Gitchi broke into a dead run.

The wolf shot around the pond like a silver arrow, its lean body gleaming in the night. Ohsinoh chuckled and took one last look at Odion. He would always be Odion to Ohsinoh, never Sky Messenger. Odion, the boy who was always afraid.

He'll be even more afraid. Very soon.

Long before Gitchi rounded the pond and hit the trail to camp, Ohsinoh turned and trotted into the deep forest shadows.

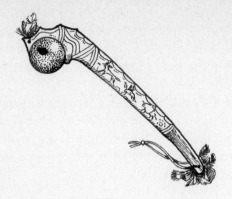

Forty-seven

High Matron Tila lay on her sleeping bench with her great-granddaughter Kahn-Tineta snuggled beneath the hides beside her. Morning sunlight streamed around the leather curtain that led outside, casting lances of pure gold across the longhouse floor. As they flashed across the little girl's face, Tila's heart ached.

Many people scurried to and from the house today, securing the village, hauling in pot after pot of water and armloads of wood. Each time a person walked through the blue clouds that rose from the fires, smoke swirled and snaked upward toward the smoke hole in the roof high above.

She weakly stroked Kahn-Tineta's long black hair. "I know these are hard days, child, but things will get better."

In a pitiful voice, the eight-summers-old girl said, "No, they won't. Mother and Father are going to die, Great-grandmother. Just like my sisters."

Tila frowned. From this view, she could just see Kahn-Tineta's profile. Tears sparkled on the girl's long eyelashes. "What makes you say that? Your father is a great war chief, one of the most respected men—"

"When Father left, he barely had the strength to lift his war club! Didn't you see him?" Kahn-Tineta rolled to her back to look at Tila. Her small face was white and strained. There was a luminous look of stunned disbelief in her eyes. The innocence of her expression struck Tila like a blow.

"I did see him." Tila shoved away the hair that had glued itself to the girl's wet cheeks. Zateri and Hiyawento had both come to bid her good-bye three days before. Though she was almost beyond feeling anything except her own agony, Tila had hurt for them, but especially for Hi-yawento. The man who'd stood before her had been a pale haunted shadow of what he had once been. "I think your father's souls split apart for a time after your sisters traveled the Path of Souls. It will take time for them to weave back together again, but they will."

"But mother never cried. Not at all. Father—"

"Child, what your mother has to stand, the ancestors have given her the strength to stand. Women were born to carry heavier loads than men."

Kahn-Tineta let out a tired breath and stared up at the sunflowers hanging from the roof poles. "Do we get that from Dancing Fox and the Wolf Clan matrons who lived long ago in the ancient darkness?"

"Yes. We do. The loss of your sisters has broken your mother's heart, but she'll bear that burden with a straight back and clear eyes. If for no other reason than your father needs her to."

A moment of pride warmed Tila's heart. Yes, no matter what came, Zateri could and would bear it. Wolf Clan women bent with the winds of change, but when the storm passed they stiffened their spines and got back to work building a better world for their clan and people.

"Great-grandmother? Why did Mother have to go with Father? She almost never goes on war walks."

"Well, this is different. If we are successful, the full Ruling Council will need to be present when the Standing Stone nation falls. Your mother will stand in for me. Decisions may have to be made on the spot."

Kahn-Tineta anxiously ran her tongue through the gap left by her missing front teeth. "I wish Mother was home." Tears filled her young eyes.

Tila hugged her more tightly. "Can I tell you a secret?"

The girl's eyes widened. "What is it?"

"I'm going to name your mother as matron of the Wolf Clan when she returns, but you mustn't tell anyone. Can you keep my words locked in your heart until it is announced?"

"Oh, yes, Great-grandmother," Kahn-Tineta said earnestly. "I'm good at keeping secrets."

"I'm glad to hear of it. Many people are not."

Kahn-Tineta's eyes narrowed slightly, as though something had oc-curred to her but she wasn't certain she should say it.

"What's wrong?"

Kahn-Tineta glanced around the house to make sure no one could hear her; then she cupped a hand to Tila's ear and hissed, "Great-grandmother, I'm not sure Mother wishes to be high matron."

"That's not a surprise. No one does." Tila poked a skeletal finger into Kahn-Tineta's young chest. "You remember I said that. Someday you will have to make the choice of whether or not to lead your people. It is an overwhelming responsibility. But I suspect in the end you will choose to place the welfare of the Hills nation above your own. You will shoulder the burden for the nation's sake. Just as your mother will."

"She will?"

Tila nodded. "I'm sure of it."

Kahn-Tineta crossed her legs and shook one moccasin while she frowned at the swirls of blue smoke gliding above her. "But Great-grandmother, Father doesn't wish to move to this village. I've heard Mother and Father talking late at night when they think I'm asleep. Father hates Grandfather Atotarho."

At the mention of his name, anger filled Tila, and she could not afford the energy it required. She closed her eyes for several heartbeats to let it drain away. "My grandmother—that would be your great-great-great-grandmother—used to have a saying. She said that for every one person hacking at the roots of hatred, there were thousands swinging in its branches. She told me the only way to survive in this world was to make sure I was the one with the hatchet."

Kahn-Tineta rolled to her stomach and looked at Tila. A faint smile came to her lips. "I like that."

"I thought you might. You have a pure heart. But you're going to have to work to keep it that way. Don't swing in those branches or you'll fall and break your neck."

Brilliant sunshine flared when Pedeza pulled back the door curtain and stepped inside the Wolf Clan longhouse. She looked exhausted, her face drawn and jaw clamped. But when she saw Kahn-Tineta she forced a smile. "Are you ready to go home? The high matron needs to sleep."

Tila gave her a grateful look—she did need to sleep—but more than anything she longed to keep talking with this precious little girl.

Kahn-Tineta sat up. "Great-grandmother, may I come back tomorrow?"

"You will have to ask Pedeza, but I would so love to see you."

Kahn-Tineta smiled and slid off the sleeping bench. When her moccasins struck the floor mats, she turned, leaned over Tila, and kissed her cheek. "I love you, Great-grandmother," she said, and trotted to Pedeza's side.

Tila extended a gnarled hand to her. "I love you, too, child. Don't forget the things I told you."

Kahn-Tineta glanced up at Pedeza, then back at Tila. In a conspiratorial whisper, she said, "I won't. I promise."

Pedeza bowed. "Good day, High Matron. Sleep well."

"I'll try. Be careful going home."

"Yes, we will."

Pedeza took Kahn-Tineta's hand, and they walked away down the longhouse.

When they were out of sight, Tila curled into a tight ball and fought to keep the pain at bay. She felt like sharp fangs were ripping at her organs. If only she . . .

Something caught her attention. Tila focused on the door curtain. In the slender space where the curtain rested against the door frame, one eye gleamed. It was large and shone with an unearthly light. It seemed to be fixed upon Kahn-Tineta and Pedeza. Then it turned to Tila. It watched her for a time.

When the man ducked beneath the curtain and into the house, her gray brows knitted. He wore a plain buckskin cape with no clan symbols. White and black paint decorated his triangular face. "Who are you?"

He had a strange manner about him. As he searched the house, only his eyes moved. His tall body seemed to be carved of wood.

"I asked for your name."

"Yes, I heard you."

With the silence of a big cat stalking prey, he entered her chamber, walked to her side, and pulled the hides up, as though to keep her warmer. Then suddenly he pressed them over her mouth and nose and whispered, "It's me, Grandmother, your long-lost grandson."

Horror flooded Tila. She fought, thrashing about with the strength of a newborn, trying to suck air into her lungs so she could scream. She was so weak, it didn't take long.

The cold black shadow of Sodowego fell upon her, and the darkness came like a soothing whisper. . . .

Forty-eight

Conversations filled the cold night, meshing oddly with the war songs that drifted lazily across the hills, moving with the dark shapes of thousands of warriors. The smoky air was sweet with the smell of squash baked in ashes.

Zateri watched War Chief Sindak rise from where he'd drawn the battle plan in the thin layer of snow on the ground and scan the seven people standing in Zateri's small circle. His gaze remained the longest on war chiefs Thona, Waswanosh, and Hiyawento, clearly judging their emotions—then his eyes flicked to matrons Gwinodje and Kwahseti, took in Chief Canassatego's expression, and finally came to rest upon Zateri.

"Does everyone understand?" Sindak propped his hands on his hips. He'd pulled his black hair back and tied it with a cord. The lines around his deep-set eyes resembled dark chasms in the firelight. Behind him, a blanket of campfires rose and fell with the hills, stretching to the star-spotted eastern horizon.

"Oh, I think we understand perfectly," Matron Kwahseti said with a thin smile. Gray strands of hair fluttered around her oval face.

"Good. Sleep well." Sindak bowed and walked away.

Zateri crossed her arms beneath her cape, waiting before she spoke, giving herself time to digest what had just happened.

"I don't believe it," War Chief Thona said through gritted teeth. The white ridges of scars crisscrossing his indignant face resembled writhing amber-colored worms. "Does he think we will stand for this?"

Kwahseti's attention had fixed on Sindak as he made his way across the huge camp, talking to warriors, sharing jokes, occasionally slapping a man on the back. "It seems that Chief Atotarho doesn't trust us."

"It's an outrage." Thona straightened to his full height, towering over everyone else in the circle. "We should—"

"No." Kwahseti put a hand on her war chief's muscular shoulder. "Be calm, Thona. Emotion only clouds our thoughts, and we must all think straight tonight."

Thona tried, but continued to seethe.

War Chief Waswanosh from Canassatego Village hissed, "This is unacceptable. How dare he tell us to stay out of the fight!"

"That's not what he said," Zateri softly reminded. "He said Atotarho wishes to keep our forces in reserve until we are needed."

"In reserve?" Waswanosh growled. "He ordered us to stay in camp. To remain behind when everyone else marches off to the fight! It is an insult!"

Chief Canassatego gave them a resigned smile. He had seen fifty-seven summers pass, and had once been a renowned war chief. A long gray braid snaked over his shoulder, looking like a silver snake against the black-painted hide of his cape. As his smile faded, his wrinkles rearranged into somber lines. "Well, War Chief Hiyawento, it seems you have your wish. We will not fight the Standing Stone People."

"Not fighting isn't the same as making peace. The only way we will ever be safe is if the fear of attack vanishes for both our peoples. We must end this war."

Zateri noticed that his fists were clenched at his sides, and his narrow beaked face had flushed. Sindak's orders had surprised him, as they had everyone else.

Gwinodje said, "What shall we do about it? Are we going to obey?"

Short and slight of build, she appeared childlike standing between Chief Canassatego and War Chief Waswanosh. In the darkness, one could have mistaken her for a frail girl. But her expression belied any such notions. Indignation actually shook the clamshell comb that held her black hair on top of her head, causing it to shimmer like a prism. Colors flashed.

Zateri said, "Each of our villages joined the Hills alliance. If we disobey, it will be viewed as a withdrawal from the alliance. Do we wish to do that?"

Kwahseti massaged her brow. "No, not yet. Our three villages could not stand alone. We would be vulnerable to anyone who wished to destroy us. Assuming Atotarho didn't beat them to it, the Mountain People would be the first to take the opportunity."

"Yes," Zateri added. "I've heard they're desperate. They've been so sick with the fever that they could not even harvest their crops. Their corn is moldering in their fields, and their sunflowers have all been plucked clean by birds. As winter deepens, they'll have no choice but to take what food they need from other nations. We—"

Hiyawento interrupted, "They shouldn't have to."

His deep voice had been so low, the others in the circle unconsciously leaned toward him to hear him better. Chief Canassatego asked, "What did you say?"

Hiyawento lifted his head. A somber emptiness had possessed him. It wrenched Zateri's souls. The loss of her daughters was like a knife slashing inside her, but duty demanded she set it aside until this was over. Then she would find a quiet place to hurt until she could bear it. The difference between them was that she *could* set it aside. He could not. All his life, he'd fought to protect his family and friends, offering his own life in their stead many times over, and his courage had always carried everyone around him to safety. Except for his baby daughters. Zateri knew that somewhere deep inside him, he blamed himself for their deaths. He must be saying, "If only I'd been vigilant, I would have known . . ." or "I should have killed him when I had the chance; then my girls couldn't have . . ."

A lump formed in Zateri's throat, making it hard to breathe. Guilt had eaten a gaping hole inside him, and he was being consumed by the darkness.

For her, the pain provoked another response. She became unnaturally focused and clear-headed—a lesson she'd learned in Gannajero's camp, where she had endured things that had killed other girls. She would single-mindedly, with the patience of a hungry wolf, hunt her father until she could destroy him, even if she had to turn the world on its head to do it. It was this pursuit that gave her the strength to face anything she had to.

"I said"—Hiyawento inhaled the smoky night air—"they shouldn't have to. If they attack us, it's our fault. By our own greed, we've forced them into desperate acts to feed their children."

Thona stiffened as though he'd been struck. "What are you saying? That because we need the food for our own children we are somehow to blame—"

"Yes." Hiyawento's red-rimmed eyes rested on Thona without emotion. He might have been gazing far out into the distances instead of at a livid opponent. "Don't you see? If we helped each other, we would all have enough. We might not have an abundance that we could hoard and smile at in the dead of winter, but we would survive. As it is, I'm not sure any of us will make it through this."

Thona snorted. "You sound like you're repeating the words of your demented friend, Sky Messenger."

War Chief Waswanosh let out a low disgusted laugh. "His vision is nonsense. I heard one of the Traders say he'd seen Elder Brother Sun flee into a black hole in the sky. Ridiculous."

Hiyawento's chin lifted. In a deep reverent voice, he replied, "When the Great Face shakes the World Tree, you will believe. There is a terrible storm coming. We will all be swimming in a cloud-sea when the eerie silence descends and Elder Brother Sun blackens his face with the soot of the dying world."

Zateri glanced around the circle. No one seemed to be breathing. They were hearing Sky Messenger's vision for the first time, or at least part of it, and none could turn away. Kwahseti's face had slackened, as though she felt the truth of it rising up from the dark place between her souls. Chief Canassatego was listening with his eyes closed.

"The sky will split wide open," Hiyawento continued, "and a snowy blanket of thistledown will fall. As it spreads out all over the world, the judgment will take place."

Thona uneasily shifted his weight to his other foot. Waswanosh observed him from the corner of his eye. Both men appeared chastened, half-believing, but not quite.

Awed, Gwinodje murmured, "It—it's Powerful."

Kwahseti nodded. As she brought up a hand and touched the cape over her heart, she said, "I don't know about the rest of you, but I want to believe. Very much."

"Wanting does not make it true, Matron," Thona remarked.

"No." A breath of wind fluttered her gray hair. She brushed it away. "But I plan to be ready, just in case."

"What do you mean, ready?" Gwinodje tilted her head.

Out in the forest, Elder Sister Gaha walked. The hem of her dress set the branches to swaying, and a musical shishing and clattering wafted to them. A light snow started to fall, featherlike, glittering on the branches.

"I mean that when the time comes, I will be on the right side."

"But . . ." Gwinodje looked around questioningly. "What is the right side?"

"I don't know yet, but when I get there, I will."

Still staring upward at the campfires of the dead, Hiyawento said, "The side of kindness. Which is, I regret, a side I have not always fought for."

No one responded, but Zateri could tell from their expressions that some of them were thinking that good war chiefs couldn't afford such weaknesses. Thona scowled. Waswanosh had a faint sneer.

Slowly, each person in the circle followed Hiyawento's gaze, looking upward into the night sky where a thin layer of Cloud People pushed southward, fuzzing the campfires of the dead, rushing away as though fleeing the supernatural storm to come.

"I'm going to find my blankets." Kwahseti lifted a hand. "A pleasant evening to you all."

"Before you go . . ." Hiyawento quietly said. Kwahseti turned back to face him. "If you could form an alliance with the Standing Stone nation to defeat Atotarho, would you?"

Kwahseti stared at him as though asking the question proved beyond a doubt that Hiyawento's soul was out wandering lost in the forest. But there was something else in her eyes—some hesitation that made Zateri's blood rush.

"Kwahseti," Zateri whispered, "just consider—"

Kwahseti turned her back and walked away. One by one, the others said good night and followed her, plodding across camp to their own fires.

When they stood alone, Zateri moved close to Hiyawento and slipped her arm through his, holding him. Quietly, she asked, "Are you all right?"

He blinked at the sky as though puzzled by what he saw there. His narrow face and hawkish nose reflected the flickers of firelight.

Finally, he answered, "My souls are broken, Zateri, and I cannot find a way to pull the pieces together."

"Well . . ." The word condensed and sparkled. "Perhaps you shouldn't try to."

"Why not?"

She squeezed his arm. "My husband, kindness does not dwell in souls that are whole."

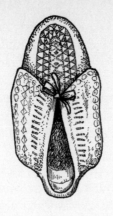

Forty-nine

Sky Messenger

The milky light before dawn casts a soft pearl glow over the snow-covered hills.

As I follow the trail up over the rise and look down across the valley to the south, an inexplicable dread fills me. I halt on the rocky ridge, waiting for Taya, who plods up the trail behind me.

Rose-colored mist eddies close to the ground, twining around trunks and boulders. In the distance, leafless trees rise and fall like gray waves, dipping down to where Yellowtail Village and Bur Oak Village nestle side by side, their palisades sheathed in frost. Reed Marsh curves around the western and northern edges of the villages, cupping them like a protective hand. Dark Cloud People blanket most of the morning sky, but a thin band of pale purple swaths the eastern horizon.

Movement. Down in the dense maples. Only my gaze glides across the landscape. After ten heartbeats, I whisper to myself, "Warriors."

As the morning light brightens, my trained eyes begin to pick them out. Visible through the trees are line after line of archers. Four lines that I can see. As one line fires, the next will move up, and so on, until the first line must again face the enemy.

Taya's steps pat the soft earth behind me. She slips an arm around my waist and lets out a peaceful sigh. It surprises me a little. "I'm glad we're almost home."

She doesn't notice anything amiss, but why would she? Though I've been working hard to teach her to *see,* the skill takes time.

I drape an arm over her shoulders and softly say, "I want you to be calm. Can you do that?"

She tips her face up in confusion. "What do you mean?"

I kneel and draw the lines of archers in the thin snow, then make a crescent for Reed Marsh, and circles for the locations of the villages. "Do you see them?"

Taya lifts her gaze and scans the hills, glances back at his map, looks up again. Slowly, the joy drains from her beautiful young face. I see her eyes stop at each place where warriors are clearly visible in the forest.

"Oh, no. Grandmother must have received word that we're about to be attacked. We have to hurry. Let's run!"

She starts to launch herself down the trail, and I catch her arm and pull her back. "The warriors are jittery, worried about their own lives and the lives of their families. Never run into a line of archers."

"But they know me! Every warrior out there has—"

"Fear creates a strange kind of blindness. Your eyes are wide open, but the only thing you see is your own weapons. Your ears hear only your heart pounding. Let's continue walking down the main trail in clear sight. They've already seen us. They'll be watching, monitoring our movements. Keep your hands open at your sides."

For the first time, she looks up at me as though I know more than Elder Brother Sun. A swallow bobs her throat. "I will."

I put a hand lightly on her shoulder to encourage her to walk at my side, and she clings to me like a shadow.

We've gone no more than one hundred paces when the trail curves and I see an eerie sight behind us. To the west, a cloud of snow billows over the trees. But it's not falling from the sky. It rises from the ground, like summer dust, kicked by the trotting feet of warriors. Because of the way the hills fold, I doubt the Standing Stone archers see them yet. I swing around to look at the Standing Stone lines to the north of the villages, then back at what must be the enemy. I can hear them now. Beneath their pounding feet, Great Grandmother Earth rings like a drum being struck. The thunderous roll echoes.

"What is that?" Taya turns to look over her shoulder.

"Just keep walking. We'll be home before they get here." I grip her hand to keep her from running.

She jerks around to look back at the billowing snow, and when understanding dawns, I feel her heartbeat stutter in her wrist.

"Are those . . . warriors?"

"Yes, but—"

"Enemy warriors?" she cries. "They're coming right at us!"

My grip on her hand tightens. "Do you see where the trail to Hills country meets the main trail that curves around the eastern side of the villages? When we hit that, we'll run. For now, just walk."

I lead her down the trail.

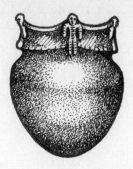

Fifty

Elder Brother Sun blazed scarlet and gold into High Matron Kittle's eyes as she marched along the outermost catwalk of Bur Oak Village, speaking confidently to her warriors, judging their moods, making her way down to where Skenandoah stood. At regular intervals, jugs of water and cups hung from the palisade, at hand for later when thirsty warriors could not leave their posts. Beyond the palisade, thick morning mist curled and spun across the valley.

When he saw her, Skenandoah bowed. "High Matron?"

In the glistening vapor, he more closely resembled a pale-faced phantom than a war chief. Muscular and of medium height, he had seen thirty-four summers pass. Short black hair, cut in mourning for the many friends he had lost in the long war, clung damply to his square face. Red feathers, ornaments of war, fluttered at the bottom of his long war shirt. He had his bow slung over his shoulder and carried a quiver bristling with arrows. A war club, ax, and two deerbone stilettos hung from his belt.

Kittle smiled. "What's going on out there?"

He propped an elbow on the palisade and gestured to the hazy battle-field. "Our archers are in place, but the fog is so thick in the valley bottom they won't see the enemy warriors until they emerge like fanged wolves from the gray."

"You've seen no Traders, no travelers, no messengers traveling under white arrows? Nothing?"

Skenandoah gave her a sad look, seemed to be debating with himself, then clearly decided to ignore her implication that she was waiting for a messenger from Atotarho, hoping to end this before it began. "No, High Matron. Just the two terrified sentries who ran in at dawn after sighting the approaching army."

Her heart sank. She didn't know what she'd been hoping for, perhaps that Atotarho wished to make peace, which was as unlikely as seeing summer replace the winter solstice. Had she grown so desperate she'd started believing in fantasies?

A slight breeze rustled across the marsh and swept the fog aside, driving it through the reeds and cattails like smoke from a bonfire. She watched it trail down the valley. Just as quickly, more mist rolled in to fill its place. The frosty world dazzled.

"How are our warriors holding up?"

Skenandoah gave her a firm nod. "They will do their duties, High Matron. They will stand until they cannot stand any longer."

Kittle braced her arms on the palisade beside him and stared out at the morning. As he climbed into the sky, Elder Brother Sun blazed through the mist like a ball of flame in the middle of a great cloud.

"High Matron," Skenandoah said cautiously. "I've heard the elders whispering. May I ask you something?"

"Of course."

For a moment, he appeared to regret that he'd said anything. His lips pressed into a bloodless line, and he frowned down at the warriors stationed at the base of the palisade. For her ears alone, he asked, "Is it true that the Ruling Council has already decided we will surrender at nightfall?"

Blood rose to Kittle's face. She felt lightheaded. She prayed they would not have to resort that, but . . . "It is most certainly *not* true. Who told you that? No, never mind, it doesn't matter." She stabbed a finger at him. "We will fight until our last breaths. Is that clear? You tell your people that at this very moment the council is planning a great victory celebration."

A faint smile came to his lips, as though he knew she was lying, but appreciated it just the same. "I will tell them, High Matron."

To cover her discomfort, she reached for the cup that hung from a peg on the palisade, filled it from the water jug, and drank. She felt wide awake. More alive than ever before. As she returned the cup to its place, she saw clouds of snow billowing over the western ridge, then a slither on the far side of the valley. The mist eddied and swirled as though brushed by a huge hand.

Kittle froze, staring. Elder Brother Sun climbed into a gap in the mist and seemed to explode. Brilliance surged across the valley. The land became a flowing field of diamonds, whiskered with frost-bright trees. The stone arrow points of her archers glittered as they aimed their bows.

She gripped Skenandoah's wrist so hard her nails drove into his flesh. "They're coming."

He nodded. "Yes. I saw them a long time ago."

Fifty-one

Skenandoah disentangled his wrist from her fingers and dragged an arrow from his quiver. "Please find a safe place, High Matron."

Kittle inhaled a steadying breath and marched away down the catwalk. As each warrior saw the enemy, sharp calls went up, and arms flung out to point. A breathless sort of anticipation filled the cold morning air. The prayers being Sung up and down the line sounded for all the world like the sweet notes of flutes.

Just as Kittle reached the ladder and started to climb down, Skenandoah called, "High Matron! Sky Messenger and Taya just rounded the Yellowtail palisade. They're running for our gates!"

"Thank you, War Chief." Kittle descended the ladder with forced dignity and walked to meet them.

Warriors opened the outer gates, and Sky Messenger shoved Taya through first, then backed in and spun around. "Utz, Hannock, there are two war parties less than one finger of time behind me. Bring more planks to barricade these gates!"

"Yes, Sky Messenger!" Utz ran to grab another plank from the pile inside the second palisade ring.

His voice had been commanding, that of a deputy war chief, and Utz and Hannock had obeyed him as they always had. It surprised Kittle, but if he wished to command in this current situation, she had no objections.

Sky Messenger strode for her granddaughter and with soft urgency said, "Taya, I must get to a high point where I can see over the fog to judge the battlefield."

"Go. I'll speak with Grandmother."

Sky Messenger touched her shoulder, a tender touch. "One last thing. Please take Gitchi with you? Make sure he stays in the longhouse. He's old. He—"

Taya nodded. "I'll take care of him, Sky Messenger. Don't worry."

Sky Messenger knelt and ruffled the fur at Gitchi's neck; then he hugged the wolf fiercely and said, "Go with Taya. Guard her. Do what she says."

Gitchi gave him an uncertain look, but loped to stand at Taya's side.

Sky Messenger trotted for the ladder that led to the catwalk.

Kittle studied her granddaughter. Taya's eyes had a gleam. Her serious expression was that of a woman far older than her fourteen summers. "Speak with me about what?"

"An alliance to end this battle and destroy Atotarho."

Kittle's laugh had a desperate ring to it. "What would you know of such things?"

Taya stared confidently into her eyes, which startled Kittle. "We just came from Coldspring Village. Many of the other Hills villages were outraged by Atotarho's attack on White Dog Village. They were not involved, and would not have approved the attack if they had been. The Hills nation is on the verge of civil war over it. I believe the time is ripe to make alliances with those opposing Atotarho. If we can, we may be able to destroy the chief on this very battlefield."

Taya spoke like a leader. Pride filled Kittle. "I fear it is too late for that, my granddaughter, but I will hear you out. Come to my chamber. I must dress for the battle. No matter what else happens, if I am captured I'm going to look splendid for my execution."

Fifty-two

Sky Messenger

Where I stand upon the catwalk, I grip the palisade and gaze out at what is surely oblivion. Past the marsh the ground slowly tips up, gently rolling until it collides with the rocky ridge to the west—the crest where Taya and I stood less than one hand of time ago. Despite the cloud cover and mist, the morning light grows brighter, revealing the enemy's lines. Thousands of Hills warriors, row upon row, march over the ridge and head down into the valley. The mist moves with the lines, slithering back and forth like a din of serpents. Clan flags drape uplifted spears, creating a panorama of red, blue, yellow, green, white, and black. In the shifting fog, the flags have an odd fluttering iridescence that resembles the disembodied wings of a thousand songbirds beating in unison.

Skenandoah comes to stand beside me. As his grip tightens on his bow, his fingernails go white, but that anxiety never reaches the calm of the war chief's face. He is a tactician and probably already four or five steps into the battle that has yet to begin. The only outward sign of worry is the short black hair that has glued itself to his sweating brow.

"When you were out there, could you count them? How many do you think there are?" he asks without taking his eyes from the battlefield.

"My guess is around six thousand, but there could be more in reserve."

Skenandoah's head dips in a barely discernible nod. "That is my guess as well."

"How many warriors do we have?"

"All of the surrounding villages sent warriors. They know if we fall it's over. We have three thousand two hundred, if we count every boy with a toy bow. But one thousand of those are inside the villages, five hundred in Yellowtail and five hundred here. So there are only a little over two thousand out there."

I can't help but glance down at the crowded plaza where warriors huddle, waiting for the time when they will be called to the palisade to replace a man or woman who's been killed or wounded. Boys and girls clump awkwardly around the warriors, their childish war clubs clutched in small fists, or plucking slack bowstrings like musical instruments. A few girls race around the plaza with dogs chasing them, laughing. Though they have endured attacks upon their villages, these children had never been called upon to help defend them. They have no idea what is coming.

But their parents do. Men and women stand before the central bonfire, their arms around each other's waists, watching their sons and daughters with glassy eyes, memorizing their faces. Huge pots of cornmeal mush bubble beside the fire, warm food for starving warriors with just enough time to gobble a few bites and race back to defend the walls. A low hum of frightened voices rides the wind.

Then . . . from the distance, a long drawn-out howl. The distinctive call of the Wolf Clan.

I look back over the palisade. The enemy line breaks apart and re-forms into three lines, one to the north, one trotting east, the other coming straight at them from the west. Those warriors will greatly regret it when they encounter the sucking mud of the marsh.

Unconsciously, I turn to the south, wondering who is out there. They must already be in place. I can't see them, just the pale glimmers of campfires sparkling amid the trees on the horizon.

Shouts go up. I turn back to look westward. Far away, I can identify the clan factions. As they run forward, the symbols on the darkest war shirts crystallize, stark against the dead grass, and I smell the salty stench of fear on the breeze.

Another wolf cry . . . then the long roar as every clan joins in and the small valley rumbles. The Hills warriors outnumber the Standing Stone by at least three to one. It is an awful sight.

The Standing Stone warriors let fly. As the arrows slice through the mist, it shreds and seems to boil.

Sharp surprised cries ring out, the yips of warriors who've just taken an arrow in the belly or chest but don't know yet that they are dead on their feet.

As the enemy runs forward, the archers who've just fired sling their

bows and charge out to meet them with war clubs in their fists. A grunting, gasping bellow rises, followed by the mushy thuds of clubs smacking
skulls. I've given and taken such blows often enough that I can see the
expressions of the wounded right behind my eyes and feel the momentary relief of the attacker in my heart.

"Hold," Skenandoah whispers through gritted teeth. One of his hands,
propped on the palisade, clenches. *"Hold."*

The Hills warriors shove them back, slowly at first. The lines surge and
withdraw, as though breathing the death of the world, and it is a labored
death. My lungs work with them. The wounded stagger away, trying to
get back, looking toward home. Some of the Standing Stone warriors
reach out to Bur Oak and Yellowtail villages, as though begging their relatives for help.

The first line breaks. As Standing Stone warriors race back, the second line of archers lets fly into the screaming horde chasing them; then
they charge out to meet them. The whooping, grunting struggle begins
again. The line holds long enough for the wounded to flee. A new sound
grows—the sound of limbs ripping from trees, feet scrambling through
deadfall, and finally, the hopeful cries of people rushing toward the gates
of the villages.

Skenandoah cups a hand to his mouth and calls, "Utz, don't open the
gates until the wounded are plastered against them. Do you understand?"

Utz lifts a hand and runs to press his eye to the crack between the
plank gates, waiting. When the crashes of people hitting the gates drive
him backward, he shouts, "Hannock, help me!"

It takes both of them to shove the locking planks aside and open the
gates. The panicked group of warriors who rush through supporting their
injured friends stuns me. There are so many. Blood drenches war shirts,
stripes faces, clots on broken skulls. A few shove captives before them.

"Get them to the council house!" Skenandoah orders. "Bahna and
Genonsgwa will care for them there!"

The arms and legs of the hardest hit dangle as their friends struggle to
carry them across the plaza.

"Blessed Spirits," Skenandoah whispers. "We don't have long."

I turn back to the battlefield. The second line has broken. Warriors
flee. Arrows from the third wave of archers glisten as they puncture the
mist and arc downward toward their targets. Despite the numbers of
Hills warriors that fall, the onslaught roars forward, barely slowed as it
crashes through the third wave and lunges for the last line of Standing
Stone archers.

"Gods," Skenandoah says. "They'll be here in less than one thousand heartbeats." He spins and calls, "Yonto, inform High Matron Kittle that our first three lines have broken, and the last is wavering. The enemy will hit the village *soon*."

The young woman warrior runs for the ladder, climbs down three rungs at a time, and dashes for the Deer longhouse.

Skenandoah faces me. "I need every experienced warrior I have. Will you serve as my deputy war chief?"

I throw out my hands as though to push him away. "I—I can't."

As Skenandoah strides toward me, he says, "Then get out of my way."

He shoves me hard against the palisade and continues down the catwalk, speaking to his warriors, probably selecting another for the job he offered me.

A numb sensation of helplessness fills me. My nerves hum. All down the catwalk, warriors stare at me. The revulsion is close to hatred. At this moment, many of my old and dear friends wish to crush my skull with their war clubs.

Their focus quickly changes when the first arrows rain down in the marsh to the west. The enemy archers can't see across the thick reeds; they don't have the distance yet. But they get it quickly. The next arrows slam the palisade and sail over the walls, where they drop into the plaza. People shriek and scatter like a school of fish at a thrown rock, running for cover. Many do not make it. By ones and twos, they fall. People race back, trying to drag them to safety. When another barrage of arrows flickers through the fog over Bur Oak Village, there is nothing for them to do but lie flat and hold the ground. Arrows lance the plaza, thudding on longhouse roofs, sending up puffs of snow when they don't strike flesh. A dog howls. I see it struggling toward the central fire with an arrow all the way through its right hind leg.

The shouting and screams go on and on. I lose all sense of time. Arrows fall like the endless rains at the dawn of creation when the hero twins fought the monsters. Fight the monsters. Fight . . .

More arrows zizz as they cut the air over my head. Down the catwalk, Skenandoah walks through the mist. Unbelievable. He walks slowly, slowly along through the hail of arrows, chatting with his warriors, bending to talk to men who'd hunched down, hiding behind the wall, convincing them to stand up again, to nock their bows. To fight.

Out in the marsh, calls go up. Two men materialize from the mist, slogging through the reeds, their bows held over their heads. Then more . . . and more. Hundreds. Several carry ladders. Others hold pots, probably filled with pine pitch. As the warriors on the palisade sling arrows at them, they continue coming, unconcerned, wave upon wave. An incredible sight, dreamlike.

An arrow slices the air over my left shoulder. I dive for the catwalk. More arrows clatter. I watch one skip down the catwalk before it cuts a bright furrow in the planks and snaps in two. I roll to my back and lie for a time blinking up at the arrows as they pass overhead. They make different sounds. Depending upon how they are fletched, some whisper, others hum. I most hate the thin breathless shrieks made by the arrows fletched with crow feathers. For the first time, I become aware of the different notes that make up the roar. It's composed of thousands of gasps, barks, war clubs cracking together, fragments of Songs, the flat splats of war axes striking bone, curses of the warriors trying to cross the marsh. Children sobbing. Like a great dying beast, the battle keens through the morning mist.

Several of the warriors standing near me on the palisade cry out and collapse. Two topple from the catwalk and crash to the plaza below. People dash to get to them, then carry them in their arms to the council house.

A dropped bow and quiver gleams not two paces from me. Actually gleams—the polished wood shines as though coated with liquid sunlight. Beads of mist sparkle on the red cardinal feathers tied to the bowstring. Just below my hearing, as though calling to my soul, the weapon's quiet voice urges: *Pick me up. Fight.*

As though competing for my loyalty, Shago-niyoh whispers, *"You are no longer a warrior."*

Skenandoah crouches with his back to me. Black. Unmoving. Speaking softly to a dying youth huddling against the wall. The young warrior has seen perhaps fifteen summers.

A wail erupts just before the enemy horde strikes the palisade. As though an earthquake has heaved the world sideways, the catwalk trembles. I get to my feet, leap over the bow and quiver, and run to look.

Below, Hills warriors slam ladders against the walls. In less than ten heartbeats, several have vaulted over the palisade and landed upon the catwalk. Eyes gleaming wildly, they whoop and charge. People rush by me. As they kill the invaders, they shove their bodies back over the palisade and push the ladders away. I look down. Gray shapes, boulder-like, scatter the edge of the marsh. More pile against the base of the palisade. Bodies. The snow is gone, beaten away by desperate feet. Blood soaks the earth.

In Yellowtail Village, thirty paces distant, melody lofts into the roar. Musicians play drums and flutes. A conch-shell trumpet blows. The haunting sound wavers through the death cries like fluttering ribbons.

As though I have stepped into another world, the chaos suddenly increases, drowning out everything but my own hammering heartbeat.

Out across the misty forest, the enemy is closing in. Warriors plant the spears sporting their clan colors, claiming this territory. The flags hang limp. No wind at all now. Just shining mist and sickly sunlight.

Only the far northern line still holds. And it can't last for long.

Fifty-three

Take him away," Kittle said with an impatient wave of her hand.

"Yes, High Matron."

The two warriors spun the Hills prisoner around and shoved him through the door curtain back out into the chaos of the plaza.

Kittle looked around at the other five matrons. Their dire expressions seemed frozen. They sat so still their white hair caught the firelight and became threads of gold. The warm air felt suddenly hot. Kittle pulled her cape open beneath her chin. "I say we do it."

Sihata, matron of the Hawk Clan, shifted on the floor mat. "You would risk your granddaughter's life on the word of a terrified prisoner?"

"Someone must do it, Grandmother!" Taya insisted. Her young face looked older. Her jaw was set, and her eyes blazed with certainty.

Kittle rubbed a hand over her face. The captured Hills warrior had been so frightened, his teeth had chattered incessantly. He'd have told them anything he thought they wanted to hear, but she suspected he'd been telling the truth about this. "Yes."

Taya, who stood to her right behind the circle of matrons, heaved a breath. Gitchi lay at her feet, guarding her as Sky Messenger had instructed. Taya gazed fearlessly at Kittle, but she had her fists clenched, clearly annoyed the deliberations were taking so long.

She said, "Grandmother, please, if I'm going, I must go now, before they've completely surrounded the village."

Matron Dehot murmured, "She's right. Send her. At this point, what harm could she do?"

Sihata smoothed white hair from her forehead. "There is one thing." They all turned to listen. "She is the high matron's granddaughter. She would make a fine hostage."

A small tremor went through Kittle, but she didn't think anyone noticed. She looked straight at Taya. "I won't let them use you against us. Do you understand, Taya? If we do this, as of this moment, you are dead to me. No matter what they threaten, I will do nothing to save you."

"I understand, Grandmother." She gave Kittle a clear-eyed stare.

Kittle held her gaze for a long time before saying, "Promise them anything you have to. Hurry."

"Take care of Gitchi for us?"

"Yes, of course." Kittle put her hand on the wolf's soft back and stroked it. "Stay with me, Gitchi."

Taya grabbed her cape from where it rested beside the fire, rushed to the door curtain, and disappeared outside.

Kittle watched the leather curtain swing. Outside, she caught glimpses of children running, dodging falling arrows, followed by shouting warriors trying to herd them to safety.

Sihata threw another branch on the fire. As sparks rose into the smoky air of the longhouse, she tipped her wrinkled face up to watch them climb toward the smoke hole. She softly said, "I think she'll make it. She has courage for one so young."

Kittle replied, "Yes. She'll make it. She has to."

Fifty-four

War Chief Sindak clutched his nocked bow and turned to look back. A solid line stretched out across the valley behind him, coming on fearlessly. The other war chiefs were keeping tight control of their warriors, not an easy thing with the enemy fleeing before them. Good men and women, every one. Despite the heavy losses they were taking, they would hold it together long enough get into position around the villages. Then it would become a different fight. He wiped stinging sweat from his eyes and licked his chapped lips. Each village had three rings of palisades. Breaking through them would be even more costly in blood and time. Gods, he wished he didn't have to do this. He wished it hadn't come to this. War Chief Koracoo, now Matron Jigonsaseh, was an old ally. He did not wish to kill her, and that's what would happen when they won. All of the matrons and chiefs would be lined up and their throats slit as their people watched. Atotarho had already given the order. "Leave the enemy headless. That way when we march the captives home, they will be lost, their souls too broken to cause us problems. We'll pack their backs with every basket of food we can find, and they'll bear their burdens without a word."

Sindak frowned at where Chief Atotarho stood with his personal guards on the crest of the rocky ridge. He could just make them out in the shifting mist. The black flag of the Wolf Clan flew over his head.

Sindak turned back. A new roar and the clattering of war clubs rose when his forces cut through the third wave of archers and approached the last Standing Stone line waiting in the trees, their bows aimed, waiting. A roar went up. Elder Brother Sun, shining through the fog, cast an eerie diffuse light over the participants. Warriors' faces—some painted, some tattooed—glowed bloodred as they appeared and disappeared in the mist. His forces pushed closer, closer. One of the enemy war chiefs shouted, and the archers let fly. At that range, if they could aim at all, they couldn't miss. His stomach knotted as he watched hundreds of Hills warriors topple. They went down as though swathed by a huge flint scythe. The rest of his forces charged forward.

Most of the Standing Stone line broke and fled, but a portion of the line to the north held. Strong men and women. Good leadership to keep them in position while everyone else ran away. That wasn't Koracoo herself out there, was it? Surely they wouldn't let their new matron command, would they? No, he couldn't imagine it. Gonda? A sad warmth filled Sindak. Yes, maybe. Gonda had warred with Koracoo for many summers. He knew her tactics well.

Sindak lifted a fist and turned to yell to the war chiefs behind him, "Keep your lines tight. We will strike the last of the northern line, then push for the villages."

He yipped a shrill war cry and charged down into the battle, his warriors pounding the ground behind him.

As he ran, he gave the other war chiefs hand signals, and the whole line shifted northward, closing gaps, moving like one huge animal. It was beautifully done. Artwork. Even after the arrows began falling like a hail of stilettos, the line still moved steadily onward.

When they got closer, a few men stopped to fire back; then more stopped. Sindak shouted at their commanders. Too far. They were too far away. If they hit anything it would be sheer luck. Move. Keep them all moving. The terrifying sight of so many enemy warriors coming at them should send the Standing Stone warriors fleeing before they even arrived.

But they held. To his amazement. Even in the face of overwhelming odds, the remnant northern line held. They were about to be swallowed whole. But they held. Admiration filled him.

He winced when, to his right, he saw his own line breaking. Warriors too eager for blood clumped together and lunged ahead. They must have planned this, their own moment of victory. Nothing he could do about it now. They were too close. Almost upon the enemy. The northern line concentrated their fire on the men running out in front, and the heroes dropped like flies after the first hard frost.

"Come on!" Sindak shouted. "Now is the time for courage! Make your clans proud."

The Standing Stone archers tossed aside their bows, drew their war clubs, and clan cries shredded the air as they charged out to meet Sindak's forces.

Fifty-five

Stay down!" Gonda ordered.

Warriors scrambled to obey, throwing themselves to the earth, covering their heads until the endless volley slicing the air overhead ceased.

He hid behind a boulder, staring for so long at the orange circles of lichen and shiny flecks of mica in the granite that when he dared lift his head and look out across the valley at the men moving among the trees, hunched, hiding, he felt too tired to move. Many warriors had covered themselves with leaves, praying the attackers would pass them by. A bloody deer thrashed through the brush to his right, three-legged, a wrenching sight. Five paces away a man with no head lay like a torn cornhusk doll. And all around him, all around, mist eddied and roiled. Fine snow filtered down everywhere, coating faces, capes, settling into unseeing eyes. The western lines had collapsed first, followed by most of the northern line. Standing Stone warriors were fleeing for their lives, trying to reach the villages before they could be cut down. The enemy formed up behind them and let fly at their backs. A new sound. Stuttering wails. Ghostly forms staggered through shifting fog, visible one instant, gone the next.

Gonda blinked. As the enemy raced by on their way to attack the villages, he breathed out. Gradually, the air softened and the battle sounds transformed into a distant roar.

Gonda stepped from behind the boulder for a better look.

A young boy, twelve maybe, crouched to Gonda's left, sobbing without making a sound, staring out at the rows of dead that littered the foggy vista. Gonda walked over and put a hand on his shoulder. "It's all right. It's over for now."

The boy lifted his face and gazed at him, his soft black eyes like polished jet. Stunned eyes. Uncomprehending. Gonda patted his shoulder. "Just sit here for a while. If you have any food in your belt pouch, eat. You need something in your stomach. It will help."

The boy's jaws worked, but no sound came out. Gonda patted his shoulder again, said, "You fought bravely today. No man could have done better." He moved on, stepped between two dead bodies, headed for War Chief Deru.

Deru had just stood up thirty paces away. His massive shoulders bristled with old leaves. In profile, his face was dark and still, his caved-in cheek nothing more than an oddly misshapen shadow, a hole in his head. He clutched his war club in a bloody fist.

Warriors slowly moved among the thick brush and piles of boulders, getting to their feet. Their faces had flushed, their eyes gone blank with shock. Lips moved; tears ran down cheeks. Friends covered the dead grass, their arms and legs twisted at impossible angles. For as far as any of them could see . . . bodies. Hundreds. No, thousands. They filled the valley. Great swaths of blood had turned the snow the shade of fire.

Gonda walked to Deru. They stared at each other. Despite the fact that they faced each other from less than eight hands away, Gonda was having trouble focusing his eyes. He kept blinking, trying to clear them. Over Deru's shoulder he saw the woman warrior, Wampa, standing with her feet braced, her shaking bow pulled back, guarding four wounded warriors, men with barely the strength to weep and stare up at her with utter devotion in their eyes. She had perhaps been the only thing that had stood between them and death.

From deep inside him, Koracoo's long-ago voice whispered, *"Like stunning beauty, true bravery has no cause, no reasons or motives. It is an offering, given without a thought."*

Gonda hung his head.

Deru looked at him with a tight expression Gonda had never seen—the expression of a man bleeding to death inside. Deru said nothing, just stared. Gonda felt an eerie turning, like a mortal wound pumping the heart dry. Then he saw Deru was crying. The war chief was crying. Gonda moved closer and said sternly, "We're not finished. Not yet."

Deru lightly shook his head. "No, we are not."

"We need to form up our warriors. We'll attack the flanks. Pick off as many as we can."

Deru wiped his face on his sleeve. "How many are well enough to fight?"

Gonda looked around. He counted perhaps thirty warriors on their feet. Thirty. Thirty out of five hundred. The rest . . . the rest would never fight again. "Enough to hurt them."

Deru gave him a grim smile, and the gesture made his crushed cheek twitch. He called, "Gather as many dropped arrows as you can. Fill your quivers! We're heading back into the fight."

Warriors gave each other empty looks and slowly turned to collect arrows, war clubs, axes. They moved like dead men still on their feet, but just barely.

Gonda said, "What's your plan?"

Deru squinted at the thousands of Hills warriors rushing toward the villages. Though Atotarho had taken heavy losses, there had to be four thousand warriors still in the fight. Four thousand Gonda could see, which didn't count whatever the chief had in reserve waiting in the forest to the south. Deru didn't seem able to speak. He kept shaking his head, swallowing.

Gonda cast a glance at the men and women beginning to crowd around them, waiting for orders. He moved closer to Deru and whispered, "I say we swing around the western edge of the marsh. Come up from the south using the cornfields as cover. Then decide what to do. What do you think, War Chief?"

Deru stared at the marsh for a long time, as though trying to see it in his souls. "Yes. Yes, let's do that." He turned to his warriors. "Follow me. We're going around the marsh!"

He lifted a hand, waved his warriors forward, and took off at a slow trot, heading for the dense stand of cattails wavering through the mist.

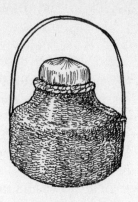

Fifty-six

Zateri watched the battle with her arms folded tightly beneath her white cape. Each time she shifted, the blue wolf paw prints that encircled the bottom of the cape seemed to be running, trying to escape. She felt sick. The people standing around the fire with her seemed as stunned as she was at the swiftness of their progress. The worst part of the battle remained ahead, however. Laying siege to fortified villages was usually a waste of lives, not that her father cared. All he wanted was to destroy the Standing Stone nation.

As War Chief Sindak re-formed the Hills lines around Yellowtail and Bur Oak Villages, there was a brief respite in the fighting. The shouts and war cries yielded to the low moans of the injured and dying still on the battlefield.

Zateri studied her comrades' faces. Kwahseti, Gwinodje, Hiyawento, and Chief Canassatego stood quietly, warming their hands before the flames or sipping cups of rosehip tea while they waited for the next assault to begin. Hiyawento's dark eyes had a glazed look, as though he was seeing through the battle to something far beyond, and she wondered if perhaps he was not living in the past with his daughters. Just behind Zateri's eyes, their sweet faces were always there, their arms lifted, begging to be held. Their bubbling laughter filled her ears. Hiyawento had always been able to smile Zateri out of her fears, to comfort her. She longed for the feel of her cheek against his broad chest and his strong arms around her. But when she looked at him, she knew this man was not going to smile, or offer comfort, for his own unbearable pain had swallowed his world.

Zateri turned to see her father. He rode upon his litter with a regal tilt to his gray head. Carried by four warriors, the litter jostled and rocked as the men maneuvered it into place three hundred paces from Bur Oak Village. When he slid his crooked body off the litter, his black cape looked stark against the snow. A log bench was immediately constructed so he could sit down. From there, Atotarho would observe the final collapse of his enemies. He must be gloating, laughing. As she watched the chief's personal guards setting up his war lodge—little more than tented poles covered with deer hides—hatred seeped through Zateri's grief.

Kwahseti gestured with her chin. "There's a runner coming."

The runner slowed thirty paces away and walked the last distance to reach her fire, where he bowed deeply. "Matrons, the chief wishes you to move your forces into position south of the villages. When the cowards try to flee, he wants the leaders captured and held."

Zateri nodded. "Very well."

The runner looked around nervously. He'd seen eighteen or nineteen summers. Irregularly chopped-off black hair hung around his narrow face, which made his nose look abnormally long. "There is one other thing, Matron Zateri."

"Yes?"

He wet his lips. "The chief wishes me to inform you that he has received word that the high matron is walking the Path of Souls."

The ground seemed to fall away beneath her feet. After her mother's death, Grandmother had been the only person in the world who'd cared enough to help her heal after Gannajero. She'd nursed Zateri when she'd been sick, taught her everything about clan politics, and held her when her heart had been broken. The loss, along with that of her daughters, seemed to open a gaping black chasm in her souls. She had the uneasy sensation that she was teetering on the edge, about to fall in where she would lose herself in the icy darkness. She said, "When?"

"Four days ago."

Zateri straightened. "Thank you, warrior. When we return home, I will call the Wolf Clan—"

"That won't be necessary," the warrior interrupted as though he knew he had to get it out now, or he never would. "The chief says you should not worry about the succession. The former high matron left instructions that she wished Matron Kelek of the Bear Clan to replace her as high matron. She—"

"What!" Kwahseti lunged forward to stare with her fists clenched. The runner looked like he wanted to crawl under a log. "She would never do that! It's a betrayal of the other Wolf Clan ohwachiras!"

"Nonetheless, Matrons, the chief has already spoken with Matron Kelek. At this very moment, she is—"

"She had better not be making preparations!" Gwinodje's voice seethed. Her face had gone livid. "Our clan will not give up rulership so easily, and you can tell that to Chief Atotarho!"

"I understand." The runner bowed again, turned, and jogged away.

Everyone turned to Zateri. Their expressions were outraged. Gwinodje's thin girlish body was shaking.

Kwahseti waved a hand. "Zateri, why didn't you say anything? You know your grandmother wished you to replace her. She said as much at the last meeting of the ohwachiras!"

A sudden frightening sensation rose and pervaded everything, stealthily closing in around her. When it settled into her chest like a frozen stone, she shivered. "He's been clever, hasn't he?"

Kwahseti frowned. "What do you mean? He just stole your inheritance. You are the rightful—"

"He's been planning this all along, and I did not guess it. Perhaps I am not fit to lead anyone."

"You no longer have the luxury of speculating, Zateri," Kwahseti said. "Will you or won't you lead the clan?"

Gwinodje was staring at her, waiting. "You must decide, Zateri. Once you accept, we can begin organizing the ohwachiras and pulling the little clan matrons together."

Zateri stared out at the battlefield. Grandmother had wanted this. In fact, the False Faces had come to her . . . Zateri looked down at her white cape, and a flood of certainty rushed through her. "Yes! I accept. If the ohwachiras will have me, I will lead them. Now, what do we do about Atotarho's order?"

Chief Canassatego's leathery brown face tensed. He glanced down the hill at Atotarho, sitting hunched over on his log bench, then back at those gathered around the fire. "I, for one, refuse to accept this farce. I will not support a chief who moves without the consensus of the Ruling Council. He consulted no one, not about the high matron's position, nor about the attack on White Dog Village. Does he think he alone rules this nation?"

Gwinodje added, "I agree. Either the chief follows the will of the people, which is guaranteed by the Ruling Council's efforts to seek the consensus of the people, or our alliance crumbles."

Kwahseti stood irresolutely for a moment. Then, bracing herself as though for a fistfight, she said, "Well, what are we going to do about it? We're in the middle of a battle. We've just been given orders."

"Orders we should refuse to obey." Hiyawento seemed to have come back to himself. His voice sounded strong, confident. His dark eyes flashed. Though he'd said nothing during the exchange, his indignation was palpable. "Matron Zateri, is it your decision that I lead the Coldspring Village warriors into this fight?"

Zateri watched the mist moving through the valley below. The sky was completely overcast now. Elder Brother Sun's gleam had all but vanished, leaving the land gray and dim. The temperature was also dropping. The fog seemed to be growing thicker, filling the valley like dove-colored smoke.

"I must consult with Chief Coldspring and the other village clan matrons."

"As we all should," Kwahseti said.

"Then let us do so immediately," Gwinodje urged. "We don't have much time to get organized. You all know, don't you? If we do this, Atotarho will label us traitors and turn his forces against us. We had better be ready. In fact we had better—"

A sharp cry rose from down the hill near last summer's cornfields. Zateri spun to look and saw two of her scouts hauling a young woman up the hill. The woman was struggling against them, fighting, and the warriors seemed to be enjoying themselves, hurting an enemy woman.

Hiyawento's eyes suddenly flared, and he shouted, "Release her, now!"

The warriors dropped her arms as though they'd turned red-hot and stared at their war chief in confusion. As soon as she was free, the young woman lifted her skirts and ran up the hill like a boy, trying to get to Hiyawento.

"Do you know her?" Zateri asked. She was beautiful, with an oval face, large dark eyes, and . . . "Blessed gods, that's High Matron Kittle's granddaughter, isn't it? She looks just like her."

"Yes. And Sky Messenger's betrothed. Her name is Taya." Hiyawento ran down the hill to meet her, took her arm, and led her to the fire.

Taya was crying. Tears traced lines through the dust on her face. "I'm sorry, I—I didn't know how else to get here without being killed. I told the guards I needed to see you, that I knew you."

Gently, Hiyawento said, "That was the right thing to do. You do know me. Why are you here, Taya?"

She wiped her face with her hands, sniffed her nose, and stiffened her spine. After a few heartbeats, when she'd controlled herself, she said, "The Ruling Council of the Standing Stone nation wishes to make you an offer."

Fifty-seven

You may go." Atotarho waved an impatient hand at the messenger who
had just returned and gazed to the south, to the hilltop where the Wolf
Clan matrons stood around a small fire. A chuckle rumbled his chest.
They must be furious, plotting against him, but it didn't matter. It was
almost over. After he'd destroyed the Standing Stone people, there'd be
nothing to stop him from conquering every other paltry contender. Within
two or three summers there would be only the People of the Hills. All other
nations would have been conquered, their women and children absorbed
into new Hills villages, their men killed or enslaved.

Negano's long black hair swayed wetly as he strode up to Atotarho and
subtly jerked his head toward the war lodge. "While you were busy with
battle . . . ," he said cryptically.

Atotarho turned to look. The lodge stood fourteen hands tall and
spread twenty hands in diameter. Painted deer hides, decorated with
symbols from each of the six clans, covered the pole structure. "Thank
you, Negano."

He careened to his feet, wobbled, and had to brace his walking stick to
keep standing. "Inform me when the battle begins again. I need to rest."

"Yes, Chief." Negano bowed.

Atotarho slowly, painfully, made his way to his war lodge, drew back
the hide over the door, and stepped into the darkness. In the rear, shapes
moved. The blackness seemed to fold in upon itself, then unfold.

"So," he said as he let the door curtain drop. "You finally got here. I was beginning to wonder."

The man didn't answer. Instead, like oil oozing from a midnight ocean, Ohsinoh arose. His bluebird-feather hood had been pulled so far forward it was difficult to make out any of his features, though he'd painted his triangular face; the lower half was red, the top half white.

As Atotarho's eyes adjusted to the darkness, he saw an eight-summers-old girl on her knees in the rear. Eyes huge and wet. Tiny whimpers eddied through her gag. Though she was not struggling now, she had been. Blood caked the cords that bound her hands and feet.

Ohsinoh leaned forward. When his face was less than one hand's-breadth from Atotarho's, he whispered, "Kahn-Tineta has seen the Crow. She will be ready when the time comes." As he straightened, he began making soft cawing sounds. He danced like a demented stork around Kahn-Tineta. The girl tried to scream through her gag.

Atotarho lowered himself to the stack of hides that had been prepared for him, and replied, "Good."

Fifty-eight

Sky Messenger

When I deliver warm bowls of cornmeal mush to the exhausted warriors leaning against the palisade, they murmur soft thanks. I move on. There's no need to rush; everyone who was hungry has been fed. Every wound has been tended. I have seen to that. My cape is soaked with the tears of the dying, but they did not die alone. I thank the Spirits for the lull in the battle, but the calm is almost over. Far out in the dense fog, clan yells erupt. Orders are shouted. Deputy war chiefs are moving their people into position. War clubs smack against palms. Laughter trails away. We'll be hit again at any moment.

I have not seen Taya since just after dawn. I'm worried about her. Where is she? She must be safe. She has to be safe.

I wipe my sweating brow on my sleeve and gaze down into the plaza. The council house was long ago filled to bursting. There is no choice now but to place the injured outside in the cold. As space is opened in the council house, the injured will be moved in. The dead rest in mounds along the walls. Loved ones refuse to leave them. They bring blankets to keep their husbands and daughters warm. They hug them and whisper in their ears. The wails are terrible.

I turn. Out to the east, thousands of feet crunch snow. Voices call. Too much fog. They are translucent ghosts swimming in a vast gray ocean, ceaselessly moving, riding waves up and down as they dip into the main trail and soar up the bank, coming on. Flat out.

An arrow slams my arm, spinning me sideways. I look down at the blood seeping from the torn muscle of my upper arm. It's nothing. Keep moving. A man sags, almost falls over the palisade, catches himself. He sinks to the catwalk with agonizing slowness. I hurry toward him. He has blood all over his chest, blood bubbling from around the arrow shaft. I kneel beside him.

"You're not dying, Idos," I say confidently as I snap off the tip of the arrow and hurl it away. "The arrow struck too high. You will get well."

He stares up at me fixedly, straining to see my face. As he slides toward the dark, I must be fading. I can't imagine what he's thinking. He gasps a breath and with difficulty says, "Tell . . . Tutelo I love her."

My souls go numb. I hesitate, not sure of the best course; then I grip the slick shaft and jerk it from his chest. I'm sure it struck his heart, but maybe . . . maybe. He writhes, cries out. When the enemy hits the palisade, the misty world shatters and becomes one long scream.

Down in the plaza, people run in all directions.

Idos stops struggling. I feel his body relax beneath my hands. He's still staring at me, but he doesn't see me now. Sodowego has leaned over him. I whisper, "I'll tell her, Idos."

I rise to my feet. The smell of pine pitch is strong, rising from the base of the palisade. Skenandoah marches along the catwalk with arrows flying all around him, giving orders, always steady. And lucky. Lucky.

I throw up an arm to shield my face and run to look over the edge. Five warriors arrived before me. They've been loosing arrows, ducking behind the palisade, loosing more arrows for ten heartbeats. A bloody tangle of bodies sprawls below, but they succeeded in setting fire to the pitch before they fell. Bright flames lick along the wall. In the mist, they resemble gauzy orange flags. Fluttering. Climbing. The warriors must have managed to splash the pitch high. Down the palisade, more fires. They've probably been set all around. That was the point of that first shuddering volley, to allow the fire teams to get in close enough. Some of the fires will burn through. Then more teams will dart in, splash the second palisade, and fire it. Finally, they will fire the third palisade . . . and be through. On the fabric of my souls, I can already imagine enemy warriors racing through Bur Oak Village, killing anything in their path. I remember Yellowtail Village . . . burning . . . twelve summers ago.

A cold whisper of air brushes my face. I dive for the catwalk. I'm not hit. Close, though. Right beside me, a young woman goes down with a sharp cry. I scramble toward her on my hands and knees. The arrow cut the big artery in her throat; it's pumping ferociously. She shivers, suddenly freezing. "How . . . how bad? Tell me the truth!"

I gently smooth black hair away from her face. I would want to know the truth. "It'll be over soon. What's your name?"

"I am . . . Londal." She squeezes her eyes closed for a moment, then opens them and gazes up at the sky. "Thank you, thank you . . . for telling me."

She seems not to hear the ululating cries of oncoming warriors or feel the palisade shudder when they hit it and their axes crack against the logs, hacking their way through the charred patches left by the fires.

I sit down and pull her head into my lap, cushioning it as I stroke her hair.

She says, "I'm feeling . . . weaker."

"It won't last long. Just a little while. Is there any pain?"

Her lips move. She mouths the word no. A brown autumn leaf flutters through the fog and alights on the catwalk.

She whispers, "Pretty."

I pick it up and twirl it before her eyes. "Yes, it's still veined with red."

Just beyond the palisade the world is dying, she's dying, and we're talking about leaves.

"I—I'm falling." She struggles.

"Don't be afraid. I've heard it's a long slow fall, that it comes quietly and peacefully."

". . . falling fast."

"Yes, but you won't hit bottom. Soon you'll be walking the Path of Souls with people you once loved. Their campfires will be warm and bright."

The blood is jetting rapidly now, but there isn't much of it. Her heart is failing. It can't keep up. Then it's over.

I rise, mindful of the hail of arrows slicing overhead. Dead bodies crowd the catwalk. Warriors trip over them, walk on their backs. Some are crying, trying to be gentle. Most of the seasoned war veterans inside the palisade are dead. Young inexperienced warriors have replaced them. Their faces are twisted into stunned masks. What happened to the two men assigned to carry the wounded and dying into the plaza?

My job now. I bend and lift the woman warrior into my arms. Walking hunched over, I see Skenandoah. He's firing one arrow after another at the base of the palisade. His war shirt has a dozen ragged holes down his arms where his cape has been clipped by arrows. His square face is hard and red, his brown eyes glittering.

As I struggle to move by him, to reach the ladder, Deputy War Chief Leep cries out. Four paces away, he staggers backward and falls off the palisade with an arrow through his skull. Skenandoah looks for an instant too long. The arrow strikes him squarely in the lungs. As he grabs hold of the palisade, his bow drops from his fingers and clatters on the catwalk. A strange, almost amused expression touches his face. It's a mortal wound. He must know it. He straightens to his full height, as though making a target of his broad chest, and shrilly roars a defiant war cry. Within moments three more arrows slam into his body, each knocking him back a step. He crumples like a dry blade of grass beneath tramping feet.

Every warrior on the catwalk stops. They've lost both their war chief and deputy war chief in less than twenty heartbeats. Most have seen fourteen or fifteen summers. There's no one left to lead them. I can see it in their eyes. They think it's over. There's no hope.

One youth throws down his bow and flees. Two follow him. The rest are backing away from the palisade.

I hastily lay Londal's body down and grab Skenandoah's bow. Sick helpless rage fills me. As I tug the quiver from Londal's shoulders and sling it over my own shoulder, I shout, "Get that look off your faces! There are Hills People to kill! Nock your bows!"

Young warriors suck in air. They stare at me.

"Do it now!" I shout.

As though they've been slapped from a nightmare, they scramble to obey me.

A strange madness filters through me. An old familiar madness. My practiced hands work automatically, pulling arrows from the quiver, nocking, letting fly. As I watch man after man fall to my arrows, the fever builds. I'm on fire, and the sparkling mist is so bright it hurts.

"Sky Messenger!" Yaweth cries. "They're coming through!"

I swing around and see enemy warriors flooding through two holes in the innermost palisade, streaming across the plaza. The few Standing Stone warriors run to meet them. It is a disorganized rabble. As more of the enemy floods inside, the Standing Stone warriors break and run. The enemy pursues. The sodden thuds of war clubs striking flesh rises. The victory cries of the Hills warriors are like a Spirit Plant surging through my veins.

I throw my head back and shriek a war cry. Every warrior turns to me. Aims shift. Enemy arrows stream around me.

"Yaweth!" I shout. "You're my new deputy. Pick twenty people and form teams to cover every place where they might come through the inner palisade."

"Yes, Sky Messenger. What about you?"

My eyes must be blazing. An appreciative smile crosses her face. She knows this look. We are going to win. "I'm going down to lead the warriors in the plaza. Now move! They're coming."

I charge for the ladder.

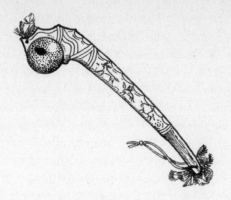

Fifty-nine

Sky Messenger

I leap off the rungs and hit the ground running. Skenandoah's bow sings in my hands. Standing Stone warriors flee around me, their faces stunned and gray, a slack-jawed mob. Most are very young, little more than terri-fied children. But I, above all, know what children can do when they must.

A bony girl in a torn dress has hold of an older man's arm. She is per-haps thirteen, crying, trying to drag him backward into the fight. He's seen around sixteen summers. "Please, my brother, they'll kill Mother and Father!"

He screams, "No!" shakes off her hands, and runs.

I grab the youth as he darts by and swing him around to glare full in his face. "Pull that war club from your belt! You're a Standing Stone war-rior. Fight!" The man is shaking badly. "What is your name?"

"P-pato."

I release him and step into the falling arrows to shout, "I am Sky Mes-senger. Follow me! Now is the time to save your families from slavery and death! *Follow me!*"

I shriek another war cry and pound into the plaza battle, loosing ar-rows on the run. I may not know these children's names, but they know mine. I hear them coming on behind me, my army of children. Bravely following. May the ancestors protect them. I cast a glance over my shoul-der. Perhaps forty. That is all the help I have to drive back the endless stream of warriors. It must be enough.

Yaweth's people race along the catwalk, getting into position. Every time Hills warriors duck through a hole in the walls, her warriors cut them to pieces. That leaves perhaps one hundred of the enemy in the plaza. Men who know the only way they'll get out is to kill every man, woman, and child in the village.

My quiver is empty. I toss it aside, scoop a war club from the ground, and lead my young warriors into the fight of their lives. My skills with a club were honed by the best: my father, Gonda, and my mother, the legendary war chief Koracoo. They taught me every nuance of the weapon.

A filthy warrior with rotten teeth charges me, roaring, his war club swinging for my shoulder. I parry the blow, shove him back, and level my club at his side. When it connects, a massive gush of air explodes from his crushed rib cage. He drops to his knees. Two more rush me.

I fight like a man possessed by an evil Earth Spirit, insanely twisting, dancing in to deliver blows, and leaping out beyond my opponents' range. They both come at me at once. I cave in the closest man's forehead and spin on one foot, ducking low, avoiding the blow that cuts the air over my head, to hammer the knees out from under my attacker. Bones crack. He falls, tries to drag himself away. He'll never walk again. But he won't have to. I crush his skull and move on.

"Sky Messenger!" someone behind me screams.

I glance back and see the youth I forced into the fight, young Pato, being beaten to the ground by a muscular Hills warrior with a triumphant grin on his face.

I'm there in three bounds. My club whispers through the mist as it slices for the man's arm. He dives, rolls, and jabs his club at me, forcing me back until he can get to his feet again.

"You pathetic worm!" the man shouts. "Do you think you can defeat the greatest warrior in the entire Hills nation? I am Ponkol of the Snipe Clan!"

When he starts to stand, there is an instant when he's off balance. I use it to rush him, hit him hard with my shoulder, and send him stumbling backward. Before he can regain his footing, young Pato slams him in the side of the head and staggers back. Pato looks dazed, stares at the dead man on the ground.

I shout, "Keep moving, Pato! Don't slow down."

As he turns to face his next opponent, an arrow rips the hide war shirt near my knees. I turn to . . .

Outside the walls, a horn trumpet blows three times. The blasts seem muffled by the fog, muted and haunting. The Hills warriors in the plaza jerk around in unison to stare. They look confused. Then there is a rush, an onslaught, dashing for the holes in the palisade. Yaweth's people kill as many as they can, but the warriors push outside.

I blink. A few are fighting a retreating action, covering their friends as they escape, but most are gone. My young warriors stagger, staring at dead friends. Disbelieving looks carve their faces.

I shout, "Stop looking at your fallen friends. We can't let anyone escape! Follow me!"

I pound toward the last four warriors who are covering their friends' escape. By the time I arrive, Yaweth's people have killed two. Two left.

With a single blow, I snap the spine of one man, then launch myself at the last Hills warrior standing in Bur Oak Village. He looks horrified. He knows what's coming. Before I can crack his skull, someone on the catwalk shoots an arrow through his belly. The man cries out in shock, throws down his bow, and charges through the charred hole in the palisade, try-ing to make it to his friends.

I chase after him. Just as he lurches through the last palisade, I crush his shoulder. He staggers back against the wall, calling desperately to his friends who are far out ahead, charging away. When he turns, his gaze flashes over me and fixes on something over my shoulder.

"No," the man hisses. "No. They're doing it!" He collapses to his knees. "I don't believe it!"

I turn to look toward the southern hills, following his gaze. A slight breeze has kicked up, swirling the fog into wavelike patterns that seem to ebb and flow. As it shifts, gaps open in the mist, revealing a sight that leaves me shaking my head, trying to decipher what's going on. Two sides are lining out. To the north, I see Sindak stalking down the lines, waving his war club. *Atotarho is to the north.*

I glare down at the wounded Hills warrior. "What's happening? Who is that to the south?"

He rocks back and forth, his hands clutching the arrow protruding from his belly. "Treasonous dogs! They deserve to die for this!"

"Who is that?" I draw back my war club to kill him if he doesn't answer quickly.

In a pathetic whimper, the man responds, "Chief Atotarho pulled three villages out of the battle because he thought they might refuse to fight. He ordered them to remain in camp! But they didn't. You can see that! They're marching out to face him down. The filthy traitors! Civil war is inevitable now!"

"Which villages?"

He lifted a trembling arm to point. "See there? That's War Chief Hi-yawento. He's leading warriors from Coldspring, Riverbank, and Canassatego villages!"

The wind changes. The mist blows back across the field to chill my face. The clan calls are easing off as warriors receive new orders and realign. The world goes soft and still.

My hands shake. I don't know what this has cost Hiyawento—I may never know—but the fact that he and Zateri have managed to pull the disaffected Hills villages into an alliance to fight against Atotarho . . .

After all my words about standing up for peace, this is where we are—locked in a death struggle.

From my right, a voice calls, "Sky Messenger!"

Father trots around the palisade with thirty or so warriors behind him. His wet cape sleeks down over his thin wiry body. His round face is haggard, his short black hair matted.

"Father! You're alive."

We throw our arms around each other in a bear hug. He laughs. "So far. Don't get your hopes up. I'm certain the Hills People would like to change that."

War Chief Deru comes to stand at my side. His eyes narrow at the sight of the wounded Hills warrior. Unceremoniously, he crushes the man's skull, then turns back to the battlefield. "What's going on out there?"

"Civil war, I think."

"They're fighting each other?" he asks in disbelief.

"So it seems."

Father's expression goes tight and sad. He says nothing for a long time, then whispers, "Warriors are asked to bear too much."

Neither Deru nor I have to ask what he means. Along with exhaustion, hunger, and the rage that leaves the heart a barren wasteland, these men and women will also have to live with the knowledge that they killed their loved ones with their own hands.

As the war fever begins to drain from muscles and sinew, my skin tingles. Those are my cherished friends out there, willing to fight their own people to save me and the entire Standing Stone nation.

My grip tightens on the bloody club in my fingers.

From out of nowhere, Gitchi glides along my leg and looks up at me with soft yellow eyes. He limps, but his tail wags, ready to follow as soon as I give the order. I don't know where he came from. One of the longhouses. Where's Taya? I turn to look, but I do not see her. High Matron Kittle must have ordered her lineage to remain within the walls of the longhouses.

I gaze down at Gitchi. "Hello, old friend. I missed you." I gently stroke his head. He leans against my hand and sighs, as though being with me is all he's ever wanted in his life.

"Well, what are we doing standing here?" Father looks around, searching each warrior's face. "If they're fighting Atotarho, they're on our side. We should join them. War Chief, what do you think?"

Deru inhales a breath and exhales it slowly; then he nods. "It seems we have just joined a new alliance—a strange one. Us and Hills People? Who would have ever thought? But Gonda is right. If these new allies are willing to die for us, we owe them no less."

A ragged, exhausted cheer goes up from his warriors. They shake bows and clubs in the air.

Father turns to a young man. "Risto, run to Matron Jigonsaseh. Tell her we join the fight on Hiyawento's side."

The warrior bows and runs as hard as he can toward Yellowtail Village.

"All right, let's go." Deru waves his warriors forward and leads them out onto the battlefield.

Father says, "Are you coming?"

I breathe, "Yes. Soon."

He frowns, then nods, understanding there is something I must do before I can follow him. "Don't be long." He trots away.

I crouch before Gitchi. The old wolf licks my face, and his tail wags. "I know you want to go, Gitchi. You are a great warrior. But I couldn't bear it if something happened to you. I want you to stay here. Don't follow me."

Gitchi's ears droop. He drops to his haunches and whimpers as he watches me pound away into the cold swirling fog.

Sixty

Where he stood in front of Chief Atotarho, Negano rubbed a hand over his face. In all his thirty-two summers, he had never imagined that a day like this would come. He had many cousins in Riverbank Village, men and women he'd loved his entire life. He could barely stand to watch. Blessed Spirits. He had to come to terms with this, or he would . . .

Atotarho vented a low laugh.

Negano turned around to stare at him. The old man had braided so many rattlesnake skins into his gray hair that it gave his skeletal face a serpentine quality. Granted, they were symbols of war victories, but this was garish.

Atotarho maneuvered his crooked body forward, carefully placing his walking stick, until he stood less than one pace from Negano. His eyes had a cold inhuman gleam. "Find a runner for me."

"Yes, my chief." Negano lifted a hand, calling, "Qonde?"

When the guard trotted over, Atotarho said, "Grab a white arrow. I wish you to deliver a message to my daughter, Matron Zateri. Tell her I wish a short truce to speak with her."

Qonde gave Negano a relieved look, bowed, and trotted away.

Negano turned to Atotarho, hopefully asking, "Will we make peace, Chief?"

"Oh," Atotarho nodded fervently, *"they* will make peace." Atotarho gripped his walking stick as though to strangle the life from it. "The arrogant fools. Did they think I would not foresee this treachery?"

From within the war lodge, a deep-throated laugh rumbled.

From where he stood on the tree-covered eastern hill, Sonon could look down across the misty battlefield. He watched his brother's messenger trot toward Matron Zateri's camp, weaving through thousands of warriors, men and women preparing for the final confrontation. The fog-shrouded field echoed with their efforts: damp bowstrings whined as they were drawn back; arrows rattled in leather quivers; wooden-slat body armor clacked. The low, dreadful groan of the battlefield hung over everything like the death wails of soon-to-be-forgotten nations.

Ohsinoh laughed, and it made Sonon go still. It was like the hiss of a poisonous serpent, quiet with the promise of death. It made the skin creep.

Sonon's gaze moved to the war lodge where his brother, Atotarho, stood. He granted himself a moment to wonder what if . . .

What if Atotarho's afterlife soul had not been chased from his body? What if the stream of their lives had not been broken? That boy, his brother's son, would have been a greatly beloved member of Sonon's family. Sonon would have helped raise him, would have taught him to fish and hunt, would have comforted Hehaka's tears. If he'd had the chance, Sonon would have done everything in his power to keep that boy from harm.

But Atotarho's soul had been shaken loose. The stream of their lives had been sundered. Sonon and his twin sister were sold into slavery at the age of eight, and Hehaka at the age of four. Their three lives had become a diabolical monument to Atotarho's loose soul—a soul that continued to wander shadow-like through the forests.

Sonon's soft exhale frosted and blended with the eddying fog.

Behind him, coming up the main trail, hundreds of moccasins thumped the frozen ground. Weapons jangled with their quickstep. They must have run all the way to get here, for the salty scent of their sweat wafted on the light breeze.

He didn't turn. Soon, it would all begin again.

He wanted to look for a time longer.

Sonon kept his gaze on Atotarho's crooked, misshapen body. Strands of Atotarho's gray hair had come loose from his bun and stuck wetly to his wrinkled cheeks. The war lodge shadowed most of his expression.

Sonon cocked his head.

How strange that the most important lessons lived in shadows. To see anything important, a man had to be willing to stare full-face into the living darkness.

As he stared at his brother, Atotarho turned, and Sonon found his own living darkness staring back. He was looking into the black abyss that had swallowed him when he'd seen eight summers.

Someday, someday soon, he would have to confront his brother . . . but not today.

The warriors coming up behind him veered off the main trail and trotted toward the hilltop where Sonon stood. Their breathing was coming hard. Their clan flags flapped as they ran.

Sonon tore his gaze from his brother and swiveled to watch their approach.

Sixty-one

The mist moved as a great white ocean, waves surging and retreating, leaving lacy patterns like sea foam in their wake. Tree branches dripped incessantly. Chief Cord shivered. The damp cold ate at a man's bones.

"I don't understand this," War Chief Baji said.

Cord rubbed the back of his neck. "I doubt anyone does. Especially the warriors on that battlefield."

Where they stood upon the hilltop to the east of Bur Oak and Yellowtail villages, they could look out across the misty battlefield. The dilemma was clear. Both sides were Hills people.

"Ah. Maybe I do understand." Baji's gaze scanned the principal figures, men and women standing out in front of their forces, preparing to give orders.

"Well, explain it to me."

His adopted daughter had grown into a strong muscular woman, broad-shouldered with long legs, and the face of a Sky Spirit. Oval, with large black eyes, high cheekbones, her face would have been perfect were it not for the white knife scar that slashed across her pointed chin. She did not wear a cape, just a knee-length buckskin war shirt and high-topped black moccasins. Weapons dangled from her belt. She carried a bow and quiver over her left shoulder.

She tipped her chin. "To the south, do you see the tall man with the war ax? That's Hiyawento. The short slender woman to his right is Zateri."

Cord gave her a curious look. "We're too far away to see their faces. How could you possibly know that?"

Her gaze moved across the battlefield and seemed to fix on some far point. Her voice turned soft. "The same way I know that that's Dekana-wida trotting out from Bur Oak Village. I know them, Cord. In ways I will never know any other human beings. The motions of their bodies live in my souls. Every tilt of their heads, every wave of their hands, the way each stands, is part of me. I might as well be looking at myself in a slate mirror. I know that sounds strange—"

"No. It doesn't." Cord nodded his understanding. They had gone through so much together as children it made sense that they would have a mysterious sort of connection.

He gave her a sidelong look. "Very well. Then we know a little more about what's happening. War Chief Hiyawento's forces are to the south." As he said the words, Hiyawento's archers trotted down the hillside. When they knelt with their bows aimed, waiting for the command to let fly, Cord asked, "Are you suggesting a course of action?"

She didn't answer right away. Her gaze tracked Dekanawida's progress across the field and up the hill toward Hiyawento. When the two men embraced, tears welled in Baji's eyes. Pain and longing, and something Cord didn't understand, tightened her expression. For just a moment, she seemed to be looking backward to another time, another embrace—one that had wrenched her heart.

Cord's attention shifted to the warriors to the north. Lines slithered into position. While archers trotted out and stationed themselves fifty paces in front of Hiyawento's line, men with war clubs snugged up behind them. An old man in a black cape drew Cord's attention. Where the main trail cut through the flats to the east of the villages, a single war lodge stood. The man stood outside it, surrounded by warriors, probably personal guards.

Cord said, "Is that Atotarho? Standing before the war lodge?"

Baji turned. Hatred hardened her features. "Yes. It must be."

"Then Hiyawento's forces are standing against Atotarho's?"

As though a plan was forming right behind her black eyes and she didn't wish to be disturbed, she softly replied, "Yes."

Cord noted, "Hiyawento is greatly outnumbered."

Shouts erupted. Orders. Both sides let fly.

The mist seemed to rip apart, punctured in a thousand places by streaks of silver. The warriors with the clubs charged into the fray. The line to the south wavered, ragged now; many had fallen. Frightened warriors ran, strides eating the distance to the tree cover, shorter legs falling behind, being cut down. Long gaps appeared in the lines on both sides, leaving warriors scrambling to close them. The mixed howls of victory and anguish resembled the peculiar serenade of panicked wolves.

As though Matron Jigonsaseh had been waiting for this exact moment, warriors flooded out of Yellowtail Village and flanked Atotarho's forces. Shrill war cries split the day. The low growl of hundreds of clashing war clubs rumbled. The Hills warriors had been surprised. Many ran in confusion. Others turned one way and then another, not sure who to fight first. Inexorably, the Yellowtail warriors pushed Atotarho's forces toward Hiyawento's, trapping them in the middle.

A slow smile of appreciation came to Baji's lips. "That's Koracoo."

"Where?"

She pointed. "In the red war shirt, leading the Yellowtail charge."

Cord saw her, and nodded in respect. It did not matter that she was the village matron now. She had a warrior's heart. The situation was desperate. She knew it. She would not let her warriors go into the fight without her.

"Do we join the battle, War Chief?" Cord asked. "Or bide our time and wait to see what happens?"

Baji's eyes narrowed. Her blood was up. The vein in her throat pulsed. She slid her bow from her shoulder. "We fight on Hiyawento's side."

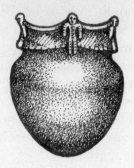

Sixty-two

Zateri watched the battle with her heart in her throat. She couldn't let herself lose sight of Hiyawento. She feared if she did, he would vanish like so many other friends had today. Keeping him in view wasn't easy. The mist was like a giant undulating beast, constantly shifting, gobbling one portion of the battlefield, then twisting to swallow up another.

Someone sobbed. She did not turn.

Wounded warriors lay on the wet ground all around their camp, dragged in by their friends, who had spoken softly to them for as long as they could before they had to charge back into the fight. Some wept inconsolably.

A monstrous disgust caused Zateri's hands to tremble. She tried to keep them hidden beneath her cape. *You can't afford to show any weakness. Not now.*

Kwahseti stood beside her in front of their fire. They had not spoken in a while, but she could hear Kwahseti's ragged breathing.

"Who is that?" Kwahseti asked, and pointed at a man running hard along the western edge of the battlefield. The blue and yellow shapes on his cape had blurred to a green smear.

"I can't tell."

"Qonde, maybe? Isn't that his cape?"

Zateri shook her head like a woman trying to get rid of a deafening ringing in her ears. The runner swerved wide around the battle, holding his white arrow over his head for all to see.

"It is Qonde; I'm sure of it. What does he want?"

Zateri pulled her gaze from Hiyawento's broad back long enough to glance at Kwahseti. The Riverbank Village matron's face had flushed. Short hair lay wetly against her forehead and curved down over her cheeks, wreathing her dark eyes like gray paint.

When Qonde finally made his way around the battle and trotted up the hill to the west, two sentries grabbed hold of his arms, searched him for weapons, and escorted him the rest of the way.

Kwahseti's jaw set. "It can't be an offer of surrender. Atotarho would never give up so easily. His huge pride—" She stopped short and her eyes flew open. "Who's that? Blessed ancestors, are those Flint People?"

Zateri swung around to stare, and Taya hurried forward with her long black hair swaying around her slender waist. She was so pretty. "They came! I don't believe it!"

"What do you mean?"

Taya whirled to face Zateri. "Matron Jigonsaseh went to Flint country to ask them to form an alliance with us to fight Atotarho."

Zateri breathlessly watched the tall woman in the lead. There was something . . . "Oh." She put a hand to her lips as tears constricted her throat. "That's Baji. Baji and Chief Cord."

As though time had mysteriously reversed, Zateri found herself sitting in a birch bark canoe twelve summers ago, with Baji's strong arms around her. The moonlit night had been quiet and cold. Mist hovered just above their heads, slithering along the course of the river. She could see it all again. War Chief Koracoo had paddled in front, and War Chief Cord in the rear of the canoe. *"I am your friend forever,"* Baji had said, and tightened her arms around Zateri. Tears had filled Zateri's eyes, for it had been the first time in moons that she'd felt truly safe.

The same feeling stole over Zateri now. It was irrational, even ludicrous, in light of everything happening on the battlefield, but she couldn't help it.

She watched as Baji dispatched a runner to Hiyawento, probably to announce herself and her intentions—so Hiyawento wouldn't mistakenly turn his forces on Baji's.

Though it wasn't necessary. Both Hiyawento and Sky Messenger were staring at Baji where she stood on the eastern hilltop. They had recognized her instantly, just as Zateri had.

When her runner returned, Baji led her forces down onto the battlefield. There had to be six or seven hundred Flint warriors. Ecstatic roars went up from Hiyawento's warriors, and on the far side of the field, Jigonsaseh's warriors whooped. They had Atotarho's forces completely surrounded.

"Chief Cord from Wild River Village?" Kwahseti asked.

"Yes," Zateri replied, and when she turned to look at Kwahseti, she noticed that Taya's young eyes had riveted on Baji.

Taya straightened. With dignity, she asked, "She's a war chief? Not just a warrior?"

"Apparently. I didn't know it myself until just now."

Taya seemed to wilt.

As the sentries shoved Qonde toward Zateri and Kwahseti, the man clutched his white arrow in both hands.

"What is it?" Kwahseti asked.

"I bring a message for Matron Zateri. Your father asks for a short truce so that he might speak with you."

"Why?" Kwahseti demanded to know.

"He did not give me that information, Matron Kwahseti."

Kwahseti turned to Zateri. "Perhaps now that he's doomed he wants to negotiate with the rightful leader of the Wolf Clan and the nation?"

Zateri ground her teeth while she gazed across the battlefield. As the mist eddied, her father's black cape appeared and disappeared. He couldn't negotiate. He *had* to win. If he didn't, he would no longer be the chief of Atotarho Village. In fact, the clan mothers would strip him of his name. He wouldn't even be Atotarho. The name would be taken back and eventually given to someone more deserving.

Zateri said, "Tell my father there is nothing to discuss."

Qonde's heart seemed to sink. His expression sagged, but he bowed. "Very well, Matron."

As he sprinted down the hill, Kwahseti said, "Good for you. We're winning and he knows it. It will be over soon."

In a soft voice, she said, "Not soon enough," and her gaze returned to Hiyawento.

He stood in the midst of a tormented knot of warriors that clashed not more than fifty paces from Atotarho's war lodge. The fighting was desperate. Through the blowing fog and smoke from the burning villages, the figures were somehow unreal, just floating phantoms, condemned to forever fight a battle no one could win. They were killing aunts, uncles, cousins, brothers. In a fight such as this, victory was impossible.

Hiyawento and Sky Messenger fought side by side, guarding each other's backs as they had done since they'd seen eleven summers. Slowly, inexorably, they were closing in on her father's position. When they got there . . . when they got there . . .

Zateri closed her eyes and let the darkness soothe her fear and hurt. She didn't want to see any more of this. Dear gods, *no more of this*!

Sixty-three

Sky Messenger

There is a sudden deafening roar when the sides converge. War Chief Sindak is in front of me, blocking the path to Atotarho, who has retreated into his lodge as though the thin deer hides will protect him.

I glance to my right, where Hiyawento swings his war club. He needs no help from me. Someone yells, "Got to pull back!" Another shouts, "No, no! Can't. Nowhere to go!" The Hills warrior in front of me has wild eyes; his head shakes violently. He leaps for me with a stiletto in his fist. The sharpened white bone shines as it plunges toward my heart. I flip sideways and he crashes by. My war club crushes his hip. Ten paces from the war lodge now. Sindak's face, the face of the man I consider to be one of my saviors, is raw and determined. He'll never let me pass, never let me get to Atotarho.

I am aware suddenly of the cold tears blurring my eyes.

As though the world has slipped sideways, from the corner of my eye, I see Atotarho step from the war lodge hauling a little girl by the arm. She is perhaps eight or nine, gagged, but when she spies Hiyawento, she goes crazy, trying to scream, twisting to get away from Atotarho, falling to the ground kicking. Hiyawento is occupied, running down a wounded man. There's something familiar about her, but I can't place it. She looks like someone I know.

From the lodge behind her steps a man. His cape is stunning, made of thousands of bluebird feathers. He has his hood pulled up. The blue fluttering around his hidden face and down his chest creates a sensation of movement, as though he's about to lift off the ground and fly away. When he sees me, he tilts his head like a man who has heard a blast of thunder right over the top of him. As though he can't quite hear, or is deaf and trying to understand the world through sight alone.

When people see him, a hiss erupts, the gasps like a beating of great wings.

Then . . . a cry. A long, shuddering, deep-throated wail.

Hiyawento lurches past me.

The next few moments happen so quickly, I can't move, can't . . .

Hiyawento throws himself at Sindak, and Sindak pivots and swipes Hiyawento's feet out from under him with his war club. Hiyawento lands hard. As Sindak brings his war club into position for a killing blow, there is an instant of hesitation. His eyes tense. I unthinkingly jump between Sindak and Hiyawento, my club cutting upward, crashing into Sindak's. We are eye to eye, shoving each other, trying to gain leverage, but I can see it in his face. He wishes he didn't have to do this. From the edge of my vision, Hiyawento leaps, slams Atotarho to the ground, and roars like a wounded grizzly as he grabs the old man around the throat.

"Help! Help . . . me!" Atotarho cries. He's choking. Struggling.

"Leave my daughter alone! Leave her alone, you—"

Negano's club takes Hiyawento squarely in the left shoulder, knocking him off Atotarho and sending him rolling.

"Hurry, my chief, get up!" Negano shouts, and drags Atotarho toward the lodge.

Hiyawento slowly crawls for the little girl. Tears are streaming down her face. She's trying to wriggle free of her bonds to get to him.

Blessed gods, that's why she's familiar. She looks like Zateri. Zateri as a child. *She's Hiyawento's daughter. His oldest daughter. Kahn-Tineta.*

"Sindak," I hiss through gritted teeth, "let the girl go."

So low no one but me can hear it, he says, "I knew nothing of this. Give me a chance."

Our eyes lock.

Negano runs back, jumps between Hiyawento and his daughter, grabs her, and suspends a stiletto over her heart.

The ragged cry that escapes Hiyawento's throat could sunder the world. Two of Atotarho's guards grab him and haul him four paces away from his daughter.

Atotarho cries, "Drop your weapons! Do it or the girl dies!" He lifts a hand, ready to give the order to plunge the stiletto into her heart.

Negano is ready, the stiletto poised for a lethal blow.

I shove away from Sindak, pause for only a moment, then my war club drops from my hand. Every other Standing Stone warrior follows my lead. Dull thuds sound as the weapons fall.

Atotarho turns to Hiyawento. "Order your warriors to cease fighting! Retreat!"

Without an instant's hesitation, Hiyawento turns to a warrior I do not know. "Call retreat."

"But War Chief!" the man objects.

I bellow, *"Do it now!"*

The man hesitates for a moment; then the horn trumpet blares three times. Warriors turn to stare, confused, afraid to step away from their opponent for fear their skulls will be crushed.

The words go down the line like dropped rocks, *stop, stop, retreat.*

Gradually, like a gigantic monster dying, the roars and grunts dwindle to an agonized base note of moans spiked with sobs. The battlefield seems to churn as the mist swirls around retreating men and women.

A breathless silence descends.

I am sucking air, my exhausted arms like dead weights.

Atotarho careens as he turns and sternly orders, "Bring me that child." The rattlesnake skins flash and flutter in his hair.

Negano carries her over and dumps her at Atotarho's feet. A hoarse cry explodes from Hiyawento's lips, and he struggles ferociously against the muscular arms that hold him. The little girl's sobs shred my heart. They must be tearing Hiyawento apart. His face has twisted with a mixture of rage and hate.

"Kahn-Tineta," Atotarho says in an affectionate voice. "You're such a pretty child."

I look at Sindak and find him staring at me. His eyes plead for me to wait, wait.

I know if I make one wrong move, that little girl will be the first to die.

Now that we've stopped fighting, my body is cooling down, the sweat chilling on my skin. A rhythmic whooshing thump pounds in my ears. After several heartbeats, my vision goes strangely gray and shimmering, as though a veil of tears wavers between me and Wrass. He has not looked at me. He has eyes only for his daughter. She's reaching for him with her bound hands, her fingers flexing in a *please, please* gesture, crying against her gag.

Atotarho twines clawlike fingers into her sleeve and drags her to her feet. Holding her, he says to Hiyawento, "You dare to defy me! I should kill your daughter before your eyes! I will kill her if your forces do not surrender and pledge themselves to me."

Hiyawento's face twists with hatred. "I don't have the authority to—"

"I know that! Get it!"

Hiyawento turns to look out across the battlefield toward where Zateri and the other matrons stand on the southern hilltop. He's dying inside. I can feel his agony in my own strangling heart. He gives Kahn-Tineta a desperate smile. Nods. "Tell your forces to stand down and I'll speak with the matrons."

Atotarho nods to Sindak.

Sindak turns. "Saponi, tell them to back away!"

Saponi trots out onto the field, and the order flies through the ranks like swallows diving. Men and women step back.

Atotarho flicks a hand at the men who hold Hiyawento, and they release his arms.

Hiyawento braces his feet, seems to be trying to resign himself to this last betrayal, and slowly trots away. He does not even look at me.

A strange crawling sensation, like icy ants, runs up my neck. My head swivels toward the war lodge. The Bluebird Witch is staring at me. When he walks toward me, it is as though he's gliding on air. His feathered cape faintly rustles as he spreads his arms like a huge bird and hops around in a bizarre dance that resembles Crow hunting mice in a field. Shrill caws rip from his throat. "I saw it, you know," he hisses. "I saw what he did to you after he dragged you into the forest."

I can't feel my body. Just the air cooling, growing unbearably icy. My insides are freezing into amber pools of brilliance. Images flare . . . *A muscular giant swaying, his eyes rolling . . . "You, Standing Stone boy, go with War Chief Manidos. Get up, boy!" . . . Tutelo wailing in a high-pitched voice I've never heard before, "Leave my brother alone! Leave him alone!"*

I stagger backward. As though to defend myself from the memories, I thrust my hands out before me.

Manidos crushes my hand, drags me away into the forest. My heart is thundering. He's walking very fast. I keep tripping. I . . .

Atotarho says, "What's wrong with you? I asked you a question."

Facedown. His heavy body crushes me. A rough hand covers my mouth. Lips against my ear. "Lie down, boy. Stop crying or I'll cut your heart out."
. . . Pain. Shock.

I twist my head, looking for Wrass. Watching him as he stumbles out into the warriors' camp. Dumping the bag of poison into the stew pot. If I can just . . . see him . . . I can . . . stand this—

Sindak's voice breaks in. "Chief, end this battle. You're asking your warriors to murder their cousins!"

I look at Sindak, at the warriors behind him, and shout, "Sindak's right. Chief, clear the battlefield so we can talk to one another. Please, just give me fifty heartbeats to—"

Atotarho laughs, the sound low and disdainful. "Clear the battlefield? You've always been a coward. I remember when you were a boy, you . . ."

I'm trembling all over when I turn eastward and lift my arms into the air, as though reaching out to touch the Sky World. I shout, "This war must end! We're killing Great Grandmother Earth!"

There is a momentary hush.

A curious far-off rushing sound echoes to the east. Everyone hears it. The battlefield whispers as warriors turn, their eyes wide, asking questions. It is as though the mist has been suddenly sucked away, leaving cold sparkling sunlight behind. I squint against the brilliance. The rushing grows louder, like a tidal wave coming in, and a black wall boils over the forest canopy, swelling into the sky, rising so high it blots out Elder Brother Sun's face as it floods toward us.

"What is that?" Atotarho props his walking stick and shifts to look at it.

Sindak's dark eyes narrow. He shouts, "Get down! Everyone get down!"

A few people obey and hit the ground, but most run, trying to find cover before the leading edge of the blackness strikes. At the first opportunity, Sindak pulls a chert knife from his belt and cuts Kahn-Tineta's bonds, but orders, "Stay down!"

She flattens on the ground.

I seem to be frozen, my hands extended over my head, as though I am the first to surrender to the monstrous storm. Shocked cries erupt. A torrent of fleeing warriors floods around me, the Standing Stone warriors trying to get back to the safety of the villages, the Hills warriors just running, running with all their strength. A few dive behind boulders; others crouch near the most massive tree trunks.

I turn to the east. Into the storm. Close my eyes. Voices fill the wind—powerful, hushed, as though the ancestors have walked the Path of Souls back to earth and are riding the backs of the Cloud People, soaring straight for us. For me. The thundering of their ghostly feet pounds in my chest.

"Blessed gods," Sindak shouts. "Run!"

I open my eyes. The men who'd thrown themselves to the ground rise and flee. One carries Chief Atotarho over his shoulder. There are only two people before the war lodge now. Two people left in the open. I kneel before Kahn-Tineta. She seems too terrified to breathe. "I'm Sky Messenger. Stay with me. You're safe with me."

Her tear-streaked face is disbelieving. She looks over my shoulder just as the trees on the eastern hills explode. Dark fragments of branches and leaves blast upward into the spinning darkness and vanish, crushed to powder.

"Please, let's go. We have to run!"

"No, don't run."

"It's coming! It's going to kill us!" Kahn-Tineta throws her arms around my neck in a stranglehold.

I clutch her tightly against me, whispering, "Just listen, Kahn-Tineta. Close your eyes and you'll hear them. Our ancestors are telling our story on the wind."

Against my cheek, I feel her squeeze her eyes closed, and I lift her into my arms and stand up to face the telling. All stories are lived between the listener and the teller, but until this moment I have never realized there is a third person in the story. The silence. Just before the ancestors enfold us in their arms, silence steps into the space between us. It is a pause in the heartbeat of the world. But I feel it like muscular arms tightening, pressing us close, encircling us with an invisible palisade of human bodies.

And perhaps that's what it is. Perhaps the souls of the lost warriors in the palisade logs have stepped out for just a moment, just an instant in time, to defend us, as they have always defended their people.

"Hold me! Don't let go of me!" Kahn-Tineta screams.

When the blackness strikes, I crush her small body against me and close my eyes.

Sixty-four

Hiyawento threw his arms around Zateri and dragged her to the ground as the blackness swept over them. All around, people in the camp shrieked, racing for whatever cover they could find.

Hiyawento never closed his eyes. He kept watching, watching Kahn-Tineta and Sky Messenger. A thin spiral of mist rose from the ground and seemed to cling to Sky Messenger's cape; then the worst of the blackness thundered down upon them, swallowed them, blackness and spinning darkness, grass and dropped arrows swirling high into the air, as though to fuel some sky war.

Then it was gone.

Passed over.

In the distance, the blackness continued to uproot whole trees and cast them about like corn-husk dolls, but the deafening roar receded, slowly, until all that possessed the world was blinding sunlight and the silence of the grave.

In the midst of the quiet, quiet world, Sky Messenger still stood, holding Kahn-Tineta in his arms. She had her small face buried against his neck, clutching him like a frightened animal. Sky Messenger took one step toward the east, and his chin tipped up, as though he'd lifted his face to gaze straight into the brilliant eye of Elder Brother Sun.

"Are they all right? Can you see them?" Zateri squirmed beneath his heavy body, trying to turn, to look out across the battlefield.

Hiyawento softly said, "Yes, I see them. They're all right."

As he got to his feet, shocked voices erupted throughout the camp. People gasped and pointed. A few ran forward to the edge of the hill to look. Zateri staggered to her feet and grabbed his arm to steady her weak legs.

Sky Messenger set Kahn-Tineta on the ground, then took her hand and slowly started weaving through the dead bodies, now tossed here and there into tangled piles, bringing Kahn-Tineta to Hiyawento and Zateri.

Zateri threw off Hiyawento's hand and was out of camp, down the hillside, dashing across the battlefield, the fringes of her skirt slashing around her legs, running for them with her arms outstretched.

Sixty-five

Sky Messenger

Light cold rain falls, pattering through the forest, creating a melodic symphony of plops and shishes.

I flip up my buckskin hood and lean one shoulder against a sassafras trunk. Gitchi lies at my feet with his gray head braced on his paws. I have my back turned to the hundreds of campfires where warriors sit discussing what happened today. In the branches that surround me, fire shadows flutter like dark hummingbird wings, beating at the soft awed voices. I concentrate on the sensation of cold. It helps me to block out the emotion. Every voice is saturated with it. They are watching me, and have been since this afternoon when most of Atotarho's remaining forces trotted over the hills, heading home.

"I tell you, I saw it. I was there. He told Sindak to clear the battlefield, and when Atotarho laughed . . ." The warrior hesitates, as though reliving the moment. "Sky Messenger opened his hands to Elder Brother Sun, and it was as though thunder was born in the heart of the mist. The sound—the sound was like Great Grandmother Earth being ripped apart."

"You're exaggerating, Saponi," another man accuses.

"No," Saponi murmurs with deep reverence in his voice. "I *saw* it. Sky Messenger lifted his hands for help, and Elder Brother Sun answered him. And then, just before the blackness struck, clouds formed on Sky Messenger's cape. I swear it looked like he was wearing a cape of white clouds and riding the winds of destruction. Just like the old stories say. I'm telling you, he's the human False Face."

Everyone around the campfire murmurs.

There is a brief lull; then singing rises. The notes lilt through the darkness.

I feel drained, utterly empty. Like a transparent husk, useless now. I straighten, preparing to go back . . .

Gitchi lifts his head, and his tail thumps the ground.

Behind me, whispering through the grass, I hear her long legs. The muscular grace of her movements, just the feline placement of her feet, is like a physical blow. I swallow. As she walks closer, I say, "I knew you'd find me."

Her moccasins shift, as though she has braced her legs. "It wasn't hard. Every eye in the camp is upon you."

She has one of those deep female voices that seem to reach inside a man and stroke his heart.

Gitchi trots away, and I turn to see him leap up to place his big paws in the middle of her chest. She hugs him hard. His tail swipes the air as he whimpers his happiness. "I missed you, Gitchi. Are you all right?"

At the sight of her, guilt blends with a love so powerful it is impossible to explain. The air seems to glitter around her, playing in her long black hair, sculpting the muscles of her arms, flowing across her broad shoulders and pooling in the curves of her narrow waist. I know every line of her body, every hollow; even the slightest imperfection of her skin has lived beneath my fingertips. My gaze moves over her beautiful face, comparing it to my memory. Her black eyes shine. It's a look that trembles the blood in my veins.

Gitchi returns to my side, gazing up at me as though to say, "Look, she's back. Isn't it wonderful?"

I step toward her with my fists clenched. "I'll never be able to thank you enough for what you and Cord did today. When I saw you leading your warriors down the hill and into the fight . . . Baji . . . I could feel victory in the very air I was breathing."

A bare smile turns her full lips. "I have always been on your side, Odion. I always will be."

The faintest breath of wind brushes her hair. Jet strands flutter and seem to be suspended upon the firelight itself, pure amber silk, shimmering. They softly fall back to her shoulders.

I rush to say, "I am to be married."

"I know."

I jerk a nod. There is silence.

She smiles and walks forward. When she looks up at me, the desperate longing in her eyes is gemlike, crystal bright.

"Are you well, Baji?"

"Well enough, Dekanawida."

As though she can't help herself, she reaches up and touches my cheek. "It's all right. You did what you had to, and I did what I had to. That is how things must be."

The sensation of her fingers trailing across my skin is like the shock of the air just before lightning blinds the world.

"Baji, forgive me for what I said to you that day. I was wrong."

Her hand lowers. She closes her fingers, as though to hold onto my warmth. "I forgave you long ago. You thought the boy was better dead than a captive in an enemy village. I understood. I just disagreed."

"If only I'd had more time to think it over, I . . ."

A small voice calls, "Sky Messenger?"

I look over Baji's shoulder and see Taya. She stands four paces away, at the edge of the trees, watching us uncomfortably. I wonder how long she's been there. I pray not long.

"Taya." I extend a hand. "Please, come. I want to introduce you to War Chief Baji of the Turtle Clan of the Flint People."

Taya hesitantly comes forward. She wears a doeskin cape much too long for her; it drags the ground. She must have grabbed the first thing she could find. Which means she probably has a reason for being here, more than just finding me.

I move away from Baji, go to Taya, and put my arm around her, pulling her close against my side. She clings to me like a raft in a raging ocean. "Baji, this is Taya, soon to be my wife."

Taya looks at Baji from beneath her lashes, not sure what to say. She is barely a woman. Meeting the legendary Baji must be threatening.

Baji takes the initiative. She smiles genuinely. "You are High Matron Kittle's granddaughter, yes?"

"Yes." Taya nervously wets her lips and casts a glance up at me.

"I hope we will become great friends, Taya. I suspect that you and I have heard Dekanawida's vision so often we've both memorized what's coming. We will need to be friends. The road ahead is not an easy one."

Taya's face slackens. "Does that mean you've decided to join the peace alliance?"

Baji blinks in surprise. "Our Ruling Council approved it with barely any discussion at all. Dekanawida is a hero among our people. They believe his vision."

With childlike excitement, Taya rushes to tell me, "That means we have the Flint People and Zateri's faction of Hills People. Now all we need to do is get the People of the Landing, and the Mountain People, and surely we will be able to destroy Atotarho!"

I brush black hair away from her young face. "All in good time, Taya." I let out a slow breath. "For now, let us just enjoy the night."

"We can't yet. I'm sorry. Grandmother requests that you come and tell your vision to the assembled chiefs and matrons."

Baji is watching me. I feel her gaze. It is life itself.

"I'm grateful to have the chance. Lead the way, Taya."

The three of us walk out together, with Gitchi trotting at my side, but as we proceed across the cold battlefield to find High Matron Kittle, Baji drops behind. After ten heartbeats of not hearing her steps behind me, I glance over my shoulder, looking for her. She's gone. Probably wandering among the warriors. She is war chief. She has duties. And more than that, this is as hard for her as it is for me.

"Hiyawento told me what you did today, Taya. It was very brave, and very dangerous. I don't know what possessed you—"

"I was the best choice."

"Yes," I answer. *But you knew it. No one had to tell you. No one had to convince you to risk your life. It never occurred to you that it might not be worth it.* "Someday, you will be the greatest of the matrons of the Standing Stone People."

She stops and searches my expression, as though greatly surprised, perhaps because she just saw me with Baji. She seems to be trying to determine if I am telling the truth. "Did you Dream this?"

"No. But I know it just the same."

She slips her arm around my waist, and we start climbing the southern hillside. On the crest of the hill, a large fire blazes. I see Mother sitting beside Chief Cord, smiling. Father and his wife, Pawen, nestle beneath one blanket to their right. Pawen is much stronger, getting well. Hiyawento and Zateri lean together, their shoulders touching, as though they need to know the other is close. Kahn-Tineta sleeps in Hiyawento's arms with her mouth slightly open. There are many people around the fire that I do not know. It makes me slightly uneasy. High Matron Kittle stands a short distance away, smiling a little too eagerly at Sindak, who seems to have no illusions about the game that is afoot. He smiles back.

"Has War Chief Sindak decided what he's going to do yet?" I ask Taya.

"I don't think so. After he deserted Atotarho's forces, Gonda offered to adopt him into the Standing Stone nation, but so far Sindak has declined. The last I heard, he said he might go off and become a Trader with his old friend, Towa."

Warmth seeps up around my souls. "I hope so. He deserves—"

"Sky Messenger," she interrupts. "Look at me."

I frown down at her.

She swallows hard, obviously preparing herself. "I . . . I've grown up some. I don't know if you noticed—"

"I noticed."

"Well . . ." She nervously licks her lips. "Among our people, marriages are matters of status and duty, not love. I know—as I did not when we started this journey—that my responsibility is to my clan, and to your vision. I will help you as much as I can, and I expect the same from you." Her expression is serious, somber. "But that is all I expect."

Above us, a great horned owl calls, *hoo, hoo-oo, hoo, hoo*. We both look up to watch it sail over the battlefield with its wings tucked.

I am so hollow I can hear my heartbeat echoing. I put my arm around her again, and as we walk, I say, "Let's take it one day at a time, Taya."

Our moccasins crunch the frost as we climb the hill. Ahead, there is firelight. I look at Zateri and Hiyawento. My muscles relax. My breathing is easier. I am not alone. Trust is no longer in exile.

Taya says, "Before we get to the fire, you need to know several people. The tiny woman sitting beside Zateri is Matron Gwinodje of Canassatego Village. On the opposite side of the fire, the woman with gray hair is Matron Kwahseti of Riverbank Village, and beside her, the elderly man is Chief Canassatego. Kwahseti's war chief, Thona, is the heavily scarred man with the scowl on his face. He—"

"You've become quite the politician," I praise. "Thank you for helping me."

She tightens her arm around my waist. "I've been listening to Grandmother speaking with the other matrons. You're going to need a good politician. Keeping this alliance together is going to take a miracle. And *I* am going to make sure it happens."

I stop for a moment. Her eyes are filled with determination. I run my hand over her soft hair. "I believe you."

Sixty-six

Sky Messenger

Around midnight the Cloud People part and the campfires of the dead become a conflagration. The light is so brilliant every branch casts a shadow.

As I walk the battlefield, I unconsciously stroke Gitchi's gray muzzle. He licks my palm. Across the meadow bright lights bob and sway. Many cluster near the villages, moving in and out of the palisades, perhaps saying good-bye to loved ones. Others roam aimlessly, confused, waiting for the deer.

There is a sound on a battlefield that's hard to define. The dead are not silent. As muscles go rigid there are thumps, whispers. Teeth grind in tightening jaws. Wings. Wings flap as night birds feed.

I study the wide cold eyes on the ground. I will keep them in the space between my souls, the place I keep all terrible things, to be taken out and contemplated when I think I cannot go on, because it's too hard, or I'm too tired, or the loneliness has become too much to bear. These men and women will remind me that the nearness of death is grace on fire, and I must learn to live the flames. I, at last, understand Bahna's words.

A warning growl rumbles Gitchi's throat.

I turn. In the trees to my right, the moonlight seems to shudder. A man stands out there, in the cold darkness, all alone.

There is a low insidious laugh. "It's Odion, the boy who was always afraid."

His feathered cape whispers. I can't tell if he is coming toward me, or just shifting positions. When I dropped my war club today, it was truly for good. I have only my words to protect me now. Words and an old wolf whose life I will not risk, not even to save my own.

"I'm still afraid, Hehaka."

"But why? You are the great man now. Elder Brother Sun obeys Sky Messenger's commands." His laughter is mocking, filled with disbelief. "Isn't that enough?"

I tilt my head. Enough? All night long—in glimpses—I've been reliving the horror of War Chief Manidos. I'm grieving, feeling wounded; it clouds the thoughts. What is enough? I pause to consider. In a man's lifetime, is it enough to forgive just once when one did not have to? Or perhaps "enough" is only reached when a person makes forgiveness his Road of Light, and spends every day walking to the Land of the Dead, expecting nothing more.

I say, "I know where it is."

He doesn't answer at first. Then, "Where what is?"

"Her pot."

He takes a quick step forward. I see wide eyes shining in his hood. His voice replies from the midst of rustling feathers, "Which pot?"

"You know the one I mean. Her soul pot."

The witch twists his head in a birdlike manner, observing me through one eye. He must be trying to figure out why I would tell him. We have never been friends. Even when we were in agony together as children, he was never one of us. Never one of the trusted few for whom we would have willingly given our lives. And perhaps that is the reason to choose the Road of Light.

"Why do you tell me this?" he asks.

"You've been searching for it for many summers, haven't you? If I'd known, I would have told you sooner. Do you remember our last camp on the river where she ambushed us?"

His voice is soft. "I do."

"Walk due northeast about one thousand paces, and you will see a small oval clearing on a hillside surrounded by maples. There are three rocks in the middle of the clearing. That's where she died. Just before Mother found us, Zateri took the soul pot from the old woman's pack and buried it between the rocks." I turn to look at the darkness in his hood. I can't see his face at all now. "Do you want me to go with you?"

Silence, for a long time.

"No, Sky Messenger."

I nod and lift my eyes to study the star-silvered heavens. The dead ferns beneath the trees thrash. He is gone, vanished like a shadow eaten by utter darkness.

I continue my walk across the battlefield, periodically petting Gitchi's head or halting to study a frozen face before I continue on. One hand of time later, when I finally look up, I discover that my feet have taken me to a high point above the Flint camp.

As I gaze out over the sleeping warriors rolled in blankets, I try to imagine where she is. Moonlight gleams from hundreds of upturned faces.

Tomorrow, I will find her. Tomorrow, we will talk.

Somewhere ahead of me there is a black sun and a crack like the sky splitting. Will she be there with me? I have not seen this. She isn't in any of my Dreams.

But I believe in things seen and unseen.

I pray the Spirits will show me the path.

In *The Black Sun,* the fourth and final book of the People of the Long-house saga, the ravages of war have left the Iroquois standing on the precipice of self-destruction. The eerie holy man, Sky Messenger, along with his cherished friends, will manage to pull four warring nations into a fragile peace alliance. There is only one holdout: A very powerful faction of the People of the Hills, led by the insane sorcerer, Chief Atotarho. Atotarho has another agenda. He seeks domination of the Iroquoian world, and will stop at nothing to attain it.

Sky Messenger and his friends will risk everything to stop Atotarho.

It is only at the end, after the great forces are aligned, and the earth-shattering final battle is about to begin, that they will, at last, understand the true, unbearable cost of peace.

The truth will appear in a single blinding instant when the Great Face shakes the World Tree, and Elder Brother Sun blackens his face with the soot of the dying world. . . .

Glossary

Flying Heads—Just heads with no bodies that thrash wildly through the forests. These fearsome creatures have long trailing hair and great paws like a bear's.

Gaha—The soft wind. She is spoken of as Elder Sister Gaha.

Gahai—Spectral lights that guide sorcerers as they fly through the air on their evil journeys. Sometimes gahai lead their masters to victims, other times to places where they can find charms.

Hadui—A violent wind.

Hanehwa—Skin beings. Witches sometimes skin their victims, enchant their skins, and force them to do their bidding. Hanehwa warn witches of danger by giving three shouts.

Hatho—The Frost Spirit.

Haudenosaunee—The People of the Longhouse, called "Iroquois" by the French.

Ohwachira—The basic family unit. An ohwachira is a kinship group that traces its descent from a common female ancestor. The ohwachira bestows chieftainship titles and holds the names of the great people of the past. It bestows those names by raising up the souls of the dead and requickening them in the bodies of newly elected chiefs, adoptees, or other people. In the same way, if a new chief disappoints the ohwachira, after consultation with the clan, it can take back the name, remove the soul, and depose the chief. It is also the sisterhood of ohwachiras that decides when to go to war and when to make peace.

Otkon—One of the two halves of Spirit Power that inhabit the world. The other is Uki. Don't think of these as good and evil, however. Both powers share equally in light and dark. Otkon and Uki form a unified spiritual universe that must be kept in balance. Otkon has a trickster-like character. It's unpredictable and can be either beneficial or harmful to human beings. Its half of the day lasts from noon to midnight. Otkon is often associated with the Evil-Minded One, the hero twin also known as Flint.

People of the Flint—The Mohawk nation. However, the word *Mohawk* is an Algonquian term meaning "flesh eaters." They call themselves the Kanienkahaka, or Ganienkeh, meaning "People of the Flint."

People of the Hills—The Onondaga nation. The word *Onondaga* is an Anglicized version of their name for themselves, *Onundagaono*, which means "People of the Hills."

People of the Landing—The Cayuga nation. Including People of the Landing, several other possible derivations have been offered for the word *Cayuga*, including, "People of the Place Where Locusts Were Taken Out," "People of the Mucky Land," and "People of the Place Where Boats are Taken Out."

People of the Mountain—The Seneca nation. They call themselves the *Onondowahgah*. Their name can also be translated "People of the Great Hill."

People of the Standing Stone—The Oneida nation. The word *Oneida* may be a rather poor Anglicization of their name for themselves, *Onayotekaono*, meaning "Granite People," or "People of the Standing Stone."

Requickening Ceremony—The raising up of souls for the purpose of placing them in other bodies, such as those of adoptees. This concept does not exactly correspond to the eastern religions' concept of reincarnation. For example, there's no idea of karma to be accounted for. Being reborn is neither punishment nor reward. Instead, there is a strong concept of duty to the People. Only strong souls were requickened, usually within the same maternal lineage. The ceremony was performed in the hopes of easing grief and restoring the spiritual strength of the clans, but a returning soul also had an obligation to help the People in times of crises. Many "Keepings" of the Peacemaker story say that Dekanawida was the returned soul of Tarenyawagon (also spelled as Tarachiawagon), the cultural hero also known as Sapling, the Good-Minded One, who served as the Creator. Those same traditions identify Atotarho as Sapling's troublesome younger brother, Flint (Tawiscaro/Tawiscaron), who was called the Evil-Minded One. Jigonsaseh, similarly, was the returned soul of Sky Woman's daughter, the Lynx.

Uki—One of the two halves of Spirit Power that inhabit the world (see *Otkon*). Uki is never harmful to human beings. Its half of the day lasts from midnight to noon. Uki is often associated with the Good-Minded One, the hero twin also known as Sapling, or Tarenyawagon.

Selected Bibliography

Bruchac, Joseph.
   Iroquois Stories: Heroes and Heroines, Monsters and Magic. Freedom,
   CA: The Crossing Press, 1985.
Calloway, Colin G.
   The Western Abenakis of Vermont, 1600–1800. Norman: University of
   Oklahoma Press, 1990.
Custer, Jay. F.
   Delaware Prehistoric Archaeology. An Ecological Approach. Cranberry,
   NJ: Associated University Presses, 1984.
Dye, David H.
   *War Paths. Peace Paths. An Archaeology of Cooperation and Conflict in
   Native Eastern North America.* Lanham, MD: Altamira Press, 2009.
Ellis, Chris J., and Neal Ferris, eds.
   The Archaeology of Southern Ontario to A.D. 1650. London, Ontario,
   Canada: Occasional Papers of the London Chapter, OAS Number 5,
   1990.
Elm, Demus, and Harvey Antone.
   The Oneida Creation Story. Lincoln: University of Nebraska, 2000.
Englebrecht, William.
   Iroquoia: The Development of a Native World. Syracuse: Syracuse Uni-
   versity Press, 2003.
Fagan, Brian M.
   Ancient North America. The Archaeology of a Continent, 4th ed. Thames
   and Hudson Press, London, 2005.
Fenton, William N.
   The False Faces of the Iroquois. Norman: University of Oklahoma Press,
   1987.
———.
   The Iroquois Eagle Dance. An Offshoot of the Calumet Dance. Syracuse:
   Syracuse University Press, 1991.

———.

The Roll Call of the Iroquois Chiefs. A Study of a Pnemonic Cane from the Six Nations Reserve. Cranbook Institute of Science, Bulletin, No. 30, 1950.

Foster, Steven and James A.

Duke. *Eastern/Central Medicinal Plants*. The Peterson Guides Series. Boston: Houghton Mifflin Company, 1990.

Hart, John P., and Christina B. Reith.

Northeast Subsistence-Settlement Change: AD 700–1300. Albany, NY: New York State Museum Bulletin 496, 2002.

Herrick, James W.

Iroquois Medical Botany. New York: Syracuse University Press, 1995.

Hewitt, J. N. B.

"The Iroquoian Concept of the Soul." *Journal of American Folklore*, VIII (1895): 107–116.

———.

"Orenda and a Definition of Religion." *American Anthropologist*, N.S., IV (1902): 33–46.

———.

"Status of Woman in Iroquois Polity before 1784," in Smithsonian Institution, *Annual Report of the Board of Regents*, 1932, (Washington, D.C. 1933) 475–488.

Jemison, Pete.

"Mother of Nations: The Peace Queen, a Neglected Tradition." *Akwe:kon* 5 (1988): 68–70.

Jennings, Francis.

The Ambiguous Iroquois Empire. New York: W. W. Norton, 1984.

Jennings, Francis, ed.

The History and Culture of Iroquois Diplomacy. Syracuse: Syracuse University Press, 1995.

Johansen, Bruce Elliot, and Barbara Alice Mann.

Encyclopedia of the Haudenosaunee (Iroquois Confederacy). Westport, CT: Greenwood Press, 2000.

Kapches, Mima.

"Intra-Longhouse Spatial Analysis." *Pennsylvania Archaeologist*, XLIX, no. 4 (December, 1979): 24–29.

Kurath, Gertrude P.

Iroquois Music and Dance: Ceremonial Arts of Two Seneca Longhouses. Smithsonian Institution, Bureau of American Ethnology, Bulletin 187. Washington: U.S. Government Printing Office, 1964.

Levine, Mary Ann, Kenneth E. Sassaman, and Michael S. Nassaney, eds.

The Archaeological Northeast. Westport, CT: Bergin and Garvey, 1999.

Mann, Barbara A., and Jerry L. Fields.
    "A Sign in the Sky. Dating the League of the Haudenosaunee." The
    Wampum Chronicles, www.wampumchronicles.com/signinthesky.html.
————.
    Iroquoian Women: Gantowisas of the Haudenosaunee League. New York:
    Peter Lang, 2000.
Martin, Calvin,
    Keepers of the Game. Indian-Animal Relationships and the Fur Trade.
    Berkeley: University of California Press, 1978.
Mensforth, Robert P.
    "Human Trophy Taking in Eastern North America During the Archaic
    Period: The Relationship to Warfare and Social Complexity," chap. *The
    Taking and Displaying of Human Body Parts as Trophies by Amerindians,*
    edited by Richard J. Chacon and David Dye, New York: Springer, 2007.
Miroff, Laurie E., and Timothy D. Knapp.
    Iroquoian Archaeology and Analytic Scale. Knoxville: University of
    Tennessee Press, 2009.
Morgan, Lewis Henry.
    League of the Iroquois. New York: Corinth Books, 1962.
Mullen, Grant J., and Robert D. Hoppa.
    "Rogers Ossuary (AgHb-131): An Early Ontario Iroquois Burial Fea-
    ture from Brantford Township." *The Canadian Journal of Archaeology/
    Journal Canadien d'Archeologie,* Vol. 16, (1992): 32–47.
O'Callaghan, E. B., ed.
    The Documentary History of the State of New York. 4 vols. Albany:
    Weed, Parsons and Co., 1849–1851.
Parker, A. C.,
    Iroquois Uses of Maize and Other Food Plants. Albany: New York State
    Museum, Bulletin 144, 1910.
————,
    writing as Gawasco Wanneh. *An Analytical History of the Seneca Indi-
    ans,* 1926. Researches and Transactions of the New York State Arche-
    ological Association, Lewis H. Morgan Chapter. New York: Kraus
    Reprint Co., 1970.
Parker, Arthur C.
    Seneca Myths and Folk Tales. Lincoln: University of Nebraska Press,
    1989.
Richter, Daniel.
    *The Ordeal of the Longhouse. The People of the Iroquois League in the Era
    of European Colonization.* Chapel Hill: University of North Carolina
    Press, 1992.

Snow, Dean.
> *The Archaeology of New England.* New York: Academic Press, 1980.
———.
> *The Iroquois,* Oxford: Blackwell, 1996.
Spittal, W. G.
> *Iroquois Women: An Anthology.* Ontario, Canada: Iroqrafts, Ltd., 1990.
Talbot, Francis Xavier.
> *Saint among the Hurons. The Life of Jean De Brebeuf.* New York: Harper and Brothers, 1949.
Tooker, Elizabeth, ed.
> *Iroquois Culture, History, and Prehistory.* Albany: The University of the State of New York, 1967.
Trigger, Bruce.
> *The Children of Aataentsic: A History of the Huron People to 1660.* Montreal: McGill-Queen's University Press, 1987.
Trigger, Bruce, ed.
> *Handbook of North American Indians. Vol. 15: Northeast.* Washington: Smithsonian Institution Press, 1978.
Tuck, James A.
> *Onondaga Iroquois Prehistory. A Study in Settlement Archaeology.* New York: Syracuse University Press, 1971.
Wallace, Anthony F. C.
> *The Death and Rebirth of the Seneca.* New York: Vintage Books, 1972.
Walthall, John A., and Thomas E. Emerson, eds.
> *Calumet and Fleur-de-Lys. Archaeology of the Indian and French Contact in the Midcontinent.* Washington: Smithsonian Institution Press, 1992.
Weer, Paul.
> *Preliminary Notes on the Iroquoian Family.* Prehistory Research Series. Indianapolis: Indiana Historical Society, 1937.
Whitehead, Ruth Holmes.
> *Stories from the Six Worlds. Micmac Legends.* Halifax: Nimbus Publishing, 1988.
Williamson, Ronald F., and Susan Pfeiffer.
> *Bones of the Ancestors. The Archaeology and Osteobiography of the Moatfield Ossuary.* Gatineau, Quebec: Canadian Museum of Civilization, 2003.

About the Authors

Kathleen O'Neal Gear is a former state historian and archaeologist for Wyoming, Kansas, and Nebraska for the U.S. Department of the Interior. She has twice received the federal government's Special Achievement Award for "outstanding management" of our nation's cultural heritage.

W. Michael Gear, who holds a master's degree in archaeology, has worked as a professional archaeologist since 1978. He is currently principal investigator for Wind River Archaeological Consultants.

The Gears, whose North America's Forgotten Past Series are international, *USA Today*, and *New York Times* bestsellers, live in Thermopolis, Wyoming.